The Secret Keeper
of Main Street

Also by Trisha R. Thomas

The Secret Keeper of Main Street

A Novel

TRISHA R. THOMAS

wm

WILLIAM MORROW
An Imprint of HarperCollins*Publishers*

THE SECRET KEEPER OF MAIN STREET. Copyright © 2024 by Trisha Thomas. All rights reserved. Printed in the United States of America. No part of this book may be used or reproduced in any manner whatsoever without written permission except in the case of brief quotations embodied in critical articles and reviews. For information, address HarperCollins Publishers, 195 Broadway, New York, NY 10007.

HarperCollins books may be purchased for educational, business, or sales promotional use. For information, please email the Special Markets Department at SPsales@harpercollins.com.

FIRST EDITION

Designed by Bonni Leon-Berman

Library of Congress Cataloging-in-Publication Data

Names: Thomas, Trisha R., 1964– author.
Title: The Secret Keeper of Main Street : a novel / Trisha R. Thomas.
Description: First edition. | New York, NY : William Morrow, 2024. | Summary: "From acclaimed African-American novelist Trisha Thomas comes the story of Bailey Dowery, a Black dressmaker in 1950s Oklahoma whose gift of "second sight" pulls her into a dangerous small-town scandal involving a society wedding, a murder, and shocking family secrets"—Provided by publisher.
Identifiers: LCCN 2023033106 | ISBN 9780063344167 (hardcover) | ISBN 9780063344181 (ebook)
Subjects: LCSH: African Americans—Fiction. | Psychics—Fiction. | LCGFT: Thrillers (Fiction) | Novels.
Classification: LCC PS3570.H5917 S43 2024 | DDC 813/.54—dc23/eng/20230728
LC record available at https://lccn.loc.gov/2023033106

ISBN 978-0-06-334416-7

24 25 26 27 28 LBC 5 4 3 2 1

For Mom and Dad,
for all the road trips looking at the stars
from California to Oklahoma

A child not embraced by the village
will burn it down to feel its warmth.

—*Anonymous*

The Secret Keeper
of Main Street

A Note from the Author

BEFORE OIL SEEPED from the first well, the people of Mendol, Oklahoma, were a community of simple traditions and quiet longings. Women went to knitting club on Tuesdays, Bible study on Wednesdays, and tabernacle praise on Sundays. Later on, those same Sunday nights, men in their wool fedoras came together for handshakes and prayer meetings in the American Legion building, seating no more than twenty at a time.

Football was their favorite sport, though the nearest team was at a college 150 miles south. Downtown housed a theater for plays and modest vaudeville acts. Next to that was the courthouse. Across the street was the post office and the First Bank. If the urge to see the cinema came about, they drove, six in a Packard or Ford, ten miles east to the neighboring city of Tulsa. A bell tower facing the center of town rang in the mornings to begin prayer service for school, with the next bell for the Pledge of Allegiance.

Mendol was merely a speck of dust on a map back then. In the neighboring Cherokee Fields, rigs had tapped into the earth five decades earlier, but those riches were divided quietly among a few good men. Unfortunately, they'd overlooked Mendol's tiny population, leaving them out in the division of wealth and plenty. No one cried about it. They were a proud group.

Once the industrial drills were secured within their boundary lines, they set about rectifying the situation. A large theater with an arched marquee was built. There were three schools now. The center of town housed more than a flagpole on a cement block. Roads were paved. Streets and sidewalks led to more streets and more sidewalks. Halls, shopping centers, and homes went up, seemingly overnight. Even while financial woes wreaked havoc on the rest of the country, the heart of Mendol continued to beat to a different drum. The rhythmic pull of rigs was heard as they punctured deeper into the earth. Pillars snaked around the flat land and could be seen on miles of skyline from any direction. Barrels of oil filled cargo docks, ready for loading onto trains headed to destinations the men and women of Mendol would never see. In exchange, the zeros rolled onto the ends of their account balances and filled their coffers.

They may not have had the Rockefellers, Roosevelts, or Vanderbilts, or Manhattan's Fifth Avenue or the Plaza, but they did have one another. It was only right that they spent what they earned and bought what they deserved. They had their photos taken and printed in the *Chronicle*'s society page. Yes, they had a society page. Charity balls and banquets. Tuxedos and gowns. Furs and cashmere overcoats. Year-round giving for the needy. Prayers and song for those far away physically, or in some cases spiritually, who'd lost their will to live in war and the Depression. Throughout it all, their foundation was built on insularity, keeping to themselves. *God bless the child who's got his own.*

WELCOME TO MENDOL, POPULATION 18,206 a sign read at the forgettable entrance off Highway 98. That was before a swollen body was found floating on top of the Red River's thick sludge. Now there was one less person. If the state prosecutor asked for the death penalty in the case of alleged murderer Elsa Grimes, that would make two less citizens in the town of Mendol.

1

IT WAS A GIFT, seeing what most people were afraid to see. It took her aunt Charlene to teach Bailey she wasn't hexed. "But did the visions have to be with naked bodies?" twelve-year-old Bailey asked one evening as she sat on the porch swing, watching fireflies.

"Turn it into what you need it to be. You have to control it somehow. Make your own signals. Make it a safe place," her auntie explained. "Your mama had the gift of sight. I wish she could've shared it with you before she passed. She used to describe people's pictures as flowers. A rose meant good things were coming their way. A thorny bush meant danger. Reading colors, auras, been in our family for years."

Bailey tried it, did her best to make the pictures into symbols. It only worked once or twice. But colors she could see. Bright blues, pinks, or grays, but unfortunately merely a haze over fleshy bodies.

She wasn't naive. She just found it hard to look someone in the eye once she'd seen them bare in her mind's eye. Especially when they were her clients. Turned out, the ladies of Mendol who came in for wedding dress fittings were far from virgin brides waiting to be declared honest women. The people Bailey saw, entwined limbs and the faces attached, weren't the same two people who were purportedly taking each other's hand in marriage. She felt like a Peeping Tom and said nothing about what she saw.

But then came Alice Ledge. Alice, dour and poised, had shown up on a Tuesday morning bright and early for the final fitting before her wedding day. Bailey and Alice were alone in the shop, just the two of them.

"Miss Alice, are you in love with someone else?" The question had climbed from Bailey's throat spontaneously.

How many times had Aunt Charlene warned her to leave white folks' business where it belonged? *"Stick to pinning and sewing the dresses, Bailey. What they do with their lives is no concern of yours."*

Bailey knew it was dangerous to speak out of turn, let alone to talk about someone's private love life. She would never forget the look of shock that filled Alice Ledge's narrowed eyes. "What do you mean? Why would you ask me that?" Red streaks of embarrassment appeared on her round face with frightful speed, very much at odds with her otherwise placid nature.

"I saw something. I know I have no right to say this, but it was you and another man. I've seen your future husband, Miss Alice. It wasn't him," Bailey said. The man Alice was to marry had made an appearance at the Regal Gown shop and had made it clear that Alice had an allowance of two hundred dollars for the dress, shoes, and veil and not a penny more. He'd accused the proprietor, Miss Jackson, of being a huckster and charlatan who caused the women of Mendol to spend hard-earned wages as if marriage were some type of beauty contest. It wasn't often Miss Jackson was left speechless. Bailey wouldn't forget Victor Kunely, or the way he filled out the check. He'd underlined the amount with three hard lines, nearly cutting the paper.

Bailey often wondered what brought two people together, especially when they appeared so different from each other.

"I have these visions," Bailey had continued that day. "They come to me in the night. Like when I do this," she said putting her hand lightly against Alice's cheek. "When I touch you, there's a charge. Just this tiny bit of light."

"But why you?" Alice asked, placing a skittish pale hand to Bailey's before pulling it away from her face.

"I don't know. Now and again, it happens. I don't have any real control over it. I thought you should know what I saw. I mean no disrespect. I just thought maybe you needed to talk to someone, or maybe—"

"He's Pawnee," Alice blurted. "I love him. We've been seeing each other only a short while," she said, her voice raspy and on the verge of tears. "He knows I'm getting married to someone else. He knows we can't be together. We just can't."

Bailey understood and nodded.

The Pawnee people were enlisted as laborers to build homes in the ever-growing outskirts of Mendol. They'd been assigned land in kind to do with as they pleased.

"I met him at our church just a few months ago," Alice said quietly. "His name is John. Everything lights up when I'm around him."

Bailey felt their connection gently, in a wave, and forced herself not to reach out for stable ground. She waited for the feeling to pass and continued to listen.

"The second our eyes landed on each other—I've never felt this way. I've never been with anyone like him." Alice wrapped her arms around herself, fighting off a sudden chill. Bold statements of love and adoration flowed until she'd gotten it all off her chest. She'd paused, and Bailey slipped in the big question.

"Are you really going to marry someone you don't love?"

"Yes. Of course I am," she answered curtly and assuredly. Her tenor could have been about anything. As if she were discussing chocolate cake versus vanilla for her reception. Carnations versus roses. There was no gray area. "This is Mendol. We don't marry for love; we marry to honor our families. For the good of our standing in the eyes of God. I can't be with John, not in public."

Interracial marriage was against the law in Oklahoma. Even a flirtatious glance might be punished. Sex between two consenting adults of different races was downright reckless, although everyone also knew that the rules were only enforced in one direction. A white man who wanted to marry or take a lover of a different race met no resistance, at least not from the law. But for a white woman choosing to be with anyone other than a white man, the road would be long, hard, and very dangerous. Alice, her entire family, and especially the Pawnee man, would pay dearly for such actions.

"I've heard some people travel to New Mexico or Kansas to be together," Bailey offered.

"Thank you. Yes. I've heard it would be easier anywhere other than here. Oh my, we best get on with this fitting." Alice turned around and waited for Bailey to close her gown. "I can't tell you what a relief it's been talking about all of this. I feel like a weight has been lifted. Can you make the hem a touch shorter? I don't want to trip going down the aisle," she added.

Bailey had spent the rest of her time with Alice silently pleading, *Please don't tell anyone what I've said here today.* "I didn't mean to overstep, Miss Alice," she eventually whispered. "Please keep this between us? I'm truly sorry if I've offended you."

"No. I would never tell a soul. Could never," Alice admitted. "Telling someone about you would mean the truth coming out about me. My fiancé is a proud man. You've met him. Not likely to let me live it down, if you know what I mean. This secret I need to take to my grave," she said with a finger to her lips. "You keep quiet and I'll do the same."

Weeks later, Miss Alice Ledge continued on her merry way, down the aisle, bouquet in hand, ignoring her true feelings. True love was a fairy tale, Bailey told herself. Lesson learned.

She swallowed the dreams and visions at night, let the tingly surge of awareness churn in her stomach, and ignored the prickly rise of hairs on her skin. She tamped down the urge to speak of warnings and soothsaying. She learned to smother the concern. *No more,* she chanted to herself. The brides were on their own. Who was she to try to open a door that had been closed and locked for decades, centuries even?

The problem was that Miss Alice hadn't kept her word. The secret was out. Suddenly, a gaggle of women, young ladies mostly, arrived with dresses in hand. Or they picked one a few sizes too large, with a bow askew, of an unflattering garish satin . . . anything they could buy right away off the Regal Gown rack so they could be pinned and *touched* by Bailey Dowery.

Not wanting to bring attention to herself, Bailey did her best to turn away the guidance seekers, even ones who offered to pay well enough for her services.

A few times she'd taken the irresistible cash pressed against her palm. *Tell me something . . . anything.*

She was enticed by the money. She could make good use of an extra twenty dollars at the end of the month. She'd also been urged along by Gabby Jones, her oldest and dearest friend. "Take the money," she'd told Bailey on more than one occasion. "Why shouldn't you be paid? You're offering a service, no different than hemming one of those gowns. It's worth more, actually. It's priceless, if you ask me."

Touching a bride and sparking a vision may have seemed like effortless work, but it left Bailey drained, exhausted. She could only read someone if there was passion and heat just below the surface. She then was forced to live and experience those emotions herself, however briefly.

Where had it gotten her? Bailey questioned the point of it all. Wishing not to see the visions didn't stop them from coming. So in turn, she was lying each and every time she said, *I can't help you*. And each time leaving pieces of herself behind.

2

THE MOMENT BAILEY AWAKENED she knew from her dreams to expect unsettled debts. Now, as she walked against the force of the wind, her hand pressed on her hat while she dodged leaves and notices sailing and bouncing in rhythm, she tried not to worry about what awaited her. She tried to ignore the cloth sign overhead, tied from one corner light post to the other, announcing the Harvest Festival. It hung upside down, the date missing except for the year, 1954, the last two numbers slashed at an angle. Everyone in Mendol knew the date and time for the festival anyway. No one needed the details. It was, however, indicative of how Bailey felt. Dislodged. Upside down. Vitally important details missing.

She kept her voice steady as she called out with a wave, "Good morning, Mr. Joe." She hoped her voice carried past the wind.

"Hey there. Morning, Bailey." Joe Patrick owned the barbershop across the street. They were both early risers. The men in town liked to get their fresh shaves before work. "You best hold on to something. Li'l gal like you likely to blow away," he said.

"Nah. I ain't going nowhere. Take more than a sweep of wind to get rid of me," Bailey replied. She was on the thin side but sturdy. "Have a good one."

"You too, doll."

There was not much traffic in downtown Mendol. Always cautious, she still looked both ways before stepping off the curb onto the street. On the other side, she slowed at the stack of morning papers in the wood crate, held down by a massive rock. The delivery boy knew the Coven Winds would pay Main Street a visit. According to folklore, the intense winds were cries from native spirits for the loss of their ancestral land. There was more written about the mayhem the winds caused than any crime or scandal in town.

The headline of the *Mendol Chronicle* read like a country club newsletter. What looked like sepia-toned senior high school portraits drew Bailey closer. She folded her lean frame to read the bold print on the front page.

ELSA GRIMES TO MARRY NILES PORTER
In one week, on October 13th, the couple will be united at the Good Steeple Church, where Pastor Jon Hoozer plans to conduct the ceremony, followed by a reception designed for a prince and princess at the Grimes estate. The children of prominent local families, Niles and Elsa were destined to be man and wife from the moment they'd first shared their lunch in elementary school.

Bailey stood straight, stretched, and inhaled the crisp gust threatening to push her back on her heels. *Destined to be man and wife.* She cinched her coat collar tighter at her throat. For a minute she was unsure if it was the cold or the memory of Elsa's last visit that chilled her bones.

The newspapers were free for the taking. She thought about scooping up a copy. But, then again, she was sure she'd learn nothing new about Elsa Grimes. What she did know was that the girl wouldn't take *no* for an answer.

For now, Bailey stepped past the stack and took a right turn to her place of work. She put the key in the brass lock of the Regal Gown and pushed in the gold-framed door.

Cool, empty air greeted her. This was her second home. Gold-and-white brocade wallpaper ran from ceiling to floor as a backdrop to dreamy wedding gowns and evening shifts. An artisan-painted cornice trimmed the high walls. If the sun was bright enough in the mornings, the crystal chandelier in the center of the showroom spun out a kaleidoscope of pinks and blues. Beaded appliqués sparkled in the glass cabinets for the extra custom touch.

Whatever the ladies of Mendol desired in the way of fashion, the Regal Gown could deliver, mostly because of Bailey.

Two years ago, she had seen the sign DRESSMAKER WANTED hanging in the window and had known the job was hers. Miss Jackson, the proprietor, had announced the required duties during the interview. "You'll always greet the customers with a smile, do the fittings, tailor the gowns, and on occasion tidy up around here. I also will require work on Saturdays."

Bailey was hired on the spot. She started working that very day and loved coming to work each morning. "Your couturier at your service." She'd seen the title written in a *Vogue* article and had practiced saying it with a cut and roll of her tongue until she'd gotten it just right. She braced herself for Miss Jackson's disapproval upon hearing the term *couturier* stated with such confidence, but the rebuke never came.

In fact, she'd heard Miss Jackson speak very favorably of her when someone questioned having a "colored gal" taking charge of a dress for their momentous occasion.

"Oh now, not to fret. You're in good hands. Our Bailey can see right away the best possible fit for your frame and style," Miss Jackson told the clients one by one when they voiced their concerns. "She is a professional tailor and dressmaker. A couturier of the highest regard."

She'd even used her word, almost bringing tears to Bailey's eyes. Appreciation was there, yes. But on the other hand, Miss Jackson never once had offered to give her a raise in the two years she'd worked there. The Regal Gown wouldn't run effortlessly without Bailey at the helm. Without Bailey's hard work and dedication, Miss Jackson wouldn't be able to sit across the street at Georgia's Diner in her favorite booth, having coffee, reading the paper, and glancing over her spectacles for all comings and goings. Bottom line, she was still Miss Jackson's *colored gal,* regardless of what fancy French name she called herself. When the ire reared its ugly head, Bailey told herself to be grateful she had a job. There was no place she'd rather be.

Business hours started at 10 A.M. Bailey used the spare time to make herself a cup of tea and plan her workday.

She slung the white sewing apron over her head before turning on the lamp in the storeroom. The bulb overhead flickered on slowly to reveal the storeroom, where a cast-iron sewing machine sat in the corner. She plugged it in and listened for the whir of a motor ready for action. She took a moment to study the garments, neatly tagged and in the order of the customers' appointments.

Her heart quickened with a snag of anxiety when she saw one tagged *E. Grimes* hanging among the garments. No doubt Elsa would be bursting through the golden doors first thing, even though her appointment wasn't until later in the week. The girl wasn't giving up without a fight.

Therefore, it made sense to swap projects to plan for the intrusion. E. Grimes now became first on her list of things to do. If . . . *when* Elsa arrived, she'd hand her the gown, complete with alterations, and send her on her way.

As she sipped her tea, Bailey mentally went down the line. She'd have to skip over the work for the lady who wanted peacock feathers sewn around the neckline of a beige cashmere coat. There was Miss Marion, who had an appointment for her second fitting. Much later would be Lucinda Ralph with the red cocktail frock, though Bailey was sure Miss Lucinda had only purchased the dress to talk to Bailey about her husband, who she suspected of having a pretty young thing on the other side of the train tracks.

Bailey had explained she couldn't read a thing happening on the other side of anything. For her ability of sight to work, she'd have to touch Mr. Ralph, skin to skin, and that wasn't likely going to happen unless he needed a dress hemmed, and she would bet he did not.

Bailey moved things one more time, only to see the feathers from the cashmere coat spit fuzz on the black evening frock. Swap. Switch. Move. Then back again.

This was why order was so important. Order made things less complicated. To have Elsa's dress finished right along with the others, Bailey would simply have to work fast and efficiently. What else was new? Miss Jackson had hired her for her efficiency. There'd been a test at the time, no different from what she was doing now. Her home economics teacher would be proud of her—cutting, ripping threads, and putting pieces back together in record speed on the machine. For the intricate details, her hands worked in knotted vigor. The ridiculous feathers caused her to sneeze every few seconds as she sewed steadily, ignoring the occasional pinprick through her thumb guard. All the while she continued to tell herself, *This day too shall pass.*

3

ELSA GRIMES CAMPED OUT at the top of the spiral staircase, not wanting to get in the way of the shuffling tradesmen whose boots were squeaking on the shiny floor. Activity. Movement. Her wedding was in five days. But this shift of bodies was owed to the pre-party before the party.

WELCOME TO THE ENGAGEMENT OF ELSA AND NILES, the engraved plaque read. The plaque had been installed above the arched entryway with screws. No one thought of or cared about the holes that would be left behind.

The staff and deliverymen took their orders from Elsa's mama—Miss Ingrid. One point or wave of her slender ivory-hued hand and her will was done.

Elsa grew up witnessing how folks drooped like water-starved flowers in her mama's presence. She knew exactly how it felt. She was an inferior version of Mrs. Ingrid Grimes, having missed her mother's genetic bonanza of grace, charm, and exquisite taste in clothing and jewelry. Those fine trappings were necessary to make a lady a *ma'am*. But they never took with Elsa, and she certainly didn't ever want to be called *ma'am*.

Elsa preferred wearing tattered dungarees and oversize plaid shirts. Her favorite shoes, shredded at the edges, were her oxfords. If she could figure out how to wear them for the ceremony, she would. She wobbled in anything with a heel. For the wedding she'd at least been approved to wear low-heeled white Mary Janes, since she and Niles were nearly the same height.

"Not here, over there," Ingrid snapped. "The library will be used as the coat check. Move the Steinway to the far-right corner of the ballroom just past the fireplace. This space will occupy the six tables with ten chairs each. Now follow me over here." Her graceful steps in kitten heels gave the impression she was charming and ladylike, but Elsa knew different. The manners and dignity her mama wore could easily be removed like an itchy sweater.

Elsa calculated the six tables times ten people. Sixty guests would be congratulating the Grimeses and the Porters, the joining of two powerful, rich families, as if they needed any more of what the other had.

"Aren't you supposed to have a hair appointment?" Her mama's voice echoed from the foyer landing when she spotted Elsa doing nothing. *Idleness is a sin.* "You're going to be late," she said after checking her thin wristwatch. Lists and schedules were her mama's true power. They were how she got things done.

Elsa leaned her elbows on the banister. "I have plenty of time."

"I think not. At least not the way you drive. Get moving."

"Yes, ma'am," Elsa calmly replied. She had plenty of time. But come to think of it, there was somewhere she needed to be, wanted to be.

"Oh no you don't. You will not leave this house looking like a scallywag."

Scallywag. The term bothered Elsa. It shouldn't have bothered her. She should have been used to it by now. Their family was considered small-town royalty; it came with the territory. Gossip, jokes, and backstabbing about every detail of Elsa's life made her an open book, from the way she dressed and wore her impossibly straight hair to how she spoke, though every possible resource had been used to fix her drawl—*as if she'd come from the swamps instead of the best of what Mendol had to offer,* she'd once overheard someone say.

"I'll be sitting in a salon chair with a cape draped over my entire body. No one is going to see me," Elsa said.

"Change. Now," her mama hissed. "I have way more to do than argue with you."

Elsa shook her head. "I'm fine as I am," she said calmly. "I'm sure no one will see me. I won't embarrass you." She snatched the keys from the drawer, then stopped before breaching the front door, already open. Defying her mama would have consequences. She always found a way to make Elsa pay for back talk and defiance.

"You go right to Lucy's and come back here straightaway," her mama called after her from the porch. "Make sure you leave the curlers in your hair for pictures tomorrow. We'll take them out ourselves. You hear me? And don't forget you have dance lessons at four thirty. But you should be back in plenty of time for that. Especially if Lucy leaves the curlers in place. You won't have to sit through her long-winded one-way conversation while she tries to style your hair."

"All right, Mama." Elsa had already made it to the brand-new Studebaker. The car was her mama's, a gift for twenty years of service. Or what some would call an anniversary present. Her mama had been pregnant when her parents got married in 1934, the year Elsa was born. Elsa had calculated the months and figured it out. Her holier-than-thou mama had obviously lost the key to her self-righteousness. Elsa never thought of her parents' union as anything but duty and presentation. If they showed even the slightest amount of affection, it was because someone was watching—guests, visitors, an audience who could report back all was well in paradise. A perfect family required admiration from others. Otherwise, what was the point?

At least they were still married. Elsa knew of three families in the last six months who'd decided to split and go their separate ways. Divorce was like a common cold, spreading in their little enclave. The men took their martinis and suits to the newly built downtown and the women kept the houses in the suburbs, clad in housecoats and sipping afternoon tequila sunrises.

When Elsa was younger, her parents often fought in hushed murmurs, rapid-fire whispers pushing past the flat walls. If they fought anymore, they were much more understated about it.

Elsa turned on the ignition and waited for the workmen to clear the way. She maneuvered slightly to bypass the fountain and she was free. Breaking out of the estate felt like winning—making it to the end of the Candyland board game she'd liked to play as a child.

She felt victorious, flooring the gas pedal, sending up gravel dust, and peeking every now again in the side mirror down the long path. Relief filled her lungs. The imaginary weight eased. She turned on the radio to hear wailing about the end of the earth and dying in sin. She turned the dial until she reached her favorite snappy jazz station.

Too many times, she'd forgotten to turn back to her mama's brimstone gospel station. Occasionally Elsa listened longer than she should have, out of curiosity.

Death by way of shame seemed to be a requirement of life, from what Elsa could understand. If so, she'd go out in a blaze of glory. It would never be said that Elsa led a quiet life. She'd make sure of that.

INGRID GRIMES WAS TOLD daughters were born to relive their mothers' old sins, a vindication of sorts. She stood at the door and watched the twirl of dust behind the wheels of the car. She'd heard the saying from her own mother a number of times throughout her childhood. Ingrid only remembered being a dutiful and agreeable daughter, one of the good ones. She hadn't done anything terrible enough to deserve a daughter like Elsa.

She'd honored her parents, just as the Bible said. She went to church every Sunday. Had proper grades in school. She'd won Miss Teen Mendol three years in a row. There might've been the rare episode of escapism, wanting to grow up and have independence, all a part of becoming mature. She started dating Matthias under the strict eye of her father, a staunch God-fearing man. Not strict enough, apparently. The first time Ingrid and Matthias were alone, parked in his coupe right out front of her home in broad daylight, their bodies entwined, and the steering wheel pressed into her back like a third hand. She still smiled at the tingling memory.

That was the day she'd gotten pregnant with Elsa, though as far as her parents knew, she was a virgin when she and Matthias were married in the Mary and Joseph Chapel. Good thing Ingrid's parents hadn't bothered counting the months down before Elsa was born. They would have understood the urgency, the need to skip the formalities and invite only the mothers and fathers of the couple to stand by their sides.

Matthias was seven years Ingrid's senior and had made a name for himself after using his tiny savings to buy a parcel of land with three abandoned oil wells. Everyone assumed the wells were tapped dry.

Fortunately, the wells had more to give. After a slow start, in which Matthias had to recruit his two closest friends to buy into the venture, oil gushed feverishly from all three wells. In turn, Senate Oil was founded with the two friends, who became Matthias's business partners. They acquired more land, more wells, and diversified seamlessly into construction. Matthias, always searching for the next holy grail of business, had even dipped his toe in the aeronautics industry. He was a risk-taker. Ingrid's job was to support his endeavors, no matter the outcome. An eagle couldn't soar with clipped wings.

Marrying Matthias had certainly been Ingrid's biggest accomplishment, and she'd made her parents proud in doing so. Maybe not at first, but most assuredly once his gamble on the wells paid off. Her parents saw nothing but moonbeams and stars when they looked at her. Especially after she'd made Matthias buy her parents the first car of its kind, a 1936 Packard, ordered in seafoam blue. The automobile made her parents the talk of the town. *Such a good daughter.* Ingrid Fredrick had gone from being a poor little girl with no future to Ingrid Grimes, woman of distinction. Certainly, she was absolved of any previous moral failings her parents might have suspected.

She definitely had done nothing to deserve the ungratefulness of her own child. From the day Elsa was born, Ingrid had pampered her plump pink bottom day and night. Then came the difficult childhood years, when Elsa wanted to climb trees and wear dirt like a second skin. The Godwin School of Etiquette was warranted. Three years of driving Elsa into the neighboring city for lessons on behaving like a proper girl who liked sugar and spice and everything nice. Feminine graces that should have come naturally to her had to be taught. Chin up. Back straight. Fork between three fingers, not five. It all turned out to be a waste of time, effort, and money. Not that money was a concern. It just turned out there was no amount that could turn Elsa into a polished debutante.

In Elsa's senior year of high school, all Ingrid had asked was that she wear the dresses they'd shopped for all summer long in Paris. A mother-daughter shopping trip in France was something Ingrid had only dreamt about for herself, and yet she'd made it come true for Elsa. But a trunkful of painfully curated couture apparel sat untouched. Elsa retreated into her big shirts and denim as soon as she could.

One could call it a miracle when Elsa showed up on a Saturday evening three months earlier with Niles, his arm wrapped around her shoulders as he helped her inside because she'd had a bit too much to drink—drunk to the point of throwing up in the downstairs lavatory. But what difference did it make how it happened? Niles, the son of Layton Porter, one of the Senate Oil partners, was a very dear friend. This new warmth between the youngsters had shown promise of something more. A blossoming romance, perhaps? Ingrid shared what she'd witnessed with Matthias and, as they say, the rest was history. She could declare victory. The Porters and the Grimeses would be united in business and family.

The promise of Niles turning their little ragamuffin into a glowing bride still brought fresh tears to Ingrid's eyes.

"Ma'am, where would you like the gifts?" The soft voice cut through Ingrid's surge of remembrance.

She wiped at her eyes and turned to see Rochelle Davis holding a box large enough to hide the top half of her body.

Rochelle was the daughter of their long-standing housekeeper, Oda Mae Davis. Rochelle attended nursing school at night, Oda Mae had explained to Ingrid when she asked why Rochelle couldn't work more than three days a week.

"My girl goes to school. She'll be a nurse soon," Oda Mae declared with an unwavering air. "Won't be keeping house for the rest of her days." Her words were resolute, emphasizing her belief that her daughter was destined for greater things. She wanted Ingrid to understand that her daughter was above this kind of work.

Ingrid couldn't help but agree. Rochelle was pretty as a doll with dark almond-shaped eyes and light dimples. Well-mannered. Smart. Quiet on her feet. If it weren't for the pageant's rules with the clear instructions on the top page that said *Whites Only,* Ingrid would have offered to guide Rochelle into the tiara world, where she surely would have won in every category. Unfortunately, Ingrid didn't make the rules and had no intention of trying to change tradition.

"Gifts. Yes. Follow me." Ingrid walked down the hall, then made a left to the storage closet, emptied for this very purpose, even though she'd specifically written on the invitations to send a donation to the Rose Society in lieu of a gift.

"Here you are. Start the stack on this side. Large to small toward the door. Things like toasters, mixers, and appliances we'll send to the Rose Society." She paused. "You know, you and your mother could benefit by signing up on their list. There's going to be a great deal of brand-new items given out this year." Ingrid had shared this information with Oda Mae many times but, to her knowledge, Oda Mae's name had never appeared on the list. Rochelle might be more receptive, less worried about appearances.

"Thank you, ma'am. I'll keep it in mind."

Something in her tone made Ingrid pause. "Is there anything you'd like to have? It doesn't all have to go to the Rose Society. It'll be our little secret."

Rochelle gave a head tilt this time with a carefully neutral smile. The silent response felt more powerful than her words. *Whatever you say, ma'am.* Or, *If you say so. But, really, no thank you.*

"That's such a pretty necklace," Ingrid blurted, having noticed the heart-shaped pendant on a thin gold chain around Rochelle's neck. She'd given one exactly like it to Elsa. Tiny diamonds set in a gold heart. She couldn't recall the last time she'd seen it, but she felt sure it was the same one. Same style, anyway. Humboldt's in Oklahoma City was a solid two-hour drive away. It wasn't as if they only sold exclusively to a certain clientele . . . perhaps Rochelle had a beau who could afford a nice thing or two. Certainly possible. A girl like her could very well snag one of the top-tiered fellas in her circle. Ingrid could think of a few, including Alston Birch, one of the young men who'd won a scholarship last year and happened to work on the grounds. The two of them would make a handsome couple, but she'd never seen them say more than a few words to each other.

"Where did you get it?"

Rochelle's hand instinctively went to the pendant, fingers pinched at its center, as if she just remembered she had it on. She tucked the chain under her white collar, uncomfortable with Ingrid's scrutiny. "It was a birthday gift from a friend."

"A friend who has expensive taste. It's beautiful," Ingrid added quickly, hoping to extinguish any feeling of interrogation.

Rochelle offered that polite smile again. "I guess."

"All righty, then. I'll leave you to it." Ingrid had known Rochelle since she was at Oda Mae's hip, too shy to step away for Oda Mae to clean effectively. Ingrid never had the heart to tell Oda Mae to stop bringing the child along. Then, before her eyes, the girl had grown into a sweet young lady. Ingrid had no reason not to trust her, not after having known her all her life.

Within minutes, she found herself rummaging through Elsa's many jewelry boxes. The search was on. She cursed under her breath while digging under layers of orphaned necklaces and bangles, untouched childhood gifts deemed worthless. Reminders of her many attempts to endear herself to her daughter with a boxed set of earrings and a matching brooch—things Ingrid would have treasured as a girl. Everything was accounted for except the diamond heart necklace.

It didn't mean anything nefarious had taken place, Ingrid reminded herself. Rochelle wasn't a thief. Ingrid would know if she was. There were a number of jewelry choices in her own collection that would have fetched a lot more money at a pawnshop. And if Rochelle had stolen it, why would she wear it in plain sight? Ingrid could only assume Elsa had given it to her.

She walked unsteadily down the wide hall to her bedroom, her daughter's jewelry boxes clutched in her hands and under her arms.

She stacked them at her feet, then found the key to open the safe in the closet. Inside were important papers like stock certificates and insurance policies, and a silver-handled gun and a box of bullets. She dumped the contents of each box into the biggest jewelry box and then shoved it into the safe.

She slammed the steel door shut. If her daughter wanted to give her precious things away, she wouldn't be needing them anymore. Taking away choices had been Ingrid's only way of dealing with Elsa. Having a say, making decisions, was a luxury and a privilege. When one was out of options, that's when understanding took place. Who was in charge? Who had the power? She was Ingrid Grimes, the one who held the cards. Eventually her daughter would learn. She'd make sure of that.

4

A LITTLE AFTER TEN, Bailey had completed alterations meant for the entire week. *Good,* she assessed. Well, *good enough.* A few slightly crooked seams, but nothing the layperson could see. She, on the other hand, knew when fabric had even the slightest pull from too much thread tension. But for the sake of speed, the work got done with the tiniest number of flaws. Her acceptable level of error meant darn near perfection in other people's book.

"Welcome to the Regal Gown. I'm Bailey, your couturier, and I'm here to assist you." She greeted each customer with an expert sensibility and a charming disposition that matched her tender voice.

"Bailey, for goodness sake, it's me!" Miss Jackson said.

"Oh. Hello. I wasn't looking up. I didn't see you. Good morning." She should have known Miss Jackson had arrived. The air in the Regal Gown now carried the scent of vanilla, making her mouth water just a little. Bailey had skipped breakfast.

Miss Jackson brought in ladyfingers, compliments of Georgia's Diner, every morning. She set them out on a china platter. A bottle of sparkling white wine sat in a bucket of ice, with crystal flutes at the ready. All of this was properly placed on an eyelet-lace tablecloth, along with a vase of fluffy white hydrangeas. Picture-perfect and ready for customers in need of indulgence or celebration.

A few minutes later, her first scheduled client of the day entered. Bailey showed Marion Carter to a dressing room, handed her a dress, and then waited outside the curtain. "May I come in, Miss Marion?" Bailey always asked for permission, giving the customer enough time to decide how much of herself she was willing to reveal.

"What do you think?" Miss Marion asked as she opened the curtain, fully zipped and ready for the final assessment.

"I don't think we're going to have to make any further changes." Bailey slipped on her gloves, then snapped on her wrist pincushion. Formalities. There really wasn't a single thing that needed changing.

In the land of opulence and oil money, Miss Marion was something of an anomaly, choosing an heirloom dress over something new. Bailey felt proud of the work she'd done. "Beautiful. Come on out. Let's get a good look," she said in a hushed voice. She didn't want Miss Jackson to hear her doting on the vintage gown.

Miss Jackson had made it clear she detested the dress Miss Marion chose to wear for her upcoming nuptials in December. She tried to pressure Miss Marion on her first visit. "My, my . . . why not a fresh start for a fresh new life?" she'd asked while staring in bewilderment at the contents of the wedding box Miss Marion had brought with her. The Victorian lace at the neck had frayed. The ivory crepe had obviously once been white. In some areas both shades existed, giving the dress a striped appearance.

"This was my great-grandmother's dress. I think it's quite lovely," Miss Marion had answered. "I've heard your girl can do wonders. My great-grandmother was a bit larger. If we can get the fit right, I believe it will work out perfectly," she'd said.

"Yes, I'm sure if anyone can do this dress justice it's my girl Bailey," Miss Jackson had said. Then, not more than an hour later, her opinion sharply changed. Her voice rose freely the moment Miss Marion walked out the door. "Gauche trash," she snapped. "With all the dresses to pick from right here at her disposal, and our supreme talents of dressmaking at her disposal, this is what she's chosen?"

Our supreme talents, she'd said. Had Miss Jackson ever sat down in front of the sewing machine or offered a hand in the process?

"We can't let her walk down the aisle in this plain-wrap garbage bag, for heaven's sake. I will be blamed for this . . . this relic," she'd said.

Bailey had worked a small miracle. She'd soaked the dress in a solution of water, vinegar, and baking soda to bring the brightness back to the gown. Once it hung dry, she steamed and stretched the fabric to its original size. Only then had she begun the alterations.

Since then, Miss Jackson's approach had softened, but not by much, which was why Bailey didn't want to be overheard offering compliments. Miss Jackson still held out the hope she could talk the bride into a new dress.

"How are we doing here?" Miss Jackson asked now. Her preened smile caused her amber eyes to nearly disappear under her pale green eye shadow.

"Everything is coming along nicely," Bailey said from where she knelt at the hem, making sure it was even from every angle.

"Yes. But I was speaking to our cherished customer, Miss Marion. You look lovely, just lovely."

The pleasant tone didn't fool Bailey. Miss Jackson still didn't want her name associated with the likes of this remade gown. Her business was based on reputation, and she never took it for granted. New. Everything must be new, shiny, and captivating. Sure, she was the only gown shop for miles in any direction. But her clientele of oilmen's wives could easily afford to shop somewhere else—Tulsa or Dallas, or even New York. It also didn't matter that the women of Mendol had practically begged Miss Jackson to open the boutique in the first place so they'd have somewhere to shop locally. As she'd once managed the ladies' formal department at Vandevers in Tulsa, she'd been perfect for the job. Bailey had heard a few ladies chatting about how smart they'd been to invest in Miss Jackson and the Regal Gown. Now any dress they desired was at their fingertips, from an Elizabeth Arden to a Givenchy gown.

Miss Marion remained poised, her arms resting at her sides. "Everything's going splendidly."

"Are you sure we can't show you something in the same style but with a border of pearls or lace?" Miss Jackson inquired.

"Absolutely not. I want to stand out. My great-grandmother's dress makes me feel connected to her. She was an amazing woman. Unique. She spearheaded the Women's Suffrage Council here in Oklahoma, you know?"

"And what will your groom be wearing? Surely he'll be in a dapper suit. Black tails, white shirt, I'm assuming. The white against your, *um* . . . beige will look a bit—" Her rapid blinking was a tell. She'd caught something else to be offended by. The cap sleeves. Bailey realized the fold remained a bit uneven and wavy. She'd gladly take responsibility for the imperfection, but later. For now she wanted

Miss Marion to feel every bit as confident as she needed to feel in her great-grandmother's dress.

"All right now. I think I have it. Now, give us a spin," Bailey said, interrupting Miss Jackson, unable to let the berating go on. Bailey stood and adjusted her work apron. Her curls had moistened a bit at the nap of her neck. A quick fan of her hand helped alleviate the stickiness.

Miss Marion admired herself in the trifold mirror. "So beautiful. Right? Isn't it?"

"You're stunning, Miss Marion," Bailey said, sincerely.

Miss Jackson let out an exasperated sigh before turning to leave them alone.

"And my fiancé, he's going to love it, don't you think, Bailey?"

"Yes. Of course," Bailey answered, peeking up to see Miss Jackson within earshot. In the mirror's reflection, Bailey could see she wore a scowl. She awkwardly organized the glass case of tulle but was surely listening. She would later tell Bailey her praise was uncalled for.

"He's the kind of man I've always dreamt of," Miss Marion said, her bluish-gray eyes suddenly dark and watering.

Bailey had anticipated this moment. Freshly folded tissues were always at the ready, stashed in her apron pocket. "Here you go."

Tears ran freely in the Regal Gown shop. Mostly out of joy, when customers saw themselves in the proverbial white gown, matched and delivered. Some cried for other reasons—unexpected ones, Bailey had found, letting out as many waistlines as she'd taken in. Releasing the seams, opening the lining around the bust or middle for an unforeseen bun in the oven, was commonplace. She often knew before the bride and simply smiled and nodded in agreement when the woman said, "I promise I will lay off the pie before the next fitting." Or, "I can remedy this. I'll simply resist my mother's pecan fudge."

"Don't you worry yourself. The dress can be fixed," Bailey would say. Anything to give them grace. What kind of torture it must have been to constantly be perfect all the time? Or at least what they deemed perfection. And yet she knew that more times than not, the tears had absolutely nothing to do with the dress.

"I'm sorry for blubbering," Miss Marion said before taking a hic-cuped breath. "I don't know what's come over me. I've wanted this for so long." She dabbed her eyes, leaving black mascara stains on the tissue. "It's just, if I was sure, absolutely sure . . ." She paused.

Don't ask. Please, don't ask, Miss Marion.

"Bailey, you know what I want to hear. Everyone knows you can read a woman's true match." Miss Marion's fingers twirled the tissue until it shredded.

Instead of taking the cue, Bailey turned the focus back where it belonged. "I think a pair of long gloves will add the sophistication you're looking for. Wait right here."

"Bailey Dowery, I've tried not to impose," Miss Marion said just loud enough to get Bailey to stop in her tracks, her pleading suddenly turned to something else entirely. Her eyes were sharp with intent. "If you don't help me, I'll be forced to speak freely about your little talent."

"I'm sure you and your fiancé will make a fine pair," Bailey said, ignoring the threat. Besides, she'd been outed for some time already. It was a miracle Miss Jackson still hadn't heard. Or maybe she had and was fully aware. Their increased business was a legitimate reason to ignore a rumor here and there.

"There are other people who would find what you do not so ac-ceptable."

Bailey folded her arms over her chest. "Everyone is *other* to me, Miss Marion. Besides, it's not something I can turn on like a light switch."

"Try."

"Try? You seriously trying to get me fired?"

"I'm sorry. I don't know what's come over me." Miss Marion cov-ered her face with both hands, wilting before Bailey's eyes. "You've been so good to me. Turning this dress into my dream gown. You've been an angel, really. I'm sorry. But . . . I have to know."

Why this sudden outburst? Why now? This only confirmed how Bailey felt earlier that morning when she stepped out of bed, tilted and out of balance. How many more times could she deny what was asked of her?

Miss Marion stepped closer. "These last few days have been filled with worry and wondering—am I doing the right thing?" New tears welled. "I simply don't know what to do. Rendel, my fiancé, and I don't know each other all that well. Not intimately. There was . . . someone else. I don't know what to expect now. What if he's not . . . desirable?"

"Come." She led Miss Marion into the dressing area, pulled the curtain closed, and removed her sewing gloves. Clean trimmed nails on slim brown fingers wrapped around Miss Marion's pale palms. "Close your eyes," Bailey ordered. "Go on, now. I gotta be quick about it." *What will come will come.*

The spark of light bolted past Bailey's closed eyes. She let the wave of energy shoot through her. *Relax. Breathe. See. Feel. Hear.* Flashes of color. Broad ranges of light. The exact pictures never came right then and there. She stored the images only to be deciphered later, in her sleep.

"Bailey," Miss Jackson called out. "Our next appointment is here."

The link of light was broken the second she heard her name. "Yes, ma'am," Bailey answered, grateful to be shaken loose from the strange entanglement. "Be right there."

"What'd you see?" Miss Marion asked.

"I don't see the full picture until I lay my head down for the night," Bailey answered. "The visions come to me at night." It was the truth. When she closed her eyes in a daze of exhaustion, the images came whether she wanted to see them or not. "I'll have answers for you when you come back for your next appointment. Your next fitting is in one week, right? I'll see something by then," Bailey said, vigorously enough to get a nod from Miss Marion.

"You're a treasure, Bailey. A true treasure," she said, her tone full of satisfaction. "I'll have something extra for you next week."

"When you come back, I'll have an answer." She repeated the same thing to all the ladies, only to make up another excuse, and then another. Sooner or later, she'd have to give them what they wanted.

5

ELSA WAS IN NEED of a sweet fix. Chocolate, vanilla, or strawberry? She wanted all three. A Neapolitan sundae would do the trick. She imagined the cold ice cream on her tongue the minute she stepped inside. Georgia's Diner had been a fixture in her life as long as she could remember. Her fondest recollection was the birthday visit. She was five or six. No gifts. Just Elsa and her daddy alone in one of the blue vinyl booths, eating French fries dipped in ketchup. Nothing about the place had changed since then.

She plopped down at the counter next to an older gentleman with hefty red ears who hunched over his soup. She considered skipping a stool but didn't want to seem impolite by leaving an empty space between them. The chalk-written sign listed the pie offerings for the day: key lime, cherry, apple, and pecan. *All of them.* Her eyes were too big for her stomach. She waved over the scrawny waiter with his red-and-white-striped shirt and white paper hat. She'd never seen him before but wasn't surprised that she didn't know him. She'd kept to herself lately.

"What can I get you?"

"A Neapolitan, double whip, with extra chocolate syrup. I'm kind of in a hurry, so it doesn't need to be pretty."

"Gotcha. You want some nuts?"

"Nope. Just whip and chocolate."

"Coming right up."

Elsa kept a steady eye on the wall clock behind the counter.

The bells on the diner door announced the entrance of a new customer. A breeze swept past her back.

"Well, look who left the reservation!" The voice came intimately close to Elsa's ear. Leo Porter looped an arm over her shoulder, followed by the acrid smell of beer and Cheez Doodles. Elsa briefly closed her eyes as if the act would block her sense of smell.

"Hey, Leo." Elsa shrugged to try to get his arm from around her. The heaviness remained. She shrugged once more before he removed his paw. "Niles with you?" she asked, trying her best to sound friendly.

"Big brother is out getting fitted for his penguin suit. You already forget? Y'all getting married. Or has somebody changed their li'l-bitty mind?" Leo flipped the empty stool around, sat on it backward, and managed to trap Elsa in his open knees. He and Niles were fraternal twins. Leo came a whole six minutes later, so Niles was designated the big brother.

The sundae appeared in front of her. She was unable to fathom one bite of the frothy dessert. She stared at it, not sure how it came to be in the first place. Had she even ordered it?

"Looks like someone lost her appetite," Leo teased. "Don't mind if I do." He reached over and grabbed the spoon. He went right into the center, breaking the chocolate shell. That was Elsa's favorite thing to do. Her heart raced at such a silly idea. Yes. She had indeed ordered it and wanted the first bite, to taste the sweetness on her tongue, but instead, she bit the inside of her cheek and welcomed the pain.

The bells on the diner door jingled again. "Aye, free ice cream," Leo announced to the extra bodies gathered behind her. They too carried the smell of yeasty beer, Cheez Doodles, and . . . black oil. The distinct harsh smell of raw crude overtook the diner's smoky scent of bacon frying in fat. Only one person in the group worked at the wells. That would be Connor Salley, relegated to a workingman's life as a laborer. The Salleys hadn't weathered the storm of the financial crisis as easily as the others. A refinery fire that Senate Oil was responsible for a few years back had bankrupted the family. Never mind that the dry winds had played a part in the destruction and lives lost, the lawsuits and liability had landed squarely on the Senate Oil partners. They all had suffered the price. The only difference was that Connor's father's bad investments made it impossible for the Salleys to recover financially. That meant Connor had to get a job.

"Elsa, hey!" Connor said directly behind her.

She visibly flinched. Hearing his voice that close to her made her want to jump up from her stool, climb into a corner, and hide. She focused and stared straight ahead, not sure what to do. *"I'll kill you, you touch me again. I swear, if you lay a hand on me, I will. I swear."* Leo and a couple of the others had witnessed her threat.

If he attempted to put a hand on her now—she felt the bile rise in her chest. What good was a threat if you didn't act on it?

"Come on, you two. Time to let all that bad blood go," Leo said.

Elsa pulled her change purse out and laid down two quarters next to the sundae. Connor stood over her, tall and brooding. He lowered his hard brown eyes and looked away when she faced him.

He was wearing his gray shirt with the Senate Oil emblem over the right pocket, an S swirled around the American flag. The shirt-tail half hung out over his dark gray pants. He kept his hands in his pockets, but she still imagined them around her throat.

Stop fighting me, Els. You just don't know what's good for you. I'll let you go when you stop fighting me.

He stepped back to give her room to leave.

Better for him to get out of her way than for her to go around him.

Leo smirked. "Y'all two like an old married couple."

Her legs weakened with each step she took to reach the exit. Getting to the door took a staggering effort.

"Don't bother. Let her go," she heard Leo say. "She's my brother's problem now. Let Niles handle her."

When she stepped out onto the sidewalk, she could breathe again and think clearly. She looked back at the diner. It was her paranoia making her think he'd come after her.

ELS, YOU JUST DON'T KNOW what's good for you.

She remembered the first time he ever said those words to her. Connor was her friend once upon a time. They'd grown up together. The Grimes, Porter, and Salley families came together every third Saturday for mint juleps and gossip. While the mothers sat in the gazebo wearing their darkest sunglasses, the fathers practiced their golf swings on the green lawn.

Niles, Connor, Leo, and Elsa ran amok in the grotto of endless trees near a rippling stream they could hear but never see. Even if they climbed to the top of a tree, there'd be no water sighting.

"You climb like a girl," Leo teased. They were all about the same age: nine, maybe ten.

"That's because she *is* a girl," Connor said, coming to her defense.

"I'm not. I'm no different than y'all. I can do anything and every-thing just the same."

"A girl with big feet and flat cakes," Leo teased. "That's why she can climb trees so good. She ain't got no boobs so she can grab a trunk good and tight."

Niles never joined in on the teasing. He was too busy climbing higher than anyone else. He'd get to the top, look down, and yell, "I'm the king of the world."

Elsa wouldn't be far behind. She kept pace with the boys until her footing slipped on one of those eucalyptus trees with peeling bark. She remembered hanging in the air, legs pedaling for something to grip, and then finally letting go out of sheer exhaustion.

She landed on her back. Her head throbbed while she listened to their laughter. Then two hands pulled her to her feet. One belonged to Leo and the other was Connor's. Niles had arrived after climbing down and jumping the rest of the way.

"You're bleeding," Niles said.

"She's all right," Leo said, brushing the dirt off her shirt and britches. "Right? You said you can do anything same as us. Little scratch won't kill ya. Come on, let's go." He took off running. Niles followed. Connor stayed.

He put his arm around her waist. "I'll get you back to the house."

"No. I'm fine," she said, squiggling out of his grip. She took one step and howled in pain.

Connor reached out to lend a hand.

"I said I don't need your help."

"Els, you just don't know what's good for you," Connor said. He shook his head like it was such a shame. He trotted off to follow the echo of boys' chatter.

NOW SHE REGRETTED stopping in Georgia's. She should have known she'd run into Leo and the gang. She hadn't considered that Connor would be hanging out with them on a Monday morning. He was the workingman, the only one who really had somewhere to be on a regular basis. She wished she hadn't run off and made him feel more important than he was.

All she'd wanted to do was get to the Regal Gown as soon as their doors opened. She arrived early enough, but she saw another customer heading into those golden doors—Marion Carter. She was a few years older than Elsa and she'd been there at the disastrous party that night. Elsa didn't want to face Marion, or any of them, sick of their judgment.

Elsa sat patiently in her car to have her chance alone with Bailey. How many pins and tucks would it take to make Marion look respectable? She guessed, a whole boatload. But Bailey was a whiz at making miracles. It wouldn't be long. She'd wait.

6

BAILEY TOOK HER TWENTY-MINUTE LUNCH BREAK sitting in the alleyway on a lone rickety chair no one had claimed in the last two years. None of the four legs matched in length, giving her a jolt off-balance with even the smallest shift or movement. The afternoon sun passed from the wedge of sky visible between the buildings, causing her to eat fast, in a hurry to get back inside, away from the cold. She checked her watch. She still couldn't believe Elsa hadn't showed up.

Bailey had been in a nervous rush all morning for nothing. She took a huge bite of her ham and cheese on toasted white bread with mustard and a pickle, her favorite. The bread held up well in the wax paper. One corner of the bread was saved for her friends, two gray pigeons that joined her regularly for her lunchtime. She broke the crust in half before tossing it, not wanting to cause a rift between the two birds, a few feet away. She assumed the rounder one was the male and the clear-eyed, focused bird, the female.

"There's more than enough for both of you."

Together they pecked at the bread in sensible, polite fashion, until a long bulky truck barreled into the narrow space, causing the birds to take flight quickly to get out of the way.

The truck's gear rammed into park. The passenger side of the door read *Wag's Handy Services* in bad handwriting.

Bailey looked down, her heart still racing. There was barely an inch between the front tire and the round tips of her leather flats.

The driver's door opened and slammed shut. A man came around, startled. "Whoa! Didn't see you there."

"I guess not," Bailey sneered. "You almost ran me and my friends over."

"Friends? I don't see nobody out here but you." His lips pushed into a one-sided smile. "Oh, you talking about them pig-birds. You need better friends." He adjusted his cap, which sat high over the curly wool of his hair. Most of the Black men around Mendol wore short, neatly edged hairstyles, as if they'd just left church. She assumed from this man's unkempt look and his risky driving that he wasn't a local, and therefore was not to be trusted.

She stood and gathered her lunch sack, which still contained an apple and a paring knife for slicing it. She eyed him while she moved her chair back. "Wouldn't want this getting crushed when you leave."

"Not going anywhere soon." His eyes rose to the sign on the back door. "Regal Gown. You going in? That's where I'm going. Got a call to fix the lights."

"The lights?" Bailey asked, surprised and thrilled. For the past few weeks she had gone home with a headache from the strobing annoyance in the dressing area. Miss Jackson hadn't mentioned anything about calling a handyman.

"You Miss Jackson?"

"I'm Bailey, the couturier," she said proudly, correct pronunciation and all. "The dressmaker," she clarified, when he had a perplexed expression. But what had she expected from—

"I'm Wag, at your service," he said in a soothing voice. She bet he could sing. An artsy type *doing this kind of work until I'm discovered,* she mocked in her head, then felt bad about her snippy assessment of the man when she knew nothing about him. He put out his hand for a shake.

She grudgingly took hold, since she wasn't wearing her gloves. The vibration shot up her hand, immediately followed by a pink burst of light. A horizon of rose color like the first blooms of spring filled her senses. She snatched her hand away.

"What? I electrocute you or something?"

"It's nothing. I . . . I'm glad you're here," she said, her tone softened. "Come. I'll show you to Miss Jackson." She led the way. "Watch your step. It's a little dark in here."

"I'll say. You work like this?"

"Yes. Well, I'm used to it."

"You need some light. Wouldn't want you sewing your hand, getting it caught up in the machine. Friend of mine sewed his fingers up. Took two of us to get his hand from under the foot clamp. Needle went clean through like a stake."

"That's not likely to happen. Really. I think Miss Jackson wants the light out here fixed." Bailey stopped talking suddenly and put up a hand for Mr. Wag to do the same. Silence.

There was the voice, familiar and expected. "Is she here? The seamstress; I need to speak with her."

"I don't have you scheduled until Wednesday," Miss Jackson retorted, with the sound of her coveted calendar pages flipping up and back. "Is there something specific you needed, Miss Grimes?"

Elsa's tone was ragged. "Yes. Well, no. But I need to speak with her. Is she here?"

"Yes. She is indeed, but I'm sure I can answer any questions you might have. Might there be a problem? The work is not scheduled for completion until midweek at your appointed time."

Bailey had heard enough. Elsa wasn't going to go away, even with Miss Jackson's determined efforts. She turned to Mr. Wag. "Wait here, please."

She pushed the curtain aside and stepped out of the stockroom. Her hands were still bare, she realized, and she quickly pulled on her gloves. "Miss Jackson, there's a handyman here to fix the lights. Oh, hello, Miss Elsa. I finished your dress this afternoon. Shall we give it one more fit?" Bailey smiled toward Miss Jackson. "Sorry I didn't put her on your calendar. She called this morning."

Miss Jackson huffed as if this small infraction had ruined her entire day, her entire week even. "I guess that's fine. We'll squeeze you in," she said to Elsa; then she turned to Bailey. "You do have Mrs. Grayson in less than thirty minutes. You'll have to work quickly."

"Miss Elsa, I'll show you to a room," Bailey said, already leading the way.

"Thank you." Elsa's wide-lipped smile was sincere. Her large, inquisitive eyes were framed by feathery thin lashes. Her freckle-tinged skin was reddened on her round cheeks from too much sun. She pushed her blunt hair ends behind her ears and looked barely twelve instead of twenty. She clearly had no intention of trying on her dress.

Her rolled dungarees, bobby socks, and oxford loafers seemed the norm for Elsa. But her oversize shirt couldn't hide the hapless shape of her scant, braless bosom. A bra was necessary, even for the less-endowed. An improper undergarment changed the fit of the dress.

"Go on, start undressing. I'll be right back with your dress. I'll also see if we have a bustier you can borrow."

"Bailey . . ." Elsa started, wanting to say more.

"I have to get the dress," Bailey said under her breath. "I can't have Miss Jackson wondering what's going on in here."

"I don't want to try on my dress. Did you have a vision? Last week, you said—did you see anything?"

"*Ssh.* I'll be right back." Whispering would only make Miss Jackson's ears perk up more, wondering what they had to privately talk about.

Thankfully, Miss Jackson and Mr. Wag were discussing his bad timing. "I specifically asked that you come early this morning."

"I'm sorry. I got caught up in a long job on the other side of town. I can be in and out, quiet like a cat. You won't even know I'm here," he said, hardly intimidated by Miss Jackson.

"I have customers now. You'll have to come back tomorrow, first thing."

Bailey took Elsa's dress and slipped it over her arm, slowing to glance up at the flickering light as she came out. At one time she'd thought she was the cause of the malfunction. It was good to know it had nothing to do with her.

"Here we are," she said with exaggerated cheer. She placed the princess-style dress on the hook. Ribbon-trimmed organza filled the space like a fluffy white cloud. "I'll give you a minute to change."

Bailey stepped out. Her armpits were uncomfortably warm. She paced and nibbled at her glove-covered knuckle. It was not like she hadn't expected Elsa . . . all day. But having been so busy preparing the dress, she hadn't figured out how to present her words to end the charade. *No. Unable. Could not see . . .*

Seeing Elsa now, face-to-face, it felt wrong to deny her. Most of the women knew their fate. Even if there was someone else out there who truly loved them, they never took the advice to heart, so what did it matter? But in Elsa's case, it wasn't as simple as second-guessing the marriage. This was different from what brought most of the women through the store's golden doors. *There's a heavy secret living in this little lady's heart,* Bailey thought.

Thinking back to their first meeting, she recalled Elsa being nervous. Her mother had picked out the dresses for her to try ahead of time. "You all right?" Bailey had asked while looping the pearl buttons in the back closed. The first dress was a strapless bodice with heavy crocheted lace.

"There's plenty of styles to pick from. I see you in something more traditional, to be honest. But your mama specifically wanted something in this style." She pulled Elsa's hair away at the neck to get to the top hook and loop. That's when she saw the purplish marks. The fingertip-shaped bruises reminded her of ink that couldn't be washed away. Her skin was beaded with moistness. "You all right, Miss Elsa?" Bailey asked again, this time with gentle concern. "You need some water, tea? I can get you whatever you like."

"No. No, thank you. Got the jitters, I guess. Marrying someone is the biggest step a girl can take. It's your entire life put into someone else's hands, isn't it?"

"That's true. One shouldn't enter marriage lightly."

"So then help me," Elsa breathed out, then faced Bailey.

This girl is wounded inside, where it hurts the most, Bailey thought. The next thing she knew her bare hands were cupped around Elsa's face. She closed her eyes and waited. It was a rare moment when she truly sensed nothing, saw and felt nothing. She didn't have to deny it with a lie.

Maybe it was because of all the worrying she'd been doing. Bailey had problems of her own she was dealing with. All her energy had been drained that day. Sparks and lightning might be dulled from sheer exhaustion. But to see absolutely nothing? It wasn't normal. Not even a hint of a vision.

"I'm just not seeing anything," Bailey had stated, and for the first time it was true.

Elsa began to well up right then and there. Those big wet eyes of hers nearly made Bailey cry too.

After the second visit, there'd been more excuses, more of Bailey offering a kind word instead of the insight Elsa wanted.

"Then what is it?" Elsa had asked. "Am I dead inside? Everyone says you can see right down to the center of someone's soul. Don't I have a soul, Bailey? I'm starting to wonder."

"What's got you so afraid?" Bailey cautiously put her arms around Elsa, thinking, *This is my last day working here. Miss Jackson's going to fire me for sure.* But she held on to her anyway. "You're going to be okay. You hear me? You're going to be fine," she told her.

"I'm not going to be okay. You have to promise to help me. Please."

This was a new day. All she could do was try.

Bailey stepped inside the dressing room to see Elsa holding the bustier in place with her arms clamped at her sides. She still wore her baggy denim jeans. Bailey began fastening the hooks, taking her time, trying to figure out what to say.

"Well? Did you see anything?" Elsa asked, decidedly done with the niceties. "I have to know."

"I . . . well, no," Bailey said. "But I have an idea. Come to my house tonight—101 Baker. The Eastside. Eight o'clock."

"Oh, thank you, Bailey. I'll be there."

"Don't worry. We'll figure this out," Bailey said, already regretting the invite. But this kind of torment Bailey wouldn't wish on anyone. She had to at least try to help her. "Now, you need to try on this dress."

"I can't. I just . . . please don't make me."

"But . . . Miss Jackson," Bailey practically pleaded. Elsa understood and let the halo of fabric fall over her head. Bailey zipped her in and looped the buttons at the top closed. Regardless of Elsa's disdain for the dress, she was breathtaking. "Look at you." She led her out of the dressing room and to the open parlor. "Step onto the pedestal."

"I can't." Elsa refused to open her eyes, knowing there were mirrors everywhere.

"All right. I understand."

The annoying alarm bell rang. Miss Jackson, with her tiny round clock in hand for counting down scheduled appointments, appeared from around the corner. "Very pretty. Beautiful. Bailey, we have a scheduled client in ten minutes."

"Yes, ma'am. I'll be right there." Bailey freed Elsa from the dress, then the bustier. "I'll meet you in the front."

Bailey rushed to the front, looking down while pulling on her gloves.

"Whoa, careful now," the handyman warned. "Hey there, you mind handing me that wrench?" he asked.

Bailey followed his voice to where he stood on the big wooden ladder that she'd almost walked into.

"Ah, come on now. Don't tell me you don't know what a wrench is."

She looked at the open rusted toolbox near her feet. The tools were all rusted too. She only had one pair of white gloves. "I know exactly what a wrench is, but I'm not touching anything in there." She stepped aside and moved back to her spot, where she would greet her next appointment.

"Thank you kindly, Miss Jackson," the handyman said.

Bailey quickly turned to see that Miss Jackson had done the honors. She stood next to the toolbox, her arm raising up the weighty wrench. Bailey was impressed. She had wondered what kind of juju Mr. Wag had working to get Miss Jackson to let him stay in the middle of the workday in the first place, but now her boss was actually helping?

Bailey stared up in wonder.

"You're welcome," Miss Jackson said.

Bailey shook her head, amused. *Who is this Wag fella anyway?*

Elsa appeared in the showroom, back in her grungy shirt and jeans. She'd missed a button. Bailey thought to tell her but felt Miss Jackson watching. She didn't want to add any details to the list of judgment. "That girl is dancing on the edge of disaster," Miss Jackson had said a month ago. "It'll be a miracle if she makes it down the aisle at all."

"Thank you, Bailey. I'll see you"—Elsa caught herself—"another time."

Bailey watched her leave. She could still see her out the window as she looked past the mannequin and thought, *What in the world am I going to tell Aunt Charlene about this girl coming to our house?*

7

CHARLENE DOWERY HAD RETURNED to Mendol fourteen years earlier for only one reason. "Your sister has died and there's business to be sorted out," the caller, a Mrs. Stuart, pointedly told her. "She needs burying. You need to be here."

It was a disgustingly humid summer in New Orleans, a solid distance away from the place and people Charlene had vowed never to see again. She wondered how the elderly neighbor had gotten her exchange or had even known where Charlene had run off to. That was what she wanted to know but didn't ask.

"Your sister needs to be buried. The church is planning a memorial on Saturday," Mrs. Stuart said before hanging up, leaving no room for questions.

Charlene automatically assumed "the business" included a last will and testament. She and her sister were hardly close. She didn't know what Sammie had gotten herself into since last seeing her. Sammie was sixteen when Charlene had left Mendol. Now Sammie had died suddenly at thirty-one years of age. How that happened had left Charlene curious, to say the least. Their mother had passed a few years earlier, at the reasonable age of fifty-two. Charlene hadn't gone back for the funeral or to pay her respects, but she at least wanted to know the real circumstances of her sister's passing. As callous as it sounded, she arrived expecting to find the washwomen gossiping and secrets revealed.

Sammie had been their mother's and grandmother's favorite. It wouldn't have hurt to know she wasn't perfect, for once. But that didn't happen.

Charlene had come for the dirt but got nothing more than squeaky-clean Sammie stories. The memorial service was an ode to her sister's perfection and gleaming spirit. Saint Samantha. Charlene sat through the prayer and speeches, waded past the arms outstretched for hugs, and found Mrs. Stuart. She wanted to know what the "business to be sorted out" was.

At the very least she expected a nice piece of jewelry to sell or the deed to the dinky house she'd grown up in. When Charlene found out the only thing her baby sister had left her was a child, she was ready to get back on the bus and let the whole situation be someone else's problem, perhaps Bailey's father's problem.

But Sammie had deliberately left Bailey's father off the birth certificate, meaning it wasn't easy to search for her next of kin. *Bailey Dowery,* it said. Another Dowery female in the family and that was that.

After a bit of snooping, though, it was acknowledged that Bailey's father, Freddy Johnson, was long gone. He'd enlisted in the army right after Bailey's birth and was never seen or heard from again. No one knew where he was, not even his own family. After conversations with two cousins, an aunt, and a distant uncle, it became obvious that all the responsibility had landed in Charlene's lap. There was no one else left to take care of Bailey.

Resentment didn't last long. One afternoon spent with the sad, rail-thin girl who had become the youngest owner of a sad, ramshackle house, and Charlene was smitten. She settled with the idea, the reality, that she couldn't leave Bailey alone. Not in Mendol. And she certainly couldn't take the child back to her unstable world in New Orleans, where she was living in a tiny apartment with two other gals and a bookie debt she couldn't pay.

She moved into the same two-bedroom house where she and Sammie had lived as children. The same house she swore she'd never step foot in again, afraid it might dredge up bad memories. For her niece, she'd decided to stay. Her most robust years of partying had passed her by anyway. Mendol was as good a place as any to do hair straightening for five dollars a head at the kitchen stove. There were plenty of church ladies in the Bible-toting town to fill her appointment book.

Once Bailey stopped crying over Sammie's death long enough to breathe, Charlene explained she wouldn't get in her way. Adults were required in name and presence only. Besides, she couldn't be bothered with disciplining a child, cooking, or ironing. As the years went on, the question of which one was the parent became a running narrative at the school and the church.

If it was up to Charlene, she would have made Bailey stop attending both. "None of the lies they teach are going to get you anywhere. Trust me. I grew up right here. You know everything you need to know to make it out of this place. You're probably already smarter than everybody here."

For the last fourteen years they'd lived together with no regrets, at least not on Charlene's part. She was happy enough. By all accounts, she'd done a fine job raising her niece. The girl had found her way. *Girl?* No. Bailey was a grown woman, a fact that filtered into Charlene's occasional thoughts of leaving Mendol. Bailey had Gabby, her school pal, someone she could count on besides Charlene. It was time for her to grow some wings and fly, meet new people, and build her life outside their tiny house. Charlene especially pondered putting distance between the town and herself whenever the Grimes family name came up.

Her customers hadn't stopped talking about the upcoming wedding.

"Did you know they built an entire stage on the Grimes estate?" Everlyne Roy said while sitting in a chair with head bent for Charlene to reach the nape of her neck without burning her. Everlyne worked nights cleaning bedpans at the hospital. But no one could tell her she wasn't going to be properly primped and polished while doing it. She came for her wash-and-press every Monday. She was the second client in one day who had bragged about getting on as a server for the grand Grimes-Porter wedding.

"Hold still, Everlyne." What Charlene meant was *"Stop moving your jaws with all that talking."*

"Use the extra-hold spray. This press-and-curl has got to keep through the weekend. I tell you, these people trying to outdo each other for their parties is a whole other opportunity. They paying fifty dollars for one day of serving. That's more than I make all week. You sure you don't want me to put in a word for you, Char? All you need is a black skirt and a white shirt. Everybody gotta black skirt and a white shirt in they closet."

"I'm doing just fine," Charlene answered. "I don't need any extra work. Straightening your hair is work enough."

"You ain't funny," Everlyne snapped. "My hair ain't no more thicker than yours. It's easy money, is all. The oil families like to show off. The more help they have standing on the line, the more they look extra rich."

Charlene wrapped the last pull of hair around the heated barrel and watched the steam rise. The very last thing she'd ever do was work as the help. Not ever again. Before the heat moved to her fingers, she blew gently, then released the clamp. A nice, silky curl bounced free.

"Didn't you use to work for them?" Everlyne asked. "Not the ones having the wedding, the generation before them? You know, before you left? I remember something about you and their son. Right?"

It was all Charlene could do not to let the hot barrel slip onto Everlyne's neck. "All right. We done here."

"Ain't you going to spray me?"

"Yes. Fine. That's another two dollars, just so you know."

"Two dollars . . . for hair spray?"

"Yes," Charlene said, already clogging the air with the sticky mist. Anything to quiet her customer. Anything to quiet the talk of the Grimes family. She'd had enough.

8

IN ITS WHITE BRICK STOREFRONT, Lucy's House of Beauty was busy for a Monday. All three washing bowls, four styling stations, and four dryer chairs were occupied. A few ladies had their heads turned toward the television, blaring the soap opera *Search for To-morrow* at the highest volume, while the others turned pages of *Life* magazine.

But then there was Elsa, legs cocked and knees bouncing, who had never been good about sitting still. She had been under the dryer for forty minutes, ears burning, scalp tingling, and nothing to do but worry. She slipped a hand under the hot helmet and couldn't stop herself from pulling the bobby pin loose from one of the rollers. The tissue wrapped around her hair felt crisp to the touch. She pushed the stifling hood up and took her first breath of cool air.

"Wait, what're you doin'?" Lucy's broad hand caught hold of Elsa's wrist. "Time's not up. If it's not totally dry, it'll be limp. Is that what you want, a head full of limp hair?" Lucy had left Betsy Childs in the styling chair to come over and inspect her handiwork. She brought a cloud of hair spray with her, probably from her own beehive, the same style Lucy had worn since Elsa was a wobbly-legged little girl getting her bangs cut.

"I honestly do not care," Elsa whined. "I have to go. I have some-where to be this evening. Didn't my mother tell you I need the pin curls anyway? I'm not having it combed out. I plan to sleep on the pin curls for pictures tomorrow."

"Yes, I know. I still got to make sure it's dry," Lucy answered.

"My scalp is burning over here," Betsy called.

"Hang on. This girl's mama will kill me if I don't send her home perfect."

"I'ma kill you if my hair falls out, Lucy," Betsy said. She spoke loud enough to catch a few smirks. "What y'all looking at?"

"Oh, hush." Lucy pulled one of the bobby pins out of Elsa's hair and placed it in her mouth. She then unrolled the hair around the curler carefully, checking for its tensile strength. Then she unrolled another and another.

"See, I told you," Elsa said, feeling lucky. "Can I go?"

"Yep. It's nice and dry. All right, you still have to wait. I need to rinse Betsy, then I'll get you in the chair and take out the rollers."

Elsa's knee bounced up and down. Her plan was to make it home to change clothes before going to Bailey's. She wanted to make a good impression on Bailey's family: her husband, children, or parents. She was ashamed to admit she knew absolutely nothing about her besides the sewing of dresses and seeing ladies' futures. "Can't someone else do it?"

"We all in here with back-to-back appointments, and you know why? Your nuptials. Ain't that right, y'all? Everybody in here going to be in attendance at Elsa and Niles's wedding." Although Lucy made her declaration loudly, no one responded. Elsa took in the faces, all eyes looking down or away, avoiding her altogether. She had a dizzying moment of concern. What do they know? Her hands slid down to cradle the imaginary roundness underneath her shirt.

"I . . . I have to go, Lucy. All right? I take full responsibility. I'll explain to my mother that you tried to stop me, but . . . I have to go." She unsnapped the plastic cape and pushed it into Lucy's hands. "I'll bring your curlers back, I promise."

Did they all know? Maybe about Connor and that night, but not everything. No one knew everything. She was being paranoid. That's all. Hurrying out to her car parked right out front, she made her getaway.

She drove with the windows up, careful to keep the loose scarf around her head, and went straight to the Five and Dime. She needed something nice to wear to Bailey's house. She sifted through the rack of dresses and couldn't bring herself to put one on.

"Can I help you find something?" a lady with an armful of folded sweaters asked.

"Yes. I like those. Where are they?" Elsa nodded to the array of burgundy and green fall colors the lady held.

"Oh, no. These are from the men's section. The women's sweaters are—"

"I like these."

Elsa bought a dark green men's turtleneck sweater. She'd also wanted a nice pair of slacks but found them all too tight in the waist. In the men's section where she'd looked, they were all too long. She stuck with her jeans, carefully unbuttoned the top button, and pulled the sweater down over the waistband. She planned to incorporate the new style into her very limited wardrobe. She thought about her mama's immediate disdain when she'd see her. But for now, she felt confident, strong.

She had a feeling Bailey wouldn't judge her anyway.

9

AS SOON AS THE LONG and short hands clicked straight down on the clock—6:30—Bailey hung her sewing apron on the hook. She moved stealthily, wanting to get out the door on time. She couldn't stay an extra hour as she'd normally done, and she knew Miss Jackson inevitably would have one more thing for her to do, even though she never paid Bailey overtime.

But not today.

All afternoon Bailey had screamed at herself in a silent battle. *Inviting Elsa Grimes to your home, are you nuts? To the Eastside—can you even imagine?* It had to be the most ridiculous thing she'd ever done. Not that her neighborhood was dangerous. Except for the dips in the road where the asphalt had given way, the Eastside had always been safe and hospitable.

But a young white woman driving alone in a nice car, gliding her way into that section of town where she'd never been before—she'd stand out like a flashing neon sign at midnight.

The clothes steamer gurgled the last spit of water from the heated tank. The scissors were wiped and oiled and placed in their felt covering. With everything in its proper place, she flicked off the light and then announced her exit to Miss Jackson.

"Bailey, hold on. I'd like to speak with you for a minute."

"Yes?" Bailey said, fully aware of the priceless value of a minute. She and Elsa were to meet at seven, and there was no doubt she'd be on time. Bailey intended to get there early enough to prep her auntie for a visitor. Aunt Charlene wasn't too keen on strangers. She kept a loaded Remi rifle under her bed and two compact pistols in her side bureau specifically for folks who'd come uninvited.

"I'm concerned about your chummy tone with the customers. I agree on the importance of getting to know the client's wants and needs. The various nuances required in figuring out style and transferring that into the client's vision are necessary; however, this is my area. You'd be better served if you put your time and efforts into pinning and sewing and not commiserating."

"I understand," Bailey replied calmly. In her mind, despite her pleasant appearance, she was counting down the time lost. Calculating how much faster she would have to drive. At which stop signs she'd wait behind the white line and at which she would only slow before hitting the gas.

She was thinking about picking up the groceries Aunt Charlene had ordered from Dixie's, or they'd have nothing for supper. She'd forgotten to stop at the APCO for gasoline on the way in. Both stops would add an hour to her trip home.

"These extra conversations must end. Being a fly in the ointment will only cause problems in the long run. You understand?"

Bailey swallowed hard with the urge to roll her eyes. "Yes, ma'am. I agree. I'll try to keep my appointments brief from now on." Bailey heard the rake of metal above her head, Mr. Wag still rummaging in the ceiling in the dressing room parlor and probably eavesdropping.

"I'll see you tomorrow. Bright and early."

"I'll see you then," Bailey agreed cordially, easing out the breath she'd held. The minute she stepped outside she smiled and thanked the sun for still being in the sky, so pleased that the "speaking to" only took three minutes of her precious time.

She took hurried steps up the block where her car was parked around the corner as Miss Jackson had requested. *So our clients aren't taken aback if they see your car out front.* The tired old automobile with the tarnished bumper and cracked seats might scare off the clientele. She'd forgotten to calculate the extra ten-minute stroll in her travel time.

"Are you Bailey?" The man's voice came from directly behind her.

Her heart was already in overdrive from rushing. Now she felt a tremor of fear. She turned around to see a slim figure, his straight black hair with a part down the middle whipped by the wind across his light brown skin.

"My name is John Smith. You met my . . . my friend Alice." He briefly pushed his hair out of his face. "She told me about you."

When Bailey stayed quiet, he continued. "Moon. That's probably what she called me. But my name is John." He stepped closer. "I mean, about who you are. You know about us."

"Yes," Bailey said, looking past him and over his shoulder. They were alone on the street, not that anyone would take notice of the two of them. After five, downtown turned into a dusty desert. She guessed no one would care. Two brown people could tend to their own business.

"Have you seen her?" John asked. His voice wavered. "It's not like Alice to disappear. We meet same time, same day of the week, and she has not come. Three weeks and she has not come. She hasn't been at church. I don't know what's happened, but this isn't right. I go there and wait, and she doesn't come."

Bailey shook her head no. "I'm sorry. I really didn't know Alice that well. I wouldn't know where she is. In fact, I haven't seen her since . . . before she got married." Alice Ledge had been written about in the *Chronicle,* her nuptials and pictures printed with her smile firmly in place. That was nearly six months ago. Not a peep from Alice ever since. Bailey's mouth turned dry. She shuddered at the thought that maybe Alice's husband had found out about her affair and something terrible had happened to her.

"She would not do this." John wrapped his arms around himself.

Bailey didn't know what to say. Her heart went out to him, distraught and obviously still in love with Alice. "I'm sorry. I really don't know anything."

"Something happened to her. She would not just disappear."

"Hey, there. Ah, excuse me?" The voice came with the rumbling approach of an engine. "Miss lady. Hey, there," the man called out.

Bailey saw Wag's Handy Service truck, now stopped across the street. She was relieved and yet didn't have the wherewithal to deal with this man too. She waved him off. When she turned to face John, he was gone.

She began her brisk walk again.

"Boy, you sure do move fast," he said from his truck window, trailing her.

"I don't have time, Mr. Wag." She stopped. "I'm in a hurry. What can I do for you? I thought I just heard you in the ceiling," she said as an afterthought. "You're the one who moves fast." She began her walk again.

"Yep. My work gets done."

"Oh. Well. Great. So, the flickering stopped?" she asked, out of breath.

"Yes, ma'am. All fixed. It was a short in the wiring. I worked on your workroom too. Did you notice it's brighter? No more stabbing yourself with scissors."

"I've never stabbed myself with anything" was her retort, instead of "thank you," which was what she honestly meant to say. *Thank you for rescuing me from having to speak with poor Mr. John and thank you for the light, but I'm in a hurry.*

"Good. Well, now you won't ever stab yourself, compliments of me."

Time was wasting. She slowed at the edge of the sidewalk and looked both ways. His truck swung around and stopped right in front of her. "You need a ride?"

Bailey looked up the street to see another block of distance to be traveled. She was out of breath, having been startled by John and his worry about Alice disappearing. She pressed a hand to her chest to try and calm herself.

"I guess a ride would be okay," she said. Any minutes she could save would be a good thing. She slid into the lumpy seat and closed the heavy door. She immediately felt the finality of being alone with him, in a truck with a total stranger. "Thank you," she said, gratefully. "I did notice the brighter work area. I'm glad the showroom lights are fixed too. All this time I was sure I was making them lights surge on and off." She let out a nervous chuckle.

"Oh yeah? You a superhero or something?" he asked with a side smile. "What other powers you got? You obviously can't fly, or you wouldn't be out here huffing it up the street."

"My car is up here in the vacant lot on Dover."

He pulled out and shifted the gear. "So, where you been, Bailey? I don't believe I know you. Who are your people?"

"I've been here all my life. Right here in Mendol. I could ask you the same question. Never heard of you, Mr. Wag."

"Walter Anderson Graves. Pleased to meet you." He put out a hand.

"Ah, your initials. W-A-G. I get it." She took his hand. The graceful pink light from earlier didn't return, but she remembered it just the same.

"Nicknamed when I joined the army and landed in Italy. I made it back, all in one piece, but decided to hang out in New York. Stayed there for five years," he said.

She lifted a finger to point. "That's my Olds parked right there. Five years? That's a good long time." She wanted to hear more of his story, but today was not the day. He turned into the vacant dirt lot and pulled up next to her car.

He reached across her and popped open the glove box. He took out a small pad. His number and name were already written on the first few sheets of paper. He tore one off and handed it to her. "If you ever in need of my services, or even if you don't need my services." He winked. "Give me a call."

"I will do just that, Mr. Graves." Now that she knew his real name, she couldn't help but use it, out of respect. She took the note paper and folded it before putting it in her pocketbook.

"Anybody ever tell you you're pretty?"

"Yep. Everybody I meet," she answered, knowing this was the furthest thing from the truth. "But thank you kindly." She waved goodbye.

While her engine rumbled to a start, she replayed every silly thing she'd said to Mr. Wag. Quite an interesting character. But no, she didn't have time for him, not now, she told herself. There was something certainly interesting about Walter Anderson Graves. There was also the pink light. She almost couldn't wait to fall asleep later to find out.

She twisted out of the dirt lot, leaving a roll of dust behind her. She noticed the car's unsteady suspension and lack of get-up-and-go. "Get me there, damn it!" At any other time, she would have offered soothing words like a good mama instead of cursing the car under her breath. "Okay. I'm sorry," she whispered to the paneled dashboard. "No pressure. Just get me home."

But the thought of Aunt Charlene answering the door and seeing Elsa, doe-eyed and casually unaware that she might not be welcome somewhere on this earth, sent Bailey's heart racing, more worried than ever she wouldn't make it on time. Her foot pressed the gas pedal nearly to the floor.

First stop, the filling station. After that, Bailey breathed a little easier but still counted down the time as she swung into the Dixie parking lot. She didn't bother to look inside the packed box of groceries she'd picked up. As she carried it to her trunk, she heard the jiggle and shake of the most important item, her aunt Charlene's beer.

Up ahead a light turned red. She came to a screeching stop, her arm out, keeping the box from sliding forward. She didn't dare turn, although it would be perfectly legal to do so. She contemplated making the turn, going up the ramp and onto the short highway. No. She couldn't risk having a run-in with the law, even if the turn was perfectly legal.

Bailey stared at the red light, counting the seconds totaling to another minute lost. With that, she turned off the radio in her car. Constantly hearing about the hostility one state over in Kansas had been unsettling. Mendol had yet to deal with the landmark case *Brown vs. the Board of Education,* which said segregation in public schools was a violation of the constitution. Pushing white folks to do what they didn't want to do always hurt the Black folks the most. The bombings and violence in Topeka were a direct result of the anger and prejudice. It hadn't yet happened in their small, sleepy town, but it would only be a matter of time. That's why, even though it was perfectly legal, Bailey wouldn't turn. She sat and waited for the green light. When it finally clicked over, she let out a hard-held breath. It was exhausting, the *never feeling quite safe* cloud hanging over her head. She started up, easily and slowly. Elsa would just have to wait.

10

THE CLAPBOARD HOUSES on Baker Street sat in a neat row with the ten feet between them required by the town ordinance. This left room for the wide gutters to catch the rain runoff so the houses wouldn't rise and float away during a springtime downpour. Tenuous foundations, thin plank roofs, and not exactly squared windows marked the otherwise well-kept neighborhood. Like the rest of Mendol, the Black residents had their own way of thriving and had built those houses long before big oil.

The men in the Eastside mostly worked on the rigs or in the railway and transit system laying roads or train tracks. The jobs sent many of the men outside of Mendol, bringing husbands, brothers, and sons home only on the weekends.

Bailey had no husband, brother, or son. She hardly remembered her grandfather, who had passed away when she was in pigtails. After that, it was her mama and grandmama and little Bailey, a complete family unit. And then came Aunt Charlene, to keep the family going.

The house, leaning slightly, had weathered two generations of Dowery women without a man to help fix things. Bailey thought of the handyman's number in her pocketbook. She couldn't afford him or anyone else to hammer a nail or stroke a paintbrush at present.

"Auntie, you here?" she called out when she entered through the back door. She placed the cardboard box filled with groceries on the cracked white tiles of the counter. "I picked up the groceries," she added after a few seconds ticked by with no answer.

An immeasurable and familiar sense of panic pulsed in her chest. "Auntie Char?" she called out again while she shrugged off her coat and tossed it on the hook.

"Right here." Aunt Charlene appeared in the kitchen doorway. She held the black handset against her ear with the rest of the telephone pressed to her chest, stretching the cord to its limit. She put a finger to her pursed lips for quiet. "That's right. Four dollars on Bluesy Ray." She paused and leaned forward to kiss Bailey on the cheek, leaving a whiff of tobacco and fruity perfume. "Man, I know. Don't worry about what I got. I'm good for it." Aunt Charlene backed into the living room to finish her call.

Bailey let out a sigh. It never got easier. She continually assumed the worst each time she entered that door. When she called for her auntie, she depended on her to be there, like a life preserver tossed out at sea. *I'm right here, baby.* It was what Bailey's mama used to say. *Right here.* But along with expecting Aunt Charlene to answer, Bailey also thought, *This time she won't be here.*

Bailey was twelve when her mother, Samantha Dowery, passed away one afternoon without being sick for even a moment. No warning. Bailey found her mama after school, sleeping, or so she thought, stretched languidly on the sofa. She'd left her there to finish her nap and quietly made tea and did her spelling homework. Only then did she go over and touch her mama's shoulder. Just a touch, then a shake. *"Mama?"* She'd never forget the lifeless wobble of her mama's head while the rest of her body remained heavy. Bailey screamed and then ran to the Stuarts' house next door, begging for someone to help her mama. "She won't wake up," she cried. Both Mr. and Mrs. Stuart followed her back inside. But it was too late. There was nothing anyone could do. Samantha Dowery would never answer her again.

Bailey questioned herself. Why hadn't she checked on her mama when she didn't answer the first time? Plainly she was there, lying on the couch. If she had only walked over, she would have known something was wrong. Very, very wrong. Could her mama have been saved? Instead of keeping quiet and studying at the kitchen table like a good girl, could she have changed the outcome? The possibility would never stop haunting her.

In church, Bailey had been taught that prayer solved all problems. Prayer gave you answers. Unfortunately, this was one problem that must have perplexed the Man Upstairs, because Bailey never received any kind of answers or solace. Never received a minute of comfort.

One day she was happily playing hopscotch and jumping rope; the next, she was a weeping shell, taken in by her mama's only sister, Charlene.

"Bluesy Ray is going to win for me. I can feel it." Aunt Charlene did a swirl and turn in the kitchen. "Come on, baby, Auntie need a new pair of shoes." She dived straight in the grocery box for one of the dark brown bottles with gold labeling. She used the tarnished opener at the ready to snap off the cap. Air escaped, followed by trickling bubbles. She took a sip.

"Auntie, it's probably warm. You should give 'em a chance to cool in the fridge."

"I like it warm." She took another sip.

"You really should stop wasting money on those horses and just buy the shoes."

"Girl, you got a lot of advice today. Besides, shoes are the last thing on my mind. When I win, I plan to make some changes around here."

"You have absolutely never won," Bailey said. "Betting is a waste of money."

"My money. So I can waste it if I want to." She leaned against the doorframe and pulled a folded bill from her bra strap. "You won't be saying any of this when I win. Maybe if you harness those mindful powers of yours, I could actually bet right for once."

"I wish. You know I've tried." Bailey moved past her to put a box of grits in the cabinet.

"You're just too pent-up. If you relaxed more . . . all work and no play make you old. Look at me, I still look twenty-five." She snapped her fingers to a beat only she could hear. She stopped suddenly and sniffed. "You smell like soot and oil. Where you been?"

"A man gave me a ride in his truck. I smell like the truck, not the man. Although I'm not sure what he smells like."

Aunt Charlene scrunched her nose. "Every man in this town smells like oil. Don't let that stop you from getting to know someone. Is he cute?" When Bailey didn't answer, Aunt Charlene picked a safer subject. "How was work?"

"Work was work," Bailey answered.

"Ah, I hear the melancholy. What that lady do to you this time?"

Bailey knew she was referring to her boss, Miss Jackson. Aunt Charlene knew Miss Jackson from her early days, growing up in the same orbit as the skinny redheaded girl with horn-rimmed glasses. In a small town such as theirs it was completely possible to know someone without ever having exchanged a word with them. Separate schools. Separate churches. Separate sides of the street. Yet Aunt Charlene knew every detail of Miss Jackson's life. "She been married three times and got the nerve to be calling herself 'Miss' and selling white dresses," Aunt Charlene had said huffily when Miss Jackson had first hired Bailey.

"All I can say is I'm happy to have a job," Bailey said as she slipped past her auntie to grab the new jug of milk. She opened the fridge and pushed it to the farthest space in the back, where it was the coldest.

Aunt Charlene handed her the brown paper–wrapped chicken.

"Oh, you can leave that on the counter. I'm frying up the chicken for dinner."

"All of it?" Aunt Charlene asked. "That's a whole chicken."

"Yeah. We can have leftovers. Something different for lunch, maybe," Bailey said, still unable to find the nerve to say out loud, *I invited a friend over.*

"You okay? You been working in that gown shop for two years now, Bailey. Coming home with the same glum face. What happened to having your own shop?" Aunt Charlene asked.

Bailey shrugged her square shoulders. "I like working there. And Miss Jackson pays me on time and adds a bonus every year. I have no complaints."

"Then why you always coming in here looking like you been held against your will?"

"It's called *a full day of work*, Auntie. I'm tired. And today was especially hard." She paused. It was the right time to say it. "That's what I needed to—"

"I see. I get it. You're a working girl. Don't worry, I'm going to have my share of the money for the tax man. I pay my share around here."

"I wasn't asking about that."

"Yeah. I know. You don't think much of my little kitchen salon business. But I been putting food on the table long before you became the seamstress extraordinaire. I work for myself. I'm not predictable and safe like you. You're down there giving all your talent and skills away for the betterment of someone else. Those gowns are pricey. You could buy yourself a new car with the price of one of them dresses. And how much do you get? None of it."

Bailey let the canned goods slam hard on the shelf. She didn't mean to put them away like that. "It's been a very long day. Do you mind if I focus on making supper and we spend less time talking about the Regal Gown?"

"Sure. Sure. Pardon me for inquiring about my dear niece and her well-being." Aunt Charlene took a long sip of her suds. "Thank you for picking up the supplies." She winked and raised the bottle higher to her lips, then checked the fill line as if already worried about not having more. Dixie's was the only place that sold her favorite beer, and when it ran out, that was that, until the next truck came through town.

"You need any help?" Aunt Charlene asked.

"I'm good. I got it."

Instead of prodding, Aunt Charlene left her alone. Off to the back porch, where she took a seat on the first plank of the knotty stairs. Bailey still had a slight window of time to say what needed to be said. She stood at the screen door and contemplated Aunt Charlene's reaction. She thought about how quickly the last fourteen years had passed. How quickly things had changed and yet stayed the same. Her auntie always saw folks as hard and unforgiving. *Trust no one.*

Bailey laid her hand on the screen door frame but waited. Her sight drifted from Aunt Charlene to the one solid tree in the backyard, stick bare, having lost its fall leaves in a harsh windstorm a few days before. The fence separating their property from the Stuarts was leaning and threatening to give up altogether. One more dry storm and it would be kaput.

As if thinking the same thing, Aunt Charlene muttered, "This place is literally falling apart."

"Auntie Char?" Bailey stepped out onto the porch.

Aunt Charlene coughed on her inhale, startled. "I don't like the beginnings of this conversation. What?"

"I have a guest coming over," Bailey said. "Um . . . she's a friend. Someone I met at the Regal Gown."

"A friend?"

"*Ahuh*. Just letting you know. A lady I met. Didn't want you to be surprised or anything when the knock came at the door."

"Oh. Okay, a friend. Nice." Aunt Charlene did a neck twist, indicating she was confused as to her role in the situation. "All right. So, she coming for dinner? You need me to spruce the place up or something?"

"She's probably coming after supper, or . . . well, I'm not sure. But no need to do anything. Just letting you know." With that, Bailey stepped back inside. She at least had told her auntie the truth, even if she had left out a small detail.

My friend is a young, rich white woman who is coming over to have her heartstrings read. No need to worry. I have it all under control.

11

EARLIER, INGRID HAD in the dimly lit library nursing a brandy and a headache. "What do you mean, she left over an hour ago? Did she say where she was going?" She checked her wristwatch again. The gold hands neatly at half past four. Elsa had left the house at nine that morning.

Lucy, on the other end of the line, simply answered, "Nope. Sorry—"

Before she could finish, Ingrid put the receiver down. On to the next call.

With each iteration of rings, Ingrid grew more angry. More thoughts of how she would make Elsa pay for this . . . this embarrassment. Ingrid slowly realized she'd lost power over her daughter. What else could she take away at this point?

"Evening, Bonnie. This is Ingrid. How're you, dear heart?" It was the proper thing to ask, although really Ingrid could give a rat's tail. After a long answer from Bonnie, she had to figure out a polite way of saying why she'd called in the first place. "That's nice. Oh yes, we're almost there to the finish line. I can't wait to see you all there. By the way, speaking of which, has Elsa been by today? Contacted Judy, or—*Ahuh*. I see."

Ingrid couldn't recall saying goodbye to her. Surely she'd said something congenial. Hadn't she?

The next call and the next had gone the same way. "No sign of Elsa," one friend after another told her. "Maybe she's with Niles?" Elsa certainly wasn't with Niles, because Niles was in the living room with the dance instructor, ready for the private lesson scheduled for four o'clock.

Her little leather-bound book held the personal information of everyone Ingrid had ever known. Names, addresses, birthdays. She slid her red thumbnail down the pages of names in her handwriting. No one on the C's. On to the D's. Annie Dune. Neither Elsa nor Ingrid had spoken to the Dune girl or her family in years, after the birthday debacle when Annie had invited everyone to her sweet sixteen party except Elsa and had called it "a mix-up." It wouldn't make sense to call Annie. Even if she had invited Annie and the Dune clan to the wedding, they were not considered friends. She simply wanted them to see how spectacularly Elsa's life had turned out. A big, beautiful ceremony, marrying the most handsome young man in Mendol. In fact, almost everyone had been invited out of spite.

Ingrid flipped through the crisp pages, realizing it wouldn't make sense to call another person. She closed the book and pushed the rubber band that was holding it together over the sides.

Elsa was a loner who never saw the value in making connections. It was a struggle to find even two bridesmaids. Eventually they'd settled on cousins from the Grimes side of the family who no one had seen since they were in training bras. Two bridesmaids were the necessary minimum for a festive presentation. Ingrid sent the young ladies handsome payments for their wardrobe, hair, and a little something extra for their travel, even though they lived only one city over, an hour's drive away. Better to call it a "travel expense" than a bribe.

"Any sign of her?" Niles asked.

Ingrid planted a smile on her face before turning toward him where he stood at the entrance of the library. "She should be here soon. Hey, how about you do a few practice steps with your future mother-in-law? Just until Elsa gets back."

His ears and cheeks pinkened immediately, but he answered confidently, "Sure, Mrs. Grimes. That'd be swell."

Ingrid drained the last remnants of her drink. A little lightheaded, the thought of dancing sent her to her feet. She took hold of Niles by the arm and led him back to the large parlor with its freshly polished floors. Her steps echoed in the room.

Rodger, a small man with glasses, came toward Ingrid with his hands prepared for a two-palm grip. "Mrs. Grimes, I'm so sorry for the mix-up. I was sure we were scheduled for four o'clock today. Niles has already explained the confusion."

"Yes. Thank you for understanding." Ingrid smiled in Niles's direction. She could kiss him for knowing exactly what to say. He'd always been the model son to the Porters. "Niles is the good one," Vera Porter always said about her son, intimating that his twin brother, Leo, cared about no one and did exactly what he pleased. On the other side of the coin, Niles lacked drive and motivation. At one point, the Porters had feared he'd need constant guidance. They certainly had all but given up on the idea of him leaving the nest and having a family of his own. A man was supposed to have a wife. There was no question that the arrangement between Niles and Elsa was the best thing for both of them. Why bother with the trouble of finding perfectly fine spouses when the match was hand-delivered?

"How about you and me, Niles? We don't want the time to go to waste. What shall we learn today? Something fun, huh?" Ingrid asked.

"Sure. Yeah," he said shyly.

"Of course. Why not?" Rodger said. "Let's not let the time go to waste. How about a beginner's waltz?"

Ingrid detected a bit of pity in his voice. "I bet I could teach you a few things. I was Miss Teen Mendol for three consecutive years. I actually won a talent competition with a swing dance and tap combo," she said.

"How wonderful! Well, for now, how about a simple waltz to start? That way, at least our man Niles will be able to lead gracefully, whether Elsa is proficient or not."

Ingrid took in a sharp breath. "Yes. Sure."

"All right, Niles, you are here. Arms up. Mrs. Grimes, step in. That's close enough. And hold. Step. And step," Rodger instructed, with his hands flowing in rhythm.

"I think we have it, right, Niles?"

"Fine. Let's give it a shot with music," Rodger said. He went to the record player and set the needle down on the vinyl.

Ingrid glided along with Niles in the two-step and wondered what could've been any easier. Nothing, really. She realized that all she was doing was stalling for time, hoping and praying Elsa would walk through the door at any moment.

Rodger lifted the needle to stop the music. He clapped. "Magnificent. Mrs. Grimes, you are indeed a natural. Niles, I could use you down at the studio. Ever consider dance as a side job?"

"No, sir," he said humbly. "Can't say it's ever crossed my mind."

"How about we move on to something with a degree of difficulty, just for fun? A fox-trot."

Rodger grabbed Ingrid's hands and spun her around. She sputtered with laughter at the unexpected step. They moved in sync, gracefully, across the floor. Another spin and Ingrid leaned into the dip.

Niles whistled. "Wow, Mrs. Grimes, nicely done."

"Thank you, Niles. Thank you," she said to Rodger as well. She couldn't remember the last time she'd danced. She and Matthias hadn't been out for a fun evening in years. Excitement tapped at her heart, revisited like an old friend. There was so much to look forward to. Elsa wouldn't ruin this. The party, the wedding, all of it was Ingrid's time to shine. She wouldn't let her daughter ruin any of it.

"All right, how about you give it a try, my friend?" Rodger said, putting his hand out for Niles to take his place.

"Oh no. That's a little too complicated for me." Niles checked his watch, then looked to the entrance. "You know, I think I'll be heading out. It doesn't look like Elsa's gonna make it back."

And just like that, Ingrid's fun sailed out the window. She saw the men out and then went back to the library and poured herself more brandy. The sun had set, leaving the room dark. Ingrid didn't bother turning on one of the Tiffany lamps on the side table. She curled herself on the sofa and sipped her drink lying down.

She heard the front door open and close and sat up. The footsteps were heavy. Matthias was home.

"Hey, girl, where you at?" he called out.

"Right here," she answered. She wiped at her eyes and fluffed her hair. She stood, adjusted herself, and made a second drink. She carried both into the living room to greet her husband.

"Hello, darling. How was your day?" She handed him one of the drinks.

"Anything exciting happen around party central?" He sounded genuinely interested.

"Everything's just wonderful. Except Elsa has gone missing. But what else is new?"

Matthias kissed her hand before pulling her down to have a seat on his lap. "You worry too much. And right now, I really want to enjoy this first sip. The first is always the best." He took his time and did just that, sipped.

Ingrid kicked off her shoes and curled herself like a cat in his lap. "She missed her dance lesson. We've had this on the schedule for three weeks. I danced with Niles. I didn't want to waste the lesson." Ingrid sighed. "I enjoyed it. I think we should have dance lessons, me and you. What do you say?"

"I say 'no, thank you.' The only dance I need to know is how to hold you tight and spin you around. I'm an expert at holding you tight." His hand slid softly against her skin while he pushed up her skirt. "Why don't we head upstairs, make it an early night?"

Ingrid climbed out of his reach. "I can't really relax at the moment. I'm worried about our daughter. She is missing."

"She's not missing. She's a woman. She can handle herself."

"Whatever she's doing, you can be sure she's embarrassing us. You can be sure of that." She let out a growl. "Why do you pretend everything is such a cakewalk? I have been dealing with this by myself and I'm absolutely exhausted. I'm counting the days until this wedding, when she's a married woman in her own house, with her own husband, and out of my hair."

"Oh, sweetie," he purred. "Come here. Come. Sit."

Ingrid reluctantly found herself back in his arms. She didn't want to relax, and yet that's exactly what being in Matthias's arms made her do. Drop her guard, lose all of her fight.

"Listen to me," he said, "We've raised a wonderful daughter. We're at third base . . . one hit away from home." He made a popping sound in his square jaw to pretend the bat had just connected to the ball. "Close your eyes. Visualize that ball, sailing over the trees. It's a home run, baby. Everything's going to be fine."

12

BAILEY ATE HER SUPPER as quickly as possible, scooping up fork-fuls of chicken, onions, and potatoes with one hand and washing it down with a glass of iced black tea with the other. The brown gravy had clumped but still tasted delicious. She responded to Aunt Charlene's trivia with *ahuh, yeah,* and *nope.* Talking would only slow down their mealtime.

She was starting to believe Elsa Grimes wouldn't have the nerve to show up anyway, so why bring it up?

When her plate was clean, she hurriedly stood and picked up her auntie's plate as well. She scraped the thigh bones, along with the end cuttings from the onions and peppers, into the small coffee can that served to hold kitchen trash.

Outside in the night air, Bailey dumped the can of scraps into the garbage can. Just as she turned the corner to return to the house, she saw Elsa approaching on the narrow brick path from the street.

"Elsa." Bailey called her name before she reached the front steps and was about to knock.

"Hey, there. I was hoping I had the right house." Elsa had changed into a turtleneck sweater, tucked and belted into the same worn jeans she had on earlier. Her hair was different, glossy and pinned in high curls, a wondrous quick change from her earlier appearance.

All this spiff and shine for her? Bailey wondered. Her hand in-stinctively rose to her own hair, which must be a mess by now. She hadn't bothered to change from her work clothes. Despite having worn a work apron, her plaid button-front dress and black Mary Janes were covered with fabric cuttings and lint dust.

Since they were already on the front steps, Bailey pulled the screen door open and then turned the front door's knob easily. The door creaked open to an empty living room. Since Bailey never entered the house this way, she saw it from her visitor's point of view. Clean. Neat. Orderly. *Jet* and *Ebony* magazines were stacked on the coffee table. Straightened pillows sat in each corner of the brown tweed couch. Family pictures were pitched on the polished wood shelf.

Besides Gabby, who Bailey had known since high school, she didn't have visitors. A wave of giddiness struck her. Her guest had arrived and nothing bad had happened. "Have a seat, Elsa. I'll be right back. You want some tea? Are you hungry? Come on in."

"No. I mean *yes* on the tea. And *no,* I'm not hungry," Elsa said, taking a seat.

Instead of going straight to the porch where she'd left Aunt Charlene having her after-dinner cigarette, Bailey went to the restroom. She took an extra minute to wipe down the tiny porcelain sink and mirror in case Elsa wanted to use the facilities. When she came out, she heard talking. *Oh no, Auntie.*

As far as she could tell, the two ladies were cordial.

Aunt Charlene faced Bailey with a hard smile. "You didn't tell me your guest was Elsa Grimes," Aunt Charlene said with sugary sharpness. "Miss Elsa here says you two met at the Regal Gown. And now you're friends. Isn't that nice."

Friends. Yes. Bailey liked that Elsa had used that word to describe their relationship.

"I was just about to make a pot of tea. Would you like some, Auntie?"

"I'll do it. I'll get the tea. You two enjoy each other's company." Aunt Charlene stood from the rigid arm of the couch. "You take sugar in your tea, Elsa?"

"Yes. And cream, if you don't mind," Elsa added.

"Of course. Cream. Special," Aunt Charlene whispered in a fantastical tone when she walked by. "Bailey, I need a little help . . . in the kitchen."

Bailey moved swiftly with the command. She had expected this private tête-à-tête.

In the kitchen, Aunt Charlene didn't waste a second. "I'm thinking this is a very bad idea," she blurted. "Earlier when you said there would be a guest, I never dreamt it was Elsa Grimes, daughter of one of the richest families in town, one of the richest *white* families," Aunt Charlene said. "Now here she is, sitting on our sofa."

"Why? You don't approve of me making new friends?" Bailey asked as she reached into the cupboard for the cups. She set them with saucers on the counter, then grabbed spoons from the drawer and looked for one that hadn't been too dulled, scratched, and bent over the years.

"Child, don't try me! Lord have mercy," Aunt Charlene said under her breath. A sheen of moisture appeared on her cleavage. She used a dish towel to fan herself. "You know what you're doing don't make no sense, right?"

"I'm helping her. She's just one lost soul and I'm going to help her the best I can, Auntie. No harm in that."

"Do you hear yourself? You can't save nobody. That's not in your job description. And even if it was," she continued to whisper, but even lower, "why would you put yourself out in the open like that? For her? All this time you've been acting like having the gift of sight was a true nightmare, and here you is sharing the ability with a complete stranger."

Now was probably not the time to tell Aunt Charlene that there were *more* complete strangers. There was no shortage of acquaintances determined to be touched and read by Bailey. There never had been a good time to confess how she'd spoken to Alice Ledge and regretted it the minute the words left her lips. She didn't want to hear Aunt Charlene scold and chastise. She hadn't wanted to hear "I told you so."

The kettle whistled. Steam swirled from the tiny hole at the top. Bailey grabbed the crotcheted potholder and poured the water into the tea server. She put everything on the silver tray and took hold of the wooden handles on the sides.

Aunt Charlene pried the tray from both her hands. "I said I was getting the tea . . . I'm serving the tea."

Bailey let out a breath and then followed as her auntie led the way.

Elsa perked up when the ladies returned, impressed with the presentation. The tray with a matching serving set had been Bailey's grandmother's. She'd always wanted to use it but never had guests for tea.

"What's this? Cloves? Herbs?" Elsa inhaled the tea steam before pouring her cup.

"Honey, that's Lipton!" Aunt Charlene rolled her eyes. "Cloves and herbs, *huh*. Bat wings too, perhaps?"

"Oh, no. I didn't mean . . ." Elsa caught a glimpse of Aunt Charlene's expression. "Thank you," she said softly.

"I'm just messing with you, darling. Wait, you asked for cream. Coming right up," Aunt Charlene said, already two steps away, back to the kitchen.

"Is everything all right? Should I go?" Elsa said gently to Bailey.

"What? No. She's cautious about meeting new people."

"Honestly, I don't want to be a thorn in your side."

"Trust me, not important. We'll be fine. You're fine. How did you hear about me, you know, when you first came to the Regal Gown?" Bailey asked, to deflect the obvious tension.

"Talk. All the ladies have heard some version of the fortune-teller at the Regal Gown. I was excited to have my chance to meet you. After one too many spritzers at lazy luncheons, the stories get a bit farfetched. What they said about you sounded sensational, but I believed it. All of it," Elsa said.

"But weren't you a tiny bit skeptical . . . about what I can do?"

Aunt Charlene returned with the cream. "Here you are." She held out the ceramic pitcher as she stared at Elsa, searching for her intentions, Bailey assumed.

"Thank you, Auntie. Me and Elsa are going to the basement," she said, standing.

"Bailey, I hope you know what you're doing."

"I do. We'll be fine," Bailey said, waving to Elsa to follow her. Now that her auntie had sobered up nicely, clear-eyed and focused, she didn't want to discuss matters in her presence. It was best to take their conversation where they'd have privacy.

"Well, then, let me know if you need anything else," Aunt Charlene said.

Bailey led the way down the narrow stairs. Their footsteps sounded too heavy for the floorboards as Elsa followed, carrying her tea. Her senses felt hyperaware. There was so much she normally didn't notice that she saw, smelled, and heard intensely.

In the dark, Bailey automatically flipped a switch. One dim light came alive overhead. Sewing paraphernalia lay strewn about. Custom-cut patterns, fabrics, magazines, and even some sketches with Bailey's signature lined the paneled walls. This space was where her grandfather once had his workshop. The smell of sawdust suddenly came to her in the cool basement air.

"I'm so excited to get this show on the road," Elsa began. "I'm a little scared—nervous, really. I figured you'd just do your thing . . . You're so talented, Bailey." She picked up a sketch pad. "Where'd you learn how to do all of this?"

"Believe it or not, I paid extra attention in home ec class. Mrs. Gorman was my favorite teacher in seventh grade and I kind of . . . I really needed her at the time," she said, remembering the kindness and extra attention the woman had given her right after her mama passed away. After school hours, Bailey would return with questions. *How do you make a ruffled collar stand? How do you hide a zipper?* The rest, she'd taught herself. With practice and diligence she turned worn tablecloths and curtains into clothes—nothing she'd want to be seen wearing in public, but things she was proud of nonetheless.

"Home economics? Wow. Well, it's obvious you're a natural."

"Thank you." Bailey cleared a space on a bench she'd reupholstered, balling up fabric scraps and cuttings. Every piece was precious and eventually found its way into a quilt or a sachet. "You sit here."

Elsa rested her tea beside her. "Now tell me how you do *this*. How do you know who someone truly loves?"

Bailey knelt in front of Elsa. "It's not easy to explain. The best I can say is that it's like being a fly on the wall. I'm the fly being where I don't belong. I see what's happening in the room that no one expects anyone else will ever see."

Elsa bristled at the thought. "Must be a scary place sometimes."

Bailey sighed and avoided answering. Instead she said, "Tell me a little bit about yourself. Do you have any siblings?"

"There's just me. I always wished I had a sister."

"Kind of lonely being an only child, I know," Bailey agreed. "Tell me about your parents."

Elsa shook her head. "I'd rather not."

"I'm sorry. Touchy subject?" Bailey asked, mostly curious. She hadn't seen Elsa's mother but had heard from Miss Jackson the strict instructions about what kind of dresses Elsa was allowed to try on. Most mamas of the bride couldn't wait for the opportunity to shop with their daughters for a wedding dress. In Elsa's case, her dresses had been picked out ahead of time, and she'd come in alone. It was Bailey who stood by, watching Elsa uncomfortably try on alluring low-cut necklines and strapless styles. Each dress was more revealing than the next, usually the opposite of what a mother would like for a daughter.

Elsa looked away. "My mother and father don't like me much," she said, wiping away a tear. "I don't see the point of this, Bailey. I thought you could just touch me and then you'd see."

"That's been the way, yes, but for some reason—I don't know—maybe I've spent so much time telling everyone I can't do it, and now I can't. My mama used to say, 'Speak your truth and it will come to pass.'" She sighed. "I just don't know. Maybe I spoke my truth a bit too much, and I just can't see anymore. It's not you," Bailey told Elsa. Their tea had cooled and the light seemed brighter in the dark basement.

"Well then, I guess we're both broken."

"We're not broken." Bailey twirled a piece of fabric between her nimble fingers. She imagined Aunt Charlene overhearing and scoffing at the word *we*. What could they possibly have in common? They were women. That was enough, as far as Bailey was concerned. "Can you tell me why you're so afraid?" Bailey asked in almost a whisper. "I mean, what's your concern, Elsa? Are you in love with someone else? Who is it you're expecting me to see?" She also wanted to ask about the faded bruises she'd seen on Elsa's neck that first day in the dressing room. Had Elsa even known the marks were there?

Watching Elsa's lip quiver made Bailey tread lightly. "Oh no. I'm sorry. I didn't mean to make you cry."

"I love someone. I think I do. It's not my fiancé," Elsa admitted with a shaky breath. She shifted on the bench. "I mean, I love Niles too, but not the same way I feel about— The problem is, I have absolutely no idea how, or if, I'm allowed to feel this way. And what if the other person doesn't feel the same about me? I'll be throwing everything away for nothing."

"Then it's the other person I should be reading. Not you. You know what you want, who you want," Bailey said succinctly, as if they'd found lost treasure, gold and riches beyond their imagining. "That's the answer, Elsa. Bring him to me. Bring him to the Regal Gown. Make up some excuse. All right? I'll shake his hand, and I'll know. That's gotta be it."

"That's gotta be it," Elsa repeated, less enthusiastically.

"Yeah. I'm hopeful, at least. Elsa, is there something else? Is there something you're not telling me?"

Elsa stayed quiet for a few seconds, then perked up. "What about this weekend? My engagement party is Friday," she said, waving her hands as if it explained everything. "You have to come. It will be small, for family and friends, a pre-wedding party. I know it makes no sense. But that's what the highfalutin' do with their money, waste it on parties and aged bourbon. You'll have a chance to see for yourself. I mean, wouldn't that work out best? If I introduce you to everyone and don't tell you who it is, it'll be perfect. The party is a tradition my mama likes where everyone witnesses the proposal and acceptance. Absolutely every soul me and my family knows will be there. The actual ceremony the next day is pretty much a formality. But if you come Friday night, I can make sure you know who to touch, accidentally maybe. Just one touch, the way you do, then you'll see. I'll accept whatever your vision shows as my destiny. Oh Bailey, this can work! This will work. I can feel it."

"Elsa. A party at your house? I don't know if you've noticed, but I'm probably not going to be too welcome," Bailey said, hesitant and retreating by the second. "I can't come to your house, Elsa. Showing up to some fancy party, me? No, ma'am."

"What?" Elsa scoffed. "You don't have to be afraid. I'll introduce you as my personal dressmaker. And most of the society ladies already know who you are, so is it really going to be a shock to have you there? It'll be like you're working. I'm begging you. I'll make it worth your while," Elsa said. "I will pay you."

"There's no amount of money . . . well, how much?" Bailey said. There was the fact that her house and car were in need of repair. The city property tax was due in a few weeks, and she couldn't depend on Aunt Charlene with her dedication to the betting track. The tax had doubled over the last few years. The Howards down the street had lost their home to auction for being unable to make the payment. The city treasurer had pulled up a podium and gavel and let the bidding commence while Sister Howard cried and had to be dragged away.

"Just how much are you talking about?" Bailey asked.

"I'll give you fifty dollars."

"Just for me showing up?" Bailey asked, her mouth agape. "For one day?"

"Not even a whole day. A couple of hours. Please. I want you there. I know if you get in the same room as . . . if you touch . . ." She trailed off again. "I just know that you'll know for sure. My life is hanging on your vision, Bailey. You just said it was the only way. I'm only asking that you try. Show up. I'll send a car for you. That way, you'll be escorted right in. Wear one of those gorgeous dresses that I know you've got in your closet. Please, Bailey."

"All right." She swallowed the lump in her throat. "All right, I'll come," Bailey said, more as a resolve to herself, ignoring the nudging inner voice telling her this was a bad idea. But no, she refused to listen. She absolutely wanted to do more than scoot by, doing the bare minimum. For some reason, Elsa's audacity gave her new courage. She didn't always want to be that person who stayed silent and well-mannered. She didn't always want to be the person afraid to make the right turn at the legal red light.

This was all Elsa's fault, wanting to be more, to be brave. Watching her lean out the window of her life gave Bailey a jolt of inspiration she didn't know she needed. She'd never felt comfortable giving orders or asking for anything. Insisting. Inquiring. All brought about the same level of angst. To survive, she'd become good at ignoring the neurotic hiccup in the back of her throat. Speaking up, asking for a hand up, a handout, meant she was vulnerable and at the mercy of whoever possessed what she didn't have. She was only calm and comfortable when there was a tomato pincushion attached to her wrist or a sewing apron draped around her neck. That had to stop.

"I'll have our man pick you up at seven on Friday," Elsa announced, full of expectation. Problem solved.

Bailey hoped she was capable of being that person for her. They were so much alike. Bailey recognized herself in Elsa, what felt like her against the rest of the world. Money or no money, she really wanted to give Elsa a fighting chance.

13

ELSA PULLED INTO THE OPEN GATE, unable to gauge the distance ahead. The darkness made her drive extra-slowly up the dark, sloping entrance. She focused on the many windows glowing yellow and used those beacons as her guide.

Each square window that shone from the monolithic mansion was designed for a specific purpose: to show off. And still, with all its greatness, there'd never been room for her. No place for Elsa to be Elsa. It was *their home,* where Matthias and Ingrid had designs on a perfect life. They hadn't planned for their daughter to be their exact opposite, unfit for this showy life modeled on pictures in magazines. Piano lessons in the parlor. French lessons in the library. Teatime on the veranda. Her parents did as most of the families in their circle did, spent extravagantly to transform themselves into worldly and cultured individuals. Priceless abstract paintings were purchased and hung on the walls for the sake of conversation. *New Yorker* magazines were placed strategically on side tables. Lilting French music that no one understood played low and slow on the intercom speakers.

Elsa shifted the car to Park in the carport. She stepped out of the car and could instantly feel her mama pacing inside. She was right. Before the front door closed, she heard the clinking of ice meeting glass, along with footsteps coming her way.

"I told you to leave the rollers in your hair. Why do you drive us crazy, Elsa Louise?"

"I'm fine. Thank you for asking." Elsa put the automobile keys back in the tiny drawer of the hall bureau. She moved quickly toward the beckoning staircase. She could taste sleep, longed for her bed with its fluffy pillows and crisp sheets. "Good night."

"Don't you dare walk away from me, young lady. You stop right there."

"There's my girl! See, I told you she was fine," Matthias announced, with drink in hand. With bourbon neat, collar open, and neck flushed, he wasn't quite the picture of a demagogue. Cocktail hour had obviously extended past eight. No doubt they'd been discussing Elsa's waywardness.

"Where were you?" Ingrid asked. "You missed the dancing practice with Niles. But you don't care. You don't care about anybody but yourself. Where were you, Elsa Louise?"

"I visited a friend."

"I called your friends. Not one of them had a clue as to your whereabouts."

"You don't know all of my friends," Elsa answered.

"Apparently I don't. I called absolutely everyone we know, and no one saw you. You left the salon five hours ago," she shrieked.

"All right now, how about we talk this out in the morning. You two need a rest," Matthias interjected, his words trailing behind him like film off the reel.

Ingrid ignored him and let out an exasperated breath. "Why, Elsa? Why can't you do one thing I ask? Why does life have to be so difficult?"

"I've done everything you've asked," Elsa said. "And you know what? I can't do it anymore. I've tried to figure out a way to not let you down, but I just— I'm always going to be a disappointment, so why bother? I'm not going through with it. I can't marry Niles. I can't marry anyone." Elsa heard herself say these words, but she couldn't imagine having really said them. It took everything in her to find the next thing, the right thing. She hated to see her mama hurt and disappointed. She hated being the cause of her bad day again and again. So all that came next was "I'm sorry."

"Are you insane?" Ingrid screeched. "Matthias, say something. I don't understand what's happening right now. Say something. Do something."

"Go upstairs and call your fiancé," Matthias offered, his only mediation between his two favorite girls. It was the best he could do. He continued to rub his wife's back. "Go on now, you need to call Niles and apologize for missing your dance lesson. You've caused enough trouble tonight, Els. Go on." The slack in his tone had not impaired his ability to give orders.

"Good night," Elsa said to her parents. This time she made her exit without interference. They could continue bemoaning the difficulties of raising a daughter like Elsa.

"Elsa is a headstrong child," Matthias used to say in her defense when Ingrid raged about the challenging job of motherhood. "Nothing wrong with that. Just too smart for her britches."

"*Smart* won't get her anywhere," Ingrid would counter. "She's going to have to learn. Her petulance will bring her nothing but pain and heartache."

Elsa had overheard the same conversation enough times. Those were the nights Ingrid would order Elsa upstairs without finishing her dinner. If it was hunger pains she'd been referring to, the pain never came, because Oda Mae would sneak milk and cookies into her room. "You are smart. Be proud," Oda Mae would say with a kiss near her ear. "Smart is good. Having your own mind is even better."

She wished Oda Mae was there to talk to, like when she was younger. Oda Mae had raised her from as far back as she could remember, from the time she learned how to count, or read, or tie her own shoe. But Oda Mae had her own smart children, and once Elsa turned thirteen, she stopped spending the night and went home to her own family.

Oda Mae's eldest son, Moses, had gone off to college in Alabama on a scholarship, to become a lawyer. The college had actually given him money just to be there. Elsa saw pictures of the family on his graduation day from Mendol Eastside High, with Moses in his cap and gown, Oda Mae smiling proudly in a sleeveless dress. The black-and-white photo made it impossible to know what color Oda Mae wore. Elsa liked to assume it was orange or peach, something very different from the starched blue uniform she worked in every day. Because Oda Mae was smiling in the picture, Elsa hardly recognized her. In another picture, there was Rochelle, standing with Moses,

Oda Mae, and Rochelle's father, Mr. Davis. Rochelle wore pigtails and shiny Mary Janes and carried a tiny handbag.

"Can I have it? The picture?" Elsa had asked Oda Mae, holding the glossy black-and-white photo in her hand. Then she quickly handed it back, feeling she had no right to claim them as her own family, though she felt exactly that way. *My family,* meaning a place where she could feel safe and secure and loved unconditionally. The next day she found the picture in her knickknack drawer. Oda Mae had left it there with writing on the back: *Oda Mae, Rochelle, Moses, and Mr. Davis 1949. To Elsa with love.*

Elsa felt a similar connection with Bailey. Actually, with Bailey's aunt Charlene too, even though she could tell the woman didn't like her much. *I resemble them,* Elsa thought. *I could be a part of their secret society.* They shared commonality, joined in a way. *Soft women.* That's the description she'd come to. Pardoning, tolerant, and easy-to-forgive type of women. She imagined spending time over on Baker Street.

Even under obvious agitation, Bailey's aunt held her tone with grace and genuine sensitivity. Elsa heard enough of their conversation in the kitchen and assumed the rest. They cared for each other and listened when the other was talking.

She shouldn't have been intrigued by such a small, dutiful trait, but as it was rare, she looked on with admiration. Most people didn't listen. Instead they simply waited for their turn to speak, ignoring any other point of view. In her family, her mama and daddy never listened to her and barely listened to each other. Good thing Elsa was a natural listener in her own right. "Listening makes you strong, makes you better," Oda Mae used to say. "Hearing is one thing. Listening is another. You listen with your heart. You hear with your ears."

Elsa couldn't stop her mind from skipping outside where it didn't belong. This must be how Bailey felt. Exactly how she described her process of *being where I don't belong.* Right then, Elsa was back in the living room with the two women, laughing and drinking tea, though she wasn't sure what she'd seen and felt had been so neatly packaged. Had anyone really laughed? The bare walls, the matte wood floor, the radio in the corner on the hutch, the framed picture on the shelf of mother and child were details she shouldn't have noticed and memorized. The bland room had overall meant nothing. It was the comfort of being in their company.

She was seeing two women living on their own without a man. An aunt and her niece doing quite nicely for themselves. They'd made their own homey nest and lived by their own rules. These two women could speak freely to each other. Even in disagreement, they could talk without being called *crazy*.

Elsa had been told in more than a hundred ways that she could not trust herself. Someone else always knew better.

Who is it you're expecting me to see? Who do you want me to see? When Bailey's and Elsa's hands touched, Elsa braced herself. Afraid. Embarrassed.

Bailey would see, for sure. The truth would come out now. But why wait?

She picked up the powder pink telephone that matched her powder pink walls to call Niles to break the news. It was oddly quick and painless. "I'm not sure we should be getting married," she announced, her voice raspy as she had lain still for so long. "I don't want to be married, all right? It isn't right."

"But our parents agreed. How is it okay to just say . . . to back out?"

"Because it's my life. And it's yours, Niles. You shouldn't let them make decisions for you."

She knew what his silence meant. Since they'd grown up together, there was very little she didn't know. His favorite food was hot buttered popcorn. He hated peas. He liked sleeping till noon and flying kites. If he could fly his kite, whatever else his day included didn't matter. He had six button-down shirts in the same shade of pale yellow. He chewed on only one side of his jaw, even when the abscess in a back tooth had made him howl in pain.

The other thing she knew was that Niles would take his place permanently in their fathers' company, Senate Oil, which meant he'd remain in their isolated town forever, something Elsa couldn't fathom.

To remain here is like drowning on dry land. She gasped in hiccuped sobs while imagining their life filled with drink socials, church, sex once a week, and baby buggies. She winced at the thought of standing in her mama's shoes. Although she did want children. She absolutely wanted a chance to love a child with reckless abandon, a chance to form a small being into a loving human to live on their own terms.

A girl, a boy—she didn't have a preference. She'd offer her children every possible way to give them a fresh start, to know what having a family truly meant. But she wanted none of this with Niles.

"I want things to go back to the way they were," she sobbed. "That's all I want."

"We'll talk more in the morning when you're rested and thinking clearly," he said. It was the most definitive thing she'd ever heard him say.

"All right. You're right. I just want to sleep," Elsa added. Two hours later, she remained awake in bed, unable to find the calm she craved. She scratched at the stiff curls covered by a bonnet. The curls were meant for the photo shoot scheduled the next day. Now there was no need, she assumed. She pulled the heavy bonnet off, removed the bobby pins one at a time, and sighed in relief when she was done.

Just make it to tomorrow, and the next, and the next, she told herself. One tomorrow at a time.

14

AFTER AN HOUR OF USELESS shifting on the lumpy mattress, Charlene finally sat up. *Elsa Grimes, the daughter of Matthias Grimes, was in my house.*

The urge to get out of bed, to find Bailey and tell her what was on her mind, was a hard one to fight. Two o'clock in the morning. Too many hours left in the darkness. She fell back against the flat pillow and closed her eyes but couldn't get back to sleep. Her fury wasn't about the girl being invited to their house and Bailey offering up her gift of visions. There was something deeper at play.

Had she done something wrong in raising Bailey? How could the girl be so naive to think she could cavort with Elsa Grimes and remain unscathed? Bailey had a sixth sense of things, visions and such. The girl had always been that way. She had *the thing*. Like Sammie, she could see someone's true motivation, what they craved in this world, see underneath to the place that most didn't even know existed, beyond their depth of comprehension. When Bailey was growing up, the other children in school called her a genie. A magical genie who could see the future and grant wishes. She could hardly grant a wish, that's for sure. Charlene had tried that, asked her a dozen times to call her numbers or pick her a horse to bet on. Nothing. She'd lost enough money on Bailey's ill-advised picks to know that wasn't part of her ability.

The girl wasn't able to see the future. What she had was a greater skill, even better than Sammie's, the ability to see what was in the past. Seeing beyond the masks and sneaky smiles and knowing the dirt hiding just below the surface.

Couldn't she see that Elsa wanted to ensnare Bailey in her troubles?

The Grimes girl was full of herself and looking down on them . . . Oh, she could feel it.

The Grimes clan as a whole were a gritty bunch, determined and full of themselves, and she was sure the apple didn't fall too far from the tree.

Matthias Grimes, Elsa's father. Charlene didn't even want to start there. Hubertus Grimes, the patriarch of the clan, Elsa's grandfather, that's where the rot started. Mr. Hubertus Grimes had been Charlene's employer. She had worked as a maid in the Grimes home when she was seventeen.

Charlene had needed one more year of schooling to graduate when she took the job. She didn't see the point of finishing high school. She started housekeeping despite her mother and grandmother wailing that she could be the first in their family to go to college. Charlene was smart enough to do it if she'd just stayed in school.

But then what? Charlene had seen plenty of hopefuls leave Mendol on the quest for an education and a profession, only to return dejected and scarred to the point they'd never leave again.

Not Charlene. She'd planned to leave on her own terms. She took the cleaning work to get her hands on enough cash to make an exit gracefully. She'd get out and from under the suffocating, dusty plains. Five dollars a house was what she earned in 1926. Not bad for a few hours of work. She arrived at 9 A.M. and would be done by lunchtime unless it was laundry day.

There wasn't much to do with just the three of them, Mr. and Mrs. Grimes and a grown son, Matthias, who enjoyed home-cooked meals and the liberal use of his parents' modest-sized home. They weren't rich by any means. At best they were considered middle-of-the-roaders. Hubertus Grimes sold insurance to the poor for policies that would never pay out, and his wife, Joann, spent her days knitting, doing crossword puzzles, and reading the Bible. Matthias, well, he spent his time chasing after girls, and Charlene had been one of them.

The day Hubertus Grimes was told about Joann's suspicion, "Matty and the Negro gal are getting it on right here under our roof," Charlene was fired, sent home without her last week's pay, as if it had been her fault. As if she were the one who'd pursued their son while she was busy cleaning their house. It never occurred to them that their son had his own mind and heart, which might take him places they didn't expect.

Now, in the dark, Charlene rolled her knees as close to her chest as her tired bones allowed and closed her eyes tight. "Matty Grimes, don't come talking to me now. I don't want to hear nothing you got to say," she hissed in the darkness. She didn't want to revisit those days.

Such a fragile young man back then. Remembering would require her to admit that she'd once loved him. Maybe that was why Bailey couldn't see him in her burst of light. It was buried too deeply. Charlene hadn't seen him face-to-face since moving back to Mendol. She knew what he was up to, because word traveled in Mendol. Senate Oil and Matthias Grimes were synonymous. If you were talking about one, you were talking about the other, but seeing him up close and personal wasn't in the cards. She wasn't in his circle, and she certainly wasn't cleaning up after his family or any others. She expected he'd never heard about her either. Who would he know who'd let the name Char Dowery pass their lips? In his part of Mendol she was as good as invisible.

A tear slid down the side of her face, remembering her ear pressed against his chest, listening to his heart beat in rhythm while he dreamt. She didn't want to relive how she went from loving him to hating him swift and hard.

All she could do was swallow the pain. All she could do was hope Elsa Grimes was nothing like her father, a dreamer who didn't care about the consequences of involving others in his schemes. She didn't want her niece to get caught up in a world where she'd only get hurt and resolved, *I won't let them hurt her.*

15

A FEW FEET AWAY, down the hall from her aunt Charlene, Bailey's eyelids fluttered in restless sleep. She wasn't afraid to see the truth, at least not yet. It wasn't her life. She was merely a visitor, after all. She had no reason to suspect or fear that what she was about to see would change her life forever.

A lightning strike, bright and blinding, caused her eyes to shut tighter. Behind her lids for those few brief seconds were the beginnings of what she usually saw and felt.

She moved freely in a room. Not hers. Not even her house. She scanned the dark paneling framed in more wood. Low light from a lamp next to a bare mattress showed two burrowing bodies. Flushed skin. Lips locked onto other lips. She heard the hushed breaths of desperation, clear and real as if she were right there in the very room.

All so familiar. But this time the throaty jerking sounds and gasps sounded different. She focused on the two people with their entangled pink-tinged limbs. There was a struggle between them. A mixture of fight and determination. The heart jolt of true love usually revealed itself by now. Sometimes it came as softly as a rose or a sunflower waiting to unfold in bloom. This wasn't what she saw. A split second showed a closed bud aging rapidly, fast-forwarding into hard, dried petals, completely unopened, clamped so tightly not even light or a saving drop of water could slip past the edges. The stem barely held under the weight. Leaves curled before Bailey's closed eyes and dropped, floating infinitely to nowhere.

Her throat went dry when she saw Elsa's face, strained and full of anger. The man with steely gray eyes, hair the color of tree bark, had paused and gripped her face and pushed his mouth against hers.

Elsa clawed his neck, leaving dark red trails against his skin.

His wide shoulders expanded until she seemed to disappear underneath his weight. He thrust back and forth, shaking the lamp off the side table. Darkness returned.

Bailey sat up, gasping. A sick chill ran through her. She wouldn't be able to sleep. *Breathe. Walk it off,* she told herself. She threw her legs over the side of the bed, pushed her cold feet into her slippers, and found her robe.

She kept her steps quiet and used her hands to navigate her way down the short, dark hallway. There was enough moonlight coming in from the window over the sink. She filled a glass with water and drank hardily. Her head swam with the image of Elsa. The man was young, the same age as Elsa, but bigger and much stronger. She had fought as hard as she could, that much Bailey was sure of. There it was, a flash of Elsa's neck in the dressing room. Was that where the bruises had come from?

But what to do with the information was the question. Who would it help to tell what she saw?

For the next few hours, she sketched under dull light to distract herself. Mindless lines came together to make elegant dress designs. The pain of what she saw in the dream dissipated, but not entirely.

When the sun began to rise, Bailey couldn't wait to get to work. She didn't bother making coffee or checking on Aunt Charlene's whereabouts. She shoved herself out the door, yawning, into her cold automobile, and headed to the Regal Gown at just past 7 A.M.

She entered the doors and wanted nothing more than to chuck herself into her sewing chair and go hard at work. Every last bad thing she'd seen or felt could be fended off with the fierce revving from the sewing pedal.

But then she stopped. An urge to speak with Elsa took over. She dropped what she was doing and rushed out to the showroom. By now the high morning sun made the dreamy space sparkle. She felt none of the usual peace and calm. She stared out the window at the diner, where she could assume Miss Jackson was already perched in her booth.

She took a few steps back in case Miss Jackson was looking her way. Miss Jackson would wonder what Bailey was doing in the front of the store instead of in the back, getting work done. Bailey went to the reception desk to get Miss Jackson's calendar. When she had it in her hands, she squatted where she couldn't be seen.

In the pages, she'd find Elsa's telephone number. She had to sift all the way back to the first appointment. September 10. It wasn't lost on Bailey that it had only been a month since she met Elsa. Such a short few weeks, and it felt like a lifetime. If there were a way she could stop caring, she would.

"Grimes residence," a woman answered.

"Hello, may I speak to Elsa, please?" Her heart raced at the request.

"Who may I say is calling?" The older woman was most likely the housekeeper. She had a strong suspicion she'd know or have heard of Bailey, since their community was rather small.

"This is Miss Jackson. I need to confirm an appointment at the Regal Gown for Miss Elsa Grimes," Bailey said in an aristocratic voice, with surprisingly perfect pitch. She sounded very much like her boss.

"Hold on," the woman said. "I'll see if she's up."

Bailey peeked out from behind the counter to make sure there was still no sign of Miss Jackson heading her way. If she caught Bailey using the phone, she could kiss her job goodbye. There was only the trashman's truck rumbling past. Otherwise the street was clear.

Elsa's groggy voice came on the line. "Hello."

Bailey peeked out again before she spoke. "I need to talk to you, Elsa." She estimated she had a safe half hour at least, but didn't want to chance it.

"What did you see?" Elsa asked calmly, as if she already knew the answer.

"You and him. I saw what he did to you."

"Connor. You saw us. We can't talk about it over the phone," Elsa said, pausing. "Later. Tonight. I can come to your house again. I'll tell you about him. About us. Everything."

Bailey rubbed her temple. "I don't understand why you didn't say something sooner. Why didn't you just tell me about him in the first place?"

"Please, Bailey. I'll tell you everything. I promise. I won't leave anything out. Meet me tonight at Georgia's, you know, the diner across the street from the Regal Gown."

"No. That's not going to work. Unless you've been under a rock, Elsa, you know I can't just walk into Georgia's and have a seat at the table." *No to all of it. Her auntie was right. This wasn't going to end well.*

"I'm just happy you saw something, anything. I guess. At least now I know I'm still alive inside," Elsa lamented.

This caught Bailey off guard. She was unsure of what to think or feel. What she saw was usually dead-on. Even when—if—it wasn't what she expected, the vision never lied. The way the man had treated Elsa, like he didn't care a thing about her. It wasn't right.

"All right, fine," Bailey said reluctantly. "We'll meet on my side of town. No one will know us—well—you. Write this down. Meet me at Queenie's on Gowan right off Highway 98. Seven o'clock. We'll sort it out then."

16

INGRID'S PALMS LEFT A SLICK RESIDUE on the plastic casing of the telephone, lotion mixed with nervous moisture. After she gently replaced the receiver on the cradle, she glided her hands against her plaid wool skirt. She'd dressed early to meet one of the contractors.

She lifted the receiver again, just in case she'd hung up too early. Dead, empty air hummed back at her.

She remained frozen, processing all of what she'd heard. She thought about what Elsa had said last night. *"You don't know all of my friends."* She hadn't meant to eavesdrop on Elsa's conversation. She'd found the receiver resting on the table when Oda Mae left to announce the call to Elsa. It wasn't Ingrid's fault Oda Mae hadn't come back to hang it up.

At any other time, Ingrid wouldn't have bothered to listen. There was nothing more mundane than eavesdropping on one of Elsa's conversations. Her daughter had never been a sneaky type, plotting or planning reckless behavior as most teens had. Elsa hadn't done much out-of-bounds besides being herself, dull and cocooned. She'd spent her childhood choosing to climb trees, dig in the mud for worms, and appear with one insect or another in her always-wounded hands. She began spending her days holed up in her room, reading books, when most girls would rather be at a sleepover playing with makeup and exchanging notes on boy crushes.

At least holed up in her room she was out of reach of peering eyes. It grated on Ingrid's nerves when someone commented on how different they were, mother and daughter. Ingrid, the blond, spirited life of the party. The grand hostess with the red-lipped smile. Rarely was anything fun or amusing to Elsa. A smile or giggle was the minimum requirement to attract a potential mate. Elsa, always so serious, knew nothing about the dance of womanhood. She didn't flirt and she knew nothing of gagging down pain while plying ahead with aplomb. Elsa didn't suffer in silence. She made sure everyone knew how she felt.

"Night and day, you two," Deanna Diplo had said once, while they waited for their daughters at the Godwin School of Etiquette. Mothers sitting together could be a contentious group. "You ever thought about having highlights put in Elsa's hair?" Deanna asked. "I know she's young, but it might do her some good, you know, when she looks in the mirror, to see some brightness staring back at her. Give her a new outlook instead of being glum all the time."

Ingrid had ground her teeth in silence. It wasn't as if Deanna's daughter Jane was winning any tiaras. The girl was skinny and buck-toothed, with her mother's lazy left eye.

Elsa's hair was just fine. She was only eleven. She had plenty of time to spruce up her looks. The dull, flat color of burnt toast had also been Ingrid's natural hair color a time ago. She hadn't decided on being a blonde until her freshman year of high school; specifi-cally, for her first pageant.

Yet, on the way home on the hour-long drive from Godwin's that day, she kept an eye on her daughter in the rearview mirror. Pale skin, reddish brown freckles the same color as her blunt bangs, and long pigtails hanging over her shoulders like banded curtains.

"Hey, kiddo," Ingrid said, "why don't we stop at Lucy's and get a wash-and-set for two? You might even like to get your hair like Mommy's, huh? You like my hair, don't you?"

Elsa shrugged her shoulders. "It's all right," she said. "But no, thank you. I'd rather go home."

Ingrid couldn't give up that easily. "Are you sure? Afterward, we can go to the Five and Dime and pick up whatever you want. Get some of those chocolate balls out of the glass jar. Your favorite."

"No, thank you."

Ingrid had seethed all the way home, furious at Deanna Diplo for making her feel less than perfect for having a less-than-perfect daughter. Just less-than in general, really. Ingrid was relentless about fixing Elsa for the next several years. The next thing she knew, Ingrid was in her late thirties and all she'd done was worry about Elsa.

The longer Ingrid stood in the kitchen with the telephone in her sights, the angrier she became all over again. *Elsa.* She'd worked so hard not to be that kind of mother, focused on her child more than herself. She didn't read diaries or search drawers. She'd only recently stepped into Elsa's room for the first time she could remember, looking for the necklace. And that too had made her livid, being reduced to such a cliché.

Ingrid felt herself being dragged into the swirling hurricane of Elsa's tiny world once again. She was so close to handing her off, sending her down the aisle into the abyss of married life. Of course Elsa was still going to be her daughter, still living close by in their sweet little town, and most likely seen in the same circles with their closest peers, but at least she would be safely tucked away under the weight of domestic bliss. Her married life would begin and Ingrid's life would finally begin *again*.

Why was she thinking about ringing the operator to ask where the call came from? Who was this Bailey person? Why was she saying she saw Elsa with Connor? The questions piled one on top of the other. Ingrid pressed a hand to her chest to calm herself. It couldn't possibly be true.

Was her daughter even capable of such a betrayal? Maybe. Wasn't everyone? She felt a headache coming on. But this would explain why Elsa suddenly didn't want to marry Niles.

This would explain so much.

Connor and Elsa. Ingrid refused to believe it was even possible. Beside the fact that Connor Salley and his family were going broke, they were hardly a match. Dull, ordinary Elsa and rugged, handsome Connor were not even a possibility. Unless he'd targeted her for her money. The joke would be on him, wouldn't it?

Ingrid had to sit. She felt her way to the long kitchen counter and eased onto the vinyl-covered stool. She whispered his name, waiting for the truth to reveal itself. *Connor Salley.*

FOR INGRID TO GO AGAINST her wedding vows, to go against God, had been out of character. Her marital oath was the one thing she held sacred. Matthias meant the world to her. She knew one day she'd have to explain everything. Apologize. Not that an apology would be enough.

It wasn't anything she'd planned. A random, ordinary day, a weekend, when she noticed that Connor had become a man. Yes. Sure. He'd always been there, a family friend from their inner circle. But right before her eyes, he'd gone from stringy and tall to athletic and sturdy. From restless to calm. From soft and malleable to chiseled-chin handsome. His voice had turned deep. His smile was just on the edge of menacing. He'd grown up right before her eyes, a scrappy kid eating ice cream cones on the lawn and being first in line for a second helping of mashed potatoes at Sunday cookouts.

The Grimes family spent their summers in Mexico, an easy trip south on a chartered plane. Elsa spent her time dredging the beach for crabs. Ingrid lounged in a cabana, sipping on straws covered by paper umbrellas. The one time they had decided to stay home for the summer was because of a tragic warehouse explosion at Senate Oil.

They'd named it the Coven Summer of 1950, the early weeks of September when winds became dry and relentless. Add in the devastation of a fire, and the gale-force winds sent black smoke around for miles. Eleven lives were lost, either from direct contact with the fire or from the hovering poison in the air. Long after the fire was put out, a yellow-and-orange haze hung in the night as if a spaceship had landed. When it finally rained, black soot left stains on sidewalks and dripped down from roofs of houses. The families of the victims wanted blood, but they had settled on money. Senate Oil was responsible.

Matthias spent every evening in the library with company lawyers and the other captains of industry, figuring out how to make the grieving families go away quietly. How much would it take to extinguish the embers right along with their voices of rage?

Ingrid couldn't go anywhere without the tragedy following her. Even in her haven, the Rose Society charity group, she endured cutting glances her way. The whispers that turned to abrupt silence when she'd approach the ladies were the worst. After one of those evenings of unbearable resentment, she ran home to Matthias with an idea. She and Elsa would go to Mexico, and if Matthias could make the trip later, great. Either way, she had to leave Mendol that summer. She couldn't take it anymore.

"I think it would be great for Elsa, for both of us," she pitched to Matthias. She continued to explain how Elsa turning sixteen was a milestone and how she pictured the two of them bonding poolside with wide hats and sunglasses.

Matthias wouldn't hear of it. He was insulted that she'd even think of leaving him in his time of need. "How will it look, y'all jetting off to Mexico while families are grieving? Don't be so selfish, Ingrid."

It was probably the meanest thing he'd ever said to her. She'd been by his side throughout the long journey from empty pockets to millionaire, the perfect hostess and trophy wife. She had the actual trophies to prove it. *Best in Swimsuit Competition* 1932 and 1933. *Best in Talent Competition* 1933. *Best in Gown Competition* 1932, 1933, and 1934.

Bitterness had filled Ingrid's chest, but she had stayed. She endured the summer with pure resentment coursing through her veins.

The decision to take Connor Salley as her lover was fueled by that resentment. At least, that's the way it began. He'd cornered her in the kitchen, grazing her as if it was accidental.

"Oh, sorry, ma'am," he'd said with a secretive smirk. He wasn't sorry, and he'd been sloppy about it. But then she'd kissed his eager mouth and tasted his inexperience. She decided then that taking him on was the noble thing to do. Edification. She'd teach, refine, and mentor a young man in need of a little polish.

That summer they would meet in the cottage in the back of the Grimes property as often as they could.

"One day you'll make a good husband to a very happy wife," she'd said, stroking his wide shoulders and pulling at his narrow jean-covered waist.

Afterward, each time they made love, she'd explain, "None of this is real. This won't last. Our time together has a defined purpose."

"Says you," he'd say with a devilish grin. "My turn," he'd say with his low, dark eyes. She loved how he'd then take what he needed, however he wanted. Afterward, his sinewy arms would wrap around her hourglass waist and they'd sleep in the afternoon heat for hours.

That summer made her long to be a girl again. She didn't have the reward of living vicariously through her daughter. Meeting Connor at the cottage gave her the chance to relive her youth, to again be the Ingrid who'd been adored and put on a pedestal.

"THE WORKERS ARE HERE to finish the arbor." Oda Mae's voice startled her. Ingrid gripped the edge of the doorframe in the kitchen to keep her balance.

"Oda Mae, do you know someone named Bailey? Someone Elsa may have recently met?"

Oda Mae lifted her eyes to think. "No. Can't say I do." She'd fully grayed over the past few years. She was older than Ingrid, but her skin was plump and free of lines as if she'd never missed a single night of sleep or agonized over a thing she couldn't control before her head hit the pillow. *What's your beauty secret?* Ingrid wanted to ask Oda Mae, but instead, she returned to the pressing issue. "Has Elsa made any new acquaintances at all?"

"No new friends that I've seen. Is something wrong?"

"Everything's fine." Ingrid tried to sound like she meant it.

"Alrighty, I'll send the workmen on around."

"Please tell them if they don't finish today, they're not getting a dime," Ingrid announced. The show must go on. She didn't care what nonsense Elsa had spewed. There would be a wedding ceremony and that was final.

17

ELSA PEERED OUT HER BEDROOM WINDOW with bleary eyes. If it weren't for the workmen banging and carrying on, she would have gladly stayed in bed past noon. Even after speaking with Bailey on the phone, all she'd wanted to do was lie there and plot her escape. But no. Planks were being laid. White lattice sides rose into place with three men hammering at the side posts. *They're building the entrance arbor. They're building the fucking arbor.*

She stormed from her room to find her mama, who obviously hadn't heard a word she'd said the night before. Elsa hadn't expected she would be so easy to find. But there she was, right outside Elsa's bedroom, as if willing her to wake up. Waiting to have her say.

"I told you there wasn't going to be a wedding." Elsa gritted her teeth and waited for the blowback. But, shockingly, her mama didn't look perturbed one bit.

Ingrid smiled serenely. "Yes. You did. Your father and I thought surely you'd sleep it off and wake up with some God-given sense. Elsa Louise Grimes, what exactly is your plan? Are you going to live here with us for the rest of your life, here in Mendol? You going to be an old maid without a penny to your name? Because that's precisely what you'll be."

"Miss Ingrid, telephone?" Oda Mae called up from the kitchen. "Telephone," she said again. "Sounds important, ma'am."

Elsa knew when she was being rescued. Oda Mae had run interference to free her from her mama more times than she could count. She made it look so easy, like throwing a dog a bright, shiny ball. *Fetch,* and off her mama went, dropping the bone that was Elsa.

"I don't think you gon' win this battle, Miss Elsa." Oda Mae had come up the stairs quietly, cutting her eyes in the direction where Ingrid had gone. "What got y'all upset this morning?"

"Oda Mae, I'm sick of pretending. I don't want to be married. I don't want to be like her."

"Shush, hush, now. Take a breath, child. Relax." Oda Mae moved in closer and put her soft arms around Elsa. "Where all this coming from?" She smoothed a delicate hand up and down Elsa's back, as she had done when she was having one of her tantrums. But Elsa wasn't a child anymore. She couldn't be soothed or talked into behaving.

"If I marry him, I might as well kill myself."

"Stop it right now. You hear? Niles Porter is a good man. You're a good woman. There ain't nothing else simpler than a good woman needing a good man. Not much else in this life to want for."

Elsa shook her head, and the wave of tears wasn't far behind.

"Your mama and daddy just want the best for you. When you know better, you do better. That's what we do for our children. When you have your own, you'll understand."

Elsa visibly flinched. She looked down at her stomach. Her breasts and her stomach had slightly plumped up overnight. Did Oda Mae know?

"Go on, now. You get ready for your day. Be grateful what God has given. All that is given is divine."

Less than an hour later, Elsa found herself sitting on Niles's lap, feeling like a showgirl. She kept her smile plastered in place and held her breath, but didn't know how much longer she could remain still. The waist of her flowered skirt grew tighter by the second. At least the wind had come and dried the sweat as it seeped from her armpits.

But she wondered how many pictures would it take to make a couple look believably lost in each other's eyes? With each click of the man's camera, she felt a sharp stab.

She couldn't believe Niles had showed up for the photo session as if the conversation they had had the night before had never taken place. Absolutely no one heard her or cared what she wanted. She could hear her mama's voice in her head: *You will be a penniless old maid. Is that what you want, Elsa Grimes?*

The entire time she'd combed her hair, put on lipstick, and dressed for the pictures, she was crying. Her eyes would be bloodshot, but the black-and-white photo wouldn't show it.

Elsa sat on Niles's lap with both her arms squeezed around his shoulders.

"Hold it for two more, just like that. Smile," the photographer said. "Eyes over here."

"Smile. Hold," the man behind the camera ordered.

"Ah, hello," the man said. "Over here."

Elsa perked up when she saw Rochelle coming up the slope, holding a tray. She rose instinctively to her feet, already picturing Rochelle dropping the heavy platter.

Rochelle was doing her best to keep the chilled pitcher of lemonade steady and balanced. The glasses filled with ice would be the first to go, sliding off the tray. Her lean, slight arms were no match for the weight she carried.

"That's enough," Elsa said quietly at first. Then she took a few steps. "That's enough—pictures. I think we're done," she announced, loudly enough for everyone to hear, including her mama, who'd been watching from a short distance away, unusually quiet.

Elsa took off in a sprint toward Rochelle. In her demure attire, a pink off-the-shoulder bodice and flowing flower-print skirt, Elsa still moved quickly and powerfully.

"What . . . wait. Where're you going? Sorry," Niles told the photographer.

She heard this and fought the urge to turn around and scream, *"I do not need for you to apologize for me. Ever!"* But getting to Rochelle was her first priority.

She reached her friend and grabbed the heavy pitcher with both hands to ease the weight just before it began to slide.

"You didn't have to do that. I had it," Rochelle said, her mouth in a pinched smile. Her cheeks turned round like small apples. Her full lips had a slight shine. "You thirsty?" she asked Elsa. When she handed over the filled glass, their fingers touched much longer than necessary.

"I'll take a glass too, Rochelle," Niles said, having joined Elsa. "Boy, I never seen you run so fast. My girl here could be in a marathon." He kissed the side of her temple. Elsa leaned away ever so slightly. Ingrid had joined them as well, one step behind Niles.

"How about you, ma'am?" Rochelle asked, already pouring.

"Lemonade, yes," Ingrid said. And then to Rochelle, "Did you make this yourself? So delicious."

Elsa stared at her mama's red lip prints on the edge of the glass and pushed back the somersault in her stomach. She'd wanted to throw up all day but it never came. Now she wasn't so sure.

"Yes, ma'am. Bart's Grocers had a tray of lemons. I couldn't resist. I thought everyone would like it," Rochelle said with a lift of her eyes toward Elsa. "I shaved the peel so it has an extra flavor."

Niles gulped down his libation and put his glass out for a second pour. "Tough duty being a happy couple," he joked with an arm around Elsa. She didn't understand this new display of affection. They'd barely touched in private, let alone in broad daylight. A chill passed through her at the thought of what sex would be like with Niles. If they ever had sex. Because Connor had been her first experience, she wondered if that was the kind of hell she'd have to experience for the rest of her life. Was that how all men did it?

"All right, folks, the sun is on the run," the photographer yelled.

"I think we're done," Elsa said. "I can't take a single minute more of posing. I'm just not feeling well."

"I agree with you, darling. The painful smiles will definitely show up in those pictures. We won't be putting those up for anyone to see," Ingrid said. "I'm going to have a discussion with Mr. Clark. I think it will be best to find a new photographer, for the wedding as well as the engagement party. He seems to not understand instruction."

"Thank you," Elsa said, astonished that her mama had been paying attention, even more surprised that she wasn't considered the troublemaker this time. But why hadn't her mama spoken up sooner? Ingrid Grimes was not one to keep her opinion to herself.

"Rochelle, do you know of any good photographers?" Ingrid asked casually.

Elsa's ears pricked up. She didn't trust her mama's suddenly easygoing tone.

"Me, ma'am? Well, yes, I do. There's someone at my church. His name is Lou. I can get his number and you can talk to him, if you'd like. He takes pictures of all our special events."

"Yes. I'd like that. This Lou, might this be the young man who gave you such a pretty necklace, the one we talked about the other day?"

Elsa saw where her mama was going now. More to the fact, where she had gone. Rochelle's hand quaked slightly while she tilted the pitcher. She spilled a bit at first, then straightened her aim as she poured another glass of lemonade.

"I know him from church, that's all," she said, answering the question and leaving it at that.

"I'm famished," Elsa said. "We should get on with this day and find some lunch."

"Lunch is ready and hot, inside," Rochelle said. "I'll see you there." She turned and trailed back to the house much faster than she had come. Elsa faced her mama.

"What was that about? Why were you asking about her necklace?"

"I noticed she was wearing one exactly like the one I'd given you." Ingrid took off her sunglasses and put the earpiece tip in her mouth. "She never had a real answer as to where it came from. The mystery remains, I guess."

"It's not a mystery. I gave it to her," Elsa snapped. She didn't know why for one moment she'd thought her mama had a soft bone in her body. "You trying to accuse her of stealing it?"

"I never accused Rochelle of stealing. I would never do that. She is like a daughter to me."

Elsa coughed her disbelief.

"I merely inquired as to who her special friend was. Had I known you'd given her the necklace, the mystery would have been solved. Seems you're in the business of keeping secrets these days."

Elsa's arms dropped protectively over her stomach. She could feel Niles staring intently, trying to figure out what the conversation meant. She tried to change the tone.

"I don't have any secrets. I just wish you'd asked me instead of insulting Rochelle."

"I will apologize," Ingrid said.

Niles cleared his throat. "Pardon, ladies, but if we're done with the photos, I've got to get going." He pulled back the sleeve of his jacket to peer at his watch.

"We're done," Elsa said pointedly. "We are definitely done."

At the same time, the photographer had arrived at Ingrid's side. "We've still got an hour of high sun we can use. Are we finished with the break here?"

"Mr. Clark, why don't you get the contact sheets together so I can take a look tomorrow by ten." Ingrid escorted him out with a hand on his shoulder. "You've been amazing. I will thank Cecilia for her recommendation."

The burly man nodded, scratching his head. "I might need another day. But. Sure. Yeah. I can have them ready by tomorrow."

"Good. Thank you for your time, Mr. Clark."

Elsa watched how effortlessly her mama had sent the man away and was disgusted by having seen Ingrid use the same power over her. Well-mannered weaponry. Just as she'd sweetly pretended to be interested in Rochelle's reference for a photographer when all she'd wanted to do was start a conversation about the necklace.

Why hadn't she listened when Rochelle had warned her? *Someone will think I stole it.*

SHE'D GIVEN ROCHELLE the necklace six months earlier.

"It's so pretty. I really can't take this," Rochelle had said, placing it back in the jewelry box. "Someone will think I stole it."

"I want you to have it." Elsa sat on her pink bedspread, the skin of her knees peeking through her threadbare dungarees. While Rochelle was supposed to be gathering laundry, they'd lain across the bed and watched television instead. Their favorite hour was *You Bet Your Life,* starring Groucho Marx, laughing at his antics and predicting which guests would go on to greater things. Elsa's favorite pastime was being a one-woman audience to Rochelle's imitations. She'd put on Elsa's many never-worn outfits, and do various skits:

The woman who'd lost her dog. The woman who'd met the man of her dreams. The woman who'd been kissed by a frog.

One dress, the navy blue one with white piping, needed livening up; anyone could see that. Rochelle was the woman who was mayor and declared that the town of Mendol would celebrate "Women's Day, their very own holiday to do nothing, or any damn thing they pleased."

"Wait. You've got to have the right accessories," Elsa said, prim and proper. "Here you go, madam mayor." Elsa lifted the top of her jewelry box and revealed a wealth of unappreciated pageantry to Rochelle and told her to pick something. The heart-shaped diamond pendant was Rochelle's choice. Elsa watched her reflection in the bureau mirror and could see how much Rochelle truly liked it. The chain clasp gave her trouble, so Elsa came and helped her, pushing the circle into the waiting loop. She wanted to take longer, make it seem more difficult than it was. The heart dipped at the center of Rochelle's neck.

"It's perfect on you. I promise no one is going to think you stole anything. You're part of our family," she assured her.

"I do love it. You sure it's okay?" Rochelle said.

"Yes. I'm sure."

"I don't want to ever take it off."

Hearing this made Elsa's heart skip. "Then don't. Don't ever take it off."

"I guess if I keep my uniform zipped up, no one will have to see it."

"Why should you hide it? It's a gift."

Rochelle smiled. "Thank you. Much appreciated."

"You're very welcome, madam mayor."

It had felt good, giving without expectation. In that moment, Elsa had felt appreciated. Now she felt no better than her mama, having ignored Rochelle's fears. Elsa knew all too well how it felt not being listened to. How would she make it up to Rochelle?

"Oda Mae, you seen Rochelle?" Elsa asked now, winded from nervously rushing inside after sending Niles home.

"Elsa. Look what's been delivered for you today." Oda Mae spun the lavish bouquet around in the vase so the large peonies faced the light at the sink window. Oda Mae reached in and took the card. She opened the envelope. *To Elsa and Niles, Congratulations, The Godwin School of Etiquette.*

"Oda Mae, where's Rochelle?" she repeated, ignoring the card. Various gifts arrived daily in honor of Elsa's wedding day. She wished she could throw all of them into an incinerator.

"I sent Rochelle home. She wasn't feeling too well. She didn't have a fever, thank goodness. But she looked like someone dragged her a country mile, so I told her to get some rest. We're going to need all hands on deck for the wedding party of yours this weekend. She's got to be in good shape."

Elsa went straight to her room. She owed Rochelle a phone call of apology.

18

THE DINER WAS DECORATED with posters of jazz greats from the 1930s, with signatures of artists who Queenie Alister had met in her former lifetime as a singer. The biggest framed picture was one of Queenie in a long red gown, her full bronze cleavage on display in a dress with a sweetheart neckline and a sweeping train. Svelte and elegant, she is leaning against a piano, a white magnolia flower in her hair. She'd performed all over the world before opening the place aptly named Queenie's.

Bailey dined there only a couple of times a month. Gabby was a server, so Bailey would normally sit at the counter, where she could chat with Gabby and not be too obvious. Today, Bailey sat in one of the booths against the window so she could keep an eye out for Elsa. The sun hovered way past dusk, causing an eerie blanket of gray fog. One lamppost in the center of the parking lot provided enough light for her to know when Elsa arrived. If she arrived.

Gabby was working her shift, busy taking plates to customers. She stopped in front of Bailey's booth. "I thought you could use this," she said, setting down a cup of hot cocoa. Gabby had plans of being a singer. Working as a waitress at Queenie's made her feel like her dreams were possible. Her shiny pageboy, clipped at the sides, along with the coal eyeliner, perfected in a swirl tip, gave her an alluring personal style. The orange diner apron on anyone else looked boring, but on Gabby it accentuated her tiny waist and curves. When musicians and old friends of Queenie's stopped in, passing through, Gabby made sure to introduce herself and take advantage of any opportunity to ask questions and get advice. With her sultry voice, there truly was nothing stopping her.

"Thank you. I haven't stopped shivering," Bailey said.

"You're just nervous. It'll be all right." Gabby added a signature wink before rushing off to pick up the next order for one of her tables.

Bailey kept her hands wrapped around the cup for warmth. With

each sip, she inhaled the fragrance of the cinnamon-sprinkled chocolate. She stirred in the whipped cream just enough to cool it and
took another sip. Between the delicious treat and Nat King Cole ser-
enading her from the jukebox, it was worth coming out to Queenie's
even if Elsa didn't show up.

"Fried catfish, two wings, and a burg and fries." Queenie Alister's
melodic voice sailed from the kitchen cutout.

Bailey hadn't ordered anything to eat, but hearing those delicious
meals called out made her want to revisit the menu propped between
the salt and pepper shakers. Eating out wasn't in her budget lately.
She'd eat at home, she thought, remembering the leftover stew in
the fridge. She doubted she'd be there very much longer, since it was
already thirty minutes past the meeting time, and still no Elsa.

Every once in a while Gabby sent a smile her way. *She'll come.
Don't worry,* her eyes said. Usually Bailey felt an obligation to keep
things entirely confidential, like a pastor who listens to the sins of his
flock. Once those dressing room curtains closed, Bailey was in charge
of protecting all that she'd felt, heard, and saw. But in this case, she'd
filled Gabby in on the mysterious Elsa Grimes and the vision.

It took a lot to shock Gabby. "Be careful. Just be careful," she'd
whispered earlier that afternoon on the phone.

"Well, fancy meeting you here."

The voice cut into the moment of tension, giving her a start and
releasing her all at once. It wasn't the voice she was expecting. She
took in the grungy overalls before she met his gaze as he looked
down at her. "Mr. Graves."

"Wag," he corrected her. "Don't get all formal on me. We old
friends now." He removed his hat and sat in the booth. "You all by
your lonesome?"

"I'm waiting for someone. A friend."

"I see." He began to scoot out of the booth, much slower than he'd
arrived.

"You don't have to leave. I mean, I'm not sure if she's going to
make it."

"Oh. A *she* friend."

"Yeah. How about you, getting your supper ordered?"

"I eat here more than I eat at home."

"I'm sorry to hear that." Bailey wasn't all that sorry. For whatever reason, she was glad to see him there.

"I like Queenie's cooking." He leaned back and stretched his long arms across the back of the booth. "I haven't had a cough or a fever since I been eating here. Queenie's cooking do right fine by me."

"Okay. I just meant you must be alone. No one to cook for you at home." She heard the words coming out of her mouth and couldn't believe she was fishing for information. Married? Single? She scolded herself. He wasn't her type. *You don't have a type.* Her swearing off men had happened without much effort on her part. She'd simply stopped looking, having seen enough man troubles through the eyes of her clients to last her a lifetime.

His eyes crinkled, followed by a white set of teeth in a nice smile. "Ya got me. I'm all alone. Me, my dog Boz, and a cat named Cat."

Bailey snorted a laugh. "That's the best name you could come up with? Cat?"

"That's what she answers to. Who am I to change a lady's name? How about you? Any dogs, cats, husbands? I've never seen you here, so you must have someone at home."

"No pets. Definitely no husband. Me and my aunt Charlene live over on Baker."

"Charlene . . . Charlene," he said, trying to place the name with a face. "Don't believe I know her."

"I'm beginning to think you were just dropped here from outer space, Mr. . . . Wag."

"I keep to myself. That's what I like about being in Mendol, quiet. Easy to find your place. No one's looking for me unless I want to be found."

Bailey didn't know what to make of Walter Anderson Graves. His sharp wit didn't fit the soft fold of his eyelids or the lopsided smile. He was quick and focused, even with his lighthearted banter.

"Thigh and mash with two sides of okra, out the door," Queenie called.

"That's me. Better get it while it's hot. I'll see you around."

He was on his feet, headed to the pickup counter; then he turned around to see her one more time. She waved, caught in the act of feeling his absence.

Gabby rushed over to her table. "He wasn't bothering you, was he?"

"Not at all. He's nice, from what I can tell."

"Yeah. He's a flirt. Flirting in here with every skirt he sees," she said.

"He wasn't bothering me," Bailey said. "He fixed my light at the Regal Gown."

"Oh. I see. He fixed your light. Then you know what I'm talking about," Gabby said. A family of hungry patrons waved her over. "I'll be back," she announced. "But I'm not done with this one. I want the details."

Bailey reached inside her handbag, fingers searching until she landed on the slip of paper from Mr. Graves. She pulled it out for the fifth or so time and considered tearing it into tiny pieces. Each time, she'd stared at the dark ink, committing every stroke to memory, so it wouldn't matter if she threw it out. She knew his telephone number by heart: 2L-55-77. Again, she chastised herself. *What are you going to do with this, call him?*

"I'm sorry I'm late," Elsa huffed as she plopped down in the booth, across from Bailey. Her skin was translucent, with auburn freckles peeking through. She untied her scarf and pulled it away, revealing flat bangs on her forehead. The rest of her hair was pinned back at the sides. Her pin curls from the other night had disappeared.

"It's okay," Bailey announced, trying to hide her annoyance. "But I can't stay much longer. I'm sure my auntie is wondering where I am. Are you all right?"

"Yes. I'm fine."

Bailey nodded, waiting for more, but Elsa was silent. "You came to tell me about him, Connor. I mean, if you want me to help you, Elsa, I need to know who he is, what he means to you. I didn't like what I saw between you two. It felt—"

"*Ssh.*" Elsa looked around as if she were a communist spy, like someone in one of those war movies. She leaned forward. "His name is Connor Salley. I've known him forever. Growing up here as children, then to teens, and adults, we were like family." She closed her eyes. "It was just the one time. We were drunk. I was drunk. But I didn't want . . ." She trailed off. "I didn't want that to happen."

"So, he's not the one you think you're supposed to be with?"

"Our church teaches purity of the heart and body. If anyone finds out he was my first . . . I belong to him . . . he was my first. He was my first," she repeated. "I wish it hadn't happened. I can't change anything, because it did happen."

Bailey let out a breath. "I saw bruises on your neck, that first day I met you. And now, after what I saw, I have to ask—Was it him? Did he hurt you?"

The music had stopped. The sound of food sizzling in a pan and murmurs of customer conversations with forks against plates filled the space.

"Well, hello," Gabby interrupted, standing at the edge of their table with her order pad in hand. "You must be Elsa. Hi. I'm Gabby, Bailey's friend."

"Hi." Elsa recovered quickly, blinking back the glaze of tears in her eyes. "Nice to meet you."

"Y'all want to order something to eat?"

Neither of them answered.

Gabby looked between the two, worried. "All right. If you need anything, let me know." She dropped her notepad into her apron pocket and left them alone.

"So you don't want to be with Connor?" Bailey asked pointedly, finally, after holding it in. "I'm confused, Elsa."

"I absolutely don't want to be with him. I hate him," she confessed. "I hate him for what he did. Hate is a sin," she added quietly. "I don't know what I'm supposed to do because the truth is, I might be . . . I think I'm pregnant. With Connor's baby."

"Oh . . . oh," Bailey said, reaching out, feeling the pain of such a thing. She couldn't fathom living with such a consequence: having a baby with the man who'd done the worst to her. "You're certain? I mean, you're sure?" Bailey pulled her hand away from Elsa's arm where she'd touched her. She hadn't felt anything. Usually, she got a kindling, a little burst of light, for a baby. Bailey didn't mention this, realizing she'd only be confirming what Elsa had been trying to say all along: *"Am I dead inside? Do I not have a soul? Why can't you see anything for me?"*

"Yeah, I guess I could be imagining the fat growing around my middle." She swiped at her eyes. "Or that my monthly has disappeared."

"In any event, seems like you and Niles can get through this together. Your wedding is soon enough, maybe soon enough that it won't make a difference."

"I know what you're suggesting. No one will know whose baby I'm carrying. But I'll know. I'll always know. I have to decide about the rest of my life and maybe someone else's. I'm so scared. There's so much going on in my head. I told my mama I don't want to marry Niles. I told Niles too. He knows it's not what I want. But if I am pregnant, I have to be married to somebody for the sake of my child. I have to do what's best."

"So it's Niles, I guess," Bailey said, to right the ship. But Elsa was on a different course entirely, focused on what she wanted.

"I think I'm in love with someone else, though."

This threw Bailey for a loop. "What? . . . What do you mean? There's someone else?"

"That's why you have to come to the party, Bailey. Please tell me you haven't changed your mind. You have to come and touch and do your feely thing. I know in my heart there's someone who I love. I just have to know if they feel the same way."

Bailey shook her head vigorously. "I want to help. I really do. But this is a lot, Elsa. I'm not sure I can help you."

"Now you see what kind of nightmare I'm living, and you want to abandon me?"

"It's just . . . can't you talk to . . . someone? Someone else?" Bailey was thinking that this was bigger than she could fix. Elsa needed someone who could really help. How did a young woman catch a break in a town like Mendol, where nothing mattered but church on

Sunday and oil on Monday? For a moment, just a moment, Bailey thought, *I wouldn't trade places with you for all the money and status in the world.*

"Please." Elsa's jaw tightened. "Bailey, this is important to me."

Bailey snapped back to the matter at hand. "A gathering like that? I've never been around— Well, it seems like it's going to be a lot of people there I don't know," she said, taking a page out of the lessons she'd learned at the Regal Gown. Diplomacy. Tact. What she really wanted to say was how unsafe she would feel. Her aunt Charlene had told her a million times to mind her business. She was right. Picturing herself in a room full of people who might hate her just for having the audacity to sit among them made her shrink with each passing second.

"You know *me*. I promise, you will be at my side the entire time. I'll have the driver whisk you away and deliver you back home the minute you don't want to be there. I promise you'll be safe with me."

"Elsa, you know I want to help." How many more ways did she have to say no?

"A hundred dollars."

"Stop it," Bailey hissed. "You cannot buy me like some piece of land for sale."

"Two hundred."

"Are you serious right now?"

"Yes. I have money. It's my own savings account. I've had it since I was five years old."

"I don't want to take your life savings."

Elsa threw her head back. "But that's just it. I'm trying to save my life," she said. "I can't live like this. I can't live with being torn, too scared to make a decision and stick to it."

"Believe it or not, I understand how you feel," Bailey said. "I'm scared too of just about everything. But I get by. I wake up every morning and step out the door and live my life. That's all you have to do, Elsa. Live your life. You don't have to decide all of it at once. Just one day at a time."

"Three hundred dollars."

Bailey hiccuped her shock and leaned forward. "Wait a minute." She didn't need to do much math to equate that amount to six months of the salary Miss Jackson paid her.

"I'm serious, Bailey. You know I am."

"All right. I'll do it. I'll come to the party. I'll take the money. I need it, Elsa, so don't play with me."

"I'd never do that. In fact, I'll give it to you up front. I trust you. I know you'll come."

19

SO THIS WAS WHAT INGRID had been reduced to: following her daughter to get answers. Sneaking around, nearly running stoplights, and barely escaping collisions to keep up with her. The Eastside, of all places, was where she'd landed, sitting in the crumbling parking lot. Ingrid had ventured to this part of Mendol maybe once or twice when Oda Mae had car trouble and needed a ride home. She remembered being surprised how well the Negroes kept their lawns and homes.

But this place could use a paint job, and the sign over the small brick building had two letters darkened as the bulbs had blown out in the center so it said QU—NIE'S. It still read correctly, as the mind could fill in the blanks. Assumptions were as good as facts. Which was what Ingrid was doing as she sat in her car, watching Elsa sitting in the diner.

Through the window she saw her daughter sitting with a girl who at first looked a lot like Rochelle. But it wasn't Rochelle. As she did for the sign, Ingrid began filling in all the blank spaces.

This must be Bailey. She was about the same age as Elsa. Slightly older. Ingrid removed her sunglasses to get a better view. From where Ingrid was parked, and because it was nightfall, the view hadn't changed much without her dark glasses. Profiles of their faces, both of them leaning forward like old friends, made their facial expressions hard to gauge. But their body language, the way their shoulders fell forward and heads nearly pushed together, intimated there was no crisis.

Elsa seemed relaxed. Not under duress from being blackmailed, which had been Ingrid's first notion. Earlier, she had reflected on their conversation and surmised the only possible explanation was extortion, a very likely assumption. This Bailey person was blackmailing Elsa after she'd seen her and Connor in what looked like a romantic tryst. A chill ran through her body. An affair? Ingrid would rather believe anything but that. Elsa and Connor? *Anything but that.*

Ingrid had considered asking point-blank that morning, "Who is this Bailey person and what was she talking about on the phone?" She wanted to confront Elsa and ask why the girl had brought up Connor Salley. But then she stopped herself. Elsa obviously had plenty to hide. She wasn't going to tell Ingrid what she needed to know. After the blowup regarding Rochelle and the gifted jewelry—in front of Niles, no less—she knew Elsa was being secretive, on the defensive. Ingrid's list of questions meanwhile continued to grow.

She had a mind to go inside and disrupt the meeting. This Bailey did not know who she was dealing with. The Grimes family were not to be messed with. One mention of this to her husband, and Bailey—and the problem—would disappear.

Ingrid grabbed the steering wheel to keep from banging her hands on the dash. Her knuckles turned a ghostly white.

Frustration expanded through her chest, traveling to her tingling fingertips. Whatever the two of them were talking about had to do with Connor Salley, that much must be true. So maybe it was he who should be doing the explaining. He should be the one telling her what was truly going on.

She started the engine, shifted into reverse, and hit the gas. A honk sent her heart racing. She slammed on the brakes. The skid of her thick tires on the gritty asphalt caused enough noise to turn heads in the parking lot. She checked the diner window and exhaled in relief that Elsa wasn't looking out her way.

Ingrid began again, slowly back, then forward, then eased out of the diner parking lot, hot tears streaming down her cheeks and bitterness clogging her throat. *Calm down. You still have no proof of one single thing,* she told herself. Still jumping to conclusions, making assumptions. When she came to a red light, she took the time to pat her face dry. She turned down the sun visor and got a glimpse of herself in the padded mirror. A wreck. Smeared mascara in a matter of minutes.

Whatever her plan had been, she'd have to rethink it. Besides, the only place she knew to find Connor Salley at this late hour was at his parents' home. She couldn't very well go knocking on the Salleys' door looking wrung out. If she called, there'd be concern. Gweneth Salley always answered her own phone since she couldn't afford help nowadays. Did that mean she did her own laundry too? Ingrid bristled at the thought.

She'd get a message to Connor at the plant, first shift, 6 A.M. to 3 P.M., Monday through Friday. There wasn't one day that passed that she didn't feel sorry for the Salleys, having to live like paupers. At the time when the lawsuit settlements from the fire were handed down, there had been no insurance in place for such a tragedy. Not for lost lives, anyway. The insurance covered machinery, tanks, and lost revenue, but not people. Angry people. Hurting people. Mourning people. On the fourth of June in 1951, the payments to the bereaved came straight out of the pockets of Matthias Grimes, Layton Porter, and Earl Salley. An equal three-way split came to three million dollars each, an unprecedented amount, withdrawn in liquid assets in one fell swoop.

Earl and Gweneth Salley had to sell their home and their share of Senate Oil, which Matthias bought for cents on the dollar. Their wealth disappeared overnight. Matthias saw to it to keep Earl employed as a manager and hired his son at the plant. Luckily, Connor was young enough not to miss the privilege he was now denied. The Porter twins, Niles and Leo, hadn't abandoned him socially. They were all very close friends. So close, Ingrid thought, that it wouldn't make sense for Connor to have a romantic interest in Elsa. He wouldn't betray his relationship with Niles by cheating with Elsa, would he? Maybe he'd been so hurt by Ingrid breaking it off with him that this was his revenge. Or maybe he'd simply wanted someone young and oblivious to his blue-collar status. Most of the young women in Mendol were acutely aware of the pecking order— who could afford the life they wanted and who could not. Someone like Elsa, who didn't care about such things, made her genuinely unique.

Or was it just simply Elsa's youth? Ingrid suddenly felt old and unattractive. The years of stress had finally caught up to her. At the stop sign, she turned the mirror down to face her. *Get yourself together.*

The woman in the reflection wasn't bad on the eyes. She was worrying herself into a tizzy. Jumping to conclusions.

She could go on endlessly trying to fill in the blanks, or she could simply ask Connor.

It was pointless to keep speculating, and yet the weight of it all kept her asking the same question. Why Elsa? Why would Connor pick her daughter, of all people, to have a relationship with? He'd have to hate her, truly hate Ingrid, to betray her that way.

Well . . . she would find out.

20

BEHIND QUEENIE'S, Bailey and Gabby shared the swing bench, which was in need of a good sanding and a coat of paint. The stars twinkled in the black sky while Bailey filled her in on Elsa's story. Now there was a baby to boot, and she didn't want to be with either of the men in her life.

Gabby did her usual huff. "Nothing you can do about none of that. So stop worrying. You going to the party or not?"

"What happened to your warning to be careful? Now you want to watch me walk into the lion's den?"

"That was before you said the going rate was three hundred dollars. Heck, I'll go and pretend to be you." Gabby put out her hands and began to mimic Bailey. "I see you have a bright future together."

"Stop it. This is serious." It was more cash than she'd ever seen in one place, simply to show up at a party. That part was true. But in all honesty, there was more to it than showing up.

"I think you should do whatever you want. To heck with what anybody thinks. Even me." Gabby blew out a puff of smoke and then snaked it back into her mouth. "Three hundred dollars, though. That's all I got to say. That Elsa is one desperate lady."

Gabby had never stopped smoking after their one shared cigarette behind the track bleachers of Mendol's Eastside High. In their matching gray physical ed shirts and blooming white gym shorts, they'd talked and giggled, neither confessing that it was their first time smoking.

"If I go to that party and Miss Jackson finds out, she won't be happy. She scolded me about being too chummy with the clients. Can you imagine if she's a guest and she sees me walk in there all high and mighty?" Bailey asked.

"Yeah, but you'll have three hundred dollars in your pocketbook. She can scold all she wants."

"I don't know if the money will be enough if I'm kicked out on my rear. My auntie's been playing the horses. The house is one nail away from collapsing, and she's busy gambling. And lately, she's been sneaking out at strange hours in the night. I have no idea what she's up to. Somebody around here has to be the responsible one."

Gabby almost choked on her latest inhale. "Ma'am," she sang out when she caught her breath. "You sound like somebody's old grandmama. When are you going to lighten up? People have lives, you know. Just because she's not telling you all her business doesn't mean she's up to no good. Besides, shouldn't you be enjoying your own life right about now? Three hundred dollars." She spoke the number slowly. "Not to mention, you could charge the rest of those ladies. Open a shop right there in your place. If they really want to be read and know who their true loves are, you make 'em pay. Yes, and you're welcome."

"Should I really be handing out advice on love when I've never felt it, not once?" Conversations with Gabby inevitably circled back to Bailey's limited relationship status. Not by choice. "If there were a life to have, I'd take it," Bailey said to the onyx sky. Fall nights were cooler and drier. The locusts were down to single chirps in harmony, instead of a full orchestra. She pulled her shawl closer. She looked up as if heaven above was ready to take all requests. "I want to meet someone. Seems every time I try they get one good sniff of me and they're no longer interested."

"You talking about that deacon?" Gabby laughed. "Honey, he wasn't good enough for you anyway. Someone going to be lucky to have you on their arm. But no, that Wag fella, he ain't it. He ain't nothing but trouble."

Bailey sat up. "Walter. His name is Walter Anderson Graves."

Gabby faced her. "Walter?"

"WAG. The initials, get it? See. You don't know a thing about him and you're besmirching the man's good name."

"And why can't you see that he's one of those hit-it-and-quit-it misters? *Wag* is short for all the dog wagging he do. Aren't you the mind reader? If you want, I can introduce you to my cousin. He's training at Fort Sill for four weeks before heading to Texas, where he'll be stationed."

Frowning, Bailey asked, "Why would I want to meet someone who's not even going to be here?"

"Well, my cousin won't be gone forever. He's a good man. Unlike Wag or whatever."

"Thank you for the offer. But I'll be fine. What about yourself? How're you doing after your breakup with HW?"

"I'm fine. He's the one whining and whimpering, 'Please, Gabs, take me back. I promise I won't look at nobody else but you.' Pitiful."

Bailey shook her head, ashamed to be there for the mocking. "That man loves you."

"Well, he should've acted like it. Fooling around with Urma Hill, of all the hussies; he knew it was going to get back to me. That girl can't keep a secret. She was always kissing and telling. Remember she got Mr. Flournoy kicked out of school 'cause she reported him for taking possession of her goodies? As if she didn't give them willingly. He was my favorite teacher."

"Mine too," Bailey confessed. "I loved when he read out loud in that baritone voice of his." She wondered if Gabby also remembered that Bailey was the one responsible for Mr. Flournoy being fired, not Urma. There was one time that Mr. Flournoy's arm had brushed against Bailey when he walked by her in the narrow aisle of the classroom. A bright red flame of light came to her. Later that night, she saw the two of them, teacher and student, shored up against the chalkboard, panting and moaning. In the next spark, there was Mr. Flournoy, crying and begging for Urma not to leave him or the worst would happen. Bailey didn't know what "the worst" might have been. She didn't want to find out.

It had scared her. Bailey felt it urgent to tell someone. She told Urma, "Be careful, Mr. Flournoy loves you something serious. Maybe a little too much. He's a teacher and you're a student. Maybe you should tell someone about him. Be careful, that's all." That's all Bailey said. How was she to know the intercom button was stuck in the classroom, piping her voice straight into Principal Palmer's office? A day or two later Mr. Flournoy was out the door. She felt responsible but not sorry.

"Yeah, well, I'm not taking HW back," Gabby said. "I got bigger plans. I'm not trying to stay here in Mendol."

"Wait. Where're you going?" No one left Mendol. Bailey especially couldn't fathom her best gal being gone.

Gabby's cigarette flared to the end with the red glow of her last inhale before she smashed it to death under her shoe. "I've been saving up. I'm going to Chicago. There's a music company there, Cadillac Records. They're looking for singers. A national search for ladies who can sing. People like me. I can sing. I'm sitting here, letting all of this go to waste, serving hash browns and eggs at Queenie's café."

"But it's not a sure thing. Right? I mean, you'd go all the way to Chicago and not even know if—"

"Bailey, that's the thing, you don't know what you don't know. Everybody's not like you and can see the future."

"I can't see the future, Gabby."

"You can see something. You told me from the start HW wasn't the one for me, and I ignored you. And look what it got me."

"I said you loved something else more. I never said he wasn't the one."

"Well, turns out you were right. The something I love more than him is singing. Singing in a choir ain't enough. And I want to invite my best friend to come with me. When I make it big, you can make all my stage dresses."

"Gabs. You know I'd be happy to make a dress for you, anytime," Bailey said. "But I'll stay put for now." Working in the dress shop was her safe haven; that's all she knew for sure.

"That's fine, for now," Gabby said, "until I hit the big time. Then you're coming with me."

"I like the sound of it." Bailey could see the possibilities. But there was one problem: She was starting to really get worried. Her ability to see true love felt hampered and off-kilter. She thought about her handshake with Wag, long and warm. There had been the pink light cascading around him, but nothing else had come in the night. Surely the man had a love or some passion in his life? And two nights had passed and she still had seen nothing definitive for Marion Carter.

In the past, she saw only true love. Now there was the vision of Elsa being attacked by Connor Salley. There'd been no love on Elsa's part, only pain. But she saw it. Up front and brutal. Why had Bailey been able to see every moment so clearly? You didn't treat someone that way if you loved them. And Elsa had been so scared. It was quite the opposite: hate. Bailey shuddered, recalling the way Connor squeezed Elsa's face and then her neck, all to control her.

"You all right?" Gabby asked.

Bailey shook herself from her deep thoughts. She could tell from the way Gabby was facing her that she'd scared her a little, staring out, numb and frozen. "I'm fine."

She made up her mind. The next starry-eyed bride who walked into the Regal Gown would be her test. She'd slip off her gloves and force a graze of her skin. She would never let the words *I can't* leave her lips again.

21

CHARLENE HAD CHANGED EVERYTHING in her life for Matty Grimes in 1926. She would have done anything for him back then, all because he convinced her anything was possible, that the two of them were possible.

They'd been seeing each other, sneaking around, for nearly a year. She couldn't recall a single day when they hadn't found a way to put their hands on each other. He seemed to conveniently show up right when she was changing the bedsheets for washday. She hadn't believed anything would come of their tryst. She was smarter than that.

It was Matty who professed his love. He said it first while she swished the mop back and forth on the modest-sized floor in the Grimes family kitchen one morning.

"I hate seeing the woman I love doing this kind of work," he said, sitting on the kitchen counter. "We should leave here, find someplace we can be together. Really together. No more sneaking around."

Charlene laughed. But then she saw the spark in his eyes under the heavy hood of his thick lashes, and realized he wasn't just blowing smoke. She paused, using the mop stick to lean against. "I love you too, Matty," she'd said. "But do you really think that kind of place exists for us?"

"I wouldn't say it if I didn't believe it, Char."

He'd convinced her to believe it too.

Years later, when she'd returned to Mendol, she'd asked around in polite conversation about her old employers, Hubertus and Joann Grimes, and learned inadvertently about their prominent and successful son. How he became a leader, a pioneer who had single-handedly put Mendol on the map with his company, Senate Oil, one of the biggest little oil developers in the Midwest. How he'd become important enough to be spared from the early draft, since his time and expertise better served the country if he kept the oil pumping for the war effort. Quite proud they all were of their prodigal son.

Once, when she'd first returned to Mendol, Charlene had waited outside those Senate Oil gates, not one of her prouder moments. She hadn't planned what she was going to say. She'd only wanted him to see her, to know she had not been broken by him and his useless promises.

Well, she *had* been broken, but since then had healed.

She'd sat there in her dead sister's car with her best dress on, wearing a fresh coat of ruby-red lip color. When she recognized him in his shiny automobile coming straight toward her, she lost her nerve and shoved herself down in the seat. But she'd seen him, Matthias "Matty" Grimes, his hair parted on the same side, shellacked to submission. The glasses were new, making him look smart and mature. But hadn't he always been smart and mature? With him being three years older, and of course wiser, she'd listened to and believed anything he had to say. Now he was in his late forties. She peeked up for another glimpse, but he had turned out of the gate.

Naturally, she started the engine and followed him.

The road felt endless, making her wonder if he'd drive to the end of the city line. The gas gauge needle pointed down in the wrong direction. Was it really worth it to be stranded on the hot pavement? She talked herself into stopping just before he made a few quick turns into a tree-lined suburb. He made a final swoop right, disappearing up a long driveway. The peak of a castle was visible just beyond the trees. Charlene didn't dare enter. No one who looked like Charlene would be in this neighborhood unless they were on staff. With her bright lips and bold striped dress, she couldn't pass for the help anymore. Those days were long behind her. She also knew, on the cusp of twilight, that she'd better hurry back to be on the Eastside before dark.

She went home that night but returned to the industrial facility a few days later. She sat parked on the gravel road across from the entrance. There were three shifts where men came with their lunch pails, and Senate Oil shirts, and dungarees of their choice. Some wore full jumpers, gray with the emblem on the back. The white men who came in suits arrived once in the morning and left as late as seven in the evening. And, like the first time, she followed Matthias all the way back to his home. Her goal had been to find out what he did when he thought no one was watching. Three trips in all before she had surmised that he was indeed a family man, fine-tuned, better off than when she'd known him last. She wasn't out to disturb his peace. She promised herself she wouldn't interrupt his life.

Inadvertently, now he was interrupting hers. And her niece's life. She couldn't let that happen. For the past few nights, she'd found herself parked outside his grand estate. Sitting. Watching. She wasn't sure what her plan was. She for sure didn't have one.

If she got the chance, she wasn't sure what she'd say. Charlene took a long, deep breath and placed her hands on her stomach. This was her ritual at night. For a few minutes, she practiced forgiving herself for the past. *Just breathe and let it out.* She tried forgiving him too.

22

THE NOISE OF SLOWLY SWINGING HAMMERS landing against wood awakened Ingrid from the sleep she'd fought hard for, first with three tumblers full of sherry, then with two Nembutal pills followed by a shot of vodka. She felt every bit of her hangover. She squinted as she pulled the silk mask away. Oda Mae had earlier pulled back the blue damask curtains and was probably startled when she saw Ingrid still lying there, unresponsive. But she was awake now, with the memory and taste of Connor still alive in the recesses of her dream.

Picturing Connor's arms wrapped around Elsa had stopped her from falling asleep. It was too much to bear, then and now.

She attempted to rise using her elbows. The weight of the top half of her won out, sending her back, flat on the feather mattress. Was the room spinning or was she? She shut her eyes and willed herself to have a level head.

The other side of the bed was empty. Matthias had always been an early riser, having disciplined himself to arrive at his office before 7 A.M. At least he wasn't there to witness her disarray. She could only guess what she looked like, since she had neglected to roll her hair before bed.

A soft knock at the door came before it slowly opened. "Ma'am, Miss Ingrid?" Oda Mae called out. "Oh good. You up."

"I wouldn't say *up*."

"How about some coffee? Might get you moving." The tray arrived at her side without her agreement. Oda Mae poured the brew and added the cream and sugar, just as she knew Ingrid liked it.

Before Oda Mae left, Ingrid took a sip. "Much better." She let out a breath of relief, feeling the lift of caffeine. "Oda Mae, wait. You ever been to a little place called Queenie's?"

"Many times. Good food. Since when you like soul food, Miss Ingrid?"

"Well, I haven't tasted the food there. I was considering a visit. Would someone like me"—she hesitated before finishing the question— "be allowed?"

"Allowed?" Oda Mae's brows rose, amused.

"You understand what I'm saying?"

"Money is green, Miss Ingrid. Nobody'll be mad at that. A customer is a customer."

"Yes. I was hoping that would be the case. Thank you, Oda Mae."

The night before, in her dizzying state of drunken insomnia, a plan had come about. She pictured herself walking into the Eastside diner, boldly enough to ask, "Does anyone here know someone named Bailey?"

Ingrid wasn't one to jump off a cliff, eyes closed, without a parachute. Her plan would take a bit of work. What she didn't want to happen was being hurled out of the café by some No-Whites-Allowed code, even though she'd just seen Elsa there, seemingly without a care in the world.

Elsa had an ease about her that would make her fit in. Ingrid, not so much. She knew she'd stand out.

But she needed to get to the truth behind this mysterious young woman and find out exactly what hold she had on Elsa and what the truth was about Connor. Clearly she wasn't going to get it any other way.

Ingrid stretched, then marched to her closet. Looking like a dowdy secretary took effort, she realized, while sifting through her designer pieces. Couture price tags still hung from some of her garments, while others that had been collected over the years looked just as new.

In the farthest corner of the closet, a pink Christian Dior two-piece sweater tank top and cardigan hung lopsided on a velvet hanger. She'd worn the set only once, because it fit too loosely in the waist area. It could work. She then held up a pair of black pinch-pleated pants, another bad decision. Next, shoes. Polished and pointed heels wouldn't do. She found an old pair of matte leather slippers from her youth, sentimental memories attached, and considered herself appropriately styled.

An hour later, she was back at Queenie's café, this time standing at the wood-framed screen door, staring at the tarnished handle. The only thing between her and getting the information she sought was touching said handle. She considered whether it would be rude to pull out a handkerchief before touching it with her bare hands. Someone might see her, and then it would be rude.

Courage. She grabbed the handle bare and stepped inside to the scent of bacon and sweet cinnamon rolls all at once. And coffee. Everything smelled like heaven. "Hello, excuse me," she said to the woman's back.

"Go on, have a seat and I'll come over and take your order," the woman said without turning around.

"Hello, I've been sent here by the office of Jones and Neuman, attorneys-at-law." Her mouth had gone dry and her words were rigid. But this got the woman's attention. She faced Ingrid.

"*Ahuh,* how can I help you?"

Ingrid pushed her clear reading glasses up on the bridge of her nose. "I'm looking for a woman named Bailey who lives in the area. She's been left a large sum from an inheritance," Ingrid announced loudly, determined to speak over the music playing from the red jukebox in the corner. "Bailey." She repeated the first name. It was all she had to work with, but it should've been enough, considering how their town was small—their circle, even smaller. "Do you know where I can find her? This is a pressing issue that needs to be addressed. I'm sure she will be grateful to receive her check, and—"

"Where you from again?" The woman at the counter surveyed Ingrid up and down. Her name tag read *Queenie,* as in the owner of the place.

"I'm from Oklahoma City," Ingrid answered, unsure where she'd gone wrong to elicit suspicion. She tried to shield the uptick of fear and continued. "It was a long drive. I'm famished. The food smells delicious. I'll take a number one, eggs over easy, and I probably should have some coffee."

The cash register rang for an even $4.00.

Ingrid pulled out a twenty-dollar bill. "You can keep the change."

The cash drawer snapped open. "Bailey Dowery lives here in Mendol with her aunt Charlene. She over on Baker," Queenie said. "I'm not sure of the exact house." She grabbed a white cup and saucer and poured the steaming coffee.

"She work at that gown shop downtown," another woman said.

"The Regal Gown. It's on Main," a man said from the seating area. Another person was heard shushing him for his added details.

Ingrid, swelled with delight and relief, turned around to her new friends. "Well, thank you all so kindly. You know, instead of the number one, I'll take one of those sweet cinnamon rolls to go? I want to stay on schedule. You've been so helpful."

"You want your coffee?"

"Oh, no. I'll just be . . . Here you are, another tip," Ingrid said, pulling more money from her pocketbook, this time ones. She placed the bills on the counter, grabbed the pastry bag, and rushed off.

Outside, she glanced back, rethinking her free pass as a white woman in this part of town. She could be chased and robbed. Surely someone had noticed the exchange of cash for a few cents' worth of pastry and concluded there was more where that came from.

Her hands shook as she started the car and drove off. On the street, she stopped, pulled out a pen, and wrote on the moist, stained pastry bag, *Bailey Dowery works at the Regal Gown. Lives on Baker with her aunt Charlene.* She didn't want to forget a single detail, not that she would. It was too important. She needed to know what had happened between Elsa and Connor and, more important, what this Bailey knew to manipulate Elsa into walking away from Niles and the marriage.

Bailey would soon be dealt with accordingly. Matthias would hear about everything. Well, not everything. But he'd know what to do, how to handle a busybody like Bailey Dowery.

23

CHARLENE LAID THE HOT COMB on the stove, away from the flame. She was halfway through a press-and-curl on the head of Hattie Richie, a longtime customer who talked incessantly about the goings-on in Mendol. The woman spread gossip like the common cold. But it was the purr of an engine that caught Charlene's attention and caused her to stop work and shush her client. "Hold on. You hear that?" She walked over and turned off the table fan. She listened. The distinct hum told her what she was hearing was an expensive automobile that absolutely did not belong on Baker, or on any street on the Eastside. And then the engine cut off. Dead silence.

"I'll be right back," she told Hattie.

At the front of the house she peeked out the heavy curtains. As soon as she saw the sleek chrome on the golden beige car that was as long as the width of their entire home, her heart did a somersault.

She never expected to see Matthias Grimes parked outside her house. But wasn't it about time? She'd dreamt of this day, of what she wanted to say to him. And yet, her first instinct was to hide. She hadn't bothered dressing, since she was doing early hair appointments. She looked down at the dull, stained housecoat that doubled as her smock, with its hem frayed from too many washings. Bobby pins lined up in one pocket and a black plastic comb stuck out of the other. Her hands went up to her temples, where she knew her own grays hadn't been tended to in a few months.

He got out of the car and surveyed the area as if not exactly sure which house he was looking for. Now, from the short distance, she could see Matthias had aged too, but money had given him a sure advantage. He still had a head full of thick hair. *Salt-and-pepper* was the term used for men. For women, it was just *gray*. He'd filled out the way older men do, chest and stomach becoming one apparatus.

When he finally decided where he was going, he began a long, confident stride toward 101 Baker.

She rushed past the kitchen and into her room.

"Where'd you go, Charlene?" Hattie called out. "I'm sitting in here about to sweat out my hair and ruin the pressing you already did. You coming back or what? Why you turn the fan off?"

"I still need a minute, Hattie. You'll be fine. Use that magazine you reading to fan yourself. Or better yet, get up and turn the table fan back on. Oh, and do me a favor and turn off that burner." A floral scarf with peacocks revealed itself as a lifesaver. She tightened it around her head and wrapped the ends to hang over her shoulder. She peeled off the drab housecoat and threw on an orange sweater and red skirt she had worn the day before to meet Ray Ray about her payout from the track. The scent of perfume and smoke wasn't the worst thing she could smell of. Otherwise, in perfect condition for a second wear.

Charlene slipped her feet into her pink loafers, then sidestepped swiftly to the bathroom and found her red lipstick. *For what?* She suddenly slowed to ask herself, *What in the world do you think you're doing? He's not here for you.* This was about that Grimes gal. Charlene suspected Matthias Grimes had found out about Elsa and Bailey's new friendship and wouldn't be too happy about it. Now he'd come to ask questions.

Maybe he had no idea Charlene even lived there. She practiced in the mirror with a hand to her heart. *Well, as I live and breathe. Matthias Grimes, is that you?*

Matthias, you're a sight for sore eyes?

Matty . . . it's been years.

She practiced all the silly greetings in her head and concluded she wouldn't give him the satisfaction. This visit wasn't about her. And yet she continued, swiping the ruby color end to end to the corners of her wide mouth. She smacked her lips and wiped away the extra. She pushed up the sleeves of her sweater and hiked her skirt a bit and went to the living room.

Right before he could figure out where to ring the bell, she swung the door open. "Mr. Matthias Grimes, are you lost, sir? What're you doing on my doorstep? My goodness, it's been years." She realized her voice pitch was too high and mightily ripe with sweetness. Nothing like the last time they'd seen each other, when she was screaming and cursing like a banshee. *"Get out, then. Leave. Go on back to your mama where you belong. You ain't man enough for me anyway."*

"Hey, Char, I can't believe you're back," he said breezily, as if he had never broken her heart.

"Yes indeed. I've only lived here for the last fourteen years," she said, hoping there was no edge to her voice.

"You mind if I come in so we can talk? I just need a minute of your time."

"Of course. Please do," she said, making space for him to enter. She peeked out to see if anyone was watching before she closed the door behind him. Not that anyone would care that one of the richest men in Mendol had arrived at her doorstep and called her by her short name. She was *his Char* at one time just like he'd been *her Matty.*

"I have a client here," she added in case he began down the sensitive-issue road. She hoped he understood not to put her business in the street—*their* business. "I was in the middle of work. I do hair. So it'll have to be brief. Very brief."

"I would've called but—"

"Not a problem. You're here now." She searched his eyes, not nearly as wide and bold as in his youth. His dark, lush lashes were still there. *Girly lashes,* she used to tease, only now with intermittent light grays. "Can I get you something—tea, water, anything?" She kept her voice low. Maybe she sounded seductive, but her goal was not to be overheard by Hattie in the kitchen.

"No. I promised I wasn't going to keep you." He must have sensed her uneasiness. "How about you give me your number and we set up a time when we can meet, talk privately?" he asked.

"Believe it or not, it's the same exchange, I mean, phone number. I don't expect you'd remember something from that long ago." She shoved things around in a messy side table drawer, looking for a pen.

"2XL-555," he rattled off without hesitation.

She stopped searching for the pen and came back to stand in front of him, speechless.

"If I'd known you were here, I would've called," he said.

"So you *do* remember some things."

"Of course I do."

"Do you want to give me a hint as to what this is about?"

He reached behind his back and retrieved an envelope. "This is for you and your niece. We have to talk about what this money is for. It's important. Wait for my call." He looked her up and down. "Nice seeing you, Char."

"You too, Matty," she replied, not realizing her hands were shaking as she clutched the envelope. She knew money when she felt it.

"Oh, lawd, I'm dying in here," Hattie exclaimed in a desperate plea, as she hadn't turned the fan back on herself like she'd been told.

"I better get back," Charlene whispered. "I'll wait for your call."

The door of the automobile closing, the engine purring and disappearing down the street, finally gave Charlene permission to breathe. She didn't know how long she'd been standing there, pensive and blank.

A hand touched her on the shoulder. "That man got you all outside yourself. You all right?" Hattie asked, standing before her, the sheet used as a protective cape wrapped around her round shoulders. Her hair stuck up like a ball of black cotton on one side. The other side was sleek and dark, straightened by the ruthless heat of Charlene's hot comb.

"I'm fine," Charlene said. "I'm sorry I had you waiting."

"Well, who is he? Everything okay? I peeked out and saw you fidgeting with your hands. You looked scared or something."

"Oh, I'm fine. He's an old friend of the family," Charlene said, very much the truth. "I forgot we had an appointment. We're rescheduling," she said.

"An appointment? What you gonna do, straighten his hair?" she kidded. "He looks familiar. You know, I think I remember him from the fire a few years back. You remember? The oil fire, and those people died. That oil company had to pay a lot of money to the families and a bunch of other folks. I saw that fancy car he was driving. I guess he had plenty left over. What'd he want to talk to you about? Were you one of the lucky few they had to settle with?"

Charlene gave Hattie a soft pat and moved toward the kitchen. "I don't think anybody felt too lucky about what happened then. Come on. Let's get you squared away. I don't want to keep you any longer than I have to."

Back in the kitchen, Charlene lit the stove and placed the steel comb on the flame. She couldn't rush the temperature. She couldn't rush the time forward to be done with Hattie so she could talk to Matthias. She couldn't make the day go any faster so the call could come any quicker. So she might as well relax and calm her speeding mind from jumping here and there, anticipating what they'd talk about, the past or the present. *Matty.* With her eyes closed for only a moment, she could see the two of them years ago: young, happy, and hopeful.

"You think the two of you going to be together?" her mama had asked when she caught Charlene packing. "There ain't no place on this dry land where you and he can live happily ever after. Nowhere . . ."

CHARLENE WAS A CHILD in 1921 when the Greenwood District of Tulsa had been attacked by white mobs. The whites had unleashed hell and brimstone on the small community, believing a Black man had assaulted a white woman. In those days, *assault* was a widely used term to describe anything from a Black person making direct eye contact with a white person to their brushing against someone's elbow accidentally. No one could pinpoint when and how the massacre happened, but witnesses confirmed the prominent Black Oklahoman community had been decimated. Outgunned. Destroyed in a war on their own soil. Local planes were used to drop homemade bombs made of turpentine. Thirty-five square blocks of homes and businesses were burned to the ground, and innocent Black folks lay dead in the streets.

Charlene had been only ten years old when the news traveled about the horrible and heartbreaking event. She watched as her daddy oiled his gun and counted his bullets. She and Sammie were told to sleep under their bed. For weeks, they hid in their fortress at night and tried not to be afraid. But they were. After that, no one ever had to tell Charlene what her place was in the world. The loss of those lives and the destruction of property spelled it out completely. There were boundaries. Being a little brown-skinned girl meant limitations. It meant she could never step outside of herself. She surely never allowed herself to dream. What was the point?

Yet after falling in love with Matthias, she'd allowed herself to picture living outside the lines drawn around her. Matthias gave her the crazy notion she could raise her head high, peek above the walls built to hold her inside, and see what else was out there.

"We can go to Louisiana. I've been there before. You should see it. Everybody living like one big happy family. They got their own community. People aren't worried about who's what color—brown, purple, or green with polka dots. We could be a family," he'd said. *"Me and you can be together, Char."*

"Owww," Hattie howled, at the same time jumping up from the straight-backed chair. She hopped and danced, holding one side of her head.

"Oh, Hattie, I'm sorry." Charlene rushed to the refrigerator and pulled out a cold beer. "Hold still now." Redness quickly revealed where the hot comb had grazed the bulge of skin. She pressed the bottle to Hattie's ear.

"Girl, you 'sposed to be the best in town. Lawd, lawd, lawd, you trying to take my ear off?"

"I am the best, I promise. I'll do your hair free for the next two appointments, Hattie. Please don't go around telling folks I burnt your ear off." Charlene knew it was the kiss of death to have a reputation for taking someone's skin off. No point in people paying good money for a press-and-curl if they were going to come away branded.

"Free? Two visits?" Hattie asked skeptically, taking hold of the cold bottle. She repositioned it so the flat bottom covered her ear like a pointed earmuff.

"Yes. I promise to be extra, extra careful. I was rattled, you know, from the visitor, the man, earlier." Charlene clasped prayer hands at her chin. "Okay? We got a deal, Hattie?"

"All right. Fine. But I'm not paying for today either. And I'm taking this suds with me."

"It's yours. Here, I got another. You got two, one to share with Joe."

"You all right, Charlene. I don't care what people say about you. I never believed all those rumors."

Charlene let out a breath. She didn't dare ask, "What are people saying about me?" because she didn't have a spare minute to care. Matty would be calling soon, and she wanted to be sitting down, legs crossed, sweetly kissing a cigarette. She wanted to be nice and relaxed. Stress-free. Ready to hear what he'd really come for and what the envelope of money meant. *For you and your niece.*

Hopefully, she'd have a chance to say the things she'd never got to. Like how she understood why he left her in New Orleans all alone. How she'd wished she'd gone back home to Mendol with him and how she knew the moment he walked out the door that she'd made the biggest mistake of her life.

24

BAILEY SPENT HER AFTERNOON on business as usual. The only difference was, she'd brought a sullen mood to work with her. She didn't feel like smiling and being polite. Miss Jackson seemed not to notice how she'd dragged along throughout the day.

"Welcome to the Regal Gown. I'm here to assist you and your needs," she'd said consistently and convincingly. The problem was, she was operating on only a couple hours of sleep instead of her normal seven or eight. All night she'd tossed and turned, falling into an abyss, only to be jolted awake for no particular reason. It was a wonder she'd gotten through the entire afternoon, bleary-eyed and starving, having left the house without her lunch.

The day moved extremely slowly. All the while Miss Jackson was in a light and fluttery mood. Her mood, happy and optimistic, was the direct opposite of Bailey's. *Bailey, I don't know what I'd do without you. Bailey, can you believe we've been working here, side by side, for two years now? My goodness, we should celebrate. Success doesn't grow on trees, you know.*

Miss Jackson paused momentarily in front of the mirror to take stock of the dress she wore, made of rustling silver taffeta that announced her every move. She pushed at the chignon pinned extra-high, then did a half turn before going on to explain that the new customer scheduled was one of Mendol's elite. "I've already picked out a nice lineup for our new customer. I will take the lead and you will obviously run the choices to the dressing room. But I cannot emphasize this enough: Do not offer an opinion," Miss Jackson said. "You know how much I value your opinions, but today, let's leave all that to me."

"Of course," Bailey said, taking the armful of dresses. *Mendol's elite.* Weren't they all. *A new customer,* meaning Bailey knew to prepare for the unexpected. Or rather, the expected. *New* meant someone who'd heard about what she could do for them. *New* meant the silence before the storm. *Stop it,* she told herself. *Park the cynicism.* The truth was, her surly attitude wasn't only from a lack of sleep. She'd been worried about the countdown to Elsa's party. Two days. She just wasn't sure if she could follow through with it.

"This one too. When you steam it, pay particular attention to the sash. Get it nice and full."

A long cleansing breath was necessary. "Who is it, if you don't mind me asking? The new customer," Bailey asked.

"Ingrid Grimes," Miss Jackson said. "Sound familiar?"

"What is she shopping for?"

"She's the mother of Elsa Grimes. She needs a mother-of-the-bride gown," Miss Jackson answered, exasperated. "My goodness, Bailey, you were here the day she picked out the dresses for Elsa to try on. You've had molasses for brains all day today. You need coffee. Shall I run across the street and get you a cup? That tea you drink all day just isn't strong enough."

"Yes. I mean, no, thank you, on the coffee," Bailey said. *Yes* was meant to say she understood. Of course Elsa's mother would be there to purchase a dress for her daughter's wedding, taking place in three short days. After all, what did it matter if two people didn't truly love each other? Elsa and Niles would follow through and get married anyway. So why should Bailey bother going to the party Elsa had offered to pay her to attend?

"Mrs. Grimes is also one of the boutique's benefactors, if you get my meaning."

"Yes, ma'am." That too she understood. The ladies of Mendol were all benefactors, contributors, benevolent beings who could make or break the Regal Gown simply by calling in the loan they had made to Miss Jackson. At some point Bailey had melded them all into one existence, to be revered and treated with the utmost care. But Bailey treated all of her clients with the utmost respect, regardless of age or distinction, anyway.

She tried to focus on Miss Jackson's further orders: *"Keep your gloves on at all times. You don't need to offer any improvements. No suggestions. Are we clear?"*

Never mind that usually Bailey's suggestions were welcomed. Clients craved feedback, even if it was from a lowly seamstress, at least feedback in the dress department.

She moved forward and kept quiet as she looked over the selection of bold choices. Bejeweled bright colors and plunging necklines meant Mrs. Grimes had vibrant, extravagant taste.

She had an hour or so before Mrs. Grimes would show up. She began steaming the dresses but realized she was just as hot as the boiling water. She pushed the back door open to get some air. It was the briefest of breaks. Before she could take in a solid inhale, she heard her name called.

"Bailey, our client has arrived," Miss Jackson announced with crisp formality. Mrs. Grimes had showed up early, a full thirty minutes before the scheduled time.

She instantly remembered her now. Mrs. Grimes could have been a Hollywood movie star, easily one of the ladies who assisted the host on *The Price Is Right*. "Hello. Welcome to the Regal Gown. You're here to assist—I mean, I'm here to assist you and all of your needs," Bailey managed to get out.

"So, you're Bailey?" Mrs. Grimes asked once they were alone in the dressing room. "You've been helping my daughter, is that right? With her dress?" she added as an afterthought.

"Elsa. Oh, yes. She's lovely," Bailey said while spreading the skirt of the first selection. "Can I help you step in the gown?"

"Lovely?" Mrs. Grimes offered. "I don't think I've ever heard her described that way. You two must've grown close over the course of her fittings." She had stepped into the opening of the dress and turned to be zipped.

"I enjoy getting to know my clients."

"*Hmm.*" Mrs. Grimes rested her slim hands on hip bones. The sash accentuated her waistline but bunched a bit from the lack of give. Beautiful nonetheless. Bailey had bitten her tongue to keep from saying such a thing. Opinion, good or bad, was forbidden today.

"May I bring you the next selection? It's a Givenchy."

"I kind of like this one. What do you think?"

Bailey swallowed what she wanted to say. The dress could stand to be let out an inch above the hip; that would get rid of the excess gathering at the waist. "You will be remarkable in any dress, ma'am." She rushed out to gather the next selection. She was met by Miss Jackson, who waited in anticipation.

"How's it going?"

"Pretty well."

"Has she said how she feels so far? Does she approve of my choices?"

"No. Yes. I mean, *no* she hasn't picked a favorite and *yes,* I think she's pleased with the choices."

"Well, I would think she'd have one in mind, Bailey. Have you been paying attention?"

She'd been paying attention all right, to the subtle way Mrs. Grimes had asked questions about Elsa. "She's waiting." Bailey took the green Givenchy in both arms and carried it away. "Ma'am, I have the next selection," she announced before pulling the curtain aside.

"Bailey, I hear you also do custom designs," Mrs. Grimes said, standing in her rose-colored brassiere and panties.

"I do. Yes."

"And what about your other purported skill, is that something you practice here? I can't believe I'm just now hearing about you. Seems everyone else knows all about you and your ability to read heartstrings."

"No, ma'am," Bailey answered quickly.

"No? You don't tell your brides their futures? Or you don't do it here?"

Bailey didn't feel like pretending she didn't know what Mrs. Grimes was talking about. The heat around her neck had ramped up, even though she'd stopped steaming dresses some time ago. She was in no mood for cat-and-mousing around. Elsa had described her mother's no-nonsense stance. She might take evasiveness as a personal affront.

"What exactly can I do for you, ma'am?" Bailey crossed her arms over her chest.

"I want to know about Elsa and Connor Salley. Rumor has it, you have insight. You can see things," Mrs. Grimes said easily. She hadn't bothered to cover her attitude or her body as she stepped into the next selection.

"There isn't much I can tell you. Elsa seems a bit conflicted, is all I know," Bailey said.

"Conflicted." Mrs. Grimes turned around, her impressive bosom now fluffed and folded nicely in the deep-cut bodice of the gown. "What is Elsa conflicted about, exactly? What do you two have so much to talk about in clandestine meetings, heads together, plotting?"

It all came together in Bailey's mind. "You were asking about me, at Queenie's yesterday?"

Gabby had called Bailey and told her about the great news, an inheritance. The café was all abuzz about a white lady from a big law firm who was looking to track her down. "Wrong Bailey," she'd told Gabby. "Ridiculous." She didn't have any rich relatives leaving her a red cent. The phone call had been another thing she could add onto her bad night. All because Mrs. Grimes had gone in there, lying about who she was.

"Yes. That was me. I had to find out who it was influencing my daughter to make very bad decisions. Well?" Mrs. Grimes waited for the answer. "What exactly was Elsa conflicted about?"

"Ma'am, I really don't know."

"I have a proposition for you."

There was a knock on the frame of the dressing room. "Is there anything I can assist with?" Miss Jackson asked. Too much murmuring of voices had probably sent her rushing over.

"We're doing just fine, Thea," Mrs. Grimes said.

"All right. Let me know if you need another set of eyes."

"Will do."

"I can't talk about this kind of thing, here, at my work," Bailey whispered. But next she raised her voice loud enough for Miss Jackson to hear. "Alrighty then, that was the last one. Is there a preference, Mrs. Grimes?"

"Yes, actually. I'd like to try the red one again."

Bailey left the dressing room with her teeth on edge. She looked up to see the light flickering, the light Walter Anderson Graves had supposedly fixed. Far to the left, in another part of the showroom, a light dimmed and brightened in a dual rhythm. Was she imagining the lights dancing? She shook her head and closed her eyes.

Miss Jackson came toward her. "She likes the red one. Good. Very, very good."

"Miss Jackson, I'm not feeling well. I really think I need to go home. I'm . . ." Bailey peeled off her glove and pressed a hand to her neck, feeling for the heat she really hadn't expected. It was all for show, but when her hand came away sweaty, she was a bit shocked. She did have a fever. The bouncing spots of light might not have been failing electrical circuitry after all. "I think I'm coming down with something."

"Surely you can make it till the end of the hour. You don't look ill."

"I'm sorry. I need to . . . I need some water." Unfortunately, that water would have to come from home. Bailey rushed to the back room and gathered her things.

"No, Bailey. Where are you going?" Miss Jackson followed as Bailey did her usual routine of shutting down the steamer and the sewing machine and tucking her best scissors into their felt cover.

"I'll be back tomorrow. I'm just not feeling well." She flicked off the light after a few seconds of watching it go from dim back to bright again. It was the new one overhead, working in a rhythm that matched her surging heart and the pounding in her ears. "I'm sorry. I have to go," she reiterated, walking past Miss Jackson and out the golden doors. In the fresh air outside, she took a long, deep breath, only to be met with a searing pain behind her eyes that made her clench them shut. Evidently her fever came with a side serving of headache. She hadn't been sick with the flu since she was a little girl, but she recognized the symptoms. Hot. Cold. Hot again.

As her feet hit the pavement, every step she took felt like a jostling of her brain. She slowed out of necessity. She was out of breath by the time she reached the hot interior of her Olds. It took a minute, resting her head on the steering wheel, but subtly she accepted the fact she might not have a job come morning.

"Bailey," a voice called to her.

"John." Bailey said his name without bothering to look up. "I told you, I don't know anything," she seethed, facing him. "Stay away from me. Please. I can't help you."

"I hate to keep asking, but if you can see things, maybe you can—" he said, reaching for her.

"I can't do that. I don't see things like that. I'm not a psychic. I don't know where Alice is or what she's doing." She slowly backed up the car, unsteady, her heart racing. "I wish I could help, but I simply can't."

25

THERE REALLY HADN'T BEEN A NEED to visit the young woman at the Regal Gown, Ingrid knew. Elsa had already come to her senses, even if that had come by way of threats. There'd been no more back talk. Ingrid had also enlisted Matthias to pay the girl off, but it brought her a bit of joy to see Bailey the busybody squirm. Maybe it would teach her a lesson to keep her nose out of where it didn't belong. Did people really fall for the hokum of reading heart-strings? It all sounded preposterous to Ingrid.

As for Connor, he wasn't worth one more minute of her time. He wouldn't be a factor. She'd finally gotten ahold of him over the phone the night before. In a whispered conversation, he'd vehemently de-nied having a romantic relationship with Elsa. Even if he was lying, it didn't matter. The wedding would go on. The party would outshine all the others in Mendol, and Connor Salley would be the last thing on anyone's mind.

Ingrid's plans were in the final stages. Originally her goal was to outdo Joffrey and Mitzy Magpie. Their son's wedding was quite a spectacle, with horse-drawn carriages bringing in the bride and groom separately instead of their walking down the aisle. There'd been a cascade of rose petals at the altar and white doves released from cages. The antics overshadowed the entire purpose of being there. That wouldn't be the case for Elsa's soiree. Each and every detail was thought out by Ingrid herself. Classy. Stylish.

She had two more days to prepare for the engagement party and three left before the wedding, which she didn't count, because she expected to be exhausted after the first party. Therefore everything had to be complete and ready to go.

Three days, Ingrid told herself, and tried to not panic. For the most part everything was going splendidly according to plan. The coverall-clad gardeners lined the pathway with their long hedge cut-ters, clipping away, grooming the topiaries out of boxwood. Green statues were created in the shape of deer, with wired branches for antlers. Enormous slabs of limestone were laid to create a path through the emerald lawn and up to the veranda, which was framed by climbing pink clematis.

She took satisfaction in surveying all that she and Matthias had built. Not a single crack or sign of wear showed despite the home's twenty years of existence.

The mansion with too many windows to count was built out of brick to emulate the old Dutch Colonial style. Their house was one of many pristine estates erected with clay-shingled roofs, flawless white pillars, and arched entrances. Opulent castles, that's what they were. Reminders of what the Mendol rich had; also a reminder of when they'd had nothing, were nothing, and their unspoken vow never to let it ever happen again. That's why she wanted all the festivities right there at their home. Perfection.

A dusty van with the logo of Bertie & Jo's Catering, Est. 1942, sat parked along the pristine entrance. The back doors were splayed open for the men who carried wood crates stacked with glass stemware, gold platters, folded napkins, and flatware into the house.

Ingrid floated around, making sure everything was as she'd ordered. Each table was adorned with a spectacular show of yellow and white magnolias in tall white vases. The tables were placed circularly to keep the center of the marble floor clear and ready for the esteemed guests, expected to dance to the live piano medley by Howl Winzer. Ingrid had boasted to the ladies at the last Rose Society meeting that Howl had been a pianist for Frank Sinatra. He'd even been in the orchestra for Broadway for the musical *Can-Can*. She reminded herself to speak to the club about sponsoring the play in Mendol. Since the town's theater had been built and completed, more than a year ago, there hadn't been a single performance.

In the kitchen, she dipped a skinny finger in the Salisbury sauce for a taste test. Bertie had agreed to make a sampling of the engagement meal for her final approval. *Delicious.* But she only nodded approval, refusing to gush with delight. There was always room for improvement. "A little touch more salt," she said.

In the dining room she drifted to the various offerings. Appetizers were spread on small trays. She gravitated to the congealed display in the center of dusty-looking crackers. "This will not do," she announced over the dish. She sniffed at what was supposed to be caviar.

Oda Mae, who was not far behind Ingrid's every step, repeated the dissatisfaction to Bertie. "That caviar won't do," she told him.

"What's wrong with it?" he asked, already at Oda Mae's side.

"It's already stiffening. It looks putrid," Ingrid said.

"It's sad and tired," Oda Mae translated.

"It simply needs a good stir," Bertie responded, lifting the dish from the table and inhaling.

Oda Mae broadened her eyes as in, *Don't ask, just do better— please*. Bertie, with a roll of his eyes, took it away.

Ingrid appreciated having Oda Mae as her henchman in case someone had to be fired or redirected. She didn't have to be the bad guy. Next she moved into the ballroom, where the well-dressed tables could have been in the White House. She began her inspection of the flatware, also provided by Bertie & Jo's Catering. Ingrid hadn't wanted to rent it, but she didn't have sixty sets of her own on hand. She randomly chose a fork and knife that caught the light. "Oh, for heaven's sake." She used her ruffled charmeuse sleeve to rub at the water spots.

"Oda Mae, have someone polish the flatware." It sounded better than saying *"Oda Mae, do this,"* or *"Do that,"* although that someone would undoubtedly be Oda Mae. She was the only person on her staff. Rochelle made two, when she actually showed up. A few extra hands from the catering service were scheduled for the party, but not until then.

Ingrid picked up her notepad and made a few more checks down her list. "I guess that's all for now." She marched up the stairs, greeted by a breeze from an open door or window, which would let in dust. She could already feel the dry, grainy film with the crunch of her shoe on the parquet floor. Why today of all days did the winds have to pick up?

Guests weren't permitted to go up the stairs to their personal space, but there were always the one or two who ignored boundaries.

She was that person at one time, snooping through the bathroom medicine cabinets and closets during a dinner party, inspecting for weaknesses. Was their warm, sunny disposition aided by prescriptions or were they miraculously happy on any given day?

"Oda Mae, have someone come upstairs to dust," she said over the banister.

Next on the list was the garden, where the actual ceremony would take place. She had a perfect view from her bedroom balcony. But first she leaned against Elsa's door for a listen. Silence was what she expected, and silence was what she got. She stepped away and carried on to her bedroom, grateful the world was now spinning in the right direction.

The oak lattice arbor and plank landing had turned out exactly as Ingrid pictured. Countdown to sending Elsa off to her new life. By all accounts, everything was going in the order of the best-laid plans.

Ingrid looked out with a hand up to protect her eyes from the glare and appreciated the magnificence of the Grimes estate.

The sun would set at the perfect hour during the ceremony, elegant in its simplicity as the light bounced off the pond. She'd had the pond dug and filled only a month ago, but it looked completely natural, surrounded by green grass and honey golden trees that were older than she was. This was the vision. Her dream.

Ingrid had checked a number of items off her to-do list, and yet her hand shook as she glided the pen over her paper. She couldn't allow herself to revel in her success, because Ingrid knew all too well nothing could be left to chance. She wasn't the type who could lounge through her day, feet up, satisfied. She couldn't take a catnap with the sun up or go for a leisurely walk to clear her mind.

Lists. Planning. Resolve. She was the driver of her life, of Matthias's and Elsa's lives. It had always been that way. She had her hand on the gear, her foot on the pedal. Nothing got done without her effort and determination. She took pride in her ability to move the needle.

She looked down again at her meticulous notes. The list looked nearly completed. Yet there was something absent. Something undone. Unsettled. It wasn't on her list, at least not written down.

"Oda Mae," she called. "Ask Alston to bring my car around," she began before Oda Mae had answered, or appeared, for that matter. She expected Oda Mae to always be within earshot, ready and dutifully at her side.

"Ma'am, the car, your car, is with Elsa," Oda Mae answered, in a timely reframe. "You're welcome to take my car. Alston can drive you," she offered.

Oda Mae's car—which once had belonged to Ingrid—was the Chevy Bel Air parked out front. Ingrid had passed it on to Oda Mae for a reason. It was bulky and difficult to maneuver. And red. The bright shiny red beast made her feel like a moving target, going through town. During the entire time Ingrid had owned it, she felt like a show-off, asking for attention while the whole damn town blamed Senate Oil for the tragic fire and loss of their friends and family. After she had a fit of tears, Matthias replaced it with a modest pearl-tone Studebaker. He apologized for the lack of glitz. He called it a temporary gift for their twentieth anniversary until the company's financial woes were resolved. There was also the matter of her spending extravagantly: It had to stop. Fine. He could call it whatever he wanted. She'd considered the unimpressive automobile a freedom card, a pass to move about as she pleased without judgment and hearsay.

"Where did Elsa go? I've been home this entire time," Ingrid said, wondering, *How did she get past me?*

Oda Mae gave her shoulders a shrug. "Should I call Alston? He'll be a while, since he's working on the arbor. The men say they'd give him five dollars to paint, so he's painting."

"I'll drive myself. If Elsa returns before I do, tell her she's not to leave this house."

"Yes, ma'am."

What if Elsa is with Connor? It was the first thing that crossed Ingrid's mind when she sat behind the wheel. *What if nothing goes as planned?* What if her daughter ruined everything?

What if the two families didn't unite? The Grimeses needed the Porters. They needed each other. She'd threatened Elsa with a penniless future. But the truth was, it wasn't so much a threat as a likely consequence. The fire that had destroyed so many lives had also hurt the Grimeses. It wasn't only the Salleys who'd made bad investments, overspent, and lived way beyond their means.

They weren't broke by any means, but they'd sprung a leak, one that guaranteed the ship was going down over time. When Matthias, with his over-kindheartedness, purchased the Salleys' share of the business, he'd left himself and his own family vulnerable. The wells were pumping oil just fine. The problem was, Senate Oil and other midsize producers had competition. Ingrid had heard enough to understand the dilemma. Iranian oil had become available, and it was far cheaper than the American stuff. Their barrels of liquid gold were worth less with each passing day.

"We've been screwed," Matthias had vented. "If this agreement goes through, which it will, pushed by Eisenhower, it'll give control of the Iranian oil straight to our competitors. They're leaving us out of the deal. Guys like us get nothing. They'll have complete control over how much petroleum gets pumped and what the price will be to sell it."

They had to brace themselves for the fallout. They were a mere five years away from being tapped out, their accountant had warned last year. If they twisted their belts good and tight, they could at least stay comfortable. This was the kind of news that no one wanted to hear, least of all Ingrid. What was defined as *comfortable*? No more trips on their private plane? Having to do her own laundry? Answering her own phone?

Ingrid had not once questioned the grand life she and Matthias had built together. She didn't believe in fate or luck. As far as she was concerned she'd worked just as hard, and had just as many sleepless hours and days getting her hands just as dirty as her husband. She'd put in the tireless effort to be better, to do better. She fought hard to stay level-headed, to not want to set a fire to their entire world.

The wedding, the celebration of their families uniting, was the last hurrah, the big splash. Ingrid considered it her going-away party. The big bang. After that, there'd be no more lavish spending, they'd agreed. *No more.*

All she'd wanted to do was secure her daughter's lifestyle. Elsa, unconcerned with such things, needed to be squared away with a solid foundation. Settled firmly with a husband who could provide and a home filled with nice things. It wasn't too much to ask. Regardless of what anyone else believed, she loved her daughter with all her heart.

The car started up with little effort. There were trucks and vans to get around. Her shaking hand jammed the gearshift up with a forward motion, then back, because there'd been no regard for someone possibly having to leave in a hurry. She slammed her hands on the center of the wheel, blaring the horn.

"Move these damn vans," Ingrid screamed out the window. "Get the hell out of my way."

26

IT WASN'T ELSA'S FIRST TIME at the house where Rochelle had grown up. She'd known exactly how to get to the green house with gray shutters. It hadn't changed since she was a child, when Oda Mae had brought her there. The square patch of grass was mostly brown with green sprouts. Marigolds trimmed the cracked concrete walkway. Elsa even remembered the birdhouse hanging from the sugar maple in the center of the yard.

"What are you doing here?" Rochelle asked when she opened the door, shocked to see her.

Elsa ignored her obvious annoyance. "Your mama said you were sick. You weren't answering my calls. I got worried. I brought soup." She made this announcement as though she was responsible for what was in the crock. As if she'd been the one who'd roasted the chicken, chopped the carrots and minced the onions and garlic, and watched the contents simmer for hours. Chicken and broth was Oda Mae's cure for everything. It had been sitting in the Grimeses' refrigerator and Elsa figured it was the only excuse she could use for seeing Rochelle.

"You came all the way to the Eastside to bring me soup? You know I'm not really sick," Rochelle said, once Elsa was inside.

"I wasn't sure. There's something going around. And I couldn't reach you by phone."

"Sorry."

"Are you mad at me? That's why I kept calling. I wanted to apologize." Elsa's eyes dropped to the necklace Rochelle was wearing. "I'm glad you still have it on. My mama didn't mean anything with all her questions."

Rochelle took hold of the oblong ceramic pot by the handles. "I'm hungry. I can heat some up for both of us."

"Yeah. Good. I'm starving." Elsa touched her stomach for emphasis, only to be reminded she could barely hold down anything the previous night. She'd retched up her supper and hadn't eaten anything since. Oda Mae had fixed breakfast, but the odious smell of butter sent Elsa rushing to meet the toilet bowl a second time. Luckily, nothing came up. She hoped the soup would be more appealing.

Elsa followed Rochelle while taking in the cozy space. In the kitchen, with its light-blue-and-white-checkered tile floor, Elsa pictured herself sitting at the red dinette set with Rochelle, having their morning coffee, eating their jam-covered toast, and chatting about the goings-on in the world. Only the two of them alone, serene and comfortable.

"Get the bowls, up to the left," Rochelle said, pointing a graceful finger.

It was hardly *up* for Elsa, who was a head taller than Rochelle. She hadn't remembered everything being so small in the Davis residence. The appliances reminded her of a dollhouse. Miniature everything. Even ten years ago, when she'd first stepped foot inside their house, the smallness had shocked her. Oda Mae had told her to wait in the car while she ran in to make sure she hadn't left the stove on, simmering a pot of red beans. She couldn't remember if she'd turned it off that morning. Elsa sat in the car barely a minute, watching the entrance, curious. Her nature was and always had been to know what was behind a closed door. That day she'd made her way up the concrete steps, through the narrow opening, and felt like she'd entered an entirely different world. As if she'd traveled into a new dimension, like the ones in the comics she sometimes read at the doctor's office. Oda Mae's home was bright and spotless, a place where glossy, colorful candies sat in a glass bowl and freshly baked cookies were spread on a platter centered on a flowered doily. Layers of scents promised there'd be something warm and inviting for dinner. Oda Mae had jumped, startled that Elsa had followed her inside, right into the kitchen. "Well, now that ya here, we might as well taste these beans," Oda Mae had said. "Have a seat." She dipped a long-handled spoon in the pot and served up two helpings. From the first bite, Elsa wanted more.

"How come you never cook beans at our house?" Elsa had asked after she'd cleaned her bowl. At home, she never would have been allowed to lick the inside clean, her face plastered to the rim.

"I cook what your mama and daddy want to eat. They don't like beans."

"I do. Very much. Does Rochelle like beans?" She'd actually hoped Rochelle was inside the house but learned she spent the week-days at her grandmother's house in Muskogee. That way, Oda Mae and Mr. Davis could work.

"She loves everything I cook," Oda Mae said.

"I want to learn how to cook just like you," Elsa told Oda Mae. But she never had had a chance to learn. Every single minute of her time was filled with lessons and studying. If it wasn't Bible study it was piano, dance, French, etiquette, or speech. If her mama could find a class, Elsa was in it, but not one taught a fundamental life skill. She had learned basics like making rice, boiling eggs, and peel-ing potatoes, since these things happened on the rare visits to her grandma and grandpa's house, but that food tasted nothing like Oda Mae's food. She'd wanted specifically to know how to cook what Ro-chelle might like. At ten years old, Elsa had known what she wanted. There had been no doubt. She wanted to be with Rochelle, sharing their meals, sitting across from her. It wasn't much to ask.

"Want something to drink?" Rochelle now asked, shaking Elsa loose from her thoughts. She stood in front of the open fridge door. "We got soda pop. Root beer or grape? Name your pleasure."

"What do you like?" Elsa asked in return, realizing she never had accomplished her goal. All those many years and she'd never pinned down what Rochelle liked to eat, what her favorite soda pop flavor was, or anything, for that matter. Not like how she knew every sin-gle thing about Niles. But then again, wasn't that the draw? The mystery of knowing someone, but not knowing every little thing, left room to be interested, to care, to learn.

"Orange is my fav, but we're out. I drank it all," Rochelle said, behind a chuckle.

"Well, then, let's go buy some more," Elsa said.

"What about the soup? It's still heating up."

"It'll keep. Come on. Pop's on me. We can go to Queenie's and get a cream soda."

"What you know about Queenie's?" Rochelle asked.

"I know she's got ice cream and pop, right?"

"I need to change." Rochelle looked down at herself. "This is what I slept in."

She looked fine, but Elsa understood. "Well, go on and change, then. This train is leaving the station," she said with a fist tug at the air. All she wanted to do was jump in the car, ride with the windows down, and sing whatever song played on the radio.

Rochelle took her time turning off the flame underneath the pot, then checking the contents. "Good. It's not boiling yet. You should never reheat more than once."

"We don't have all day, Rochelle," Elsa announced. This was especially true considering she'd taken the car after her mama had forbidden her to leave the house. But that punitive sentence had been given days ago, when she'd come home late and skipped the dance lesson with Niles.

She figured that was an old punishment: sentence served and expired. Since then, she'd done everything her mama had asked her to do. They'd made nice that very morning. Her mama had popped around the house in good spirits with a kiss on the top of Elsa's head, followed by a hug. Though brief, a hug was still a hug. No one knew better than Elsa not to take a kind gesture from her mama for granted. She had to be back by suppertime. She had her mama's car and knew Ingrid wouldn't need it all day, while she stayed home to mind the workmen. Until then, no one would notice Elsa was gone.

In the center of the stove, the hands on the tiny clock pointed to 12:30. Elsa had another stop to make before the end of the day. Three crisp hundred-dollar bills sat in her pocketbook, fresh from the bank, the promised payment for Bailey.

"I'm ready," Rochelle sang out, arriving in the kitchen in a yellow cotton dress with a matching belt. The soft fabric made the skirt wave with the slightest movement of her hips.

Rochelle smiled sheepishly, apparently aware she was being adored. "What you staring at?"

"You."

She rolled her eyes, then led the way out the front door.

Queenie's was no more than two miles away. If not for Rochelle growing impatient with the long idles at the stop signs, Elsa would have stayed at a snail's pace. Instead, she picked up speed. Rochelle noticeably inhaled and exhaled with slow relief. The breeze from the open windows cooled them.

"You good?" Elsa asked, because she secretly feared Rochelle just wanted to get the day over with.

"I'm great," Rochelle said. "I'm glad you got me out of the house. What do you say we skip the ice cream and get some pops and sit at Brim Park?"

Elsa grew elated but kept her joy at a low temperature. "Yeah. Sure. Sounds good to me." She pressed on the gas. She knew where to go for the pops, right along with the extra gas they'd need for the ride to Brim Park, which was farther out of the way. Secluded.

"Wait here," Elsa told her, strong-arming the gearshift into park. She left the car and rushed past the attendant. "Fill her up and check the tires, please, and thank you." Inside the tiny store she went to the cold box and found two icy colas. Next to it was the freezer. She lifted the glass door and picked up a couple of ice cream bars. At the counter she added a bag of potato chips and two Butterfinger bars, her favorite.

"Two-fifty," the stoic man at the register said. "How much gas you got out there?"

"I think it's about two dollars. Tank was already half full," Elsa said.

"We'll call it five even."

Elsa took the brown sack with the cold things pressed against her arms and wondered if the day could be any sweeter.

That's when she saw the silver car pull up behind hers. The four guys sitting inside were place settings for typical young men of Mendol, with slick hair parted on the side, fresh shaves, and nothing better to do on a Wednesday afternoon than hang around. Except for Connor. He should have been at work.

Elsa tried to ignore her name when he called her. She handed the bag to Rochelle but didn't make it inside her car before someone tapped her not too gently on the shoulder.

She could guess who it was. Leo had been driving. Niles was in the front seat. Connor and Mike, who Elsa didn't know well, had sat in the back.

Rochelle whispered urgently, "Come on. Let's go. Just get in."

Elsa gave a reassuring nod to Rochelle. *I've got this.* She faced Leo, who she knew was all talk and no bite.

"You and your girlfriend got a hot date?" Leo asked, with his best smirk. He must have woken up every morning practicing that face, determined to look menacing. "Where you two off to?"

"Why? You jealous?" Elsa was in some kind of mood. This was what happiness got her. Trouble.

Niles approached. "Hey, Els. How you doing, Rochelle?"

Rochelle nodded but kept her eyes straight ahead.

Leo leaned his head inside the car. "Y'all need escorts. Pretty ladies shouldn't be driving the highways unattended."

"Where they going?" Connor asked, suddenly in the mix. He'd gotten out of Leo's car, unsteady, holding a beer close though there wasn't much left in the bottle. "You haven't learned your lesson, I see." The words were like a slap to Elsa's face.

"What'd you say?" Her heartbeat thundered inside her ears.

"Get back in the car," Niles said to Connor. "Don't pay him any attention," he told Elsa.

"Oh, now, you're trying to be the tough guy," Connor slurred. "If you was the man you're supposed to be, I wouldn't of had to—"

The fist to Connor's jaw came out of nowhere. His beer bottle shattered on the ground. Niles threw a second hard punch just as quickly as the first, surprising Elsa and Leo, who'd stepped out of the way. Connor recovered and lunged at Niles. They both went down to the pavement, wrestling dangerously close to the broken glass.

"Elsa, get in. We need to get out of here," Rochelle yelled.

But Elsa couldn't move, frozen, afraid. Niles was no match for Connor, even if Connor was drunk. When Connor was suddenly on top of Niles, she stared at a shard of brown glass and imagined how easily she could jab it into his neck.

Leo had decided that was enough. "All right. All right," he said, pulling Connor up by the collar. "I'm not going to let you beat up my brother. He's the only one I got," he said. This too sounded practiced. How many times had he defended Niles from being picked on? It was the thing Elsa and Niles had in common, being underestimated. Easy targets.

This time Niles didn't back down. He wasn't done. He reached past Leo and landed another solid fist on Connor's jaw. "You ever go near her again, you'll regret it."

"Yeah. I bet," Connor teased. "She don't want you. Ain't that right, Els? You and your girlfriend have a good time, all right." Connor puckered his bloodied lips and kissed at the air while Leo and Mike pulled him backward.

"Niles, you don't have to go with them. Come with us. I'll give you a ride," Elsa offered.

"Nah. Nah, you go ahead. Have fun," he said, almost as bitterly as Connor. He didn't mean it, she thought. Not like that. He'd never tease her like the others did. She watched Niles get into the front seat. Leo paid the attendant for his gas, then got in and sped off.

Elsa stood, shaking. Rochelle came to her side. "You all right? I'll drive. Okay?"

27

BAILEY SWORE THERE WERE HANDS pressed on her chest. That's what had awakened her from her nap, the feeling of someone's weight holding her down. But of course no one was in the room when her eyes bolted open. She was alone.

Dusk had turned the white walls a grayish hue. Had she slept that long? When she'd gotten home in the afternoon, having escaped the clutches of Mrs. Grimes, she'd come in and lain down out of exhaustion and a budding fever. The sun had been bright and high.

She sat up in bed. The collar of her dress was drenched in sweat. She usually remembered her dreams as vividly as if she had seen them in a picture book. Not this time. She only knew the danger she felt. She'd been running in her dream. And then she heard the sound of glass breaking. She realized it was the noise, real or not, that had sent her eyes wide open.

Real, she assessed. There it was again.

Was it dishes hitting the floor? A window shattering? She moved slowly out of bed, stepping directly into the slippers that faced out, ready to go. Her robe lay at the foot of the bed. She thought about Aunt Charlene calling her "predictable and safe." At a time like this, she'd take *safe* any day. Better than fumbling around rushing into God-knows-what, walking on broken glass. Aunt Charlene hadn't been home earlier when she'd arrived. There had been a hint of burnt hair in the air but no sight of her.

Now she called out, wondering if Charlene had come home while she'd slept. "Auntie? Hello?" She padded down the hall. A gust of wind swept past her, and she saw the front door wide open banging against the adjacent wall. Glass crunched underneath her slippers before she reached the door. A panel of glass had broken and fallen out of the door. She was also stepping on the remnants of a framed photo that usually sat on the side table next to the door. This was her favorite picture of her mama.

Samantha Dowery was six years old in the photo, sitting unsmiling and yet content on someone's lap—Bailey's grandmother, she had always assumed. The shiny photograph was faded, no longer black and white but more gray with beige tones. Bailey was carefully picking up the shards when a gust of wind pushed the door open again. A scattering of leaves blew inside. The winds had been unusually aggressive over the past few days. She was happy to blame Mother Nature for the event. She had no reason to be afraid of the wind.

She made it to the front door and took hold of the knob, which was shaky and loose. Obviously, the latch was the reason the door blew open so easily. She'd have to get that fixed. That, along with so much more. It was time to stop ignoring the state of disrepair. Not that she'd been ignoring it, just accepting it. She should face the fact that she'd be here for some time, probably into her old age. She'd probably die on this very street, in this very house where she was born. She went back to picking up the loose glass. She put the glassless photo back on the table.

Before she could settle into her relief, she heard another sound. Movement, shuffling, from down the short hall.

"Auntie?" she called out again as she approached the closed bedroom door, knocked, and stood to listen, but she heard nothing but outdoor noises: the rustle of trees and the whirl of debris surrounding the house.

Aunt Charlene never stayed out all day and into the night. The house was oddly missing the smoky stale scent of cigarettes mixed with perfume. Had she found somewhere else to be, somewhere else she'd rather call home? Had she met someone? The other night, it took everything Bailey had not to reach out and grab Charlene— touch, feel, see. But she realized she didn't really want to know. The possibilities, whatever they were, frightened her. For all of her auntie's chiding, Bailey had never considered a life without her.

Bailey had never been alone, lived alone, unless she counted those few short, unbearable days after her mama had died. She'd felt adrift and abandoned. But even then, she'd stayed with someone, Mr. and Mrs. Stuart, who had no children of their own. She always thought back to how perfectly they'd fed and cared for her, offering a hug when she'd cried in her sleep and space to be silent as long as she liked, as expertly as if they had raised a brooding child at one time. Those long days and nights when she missed her mama had felt like the world had ended. She shuddered at the memory. But then came her auntie, taking full rein of Bailey's emotions, reeling her in. Making her see there was light at the end of the tunnel.

Bailey walked by the telephone and acknowledged that she had absolutely no one to call to ask if they'd seen her auntie because, in all honesty, she hadn't been paying enough attention. She didn't know what Aunt Charlene did during the week besides call in her horse bets and tend to hair appointments. On the rare times she'd gone out, Bailey had no idea who she'd gone with.

A knock at the back door startled her. She kept her hand on her heart as she peeked out the shaded window. Elsa.

"What're you doing here?"

"Hi" was all she said before putting her hand out with a wad of bills. "Your money."

Bailey stayed quiet, slow to understand.

"For the party." Elsa waited with her hand steady. "Take it."

"How did you know I was home?" Bailey asked. She normally was just leaving the Regal Gown.

"Miss Jackson said you went home ill," Elsa said. "I wasn't going to disturb you. So I planned to leave the money somewhere safe, then call and tell you where it was. But when I saw all the branches and broken pots on the porch from the wind, I figured I better find somewhere else. I was going to tuck the money in the screen door," she said.

"Come in," Bailey said.

"I can't. I got to get back home." Elsa's hand remained out, holding the rolled bunch of bills. "I would've brought you some broth if I'd known."

"I'm feeling much better," Bailey said, finally taking hold of the cash. She'd never held that much money in her hands. It felt surreal. She was surprised that her heart raced a bit.

"Okay. I'm glad you're feeling better. So, see you on Friday," Elsa said, but it came out sounding like a question. Well, if it was a question, she didn't stick around for the answer.

"Yes, ma'am," Bailey said with a smile after she'd closed the door. She was so overcome by the sight of the money and all it promised that she'd forgotten to tell Elsa about the visit from Ingrid. That should have been the first thing out of her mouth. She felt remiss in not warning her. *Your mama is out for blood, honey.* She also wanted to ask her own questions. How did Miss Jackson sound? Angry? What did she say? *When you see that Bailey again, tell her no need to come back here to work. She's fired.*

But now she had a lifeline. She pressed the money to her chest. "Thank you, Jesus."

WALTER ANDERSON GRAVES didn't wait until the next morning. When she dialed his number, she thought he'd have a booked calendar at least until Monday. No way did she think he'd be standing on her doorstep at seven that evening with his hat in one hand and the other holding his toolbox.

"First thing is this doorknob. Barely closes, let alone locks," Bailey said, before he stepped all the way into the house.

He nodded. "Easy fix. Not that folks lock their doors much out here."

"I do," Bailey said. "I can't sleep with an unlocked door."

He followed her through the house as she pointed to the obvious. Up. A leak stain on the ceiling. Sideways. A crack in the window, climbing its way to the top of the frame. Down. A divot in the floor where Mr. Wag stood and bounced at his own peril. "Foundation needs to be shored up," he said.

"All right, how much is this all going to cost me?"

"I can't say for sure. I'm taking notes. I'll have to do a tally."

"A ballpark, Mr. Wag."

He shrugged. "How about I start with the front door, getting this place nice and secure for you so you can lay that pretty head down for a good night's rest, for a little of that stew you got simmering? And tomorrow I'll give you a full estimate on the rest of what needs work around here."

"How you know I got stew on the stove?"

He pointed to his regal nose. "I can smell stew a mile out."

Bailey had started the beef stew after she'd gotten back from the market. As soon as she'd gotten the money from Elsa, that's where she had headed, to buy all the goodies her fridge could hold. Calling Walter about coming over to give her a quote for the house repairs had been next on her list. It felt like Christmas being able to have all the things she'd wanted but had felt were out of pocket range. She couldn't remember the last time she'd had a good piece of chuck to brown and simmer. She'd bought the entire slab. She only used a corner of it for what was cooking in the pot. The rest she cut in pieces, wrapped in tinfoil, and put in the freezer.

"Fine. Stew's not quite ready yet. By the time you fix the lock, supper will be served."

"I'll get started," he said. He was surely the most easygoing guy she'd ever met. She headed into the kitchen, pulled down two bowls and plates, and gathered spoons. She began to set the table, unsure of where she should seat Mr. Wag. *Where do men like to eat?* It was the kind of question she thought of but would never ask out loud. Where? Why would it matter? But for some reason she believed it mattered.

As she dragged the cloth place mat from one side of the table to the other, she pictured Mr. Wag in each chair: his back to the living room, or his back to the outdoors. She saw the kitchen cabinets from one angle, with their crooked drawers and missing handles. She scooted to the other side and the view was of the ancient stove, white porcelain with black knobs. Clean. Solid. Dependable. *Here,* she thought. In some way, the kitchen told the story of who a person was. This was what she wanted Mr. Wag to see, to understand: Bailey Dowery was a solid, dependable person.

Why? Why had she wanted him to know anything about her? What did it matter, if he was the dog busy wagging his tail, as Gabby had said?

She slipped her apron on over her head and tied the back. She lifted the pot and inhaled the steam. From just a whiff, she could tell if the potatoes and carrots, added not that long ago, had cooked through to tenderness. The steam confessed that they were not quite there yet. Bailey stirred gently, then tapped the drippings away from the side before replacing the steel top. There was plenty to share. If her auntie came back in time for supper, she would have a bowlful and maybe seconds.

If her auntie came home while she and Mr. Wag were having their supper, she wanted to have an excuse, a reason why a man was sitting at their table. She couldn't think of a single thing to say except, "He is my guest."

"All fixed."

"Oh," she said, facing him. "That was fast."

"Food ready?"

"Almost."

"Good. I need a minute to wash up. I gotta clean shirt out in the truck."

"What are you doing carrying around clean shirts?" she asked, amused.

"I was hoping we'd get some time together," he said, brutally honest.

"Oh. Oh," she said again.

"When you called, I'd just come through my door after a hard job and I didn't get a chance to, you know, wash my face. I was in a hurry to get over here," he said. "Excited. So I grabbed a couple of things from my stack. You ever use Spring Laundry Service on Main? They just opened a few months ago. Everything really does smell like springtime. So, if you don't mind, I'll use your facilities to clean up. I'll be ready for supper in ten, fifteen?"

"Take your time," Bailey said. "It'll be fine. Go on. Please, take your time. I need to make some cornbread anyway. Can't have stew without some cornbread."

"You trying to steal my heart," he said before backing away, a hand pressed to said heart.

And now she needed an excuse as to why there was a man in her bathroom, she thought, if her auntie walked through the door right then. She sputtered out a laugh, then covered her mouth. *My goodness. What have you got yourself into, Bailey Dowery?*

She whipped the eggs and poured warmed butter into the mixture, followed by buttermilk and cornmeal. She'd cook it on the stove first, then brown it for efficiency's sake. That way, she'd have time to change as well.

She rushed to her room, pulled her sweater off over her head, and tossed it on the quilt-covered bed. She stepped out of the loose dungarees she'd worn while grocery shopping. Her closet was filled with dresses she'd made over the years. Church clothes. Work clothes. Dresses she'd made with no intention of ever wearing them, but which had served as good practice for the day when someone might ask to see her creations. Those creations were way too fancy for a kitchen dinner with Mr. Wag. She didn't want to look like she was trying too hard to impress him. Though she *was* trying. She just didn't want him to know it.

She settled on a black boat-neck sheath, a church dress for sure, but with a platinum-toned belt she would transform herself into a modern lady who simply had no time for fussiness, a working gal who'd made plans for an after-dinner drink. "This will work," she said. She slipped on her narrow flats, then went to the tiny mirror hanging on a nail, pulled the pins out of her hair, and gave it a fluff. *No. No. No.* She pulled the pins from her mouth and stuck them back on the sides of her hair, so it looked neater.

In the kitchen, there was no sight of Mr. Wag. She peeked out and saw that the bathroom door remained closed. Well, maybe someone was also trying too hard to make a good impression. The cornbread had a nice rise. She grabbed an oven mitt for the hot handle of the cast-iron pan and shoved the cornbread into the oven. *Five minutes, tops,* she thought. Surely he'd be finished cleaning up by then.

She slipped her apron on and began scooping the stew into shallow bowls, the ones with the pink-and-yellow flower vines around the edge. Special plates. Again, *why?*

Admit it, you like him. She could almost hear Gabby chiding her, *"Didn't I warn you? Don't say I didn't warn you."*

"Hey, there. Looks like I'm right on time," Mr. Wag announced, at her side all at once. He smelled minty and gave off heat and moisture from a fresh shave. He took the plates and bowls, and walked them to the table. He stood and waited behind the chair she'd chosen specifically for him, and she wondered how he knew.

"Go on and seat yourself. I'll get the bread." First she gave her apron a toss. He was facing the oven. He'd see her dress, the belt, her effort, and she didn't mind one bit. "Do you like butter on your cornbread?"

"I certainly do."

"How about some honey?" she asked, stacking a serving plate.

"Nah. I want to taste everything pure. Without the extras," he said.

"Well, what do you think? You like it?" she asked, when she noticed he'd already begun eating the stew. She sat down and handed him a corner piece of the buttered yellow bread.

"Forgive me. For shame, me eating without blessing the food. That's how good it is. I was only going to sneak a taste. Next thing I know I'm stuck, close to picking up the plate and pouring it down my throat. Ma'am, you are one hell of a cook."

Bailey smiled and shook her head. "So, that's a *yes*."

"That's a *hell yeah*."

She believed him and quickly ladled a refill. "I wish I'd used more meat."

"It's delicious. How was you to know you'd have a guest for dinner? I practically invited myself."

"I'm enjoying the company."

"You usually all alone about this time?"

"No. Actually, my aunt Charlene is out this evening. Just worked out that you—we are alone." Bailey broke off another chunk of cornbread and placed it on the side of his disappearing stew. "I can get you some more if you'd like."

"I don't want to eat you out of house and home. Believe me, I can eat."

From the leanness of his frame, she'd guess he didn't eat much. Or at least, not often. "What about something to drink?"

"Don't worry about me. I'm one satisfied customer. You eat. Let me get you something to drink." Before she could say otherwise, he was on his feet. "What's in here? Oh, look a there. Iced tea. Oh my, someone likes their suds. We'll save that for another day," he said, talking to himself.

A tall glass of tea appeared before her with a few ice cubes floating on top. She was about to thank him when he leaned down and kissed her. Quick and to the point, his lips met hers. A test, it seemed.

When she didn't protest, he kissed her again, slow and tender, with an open hand smoothing over her face. And then it was over, much too soon. He went to the adjacent chair, where his food remained, and picked up where he'd left off, scraping up the last bits with his spoon. "We should go out for pie," he said.

She didn't know what to make of it. One minute he was kissing her and the next he wanted to go out for pie. Did that mean she was a horrible kisser? Had it been that long?

"Or do you have something we can eat here, for dessert?" he asked. "Food this good deserves something sweet."

"I've got cookies."

"Homemade?"

"No. But . . ."

"No, ma'am. You can't ply me with this fancy stew and then try to pawn off some stale cookies as a finisher. No," he said. "Finish up and then we're heading to Queenie's for her pecan pie à la mode."

Queenie's was where Gabby would be working the evening shift. Bailey wasn't in the mood to hear or notice Gabby's concerted feelings about Walter. "Listen, you got a sweet tooth, Mr. Wag. All you need is some honey on that cornbread. I'll get you some."

"You make an excellent point," he said. "I accept."

She let out a breath of relief. "All righty, then."

"I was trying to give you an easy way to get rid of me, but now you're stuck with me," he said with a grin.

Bailey rolled her eyes and found herself shaking her head once again. Mr. Wag, she thought, was a whole mess, and she couldn't stop herself from smiling.

When they finished eating, the silence didn't last long. She stood to carry their empty dishes to the sink. She felt his arms pull under hers, wrap around her waist, and rest there.

"I always wanted extra hands," she said.

His face nestled against her neck. "Well, now you have them."

28

INGRID STOOD AT HER DAUGHTER'S CLOSED DOOR, deciding whether to knock or simply walk right in. The lock had been removed years ago, after one of Elsa's episodes. She pressed her ear against the cool exterior of the door. She heard her daughter's voice, husky and hardy, "No. No. I don't care about fitting into my dress. Genius, mixing the cream into the soda bottle. From now on, that's how I'll always drink my cola. I'm just glad we got to spend the day together."

"Do you mind telling me what's going on here?" Ingrid asked, opening the bedroom door wide.

"Excuse me?" Elsa retorted coolly, as if she'd expected Ingrid had been listening the entire time. "You want to know what's going on here in my room, or in my life?" Her voice and words conveyed contempt.

When she burst onto the scene, Ingrid had expected Elsa to look guilty, or at the very least startled. But apparently not. Ingrid stepped inside and closed the door. "Hang up the phone. Now."

Elsa sat up, took her palm off the receiver, and cheerfully said, "I'll call you tomorrow. Have a good night."

"Who was that?"

"A friend." She put the phone receiver down and folded her arms across her chest defiantly.

"Where were you? Did you have anything to do with the fight between Connor and Niles?"

"Is Niles all right?" Elsa asked.

"Well, I wasn't there. Were you? Did you have anything to do with Niles and Connor's fistfight, an all-out brawl that left Niles with a black eye? He'll have a black eye for his wedding!" Ingrid's voice rose to a shriek. "In the midst of my worrying about where you'd run off to, again, I hear about this from Vera, who, by the way, wanted to know if you perhaps knew what the fight was about, since Niles didn't want to talk about it."

Ingrid leaned forward on the fluffy bed linens, her shaky arms keeping her upright. She honestly was exhausted. Her entire body quaked as if she'd just run a marathon, but she decided to power through.

"It's time for a bit of honesty," Ingrid said. Not hers. She'd never been accused of skimping on an observation or two. It was Elsa's truth she wanted unearthed. What was crawling just below the surface? This quiet private life of Elsa's had to be tended to. There was no room for error.

"I want to know about Connor Salley—everything. I heard the conversation you had with that Bailey person. I overheard everything the other day. What have you been up to? What were Niles and Connor fighting over? You?" She refused to budge until Elsa confessed. Although she'd gotten used to her daughter's walled responses and tiny stabs of rejection, she was surprised when Elsa curled into herself.

All of it hit Elsa hard. She slumped as though all the bones had gone out of her body. Ingrid went over and closed the door, then came back to Elsa's side and said, in a gentler tone, "Oh, sweetheart, I just want to help. Whatever is happening, or has happened, can be fixed. Do you understand? We can fix this, but you have to trust me."

Little did she know that what Elsa was about to tell her would be the most horrendous thing she'd heard for a long time. She listened in shock. Sure, girls were taken advantage of, for sport or passion, by young men. Some thought it a rite of passage. *Boys will be boys.* Wasn't it the goal to be desirable? Her copy of *Look* magazine had arrived that very morning with a barely clad young actress on the cover. It may as well have read, *Something to aspire to.* Was it really what any mother wanted for her daughter? Being seen as nothing but an instrument of desire? Used and discarded?

Ingrid carefully avoided gripping her chest. She kept her hands at her sides and continued to listen as Elsa told the story with the very same cold voice she'd used when Ingrid first came into the room. "He pushed himself inside me. I tried to fight him. They were all there. They heard everything, and no one tried to stop him. We were all playing the kissing game, the same one we been playing since we were kids. Only difference was, it was kissing and drinking. The bottle spun and landed on Connor. It could've easily been Leo. It could've easily been Niles or Heidi Gillman. It could've been the hostess, Jane Merry, Christina Oaks, Billy, or Sam. Whoever the bottle pointed to, they were supposed to kiss, that's all.

"Didn't matter if it landed on a girl or a boy. Didn't matter if boys weren't supposed to kiss other boys and girls weren't supposed to kiss on girls, but we did. We did it all the time. Even if it wasn't what you wanted, wherever the bottle spun, it was your turn. But then it landed on me. This time, it was me and Connor. He clapped his hands together and said, *'Well, you don't say? Me and Elsa got us a date.'* He took me by the hands and pulled me to my feet and took me into the study. They all heard what was going on. I mean, there was music and laughter, but they had to hear me fighting him, because I was crying and yelling for him to stop."

It seemed her daughter had come to an understanding with herself that what was done was done. The flatness in her voice, in her expression, as she described the attack was oddly placid. *Choked. Shaken. Smothered.* Connor had done this to her. She even repeated what he'd said as he'd done it.

This was her fault.

My fault. I did this.

Ingrid licked her lips before she dared speak. "Where do you think he would've gotten such a thing, such an idea about you?"

"Saying I liked girls instead of boys? Saying that I was confused?"

"Yes," Ingrid said, nodding her head.

"Does it matter? He decided that I needed fixing, that I didn't know what was good for me, so he was going to fix me and show me all that I was missing," Elsa said. But this time her voice wavered. *"You just don't know what's good for you,"* she whispered. "He kept saying it the whole time."

The calm recap didn't stop the surge of Ingrid's utter loathing for Connor Salley, and for herself. Ingrid couldn't bear the thought of Elsa knowing *she* was the reason Connor Salley had done this.

"I'm so-so-sorry this happened to you," Ingrid said, feeling the beginnings of tears in the back of her throat. She would not cry here, not in front of Elsa.

"I wish I knew how to stop thinking about it. Niles was trying to protect me today," Elsa finally stated. "He's felt guilty about being there and not helping me from the start. Don't you see how all this came to be? It's wrong marrying Niles, Mama. He's only agreed to all of this because he feels guilty. Because he was there and he felt powerless to stop it. He told me that night when he drove me home, '*I know what Connor did to you. I'm going to make it right, Elsa.*' Niles kept saying it. '*I'm going to make this right.*' He was so kind, and so sweet. I mean, none of this is his fault. He shouldn't have to pay for something that wasn't his doing. Niles shouldn't have to pay with his future. It's just plain cruel." Her eyes did the pleading for her. "I'm glad you know, Mama. I've been so afraid to tell you." Her hand slid to her belly.

Only then did Ingrid see the slight swell on Elsa's straight body. Ingrid leaned over and pulled her hand away. "What're you saying? Are you pregnant?"

Elsa nodded, thick tears finally releasing and trailing down her reddened cheeks.

"It's all right," Ingrid heard herself say. "Niles genuinely cares for you. We'll go through with the wedding. No one will ever suspect that it's Connor's baby."

"I'll know. And Niles will know, because we've never had sex, and maybe never will. Mama . . . I . . . I'm—"

"No. No. Don't say another word."

"Mama, I don't think Niles is an idiot. I don't think he's going to want a wife who isn't interested in being with him. He'll also know it's Connor's baby."

Ingrid was beside herself. Her mind had already raced on. Plan B. "But Niles doesn't know you're pregnant . . ." She trailed off. "Who does know? Exactly who have you told?"

"No one does besides my friend Bailey. I told her I thought I was, but at the time I still wasn't sure."

"I don't think Bailey will be an issue. Who could she tell that would listen to her? As for Niles, yes, he'll probably go along out of sheer guilt. But his mother, Vera, such a busybody, she'll be suspicious if you're suddenly showing one month after your vows. Niles will tell his parents everything at some point." Ingrid paced. "And if those Salleys get a whiff, one whiff, that they might have a grandchild, we will never be rid of them. They used to be our people, but as far as I'm concerned, they are no longer our people. You can't be aligned with the Salleys. They're bitter and poor," she said. "Elsa, sweetheart, you deserve a decent life. We've got to get to the doctor, see if we have time to clean up this mess.

"The ceremony will go on, then Monday we'll disappear for the day. There's a Pawnee woman who does a fine job, I've been told. We'll be back before anyone even knows we're gone. It's safe. You'll be fine. And we'll be done with this forever. Problem solved." *Breathe,* she told herself. She stood but had no choice but to sit right back down.

"Mama, you all right?" Elsa was up. "I'll get you some water. Wait right here."

"I'm fine. I'm all right," Ingrid said, stopping her from leaving. This was her chance, she realized. Elsa needed to see her vulnerable, to understand what was at stake. And so she told another story. Of course it was not half as emotional as Elsa's. Nor was it all of the truth, but it was equally important. Their family wasn't teetering on poverty. But there were levels beneath them that they weren't willing to revisit. She watched Elsa's questioning face. Disbelief, really.

"I know what you're thinking: *How is it possible?* The oil business isn't what it used to be. Big oil companies have been conspiring to fix their prices to shut out smaller refineries like us. Your father had a chance to merge, to sell, and he refused," Ingrid said flippantly. There was more. She didn't want to waste time with intricate details. Demand versus supply. Cost versus revenue. Her husband's questionable investments.

Matthias had tried his best to keep Ingrid's nose out of the fine details, but she had an affinity for organizing and completing tasks. If there was something out of place or undone, she was left frayed and uncomfortable. She knew far more about the Senate Oil bottom line than she should have. The corporation, built brick by brick, had begun leaking—first a trickle and then an entire gush, like water flowing over a dam. "We might not be beggars," she explained to Elsa, "but there are other kinds of poverty, and I'm not going to be poor again. And you, my dear, could never survive in a constant state of need. You simply have to marry Niles, baby or no baby, for your sake. We're simply stronger together. The Porters feel the same way. They're in the same predicament. Maybe they'll stay afloat a bit longer, but the bottom line awaits us all."

"But, I don't care about having money." Elsa stood, rigid. Now Ingrid could see that she was barely showing. She could stand at the altar in her wedding dress and no one would be the wiser—just as Ingrid herself had not been.

Elsa's cheeks burned a brighter shade of red, which Ingrid didn't know was possible. Where her daughter's pale skin had come from had been mystifying. She and Matthias, both with dark pupils and dark hair naturally at the root, were bestowed with sun-resilient skin. Then came Elsa, bluish and lucent as a ghost. Her silver-blue eyes were traits that had to have been buried deep on both sides of the family tree. Her restless personality—that too came from some-where unknown.

"You have to marry Niles. All right. That's the end of it, Elsa. Do you understand? I don't want to have this conversation again. Ever. This is all that Bailey's fault. I spoke to her. I asked her what exactly she told you to make you so sour on marrying Niles, and she ran off. Coward. I told Thea Jackson she needs to be fired. Someone like that, spreading her insane witchcraft, does not need to be working at the Regal Gown."

"You got her fired?" Elsa covered her mouth with both hands.

"What did you expect me to do? You shut me out. I couldn't fig-ure out what was going on, you suddenly not wanting to go through with the wedding. I knew there was someone responsible."

Ingrid was losing her. "Listen to me, I'm your mother. I'm the one you should have come to in the beginning. But now that I know, I'm going to make sure you're safe and taken care of. No one is ever going to hurt you like that again. We will get through all of this together." She opened her arms and didn't have to wait long before Elsa found her way, chest to chest, heart to heart. She kissed her head and swayed her gently. She meant what she said: No one would ever hurt her baby again.

Later in the night, Ingrid was plagued by everything she'd heard from Elsa. She wanted sleep to put her out of her misery, but this was her punishment: remembering her time with Connor and how she would forever blame herself.

She could in a way blame Matthias. If he had loved her properly and given her the attention she deserved, she wouldn't have sought refuge in a young man who only wanted to give Ingrid pleasure. It was the only time she could truly be herself. Nothing to do with Senate Oil or the needs of the many. She didn't have to placate Connor with false interest in his day or week. The conversations inevitably turned to Elsa, since nothing else consumed Ingrid's time more than worrying about her daughter.

"I saw her when she was about thirteen, her and the housekeeper's daughter," Ingrid confessed. "I walked in on them, kissing, making out, going at it like they were boy and girl. *Whew,* I tell you. I've never seen anything like it. I didn't even say anything. I was too stunned. I closed the door. She never even knew I saw them."

Connor had lit a cigarette and handed it to her. "Maybe it's a phase."

"No, sir. I think Elsa is going to keep on disappointing me. It's what she was born to do. My first inclination was to fire Oda Mae; that way she'd have to take her daughter with her. But I realized it wasn't about the girl. This is who Elsa is, who she'll always be."

"Nah. She might not know what she wants 'cause she hasn't had the real thing," he'd said.

Ingrid playfully slapped him on his bare chest. "Too bad she can't have someone like you. Then she'd know what she's missing," she'd teased.

She would never forget saying those words to him. Nor the way he looked at her, like he was up for the challenge. How was she to know he'd take it upon himself to teach Elsa a lesson? To show her *what she was missing.*

She couldn't stop hearing Elsa describe what happened that night. *"He kept saying I didn't know what was good for me . . ."*

Ingrid would never stop hearing those words.

29

CHARLENE MOVED ABOUT THE DARK HOUSE on Baker Street, holding her shoes in a two-finger hook. Her footsteps were light, but still she paused with anguish when the floorboards creaked. She made it to the kitchen and filled a glass with desperately needed water. A full day with Matthias Grimes had left her with unquenchable thirst. She was frazzled and lost in her flashes of time with him.

It started with the visit, then the phone call. What profound force had brought Matty back into her life? What had happened in the universe to overcome the odds of ever seeing him again?

She opened the tap and filled the water glass again. She sipped slowly this time. She took a minute to breathe, relive the details and maybe even enjoy them.

She had told herself she wanted to know what the cash was for. Curiosity had gotten the better of her. *For you and your niece.* But why? She knew it was about Elsa, of course. Surely, the entire endeavor was about asking Bailey to keep her distance. Charlene knew all of this and showed up anyway at the 98th Street Motel. Traveling salesmen and truckers went to refuel there and sleep, but it was mostly vacant at that time of the afternoon. It was far beneath Matthias Grimes to be at a place like that, but where else were they safe to avoid being seen together? A motel—to just talk, he'd said.

She already had the envelope filled with hundred-dollar bills. Wasn't like she needed to speak to him in person. He could've told her all he had to say over the phone.

But it was that phone call, his voice breathily in her ear, when he said "Char, I think we should speak in person," that made her heart race.

She hadn't expected him to touch her the way that he had, as if he'd never stopped loving her. One brush of his lips against hers and she'd turned slippery. She hadn't expected to be aroused the minute she entered the room. His scent hadn't changed. He still reminded her of the first rain on a spring morning.

She had no plans to see him again, though when he made the request, she'd said *maybe*. Maybe. She shook her head now, ashamed of herself for leaving the door open to her heart instead of saying, *Hell, no*. She'd made one mistake; she didn't need to make another.

She showed up wearing a gingham dress she didn't know could still fit, the first two buttons left undone where she had slathered her skin with Vaseline. Brown skin coated and glistening. She wore her dark sunglasses and didn't take them off until she was safely inside room 101.

He didn't pretend for a second not to want her. He pulled her inside, closed the door, and swooped her into his arms. Once she peeled out of her dress, she'd forfeited her questions.

A ripple of wanting passed through her—the memory, the taste of his mouth on hers, as if they were still babes in the woods instead of grown and knowing better.

Meeting him had been foolish.

She wouldn't see him again, and that was final.

Funny how she hadn't bothered to ask, until after they'd spent four hours in each other's arms, what he'd given her the money for. At least there was that. They'd eventually gotten to the point of their meeting. "Your niece needs to stay away from Elsa, at least until after the wedding. Tell her there's more where that came from if she needs an incentive," he'd said, figuring it was that simple. It wasn't. She wanted to tell him that he was right, stubbornness indeed ran in the family. Her niece Bailey wasn't likely to listen to anything Charlene had to say, even if it came with the unbelievable reward of five hundred dollars. This was a new side of Matty, believing he could buy his way out of any situation.

"Dissuade your niece from having anything else to do with Elsa."

Charlene had explained how she'd already said her piece, pointing out the danger of being involved with a Grimes. "The minute I found out who she was, I tried to talk sense into her. You think I want her involved with your daughter? The first thing I thought was 'The apple can't fall far from the tree.' Impetuous. Wild. Dangerous."

He had chuckled at that, lying with one arm behind his head and the other strong arm wrapped around her. "I see you're still blaming me for everything," he'd said against her ear. "I'm not the hard-headed one in this story, Char." True, she thought, for the most part, it had been Charlene who wouldn't listen to reason.

"I lost the baby," she told him. It wasn't truly a lie.

Matty was gentleman enough not to push her for details. "I figured as much," he said. "I knew you wouldn't have run off like that unless you were hurting real bad. I never should've left you behind. I was wrong for that. When I came back and no one knew where you'd gone, I punched a hole in the wall." He lifted his right arm, where a raised, jagged scar remained.

She put her lips to the place long healed over. "I'm sorry. I should've trusted you."

He'd come back for her. That was all she knew—now. He'd come back and she wasn't there.

She would honor her word and talk to Bailey. Try to talk to her, anyway.

When Charlene looked back, as she often did, she told herself there had been no choice in the matter. All Matty wanted to do was go home and get a fresh start, and she punished him for it. He couldn't get a foothold in New Orleans, where they'd landed as a young couple in 1926. The area had just survived one of the worst hurricanes in its history. The city had taken a monumental hit to its industrial centers. None of that registered for a young couple who only had their hopes and dreams to consider.

Matty Grimes ended up washing dishes, shoveling trash and crap off the streets, and cleaning windows. The kind of work he'd been hired for made him feel small and helpless. "I can't go on like this, feeling less than worthless."

She wanted to tell him, "Welcome to my world." After six short months, he'd thrown up his hands, waved an imaginary white flag, and announced his exit plan.

"If we go back home, I can get a job at one of the wells," Matty told her. "My uncle will get me on. I can't live like this, Char. We can't live like this."

"But you're the one who wanted to come to Louisiana. I left my family with big talk of making something of myself. Now you want me to go back there? Be shamed and embarrassed like this." Her hands landed on the barely visible bump. Three months along. She couldn't possibly go back home pregnant, claiming it was all just a misunderstanding, bad timing, and whatnot. Fumbling for words, she'd have to tell her mama and grandmama that Matty needed a reset. Then they'd be together. Her mama and grandma would have laughed in her face. And Sammie . . . she was the one who'd seen everything Charlene was hiding. Just a graze against her hand and she saw Matty, the two of them. *"Oh, no, you love him. Char. No. He's just using you. Can't you see that?"*

"I promise we'll be together. I'll figure out a way," Matty had said.

"How? You know we can't be seen smiling in each other's direction, let alone touching, holding hands in Mendol. I can't go back to the way things were. Please don't make me. We can make it work here, Matty. I got two clients. I can make enough until you find your place."

"Clients? Two more houses to *clean*."

"Yeah. They are *clients*," she said. "It's paying work. Honest work."

"I promised you it wasn't going to be like this. Every day you spend scrubbing somebody else's floors makes me realize how I let you down." He went on his knees and kissed her belly. "And what about this little guy, how're we going to have a family like this? Let's get on a train, head home, and make our own rules."

"I already followed you to one place. What happens when it don't go your way again? We going to be roaming around looking for a home, looking for people to accept us?"

"I can't stay here, Char," he'd said. "I'll go, get situated, then I'll come back to get you, and I'm not taking no for an answer. Me, you, and our baby are going to be a family."

She'd snatched her wrists away from his grip. "I'm never going back there, so you go on back to your mama and daddy. And you know what? Stay there."

The fight, if one could call it that, lasted for three days. By the time he'd left out the door for the bus station, she'd made up her mind. She wasn't going to be there when he came looking. The girl who'd arrived in New Orleans with hope and love in her eyes had become a bitter, angry shell of herself.

She didn't know if Matty had come back to get her, because she wasn't there to find out. She had spared herself the disappointment.

She moved into the Broussard family home. They were clients in the quarter who'd been asking if she'd live in full-time to help take care of their one-year-old daughter. It was double the pay she'd been getting for regular day work. The Broussard family had no idea she was pregnant. They were a professional duo, considered Creole in those parts, with a large three-story home with more than enough space. She told them she would accept their offer to be a live-in housekeeper, but she wasn't planning on staying forever.

"We'll take you for as long as you will stay," Phoebe Broussard said, gladly handing over the reins to her household, toddler, and her husband, Dr. Broussard.

Charlene quickly became part of their family. House manager, nanny, and confidant to whoever had a dispirited day. The doctor was affable and energetic but could sometimes be a bit stern. Phoebe worked as a librarian and didn't see the point of giving up her love of books for her love of family. She was a college-educated woman and refused to sacrifice all her years of determination and effort to live in domestic servitude as merely a wife. The married couple had many a heated discussion over the issue. "No offense," she'd say to Charlene on a few occasions when she'd let out her dismay at her husband's gall, "but the audacity to think I'm worth sacrificing and he is not! We're past all that now. A woman has just as much a right to do as she pleases, the same as any man."

Charlene seemed to be the middle ground where both parties found a safe space to speak their minds. Eventually, they'd find themselves wrapped around each other, making Charlene feel like her work was done. She'd helped the couple in her small way by listening. "Everyone just wants to be heard, whether it makes sense or not," she'd offered to Phoebe and the doctor alike. Individually of course.

For that small gem of advice, Phoebe gave her a savings bond worth ten dollars. She called it a *work bonus*. "In twenty years it will be worth a hundred dollars," Phoebe told her one evening. She pressed the certificate into Charlene's hands as if it were worth more than gold. "You'll have something saved for your little one. You're going to make such a wonderful mother. You're such a gifted spirit, wise beyond your years."

Charlene suddenly felt light-headed. It was the one thing they hadn't discussed: her obvious weight gain and slower movements around the house. She'd never mentioned she was carrying a child and hoped she'd be gone before anyone noticed. She'd planned on Matty finding her before the baby was anybody's business but their own.

"Oh, sweetie, sit. All this time you've been working this hard just so we wouldn't notice?" Phoebe said, the realization fresh. "You shouldn't be standing all day." Phoebe pulled up a second chair and helped Charlene put her feet up. She brought her a glass of water, then sat across from her. "I think it's high time you do the talking for once. I apologize for failing to engage you. We're so busy going on and on about our days around here, we forget you have a life too."

Charlene said, "No. I'm the one who should be saying 'I'm sorry.' You all welcomed me with open arms. I didn't have the heart to tell you I was pregnant. I was ashamed because my man left me here alone. But I've been saving my money. By the time the baby comes, I'll be out of your hair."

"Nonsense," Phoebe said. "You're not about to be stressing, not on my watch. This is your home and your baby's home for as long as you need it to be." She clasped her hands together. "I've already got a bassinette and tons of baby clothes, some never touched, just sitting in the attic."

"What will Dr. Broussard say?" Charlene asked. The opportunity sounded too good to be true.

"The good doctor and I have plenty of space. This is my house as much as it is his, and you are staying. Then our little Vivienne and your new sprout will be playmates. We'll be just fine."

"It's not necessary, really. I have a plan."

"What kind of plan you got? You're seventeen. You and this little one are going to need a whole lot of help."

"I'll be eighteen when she comes, or he," Charlene said, rubbing a hand across her belly. Not that the matter of being eighteen made any difference. She could've been thirty and it didn't change the fact that she had nowhere else to go.

"So, then, what's your plan?"

Charlene held her tongue. This wasn't the time to confess that all she'd wanted to do was make Matthias Grimes suffer. She'd only wanted to disappear long enough to make him fret a bit and be taught a lesson. All she'd wanted was for him to regret leaving. It wasn't really a plan, but more like a dream, a wish, a hope, and a prayer that he'd see the light and come rushing back to her. She imagined him asking the landlord of the tiny studio where they'd been living, "Have you seen Char? Do you know where she went?" She'd even made sure to tell her landlord where she'd gone. She'd written down the address in the guise of having her mail forwarded. She'd done everything according to *her plan*. She would hear the bell ring at the Broussards' door one afternoon. She'd answer it and fall into Matty's arms, warm against his beating chest. *"I thought I'd lost you,"* he would whisper.

But after a way too long silence, Phoebe Broussard tapped her knee. "You see there, you don't have a plan, and that's all right. That's just fine. For now, we're all you need, right here."

Her pregnancy felt like a life sentence. Matty wasn't coming back: She'd accepted that. He hadn't showed up to plead for forgiveness or sweep her off her swollen feet.

Finally, on a hot yellow August morning, her baby was delivered, healthy and glistening, after hours of being prayed over and prodded by the midwife's gentle hands. Sageuine Marie Dowery made her appearance in the Broussard family's upstairs spare bedroom, where

Charlene had been living. They'd hired a midwife, Aria, a round-faced local woman thoroughly confident in her skills. Small hands were required for her delicate work and those she had, cutting the cord and washing the infant clean with meticulous attention. She handed the swaddled baby to Phoebe while she tended to Charlene.

Hours later, Charlene awakened to find Phoebe standing over her. She panicked when Phoebe leaned over to place the newborn in her arms. "It's okay," Phoebe said. "You won't break her. But she needs some of your goodness."

It wasn't much, just a few drops of nourishment. After the second day, the milk finally let down from her breasts and traveled miraculously down the baby's throat in plentiful gulps. All the while she watched and marveled at the tiny bundle of beauty. Perfection. A head full of shiny black hair swirling around a ripe pearl face. Dark searching eyes. *Are you my mama?* Charlene wished the answer was *yes,* but she was in no position to be anybody's mama. She was in no position to take care of anyone when she could hardly take care of herself.

It was an agonizing decision, leaving such a perfect, beautiful baby behind. It didn't feel right to stay, falling more in love with those round cheeks and chubby legs as each day passed. Sage, as Phoebe began to call her, was only three months old when Charlene left the Broussards' home.

She wished she could change the past. There was so much more she longed to forget. Begged to forget.

Now, she could feel the pictures forming. Bailey would know what Charlene's heart truly yearned for. She'd see that small baby, wrapped in pink, the way she remembered her. And when she asked, "Auntie, who is that child?" she'd have no choice but to tell her the truth. "*My daughter. I left her in New Orleans to be raised by another family.*" She'd explain how she'd given up her daughter, left her behind to pursue a great big life, which turned out to be quite the opposite. A frivolous life. Wasted years until she'd been called back home to take care of Bailey.

Charlene shoved the wave of memory down. Her hands rested

on her stomach, and for the first time she didn't feel the ache, the dark emptiness. There was a new feeling: warmth, love. She'd had a daughter and she did what she thought was best, out of love.

And now, she at least wanted to tell Matty the truth. She owed him that.

He deserved to know about their daughter, the child he thought had never been born. It was time.

She stood at the kitchen sink, where she finished her second glass of water. She squeezed back the tears suddenly threatening to fall from her eyes, as so many tears had fallen back then.

Useless, she thought. Tears served no purpose. The past served no purpose. Regrets. Shame. Repentance. All of them should have meant nothing. All she had was now. She drew an arm across her face, wiping away the evidence of the pain.

Charlene made her way down the hall with barely a squeak on the floorboards. She took the envelope of money and tucked it under her mattress.

By the time she closed her eyes, headed for oblivion, she heard the neighbor's rooster announcing sunrise. The sky illuminated her wall with a hazy sparkle of blue dust. She'd been afraid to close her eyes in the darkness, her memories too much to bear. But with the sun peeking over the horizon, she slept peacefully and without regret.

30

BAILEY RUSHED TO HER CLOSET at six-thirty in the morning, her mind focused on getting to the Regal Gown to make up for the work she'd missed the day before. Hopefully, she had a job to get back to.

She'd find out when she got there. If it was her last day, Miss Jackson owed her a word to her face, not to mention a week's worth of pay. Bailey had been a loyal, hard worker. If one day of sickness caused her to lose all the faith and merit she'd built up in two years, so be it.

She'd never walked out on anyone before, as in, *left them in their time of need*. She had never put her own needs before someone else's. One of many firsts, she thought, after catching sight of her platinum belt on the floor, nestled like a cat on top of her black dress. For a second or two she simply stared at the evidence of her misdeed; then she picked up the dress, inhaling the scent of Walter Anderson Graves's aftershave. After a few minutes, she hung the belt and dress in the closet.

What now? She wasn't sure what she was supposed to do. Call him? Wait for him to call her? Just because they'd shared a meal and made out like puppy wolves didn't mean she was owed anything. She wouldn't call first; that much she knew. He was supposed to come over on Saturday to start work on the house's foundation. The better thing to do was to wait. *"Have some dignity."* She could hear Gabby in her head. *"Show some respect for yourself."*

She'd call Gabby and tell her everything, of course. She'd want the details. "Just dinner and some kissing," Bailey rehearsed. The details would have to wait, though she'd committed every single moment to memory.

"So how come somebody as pretty as you don't have a man?" he'd asked when she'd finally convinced him to go on home for the night. He stood at the open front door, feet on the porch and body leaning in. He wanted another kiss, she could tell, his eyes closed, full lips slightly pursed.

She gave him a peck. "Maybe it's me who don't want a man. Ever thought of that?"

"Yeah. All right. We'll have to change that," he said. "Good night, Sweet Bailey. See you soon."

She'd also tell Gabby what she saw in the night. The pink-and-gold fusion of shooting stars swirling around Mr. Wag's aura. Nothing definitive, which was a good thing. It meant he was free and unattached. She would have seen it if there were another woman, someone he was truly passionate about. She'd seen only the fluorescent colors flowing like a river over his kind, soft face.

She'd seen Mr. Wag's light, and it was a bright, empty ball. There was no one else, no one he cared about.

But wait—did that mean she should have at least seen herself? Too soon, perhaps. Last night had only been a breath away. She could still feel his mouth on her neck, the warmth and pressure of his hand when he went there. *My, my, my, what he could do with his hands.* She let out the breath she found herself holding.

It was time to get to work. Enough of her reminiscing over her night with Walter. She checked the mirror. Her reflection showed a woman who might've stayed up an hour or two too late. Soft coal-dark eyes and a relaxed pout that had been kissed throughout the night. She showed no evidence of her evening. Miss Jackson wouldn't know she'd had a fun night when she was supposed to be home nursing a fever.

The bureau mirror reflected her unscathed. But she really could have used a few more hours of sleep.

She forced herself to pull a plain burgundy cotton shift off the hanger. It wasn't something she'd normally wear to the Regal Gown, but today she felt like trying something new.

THE SUN WAS UP AND STRONG when she left the house. Only while sitting at the first stop sign did she think, *I didn't check on Aunt Charlene.*

She considered circling the block and returning to the house.

She also considered what it would mean if Aunt Charlene wasn't safely home in her room. Stress, worry, concern: All things she couldn't afford right now. Her foot pressed the pedal nearly to the floor before the car picked up speed. One worry at a time. Miss Jackson. Her job. Then she'd return home and deal with her auntie.

A half an hour later, Bailey arrived at the vacant lot and parked. Besides her lone Olds, there were just a few tumbleweeds, ready to break away from their birthplace. Wasn't that what life was about? Breaking free from the dirt and making a way to a new destination?

Bailey began her walk. The morning chill felt glorious. She fluttered with involuntary lapses back to her time with Mr. Wag.

She arrived at the front entrance of the Regal Gown. The golden doors sealed against each other seemed solid and final. She pulled out her key and pushed it into the lock, and then blew out a relieved whistle when it easily clicked to the right. If Miss Jackson didn't want her there, she would have had the lock rekeyed: simple as that.

Bailey stepped inside, took in the brilliance of the chandelier overhead, the light reflecting on the mirror, and wondered if it could be a new chapter between her and Miss Jackson, with her role at the Regal Gown more than only as a seamstress. She'd dreamt of seeing her own gowns and designs hanging on the walls. She briefly had a flash: her name, *Bailey Dowery,* in red embroidery on a silk tag stitched into the necklines of shimmering satin, taffeta, and beaded lace gowns. She pictured rows and rows of her own creations, surrounding her.

"Oh, surely there's a better way." Miss Jackson's voice tapped at her dream state. But it was the second voice Bailey followed to the storeroom, her work area.

"Hello," Bailey said, doing her best to disguise the uneasiness in her voice. "Mr. Wag, Miss Jackson, good morning."

Miss Jackson removed her playful hand from Wag's shoulder. "Well, hello to you too. Feeling better, I presume?"

"Yes. I guess it was one of those overnight bugs. I'm feeling much better," Bailey said.

"Mr. Graves, I will leave you to your work. I need to discuss a few things with Miss Bailey."

"Oh. Okay," Bailey said, concerned. She followed Miss Jackson to the showroom, but she kept going out the front door and held it open for Bailey.

"I am not happy with your behavior yesterday."

"Miss Jackson, I really was ill. I can't apologize enough, but I also was running a fever and I—"

"If it ever happens again, I'm going to have to let you go. There are plenty of available candidates who would be grateful to have your job. Do you understand?"

"I do. I absolutely understand."

"Mrs. Grimes was extremely disappointed. She asked me to let you go. I said I would fire you, so in essence I've told a tall tale. I said straight to her face that you'd no longer be working here. I'll have to deal with that later, I suppose. The truth is, you've been such a hard worker and . . . well, honestly, you're invaluable, Bailey. You're quite good at what you do. So promise me, no more mishaps." Miss Jackson actually sounded sincere. She wanted to keep Bailey around and she meant it.

"I promise." Bailey nodded. "Thank you. I won't let you down."

"I knew you'd bounce back. Everyone deserves a second chance," Miss Jackson said, stepping back slightly, uncomfortable with their intimacy. "I'm going to leave you to your work. I'll be over at Georgia's." Her eyes darted toward the interior. "Keep an eye on Mr. Wag. Don't let him leave without letting me check his work. He also asked for a reference letter. I told him I'd write the letter, even though there's plenty of work in this town. No need to run off to Oklahoma City. We need him right here."

What she'd heard was innocent enough, yet Bailey's mood dropped, catapulting her from the satisfied place where she had re-sided a moment ago. The reference to such a personal subject left Bailey's chest wound up tight like a steel coil. *No need to run off.* Walter had never mentioned a single thing about leaving Mendol. They had spent all evening together.

The whine of the entrance door opening and closing caused him to come from the storage area. They were alone. "There you are. You all right?" he asked.

She walked past him. She sorted her sewing table and then hung up her coat, which she realized was done out of logical order.

"Hey, everything all right?" he repeated, as if she hadn't heard him the first time. She had her own noise in her head, bidding for her attention.

"Sweet Bailey, what is happening here?"

She still couldn't bring herself to face in his direction. But she spoke softly, fearing if she spoke any louder her voice would crack. "It didn't cross your mind to mention you'd be here? After I told you my concern? We talked. I told you how worried I was about having a job come morning. You and I, we . . ." She paused, unsure if she was making sense. "You could've mentioned you had an appointment with Miss Jackson last night. You told her you were leaving Mendol. I'm a fool. Gabby was right."

"Hey, there." He was standing close, both hands having taken hold of hers. "I don't know what's got you so upset here, but the last thing I wanted to mention last night was that I was coming here, especially with you already feeling some sort of way about this place. Yeah, it was on my work schedule, but it wasn't important. Not to me. I just wanted us to enjoy our evening, just the two of us."

It came to her suddenly why she'd reacted the way she did. "I've heard things about you, Walter Anderson Graves, things that don't inspire much confidence. I guess it came to the surface when I saw you here. You and Miss Jackson were quite friendly."

He coughed out a laugh of disbelief. "You've heard things about me?"

She braced herself for the onslaught of teasing. She'd made a fool of herself for sure. What was she thinking? He owed her nothing. And here she was, jealous of his affable presence.

"You ever hear something about me, ask. You want to know about this man here, ask."

She blinked away the tears of embarrassment. "All right. You moving to Oklahoma City or not?"

"I've let it cross my mind. Ain't nothing wrong with a man looking to do better for himself, especially when he's thinking about settling down, having a family."

She searched his eyes. Was he smooth-talking her? Settling down. Having a family. She didn't want to know if he was seriously saying what she thought he was saying. Not now. She skirted around the subject. "I must sound as ridiculous as I feel," she said, wanting to be done with the wayward emotions. "I have to say, in my defense, Miss Jackson don't like nobody. Her wanting to write you a recommendation puts you in high regard."

His eyes pulled to a squint before laughter followed.

"She seriously hates everybody," Bailey sputtered, her own laughter catching up to his. "You have some kind of special power?"

"Yeah. I do. Apparently, it works on everybody but you." He wiped at his eyes, the tears from a good laugh left behind. "Miss Jackson's a pretty jazzy lady. She got a bad rap."

"I'll take that under advisement."

"Yeah, well, judge not, lest you be judged, for with the judgment you pronounce, you will be judged."

"Are you quoting the Bible to me, Walter Graves?"

"Yes, ma'am. But don't worry, that's the only quote I know."

This wasn't the way Bailey saw her day going. The one thing she knew was that she was pleasantly surprised. No customers. No worrying she'd be asked to read someone's heartstrings. She sewed uninterrupted on her queue of alterations while Walter cut and nailed in the next room. His work entailed planning a second dressing room. Miss Jackson had cleared Bailey's fitting calendar. There was a sheet of paper taped to the window facing out that read *Closed for Improvements*. Miss Jackson must have posted it without her noticing. It was just Bailey and Walter, alone at their tasks in solitude.

The morning passed swiftly. At noon, outside in the shaded alley, Bailey and Walter shared her usual ham sandwich, peanut butter, and apple. "Last one," he said, holding up the perfect slice with just the right amount of peanut butter slathered over the edge. She opened her mouth just wide enough for Walter to press it to her lips.

She bit into it. He popped the other half into his mouth. She could count this time as their second meal together. There'd be more to tell Gabby, she surmised. More than she thought possible. Bailey liked him—really, really liked him. His outward carefree view matched an inner lightheartedness she'd not encountered before. For a moment, she contemplated asking him about the blank slate of light, what it meant. How could someone like Walter not have been netted and ensnared like a beautiful butterfly, captured in a jar? Had he ever been in love? There was so much she wanted to know, yet she didn't want to ruin their mood with hard questions.

She tossed the corners of her bread crusts to the pigeons. The same two pecked their way closer, eating the bits that fell and looking for more. Walter took a piece of what she had left in her wax paper and threw it toward them.

They were all friends now: Bailey, Walter, and the pigeon family. Bailey was happy. Maybe shame on her, but that's all she cared about: just herself, for the time being, anyway. Little did she know it would be a long time before she felt that way again.

31

THE LAST TIME ELSA HAD BEEN TAKEN to see Dr. Norman, she'd been left there, at age thirteen, scared and all alone. The Pridemore Hospital was a four-story white brick building with a basement Elsa remembered vividly. The mental ward was the final stop on the small elevator, the stuff nightmares were made of.

"It's just a routine checkup," her mama had said. "You haven't been sleeping. These things sometimes happen once you start your monthlies. Me and your father think you need to be examined. That's what doctors are for, to help, to fix things. Your outburst in church had us worried, baby."

The outburst, yes. Elsa had attended the Good Steeple Church every Sunday for as long as she could remember, the place where only the holy were welcome, where there was speaking in tongues, healing by faith, and the prophesy of doom if the collection plate didn't include large handwritten promissory notes. This was where Elsa had learned to expect her punishment, to own it.

Before the outburst there'd also been the issue with her bedsheets. How could a thirteen-year-old not know when to get up and use the bathroom? her mama wanted to know. They'd visited Dr. Norman a few weeks earlier for that problem. "She didn't even wet the bed when she was a toddler, and now she can't hold it?" her mama queried.

"Bed-wetting is common, Ingrid. Please don't fret. It's a phase, especially with the onset of puberty. I'll prescribe her a mild antianxiety medication to take throughout the day. That way, by nightfall, she can relax. Sleep won't be fraught with nervousness. It all goes hand in hand."

The pills came in an enormous brown bottle. Elsa took three a day. She didn't like the way it made her head swim and feel heavy and uncontrolled. Everything appeared in sonic waves. She was tired all the time. After about the second week, she threw the tablets in the toilet with a good flush. It took a few days before she was alert and back to her old self. She could think, and hear, and respond coherently. She could keep her head up in school, no longer drifting to the outside, swaying as the leaves blew on the trees. Maybe she was cured. She no longer wet the bed at night. Her anxiety dissolved, at least to a tolerable level. Just below the shell of herself, a mild paranoia remained.

But then came that Sunday sermon in the middle of a humid August. The entire congregation was hot and uncomfortable, fanning themselves and shifting in the pews. Elsa endured the sweat dripping down her back, the stream landing on her cotton training bra. The thick band grew tighter across her rib cage as it soaked up moistness.

"God only gives mercy to those who repent. If you want to see the glory of Heaven, take responsibility for your sins." It was that simple and straight to the point. Pastor Hoozer had spoken and sent a thud to Elsa's gut. She knew then that her destiny wasn't far behind.

Pleasures of the flesh are a sin. She thought of all those times she'd lain in her bed, hands and fingers at play, bringing her to a magical place deep inside herself. The sexual climax always came as a surprise, a gift. Transient. Sometimes she was drowning. Gasping. Sailing above herself was the most pleasurable place to be. Tempting at times not to do it twice or three times a day. There'd been no confession, no conference with the Lord about her sin, because if there was, Elsa knew where she'd end up. Those nights she'd awakened panicked, frozen, were out of shame and fear. She'd burn in Hell.

She'd quickly learned that Hell was one long string of events.

She couldn't help it if she'd wanted to get it over with. "Take me. Take me now. Let me die if I'm going to Hell," she'd screamed, rod-straight, standing on her feet. The congregation murmured, unsure of what to do in such a case. Speaking in tongues might be expected—desired, even—but this was crystal-clear English.

Her mama and daddy pulled her to sit, fastened themselves onto her as if smothering a fire. But it was too late.

She'd gotten away and had run down the aisle, pushed her way onto the stage, and continued her confession. "He's going to punish us. We're all going to die of our sins. You, and you, we're all going to be punished. Take me now. Hell is waiting. Hell is waiting." She'd repeated the phrase even as the church ushers grabbed her by the arms and carried her off.

Dr. Norman had been in church that day and had witnessed the scene for himself. When she'd arrived the following day at Pridemore, he'd been waiting in his office with two men dressed all in white, male nurses who escorted Elsa directly to the elevator, and down she went. The mental ward had no windows, at least none accessible to the patients. She stared at the demanding blue walls under fluorescent light for six days. A short visit. But long enough to remind her of what happened if she didn't follow the rules. Life had rules.

And on the seventh day, the work was done. She'd been forgiven for her monstrous behavior. Pastor Hoozer made a personal visit to help her repent with an hour-long prayer. She shut out the temptation and locked the door.

"You see, you're all better now," her mama had said on the drive home. Elsa, overly grateful to leave the place, promised she'd never sin again. She'd kept her word until the night with Connor. Even if she'd fought to stop him, she knew the burden of sin still fell on her. She had *let* it happen.

She was the problem.

We can fix this. Her mama's words pulled at Elsa, tugged at the corners of her mind, no matter how she tried to move away. Her mama was an undeniable force. There wasn't any doubt about what she was capable of. Problem-solver extraordinaire. And there was nothing Elsa wanted more in the world than to be fixed. Because her whole life had been a problem. She'd felt nothing but broken her entire time on God's green earth.

This pregnancy might be the one time Ingrid Grimes was outmatched, Elsa thought while she lay on the white sheet–covered table. This, Elsa, the problem wouldn't be solved by a visit to her family doctor or a week locked in a room with lights so bright she was unable to fall asleep.

Elsa stared up, allowing the row of white bulbs to irritate her eyes. She wanted to remind the doctor and her mama she was still in the room. Alive. Wide awake. It was her body they were speaking of. She blinked forcibly, rapid butterfly motions, even if that was all she could do at the moment.

"She appears to be ten, maybe twelve weeks along," Dr. Norman said. He picked up a towel and wiped off his hands.

"That's good, right? She's early enough to, you know . . . have a choice?"

"Ingrid, you know that's not something I can help you with," he answered reprovingly. He pushed away on his metal stool, giving them space to speak "privately," although Elsa was right there. He pulled a pen from his coat pocket and scratched out a note. He tore the sheet off. "This is a prescription for the nausea. I'm here to make sure she carries to term. Other than that, you'll have to go about your business." He paused, then lowered his voice. "For what you want, you'll surely have to travel a bit."

"Yes. Of course. I want what's best for her, is all. You understand. I wanted to know how much time we have. There's the wedding in a few days and—" The paper exchanged hands. "Thank you, Teddy." She folded the prescription.

"All righty then. Best of luck to you," he said before leaving the examination room without so much as a word to Elsa, the actual patient, whose womb he'd just examined.

"Get up. Get dressed," her mama said, before leaving right behind him. The door closed and Elsa stayed in the same spot, shivering, her naked feet slotted in the metal stirrups.

She shoved the sheet off and climbed down to the gray linoleum. Her clothes were on the chair where her mama had folded them, cursing under her breath, "I'm going to have Oda Mae burn these damn denims."

Elsa hadn't had a minute for it to sink in at the doctor's office. But now, in the car, Elsa's throat swelled with honest-to-goodness joy. Or was it sadness? She couldn't distinguish the two. Both feelings were not allowed.

"Oh, for heaven's sake!" Her mama snatched the tissues out of her purse that she normally used to blot her lipstick. "Wipe your face. Stop crying. We don't have time for this, Elsa."

Elsa wiped. She blew. The clog of tears stopped her from opening her mouth. The words she'd wanted to speak refused to form, for her own good. Because what she was feeling and thinking was farfetched and wholly unthinkable. *I'm keeping this baby. I'll never have another chance. You see . . . you see who I am and I know you see me, Mama. You made me wear a dress to that party. You said it was time folks realized I was a young woman. I am so ashamed, because I was actually flattered when Connor wanted to be alone with me. I thought for once you'd be proud to have me for a daughter. And then he pushed me down, pulled and scratched at that ridiculous dress, and poked himself inside of me like it was the easiest thing in the world to tear into me. That wasn't my choice. But this is. I will be a mother. This is my choice.*

Elsa shuddered and swallowed each and every word not spoken, and then she laughed. How would she even take care of a baby?

"What is wrong with you? There is not a damn thing funny."

Elsa tried to stop but the hiccuped gulps of air turned seizure-like.

"Stop it right now. I swear, Elsa . . . if you don't get it together . . ."

Elsa rolled down her window and pushed her face into the wind, instantly calming. It had always worked when she was younger. She'd only remembered right then how soothing it felt to have the dry wind lapping at her lashes and whipping her hair against her back. Her mama did the same, rolled down her window and tossed her cigarette into the moving wind.

The drive back to their house continued the long event. "Strong women and weak women. You know what the difference is between them? Choices," her mama announced. "I've been trying to teach you this simple fact all of your life. Having choices is the difference between just about everything: rich or poor, strong or weak. You have a choice here, do you understand? I'm letting you decide. If you don't marry Niles, then the baby must go."

Elsa dried her tears and thought about saying that the most important of all the facts had been overlooked. There was a real live little human growing inside *her* body. She'd made her choice. *Isn't that what strong women do?*

It was absolutely her decision. Her mama's old tricks of trying to box her in a corner would not work this time.

32

CHARLENE MET MATTY AGAIN AT THE MOTEL, even after she swore to herself she wouldn't. He was a married man. This wasn't the same as when they were teenage lovers sneaking around behind his parents' back. This was different. He truly belonged to someone else.

But nothing had changed. When Matty called, she went running. Now, though, it was under the guise of discussing Bailey and Elsa. Had she told her niece what the deal was? He wanted an update. Then, he made an offer to give her another installment. "Meet me. I have another envelope for you. Something to sweeten the pot."

She'd rolled her eyes on the phone, knowing it was just an excuse to get her there, back at the 98th Street Motel.

"I'm sorry to put you in this position, Char. The last thing I want to do is make a stink about this, but it's important to my—"

"Your wife," Charlene had finished for him while straightening his tie in the open doorway. The sun was still a yellow ball against the blue sky where Matty stood. He still looked like a dream, a movie poster at the Renway Theater—just a little bit older. "Don't worry, I'm a big girl. You're a big boy. You have a wife, a family. Good for you," she'd told him. She kept her chin up with pride. "Goodbye, Matty." She gave him a safe pat. *Goodbye.* She'd meant it.

Charlene had no plan to mention the payoff, or, kindly put, the incentive. It wasn't like Bailey to be swayed by such a crass proposition anyway. For the past few days, she'd been tiptoeing around her niece, unsure of how to say what needed to be said without showing her the money. The payoff might have been interpreted as a threat anyhow. *Do this or else.* She couldn't very well explain that she knew Matthias Grimes in another lifetime, that he didn't mean it that way. *Her* Matty had always been thoughtful and generous. Threatening? No. The money was a gesture of goodwill, nothing more. She planned to keep it safe, the envelope tucked safely under her mattress. Even with the urge to bet some of it at the track, she kept the voice in her head at bay. *This money is for Bailey.*

Charlene figured out a way to give it to her by saying she won it at the track. There was only the small price of telling Bailey, making her really listen this time. She needed to know that Elsa was bad news.

This was the conclusion Charlene had come to. If Elsa's parents were this worried about her every move, that meant she was up to no good. She practiced in her head . . . nothing good was going to come out of their so-called friendship. Whatever Elsa was up to, Bailey was more than likely going to take the blame. That's just the way it worked.

Charlene straightened her shoulders and took a deep breath before swinging around the corner to Bailey's room. She stopped suddenly to see Bailey bopping around to the transistor radio.

"Well, you're in some kind of a mood," Charlene said, plopping onto her bed. She'd been so immersed in memories and floating around in a dreamlike state, reliving her time with Matty, that she hadn't been paying attention to the status of her niece. When had this light, happy person descended into Bailey's body?

"I have a date," Bailey said, gliding an iron over a white blouse while dipping her knees with a shake of her hips.

"A date? With a man?"

"Yes. Is that so hard to believe?" She held up the blouse for inspection.

"Ah, yeah," Charlene answered with newfound interest. There hadn't been a man in Bailey's life since that Emory boy a few years back, the one who'd left her without an appetite for food or anything else.

"His name is Walter. People call him Wag. He's the one responsible for fixing the front door—the lock, if you hadn't noticed. He's also going to fix up the floor. We're sinking, also if you hadn't noticed."

"My, my, you've got a good thing going, I see."

"It's not like that. I'm paying him for the work."

"Well, you shouldn't be," Charlene replied with a smirk. "Not if you two are dating."

"It's one date. And I will be paying him for the work out of respect."

"I guess he's not charging you too much then."

"I really haven't asked. He fixed the door for a bowl of stew and cornbread. There's a drive-in theater in Mendol. Did you know about it? I had no idea. I've never been to a drive-in," she said, with an infectious smile. Bailey's dimples were showing.

Charlene kind of liked this side of her niece. Ready to crack out of her shell and step into an adventure or two. Something lightened in her heart right then. Now didn't feel like the right time to bring up Elsa or dire warnings. Or Matty. "A drive-in and a white blouse do not mix," she said, coming to Bailey's aid. She went to Bailey's closet. "Wear something dark so when you drip hot dog ketchup all over yourself, no one can see it."

Bailey's eyes widened. "Auntie, you're right, and I don't say that often enough. You said I was predictable and afraid. I can't tell you what a relief I feel, living outside of myself. I don't want to be that girl, that woman, anymore. I want to see beyond the little fort I've built." She approached Charlene, ignoring the dark sweater in her hand, and wrapped her arms forward in an unexpected hug.

"Wait," Charlene said, and tried to pull back. Bailey's grip held her firmly, followed by a flinch. A *jolt* might be a better way to describe it.

Bailey leaned away unsteadily. "*Umm,*" she said and repeated, "*Umm . . .*"

"Are you okay?" Charlene asked.

"Light-headed is all. Yeah, I'm fine," she answered, but it was obvious she'd had one of her episodes. Charlene felt a semblance of the vibration between them.

"What'd you see?" she asked, nervous. "Bailey?"

"What? Nothing. It was just light, Auntie. Bright gold." Bailey squeezed her hand. "I better finish getting dressed."

Charlene remained standing, but wobbly, as if it were she who had the power of sight. As if she'd just witnessed the inner workings of someone's heart and entangled thoughts. She marched to her room, then pressed her back to the closed door to catch her breath. She squeezed her eyes shut. "No, please, no." She hoped Bailey wouldn't see what her heart wanted. What she was lacking and, fiercely desperate with hope, needing.

She'd had plenty of time to tell Bailey about the most monumental event of her life. But she never had. How would she explain now, after all these years? If she hadn't been so ashamed of what she'd done, she could have let the story fall from her lips. *I was so young and in love.*

A baby wasn't going to fit into her life, her unmade teenage life.

There'd be no trust left between Charlene and her niece if Bailey found out now, by herself. Charlene would have to tell her before she asked, or their relationship would never recover.

33

INGRID CIRCLED, WEARING DOWN THE RUG where she'd paced into the late hours of the night. She hadn't bothered to lie down. There was no hope of sleep. The clock on the nightstand read twelve minutes past midnight. Matthias still hadn't come home.

She'd called his office throughout the day, at least five times. Once her frenzy had taken over, she lost count. His secretary, the tidy Mrs. Kenner, with her nasal tone, kept saying he was in a meeting until she had stopped answering the phone altogether. Once the clock struck six, Mrs. Kenner had surely left the building.

Matthias had a chippy on the side. Ingrid had no evidence of this. She'd suspected him of infidelity many times, suspected without proof. There was no way she could be sure of anything. He always had a ready excuse and denied everything with the same calm, logical approach he had to all of his situations. *Their* situations. And it didn't help that she was by nature suspicious. Her ability to conjure up situations was unmatched. Ingrid knew she actually had no idea what Matthias did with his time or if he had ever slept with another woman.

She heard the footsteps coming and faced the bedroom door, waiting to pounce.

"Where have you been?" she blurted. "You didn't take one of my calls. Not a single one." She stepped over and clicked the standing lamp on, a reading light, but enough to get a better look at him. She could clearly see how he'd left the house that morning was a far reach from the way he returned. His open-collared shirt was missing his tie. His hair had clearly met with water at some time of the day, the only way to remove the holding spray that kept his wild curls in place. She bet that if she stepped closer she'd smell the cheap motel shampoo.

"You scared me," he said. "What're you doing up?"

Ingrid flipped a hand. She didn't have the energy for however he planned to turn this on her. "I can't have *this* right now. I can't have you embarrassing me right before the wedding. If it's someone who will be looking me in the eye and laughing in my face, please refrain from seeing her again. Or at the very least, make sure she is not at the party or the ceremony," she ground out, nearly in tears.

"What's got you so riled up?" He came toward her, ready to console and silence her all at once. "Babe, I'm sorry I didn't call."

She took a step back, then two. "I don't want to hear it."

"I went to the club with Layton. We golfed all day, blowing off steam. Didn't even finish the back nine. I took a shower before going back to the office. We stayed, hashing some things out, having a few drinks," he said mildly, refusing to match her mood. "You know there's a lot going on. If you don't believe me, call Vera tomorrow. She'll tell you Layton came home the same time as me. That is, if he went straight home." He sat down and began to pull off his shoes, then his socks. He massaged his pinkish toes. "I've got to get me some new golf shoes. Layton took me apart out there."

"You have no idea what I've gone through today."

"I'm sorry I didn't call," he repeated. He stood. "Is there anything I can do to help with the wedding planning?"

The patronizing tone felt like a hard slap to the face. She even placed a hand there, as if it had actually happened. *How dare you?* she thought. She stared, hot with anger, at him. Mr. Good-Looking. Mr. Perfect.

He didn't care about one thing happening under their roof. About her or Elsa. Senate Oil was all he cared about. His dear company and the plummeting price of each precious barrel of crude oil. His bottom line, revenue, profits, being the king—that was all he needed. She had to confess, being the queen was all she had cared about as well. For a long time, money was the elixir that could fix anything. It took a mighty fall to learn that there were far more important things at stake. No amount of riches could fix a reputation. Ingrid cared about what people thought of her, of her family. She'd always pranced around like a show pony, head up, pretending to ignore the things said about them, about Elsa, but she'd felt each and every arrow that was shot their way.

Did he not feel any of it? The talk, the disdain? Early on in their courtship, Ingrid had heard the most appalling, rude story, something from his past. He'd run off with a teenage girl when he was a boy, she was told. He was twenty or so, far before Ingrid's time.

"She was a Negro, barely of legal age. She used to clean his family's house. I guess she offered other services as well," Deanna Diplo had told her, with a sneering grin.

Ingrid had no choice but to sit and listen, determined to shrug it off.

"He and the girl ran off against his parents' wishes. No one knew where he'd gone for close to a year. Guess you better make sure your help is of a certain age. Wouldn't want him to revisit his old urges."

Ingrid never brought it up to Matthias. She didn't want to embarrass him by discussing his past. All people had one; some were more recent than others.

"Elsa is pregnant," she announced, feeling a tinge of satisfaction. Hardly reasonable, but that's what she felt: satisfied to have hefted the bag of doom onto her husband's shoulders for a change. Satisfied that it wasn't only her problem anymore.

"All right," he said, still too calm for her taste. "You were pregnant when we got married, as I recall."

"Pregnant with Connor Salley's baby."

This got his attention. His eyes darkened with intensity. "Connor?"

"He forced himself on her. Violently. She's about three months pregnant. We visited the doctor today." Annoyed by his silence, she repeated, "He forced himself on her. Connor Salley attacked our daughter."

"This doesn't sound like something Connor would do," he finally said. "Elsa told you? She said he attacked her?"

"Yes. She told me everything. I felt the same way, in disbelief. Connor was always well-mannered. When Elsa told me, I was shocked. Turns out this has been the reason Elsa's come undone these past few weeks. All this time I blamed that woman, the seamstress, for making Elsa act this way. I had her fired."

"You did *what*?"

"It doesn't matter. I'm sure she had some kind of negative effect on Elsa. Besides, you gave her the money, didn't you? I'm sure it's enough to hold her over until she finds another job."

"You had her fired?" he repeated.

"Well, I confronted her and she was rather rude. I insisted. I'm not sure if . . . when . . . well, yes. Why is this the thing you're concerned about? What do you care? Our daughter is pregnant, and I'm absolutely sure she's thinking about keeping the baby and not going through with the wedding. I can't even fathom what goes on in that girl's head. Can you just focus on what I'm telling you?"

"What now? What is it you want me to do about Connor?" he asked, deflated. "What can we do? What would it do to Elsa if everyone in town knew that happened? If the police actually arrested Connor and put him on trial for rape?" He shook his head. "She's fragile enough as it is."

With that, somehow, the burden had fallen back on her: the how, the what, the when of all the decisions when it came to Elsa. She didn't bother telling him about the ultimatum she'd given their daughter. He wouldn't take it well. He didn't have the stomach for the hard decisions like she did.

34

NOW THAT ELSA KNEW without a doubt she was pregnant, her mind worked tirelessly around the clock, imagining what her baby would be like. Sharp brown eyes like her mama's. Fair skin like hers. There were Connor's traits to consider. Tall, brooding, and tannish. He was good-looking, she admitted to herself, even if she hated him.

In her daydreams, Elsa saw herself and Rochelle together in a cute little cottage in a shady grove not too far away from Oda Mae, who visited often, giving them advice and lessons on pinning diapers, bottle preparation, and tying hair ribbons. Ribbons? A girl. Was her baby going to be a girl?

"Elsa, you up?"

The voice calling her was real. Not a dream. Her eyes rose to the white ceiling of her room in this house built by her parents, where her dreams or future plans were not allowed.

"Yes," she called out. "I'm up. Come in."

Oda Mae entered, carrying a silver wardrobe bag with *Regal Gown* written across the front. "Your dress was delivered this morning. There's a note attached." She hung the bag on the back of her door and unzipped it. "Let's take a peek."

"No," Elsa said quickly. "I don't want to see it right now. Please. If you don't mind."

"All right." Oda Mae raised an eyebrow. "Here's the note. You feeling all right, darling?"

"I didn't sleep well." Elsa took the small white envelope with her name written on the front. She'd hoped it was a note from Bailey, but could already tell it was a standard-issue card from the Regal Gown.

Best wishes on your wedding day. It has been a pleasure to serve you.
Thea Jackson

Elsa shoved herself back under the covers. She had no desire to leave her bed, let alone her room. Then came the knock, followed by the soft voice. "Hey, there, can I come in?"

Elsa's breath caught in her throat. The gulf of space between her and the door grew to an unbearable distance. She jumped out of bed and ran to the door. "Hi," she said.

"Hi. You're still in your pajamas," Rochelle said, smiling.

She wore the necklace. Elsa's heart skipped an elated beat. The gold heart peeked out just above the blue collar of Rochelle's starched and pressed work smock. She took Rochelle by the hand and pulled her inside. "If you hadn't showed up I would've stayed in bed all day."

"I wasn't going to get away with not coming to work for three days in a row, now. You know my mama. And most assuredly you know yours." When the door closed, Rochelle looked up to see the oversize garment bag. "Gosh, can I see it?"

Elsa ignored her curiosity. The last thing she wanted to talk about was anything to do with her wedding. The dress might as well have been a bag of smelly old rags.

"Does it have one of those long trains like Princess Elizabeth?" Rochelle continued. "Well, she's a queen now. But remember when we watched the royal wedding? My mama let us stay up all night to watch the highlights. We both said we'd have dresses like that one day when we got married and was grown."

At the thought of putting on the wedding gown, a heat rash ran up Elsa's neck. The sudden urge to throw up felt like a response all its own. Rochelle stood, transfixed by the dress, too busy to notice Elsa had rushed to the bathroom, halting over the toilet.

What felt like forever was only a few minutes before Elsa came back, teeth brushed and mouth fresh with minty green mouthwash. The dress was released from captivity, a white cloud that burst into her pink bedroom. Rochelle's hands fluffed the many layers of white satin and shimmering tulle.

"What're you doing?"

"Making sure it don't wrinkle. It needs to breathe," she said, standing back to admire her handiwork.

"Put it back in the bag!"

"But . . ."

"Put it back," Elsa snapped, taking a handful by the hem, then an armful, to shove into the hanging bag.

"I'll do it. All right? Take it easy," Rochelle said, taking the dress and spreading it over the bed. She lined up the hanger with the open bag and carefully began rolling the train.

Elsa took a deep breath. "I'm sorry. I haven't been feeling well. Maybe I got your flu," she said, knowing the statement made no sense because Rochelle never was really sick. She'd only stayed away because of Ingrid's grilling her about the necklace.

"I should let you get your rest then." Rochelle finished and hung the wardrobe bag on the hook. "You want me to get you anything— water, tea?" she asked with her hand on the doorknob, anxious to leave.

Elsa swallowed the horrible pit of heat forming in her chest. "I'm not sick. I'm feeling just fine." She'd meant it jokingly. Something to lighten the air in the room. A way to apologize without looking completely pathetic.

"I'll leave you to rest," Rochelle said anyway.

As soon as the door closed Elsa dived onto her bed, pushing the pillow against her face to muffle her scream. How many screams did it take to feel better? A few more inhales, shoving the cotton of the pillow into her mouth and pushing her disappointment to the surface.

She sat up, strong, revived. If there was something worth having, you had to fight for it. Work for it.

What that would take, she didn't know. She had loved Rochelle since that night when they were thirteen. Funny how Rochelle had brought up the royal wedding. It was all anyone had talked about. The wedding had happened days earlier, but it was finally scheduled to be aired on American television. Elsa and Rochelle planned to eat popcorn and drink pop in their pj's. Oda Mae said they could stay up as long as they were quiet. She had clicked off the light, leaving the glow of the television on their faces. They watched the dramatic wedding from beginning to end. When it was over, they turned to each other, enamored by the love in the atmosphere, and said their own version of vows. "Do you take me as your wife to love and cherish?" Elsa asked.

"I will, and do you take me as your wife to love, care for, and make me laugh, always?"

"I will. I do," Elsa said, leaning in close to Rochelle, eyes closed. It happened so naturally and perfectly, the kiss perfect, as if they'd both known what they were doing. As if they had practiced all their short lives for that one kiss.

"Can we do it again?" Elsa asked huskily when they came up for air, not wanting the moment to ever end.

"Okay," Rochelle had said. Simply *okay,* though her face was flushed, her copper cheeks glowing.

It was more than their lips on the second kiss, exploring each other's body with soft, sweeping palms. They took in each other's warm breaths, only to begin again. It was the sound of a door shutting that drove them apart. With their hearts fluttering, they went back to eating popcorn with dry throats and racing minds. Elsa had never stopped reliving the moment. It seemed to her that Rochelle felt the same, but there was always something holding her back. There were plenty of times when their hands grazed and shoulders pressed each other's as they sat together, but Elsa could never recapture that moment.

35

THEY'D SEEN MOST OF THE VAMPIRE FILM. Halfway through, Walter had leaned over and stroked Bailey's face with a smooth hand before guiding her lips to his. She couldn't remember a single thing about the movie after that point. Bailey had asked Walter if he'd like to come inside after returning from the drive-in.

Her auntie wasn't home. The house was pitch-dark. She noticed the Olds was gone from the street. Normally, seeing that empty space where the car was supposed to be parked would have sent her heart reeling. It signified her auntie's mysterious night jaunts, her disappearing without notice.

Not this time. She'd almost been happy about it. That's when she invited Walter to come in. She had wanted to leave the drive-in right after intermission. She wanted to kiss him some more, but somewhere comfortable. The hard seats in his truck had springs poking her in just about every part of her back and thighs. But she didn't know what he'd make of her if she wanted to leave early. Saying she was being jabbed by steel springs might have been insulting.

It wasn't so bad waiting for the end. She concentrated on his soft lips and gentle touch. His arms were strong and firm. The way he held her made her want to curl up and stay awhile, even with the bad truck seats.

"If you don't have an early morning, maybe you'd like to come inside for some tea and cookies. And no, they're not homemade. Women have other things to do besides bake," she said when they reached her house. She didn't know what propelled those words out of her mouth.

Thankfully, she hadn't scared him away. He shifted the truck to park and switched off the engine, then lifted his hands in defense. "I didn't say a word. I wouldn't care if the cookies were made out of dirt, long as I got to spend more time with you."

He hopped out of the driver's side and trotted over to open her door. They walked the dark, narrow pathway to the back of the house, holding hands, with Walter leading the way.

Once inside, she had every intention of putting on the hot water at the stove, setting out the cups and tea bags. Every intention of sitting on the living room couch and talking, getting to know each other. That's what she firmly believed, even after they'd landed in her bedroom, his fingers feverishly pulling at her buttons. Hers, pushing his T-shirt over his head. She believed there'd be tea afterward. But until then, she passionately welcomed him against her skin. He seemed to have known or had hopes of where the evening would go. He'd brought protection and stopped all at once to ask, "Is it okay? Are you okay?"

"I'm okay," she said, grateful and yet impatient to have him back in her arms, close. She gripped his back and thrust her body against his, and before she knew it, she was the one rocking past mid-tempo. She wanted every part of him and made sure he knew it.

They lay in a heap of themselves afterward. Bailey wasn't sure which one of them started laughing first, but it hadn't mattered once they were both in spasms, neither knowing what was so funny. He rolled over and pulled her to lie on his chest. There, she listened to his strong heartbeat. When he spoke, his voice was deep and poetic in her ear. She told him the brief version of her history. Her mama's passing had hit her hard, and she still hadn't gotten over it. He told her of his parents, who were still alive but had moved to Wichita with his four sisters. He hadn't seen them since before he'd been shipped to Sicily in 1943 for the war. He anticipated her next question—why hadn't he gone to visit?—and added that he and his father were on rocky terms and he never thought he'd be welcome.

"I guess you won't know until you try," she told him. "Family's all we've got."

"I've got you now," he said in response, with a kiss.

Later, in the middle of the night, a bold, blinding flash in rolling colors came rushing toward her. She expected to see herself and Walter, because, well, they'd shared a moment, hadn't they?

But what she saw was wholly unfathomable. Unbelievable. The image of Aunt Charlene, her sweaty forehead squeezed in pain, bearing down, teeth grinding on a rag, in the undeniable act of giving birth. The picture jumped to a baby, ripe and fully happy, in another woman's arms. Not her auntie's arms. No. These arms were lean and corn-colored. This lighter-skinned woman had taken hold of the softly wrapped baby and had not let go. The ache seared through Bailey the same way it must have cut through her auntie.

The pain was so great, Bailey welcomed it, especially if it pulled her out of the dream. She covered her face, touching, feeling, to make sure she was actually awake. She shivered with cold. This wasn't a dream. It was a vision.

Walter was there by her side. She curled herself under him, burrowing to get his heat. She couldn't believe what she'd seen. How could it be true? Aunt Charlene had never once told Bailey a single thing about giving birth. Some things were private, yes. Everyone wasn't in the business of baring their soul. But this . . . this was an enormous, life-changing event. How did one go about omitting it from their memory, from their being?

Bailey hunched closer, as if it were even possible to get closer. Walter stirred slightly but didn't wake up. The cold wouldn't go away. She was chilled head to toe, her body experiencing shock as if she herself had given birth. As if she'd felt the pain, the joy, and the loss all at once.

Sheer exhaustion must have forced her to fall asleep. Her eyes stung a bit as the morning sunlight brightened the room. Walter was there by her side, sleeping soundly. Embarrassment washed over her. At first, anyway. Then she shifted and a silly grin pushed upward, turning into a full smile. She was grateful for him as well. In fact, downright giddy, really. *Salutations and good morning.*

Aunt Charlene would be—proud. *Oh, Auntie,* she wavered, remembering her dream. Her eyes darted across the room. Her bedroom door was closed, locked, to keep her auntie out. She'd made sure, not wanting any surprise intrusions. But now . . .

Now she needed to find her. Talk to her about what she saw and experienced. *A baby.*

She touched Walter's cool, bare shoulder, leaned in, and kissed the lobe of his ear. When he didn't stir, she moved carefully so as not to wake him. She pushed her arms through her housecoat sleeves and bunched it closed. The fall dawn chilled the house. The floor creaked unreasonably loudly, and she stopped in her bare feet. She listened for any sign of her auntie being on the other side of her bedroom door. What she heard was the stirring of restless birds; a car idling to warm the engine before driving; and children, the Williams twins, having a conversation as they walked by.

She continued out, down the hall. Aunt Charlene's door was closed, also locked, something she'd been doing lately. All this time there had been secrets. Bailey rested her forehead against the door for only a minute, then went to look out the window. There was the Olds, parked on the street right behind the Wag's Handy Services truck.

Aunt Charlene was home. Bailey just had to figure out how to broach the subject. She'd make her some coffee, tap on the door, and say . . . *Oh, hey there, Auntie, how about that baby you had when you were younger?* Somewhere there was a child, an adult by now, who was Bailey's cousin, who she had never met.

Knowing this truth felt as intrusive as the heartstrings she saw in the town ladies' readings. Even when they'd asked, requested to be told what her sight held, it felt invasive. Seeing their dirty little secrets. Even when there was love and passion, like in the case of Alice Ledge . . . Well, look how that turned out.

As a matter of fact, she couldn't think of a single incident where she had made someone's life better, enriched them, by learning what she had seen.

If Aunt Charlene wanted Bailey to know about her past, she'd have told her by now. It was none of her business. Painful as it might be, she would stay silent. Bailey decided in that very moment that she wouldn't speak of it. Not ever.

Tonight, at Elsa's party, will be the last time I butt into anybody's business, invited or not, she resolved.

Elsa's party was her final curtain call on the show of other people's lives. She marched to her bedroom and closed the door just as Walter was peeking up from the pillows. "Good morning," he said.

"Hi," she said, tempted to climb back into bed with him. Wouldn't it be nice if she could just forget about everything, other folks' problems, and even her own, and just cuddle the day away? Instead, she went over and gave him a peck and ran a soothing hand over his thick hair. "I have to go to work."

She sent him on his way. There had been no choice in the matter. Bailey didn't dare miss another day of work. Miss Jackson had warned her. Bailey and Walter went their separate ways, and by afternoon, with the Regal Gown abuzz, she had almost forgotten about the best evening she'd ever had—the drive-in and what happened afterward.

The ladies came, one after the other, to pick up their completed evening gowns for the Grimes engagement party, the party Bailey herself was to attend. She tried not to think about it.

She went about her day, head down, determined to believe everything would turn out all right.

36

BY THE TIME CHARLENE FINALLY DECIDED how she was going to broach the subject of what she knew Bailey must have seen, the day had come and gone. It was evening when Charlene stopped at her open door. "Going somewhere? Another date, perhaps?"

"A party."

"I need to talk to you," Charlene said, then paused. "What party?"

"Elsa's dinner party. Maybe we can talk tomorrow," Bailey said, her eyes darting away from Charlene's face.

Charlene felt the none-too-subtle disdain. This was what she'd been waiting for. Exactly what she'd expected. She had wondered when it would happen, when Bailey would finally learn her unforgivable secret. But that conversation would have to wait. Her groveling and apologies would have to get in line, far behind what needed to be said right now. She had to talk some sense into her niece mighty quick.

"Listen, this isn't a good idea," Charlene said, realizing this urgency had nothing to do with Matty's proposition. This was Charlene wanting her niece not to do something utterly wrong and dangerous. "Turn around and look at me. I'm not asking for much of your time. I just need a minute," she nearly shouted. "Please."

"The girl needs my help, Auntie. I'm trying to do the honorable thing. She gave me money that I've already spent, or have plans on spending. I won't be gone long," she said, keeping her back to Charlene while sifting through her closet. "Besides, weren't you the one who said I needed to live a little?"

"Yes. Well, you've certainly done that. You got yourself a new beau," Charlene said. "Don't ruin it before you even get going."

Bailey's back flinched; she was annoyed. Now, maybe, Charlene had gotten her attention. But no, she continued thumbing through the crowded hangers in the small closet, assessing what she was going to wear to the Grimes family's home for a dinner party. Just one more thing that had gotten past Charlene because she'd been immersed in her mistakes, past and present, foolishness either way. She had been too busy with regrets to see life happening before her eyes.

"Bailey," she said but couldn't find the words fast enough.

"This one should do," Bailey said, slipping a lilac dress off a hanger and quickly stepping into it. "You mind zipping me?"

Reluctantly, Charlene obliged. "These people will eat you up and spit you out, honey," she managed to say. "You, going there, talking about your ability to see what can't be seen, is dangerous. Why don't you go ahead and show up with a black witch hat and broom?" She chuckled. *Humor. Yes.* She kept going. "'Cause that's exactly how you'll be treated. Like a witch in Salem. Pitchforks and torches will be at your door. And what about the fact that Elsa is already spoken for, to another man? You don't want to get in the middle of none of that," she said, as nervous fingers fumbled with the set of hooks and eyes above the zipper.

The dress was perfect on Bailey. Charlene remembered the day Bailey had brought the pricey woven silk home, leftover fabric from a client, Mrs. Henley. Miss Jackson thought the shade of purple was gaudy, Bailey had told Charlene, and told her to discard the leftover cloth. The dress was born after only a few nights in Bailey's sewing nook in the basement.

"Thank you," Bailey said, touching the dress's high neck, still refusing to look at Charlene.

"What if she's there—Mrs. Henley—at the party?" Charlene offered, ecstatic to have thought of another angle. "What if she sees her same dress fabric on your back? Or Miss Jackson?" Charlene said. "Does your boss know you were invited? I can't imagine she'd be happy about you being there. What then? That won't be good."

"Miss Jackson won't do anything to embarrass herself. She might even pretend not to know me at all. But you're right about Miss Henley. She'll know this was the same fabric as her dress," Bailey said. "Unzip me."

Again, Charlene did what she was told, realizing she was getting nowhere.

Bailey slipped the dress back on the hanger and went with her next choice, a strapless shimmering gray cocktail number. "This one." Bailey said confidently. She had bought the fabric herself when it was discounted by the wholesaler.

Charlene remembered this dress as well, the day Bailey showed her a model in the pages of *Harper's* and said, "I'm going to make one just like it." Charlene had responded, "Make your own. You're talented enough. You don't need to copy anyone's designs, ever."

"This one works. Zip me," Bailey said.

As ordered, Charlene zipped her up. This absolutely was not what she meant when she'd challenged Bailey's predictability. This sudden new spontaneity and hopeful outlook could all be traced back to Elsa Grimes. Funny how everything came full circle in unexpected ways. Charlene remembered how no one could talk her out of leaving with Matty all those years ago. Not her mama, grandmama, and certainly not Sammie.

Bailey turned around and whatever else she'd planned to say fell by the wayside. Charlene felt the tears spring up and wiped furiously at her cheeks.

"Oh, sweetie." She took in the full length of the gorgeous young woman standing before her. What now? This time, Charlene couldn't help but say it out loud. "You're stunning. Wait. Wait right here." Charlene rushed off. She bolted to her closet, all the while whispering to herself, "You tried. There's nothing you can do. You tried."

She came back with a pair of black patent leather pumps. She knelt to help Bailey step into them.

"I'm not sure if I can walk in these, Auntie."

"Of course you can. Try them. Walk. Give me a twirl."

Bailey turned effortlessly. "These are nice," she admitted. "They fit perfectly. Thank you, Auntie."

"Good. Good," Charlene said, unsure who had taken over her mind and body. This was not what she was supposed to be doing— encouraging her niece to walk out that door, helping her make a huge mistake. This was the polar opposite, in fact. "Hold on. One more thing." Charlene rushed to her room again. She knew exactly where her best stuff was buried, even if she hadn't worn or used a single piece since moving back to Mendol.

"Use this," she said, handing Bailey a black rhinestone clutch.

"Oh my, Auntie! This is perfect." Bailey dumped her handbag onto the bed. A bevy of items came tumbling out. Lip balm, perfume, a wallet, tissue packets, and an enormous ring of keys.

"All of that won't fit. You have to pick a couple of things you really need. Probably the lip balm and tissues. You're not driving or going to work, so you don't need the keys. Instead of the whole wallet, take a few emergency coins and perfume . . . you won't need the rest." Charlene put the lip balm and tissues in the clutch then handed it back to Bailey. "Now. Perfection."

"Be polite and keep a close distance to your friend," she heard herself say. "Know your place, Bailey. All right? Don't forget for a second who you are. Promise you'll be careful. Keep your head on. Don't get too comfortable, you understand?"

"I do." Bailey nodded. "No one will know I'm in the room."

"I think with you wearing that dress, everyone's going to know you're in the room. Be careful." *It can't be said enough. Be careful.*

Bailey reached out for a hug. "I'll be fine, Auntie. Please don't worry. I should go wait by the door. The car will be here soon."

The sound of an automobile engine idling outside broke the silence between them. Bailey turned and walked gracefully toward the living room. *She's leaving.* "Wait. Wait a minute." Charlene couldn't help the hiccup in her chest, seeing her niece about to walk out the door. "I promise we will talk and I will tell you everything, Bailey. I know you have questions . . ."

"Auntie, you don't owe me your secrets." Bailey kissed her on the cheek and left, taking careful steps to the wide black car waiting at the curb. And just like that, Bailey was whisked away and Charlene had nothing left to do but pray. *Just this once,* she thought. She'd ask for this one thing, for Bailey to be kept safe.

She closed her eyes, having the recollection of Matty's voice in her ear, *"No one will know who we are and we can be together,"* recalling a time when she'd crossed the line like Bailey was doing now and had entered into a world not hers. It was a lifetime ago, back when she had briefly believed life was an equal playing field, but learned quickly the game only worked if everyone played fair. And since when did that ever happen? No one could have stopped Charlene then, just like she couldn't stop Bailey from walking out the door now.

She could only share what she knew to be true. When Bailey returned, Charlene resolved that she would tell her everything. She wouldn't leave anything out. Then her niece could decide for herself where she wanted to be and with whom and why it always mattered.

37

BAILEY SAT IN THE BACK of the chauffeured car as it pulled alongside many other shiny vehicles stacked in the roundabout.

"We're here," the driver announced. On the drive over, he'd introduced himself as Alston. She'd seen him around Eastside, but they had never met. He talked about how long he'd worked for the Grimes family. Eleven years, he'd said, and Bailey whistled and shook her head, unable to imagine working in one place that long. Her second whistle was at the sight of the mansion, a massive house that looked like it had swallowed five or six smaller houses.

"I'm supposed to take you back whenever you ready to go. All you got to do is have the valet toot his whistle three times. That'll be our signal," Alston said, peeking at her in the rearview mirror. "Just say, 'Three whistles.' They'll know."

The car door swung open by the hand of a darker-skinned man wearing a penguin style tuxedo. He appeared stunned to see Bailey in the back seat but recovered nicely. "Ma'am," he said, offering assistance with a gloved hand. Bailey genuinely needed his help. Her legs had gone wobbly and she hadn't even realized it.

She met his gloved hand with her own. She stood, then adjusted her fit lines, smoothing down the seams against her hips. Finally, she began her walk up the lighted path. She entered the foyer and told herself she was halfway there. *You'll do fine. Just breathe and smile. Breathe and smile.*

There was nothing fun about walking into a room full of folks she didn't know. She knew what her aunt Charlene had gently tried to say. The rich white folks of Mendol wouldn't be too thrilled to see her there, sitting at the same table, drinking from their glasses, and eating one elbow-space away. She knew they'd wonder what she was doing there, yet she talked herself out of turning and running back to the car, which hadn't gone far. Alston had said he was just three whistle toots away.

The minute she walked in, she felt the vibration of a man's voice blaring through a speaker. "You know what they say—Gawd ain't making no new land or oil. That's why this union is a blessing. A toast to my son, Niles, and his future bride, Elsa, for keeping it all in the family."

Bailey waited, nervous, with only a sliver of a view inside the ballroom. A full house, she could tell from the sounds of chatter and murmuring voices echoing off the high walls.

Was she late? The last thing she wanted was to be the center of attention. "Excuse me, hello," she said to the regal-nosed man dressed like the others in a staff tuxedo with tails. His mustache hung straight, like broom bristles. He looked up from his podium but said nothing; then he turned his head in the other direction.

Leave. Go home. This ain't your place. Bailey took a step back. The presence of new guests lining up behind her kept her from making an easy getaway.

"The party's started. You see, Mother? All that fussing over one speck of lint and we're late."

Bailey turned to see two ladies talking behind her. Their escort peeled off his coat, then theirs. The younger lady smiled. Bailey smiled back and quickly resumed her position of waiting and being ignored.

"Excuse me," the young lady said from over Bailey's shoulder. "Hello," she said to the man acting as maître d'. "We'd like to be seated."

"Good evening, miss. May I ask your name?"

"We're the Holden party. George and Mary Holden and my mother, Gretchen. And this lady is waiting as well. Tell him your name."

"I'm Bailey Dowery. I'm a guest of Miss Elsa Grimes. I'm her couturier," Bailey announced, just as she'd rehearsed.

"The Holden party of three and party of one, Bailey Dowery," the man announced to a woman standing off to the side, looking stern and dark in a long black skirt.

"Yes. I have the Holdens at table three. I don't show anyone on the list as Bailey Dowery," she said in her best posh voice.

"I . . . I'm supposed to sit with Miss Elsa Grimes," Bailey said, hearing the plea in her voice and decidedly disappointed in herself. "Can you check again? I'm her guest. I'm her attendant, for her dress, her wedding dress."

"I'm sorry, I don't have you listed."

"But . . ." Bailey let out an exasperated sigh. She did her best to see inside the ballroom. But Elsa wasn't anywhere she could see.

Mary Holden interrupted. "She can join us at table three. We'll all sit together."

"I'm not sure there is a seat available for her," the hostess started, ready with excuses. The suddenly sharp expression on Mary Holden's face gave the woman pause. "Fine," the woman said. "Follow me."

As they entered the extravagantly decorated room, another man's voice burst through the loudspeakers, startling Bailey. "This thing on?" the booming voice asked. "I'd like to say a few words. Most of y'all know one thing for sure about me . . . not one to shed any tears, but tomorrow when I watch my baby girl walk down the aisle to become a wife, I just might spring a leak." Laughter followed.

The hostess zigzagged between tables with the party of four trailing closely behind. Guests sat in rapt attention, ignoring Bailey.

Bailey took anxious steps toward a table where four perfectly empty chairs waited. The finish line was near. And then something curious entered Bailey's mind. Coincidence or a miracle that there was room for her to sit with the Holdens? Perfectly good things never happened to Bailey. Inevitably the fourth person would come with a tap on her shoulder and protest, "Someone's in my seat." Soon she'd be escorted out, with feet sliding across the floor.

But for now no one noticed her. Four chandeliers in one room, Bailey counted, as she looked up. Warm light descended over the many decorated tables where tall flower arrangements sat exquisitely in the middle. The men and women were adorned in their finest attire. Bailey spotted more than a few familiar dresses in the crowd.

The man speaking was Elsa's father. He roused the crowd to their feet with whistles and clapping. "Come on, now, a round of applause. To my beloved Elsa. You're deserving of everything rich and wonderful in this life. And damn it, son, you better give it to her."

The guests at table three were already standing and lifting their champagne flutes, joining in with cheers, when Bailey and the others arrived. And there Elsa was, only a table away, looking forlorn and out of place, her pink cheeks darker from all the attention. Her hair was pushed up high in a shiny bun.

When everyone sat down, Bailey felt a pair of eyes upon her. Was it beginning now? *Who is the colored gal? What's she doing here? Safer to look down,* Bailey told herself. The splendid linen-covered table boasted more plates, silverware, and glasses than she owned in all her kitchen cabinets. There was shiny gold inlaid trim around the bread plate. A spoon she could see her face in. A frosty crystal goblet with ice water. As thirsty as she was, she didn't dare reach for the glass. If she drank from it and then moved tables, no one else would touch it. The concern didn't last when she saw Elsa put up a hand and then smile. That was their signal. Relief washed over Bailey. She waved back, hopeful they could begin, move quickly in their mission. Who was the person Elsa wanted her to read? She gripped the tips of her gloves and began pulling them off to free her hands.

Mary Holden leaned in. "You'll be fine," she said. Even with the show of kindness, Bailey was still cautious, questioning the woman's motivation. "So you're Elsa's guest, the dressmaker. I'm her third cousin on her mother's side. Have you two been friends long?" Mary asked, once the noise and chatter slowed.

Bailey nodded. "I met her while doing the fitting for her wedding gown. By the way, thank you for rescuing me, Mrs. Holden."

"Mary. You can call me Mary. It's a pleasure to meet you," Mary whispered. "I can't wait to see your work," she said with a hint of conspiracy in her tone.

"Oh, well, I didn't design her dress or anything. I made sure it fit well, is all."

Mrs. Holden tilted her head with a knowing raised brow. "Some of us need a good fit. Don't ever underestimate the value of your work."

Bailey didn't quite know how to take what she'd just heard. Which work would that be? Dressmaker or reader of hearts? Something about the way Mary Holden said she shouldn't underestimate the value of her work, and the admiration in her tone, told her she knew more about Bailey than she let on.

Before she could think any more about it, a hand landed on her shoulder. "Hello, Miss Bailey, my name is Rochelle. Elsa wanted me to give you this."

The microphone crackled and adjusted with a piercing whistle. "Hello. Good evening, friends. Hello. Thank you so much for coming." The woman stood, regal as a statue, holding the microphone in her bejeweled hands. Bailey recognized the green Givenchy gown with the sash waist. She had known the minute Ingrid walked into the Regal Gown that she had an ulterior motive. At least she'd actually worn the dress.

"Tonight we are here to celebrate the union of my daughter, Elsa, and her fiancé, Niles Porter." She spoke in a singsong way, each word carefully delivered. "I can't tell you how proud I am of Elsa. I'm also equally proud of Niles. I watched Niles grow up and become the stellar young man that he is today." She paused, her eyes darting sharply to a part of the room hidden from Bailey's view. "He . . ." She paused. "Niles has always been an upstanding and polite young man." It took her a moment to sway back to her starting point. "May you both be blessed with a house full of love and children."

Mary Holden whispered something to her mother, their heads huddled together. Some kind of ruckus made the women perk to attention. Bailey followed their glances to see a man in a sheriff's uniform. The gray-haired officer stood out from the formally dressed guests. His height was the first thing Bailey noticed. He was taller than most of the white-gloved servers. As he crossed the room, weaving between tables, Elsa appeared to be his target.

Her father stepped forward, blocking the tall man's way. The music stopped. The crowd froze in place. The men could be heard without difficulty in the pin-drop silence.

"What are you doing here, Gale?" Matthias Grimes asked.

"We got evidence. Elsa's gotta answer to this."

"I don't care if Jesus just came down off the cross—we're having our party and you come in here now?" Matthias blurted.

The men put their heads together, leaning close to exchange more words, but the microphone nearby picked up their exchange loud and clear.

"We'll deal with this later. We already told you, nobody knows a thing about what happened to him."

"I'm sorry, Grimes. We got to deal with this now."

"The night before her wedding? Are you serious? Get on out of here. You have no right barging into our home."

Another officer appeared and stepped toward Elsa, only to be blocked, this time by Elsa's mother. "Stay away from her. What are you doing?"

"Step aside. Elsa, on your feet. You're under arrest for the murder of Connor Salley."

"You can't do that, not without a warrant," Matthias said.

"Yeah. It's called *probable cause*. Now get out of the way or we'll take you too, Grimes. Your money's no good here, not this time," the sheriff announced.

The guests crowded closer in shock, mouths covered to silence their whispers. Bailey pushed and made her way through. Elsa stood. She put her hands out in front of her as if she'd expected this to happen. As if she'd played it in her head a thousand times.

"I'm sorry," Elsa said, loudly enough for the confused guests to hear. "I'm sorry about Connor."

ELSA TRIED HARD to take in the faces of the guests, who she knew must have been clamoring to know more. Were they in the company of a murderer? Did they truly believe she could do such a thing?

She worked hard to show some type of remorse. She wanted to feel something, anything. Seeing her mama's and daddy's faces, stunned and disappointed at the same time, should have made her miserable—at the very least, regretful. She had never felt more alone.

"I'm sorry about Connor," she whispered to no one in particular.

A man fly-fishing had found Connor's body at the edge of the Red River that morning. In a short time, word had spread. Shock reverberated around Mendol. *How? Did he fall in and drown? Drinking . . . probably fell in and hit his head. He was such a good boy.*

Elsa's mama had made her say it in the mirror until she looked appropriately sad: *"I'm so sorry for your loss, Mr. and Mrs. Salley."*

"Yes, that's fine. For heaven's sake, it's better than what we're really feeling: Good riddance! But really, do we expect the Salleys to make an appearance after hearing their son was found floating dead in a river?" Ingrid had asked of Elsa's daddy.

"Better to be prepared," he'd said.

"Do not say a single word!" her mama now said to Elsa, squeezing past the sheriff. "Not a word."

Elsa knew better than to utter anything more than what she'd rehearsed.

"Stand back, ma'am." While her father continued to try to reason with the sheriff, his deputy led Elsa away with a light grip on her shoulder.

As she moved forward, the murmurs came closer to her ear, accompanied by the guests' blurry images. Everything around her was shapes and sounds, as if she were underwater. What they were saying came slowly and sounded thick to her ears.

"Oh my Gawd!"

"This is awful!"

"Elsa killed Connor Salley?"

"I heard about that night, what he did to her. I never thought she'd do this."

Her feet kept moving, though Elsa wanted to crumple. This was not how she saw the evening going. Had Rochelle given Bailey her note? Did it happen? Did Bailey get a chance to touch Rochelle?

Strangely, those were the pressing questions her mind conjured up in the midst of the disaster. And though Elsa knew it wasn't the right thing to be thinking, she didn't care.

"Stop right here," the young deputy announced. He pulled out a set of handcuffs and placed them around her wrists.

She hadn't noticed the deputy by her side. When had he stepped in place of Sheriff Gale?

"We got stairs right here. I need you to pay attention or we'll both go down," the deputy said, gripping her arm so tightly it was painful.

Elsa snapped out of the fog. He was right. She hadn't been paying attention, just putting one foot in front of the other. "I'm fine," she told him.

"Elsa, I'm Glen MacMillan. Do you remember me? I'm your family's attorney." A slender man put himself on the other side of her. She was sandwiched between the two men now. Glen MacMillan continued to talk, getting his words out as quickly as possible. "I'll be with you at the station. Please don't speak to anyone. Don't answer any questions, do you understand?"

"Yes," she replied quietly. Elsa understood. It wouldn't be hard to honor the request, since she could never tell anyone the truth.

38

"YEAH. I'M HERE." Charlene pushed the light switch to see Bailey standing in the middle of the kitchen in her stocking feet. "Why are you standing here in the dark?"

Bailey started toward her, arms outstretched in distress.

"Oh my goodness, sweetie. What happened?" Charlene asked. "You're shaking. Tell me right now." She held Bailey at arm's length to get a good look. She took her in, head to toe. Bailey looked perfectly fine. No harm had come to her niece, at least not physically. "Talk to me, sweetie."

"Elsa was arrested at the party. The sheriff walked in there and put handcuffs on her."

"For what?"

"They said she killed somebody. It's not possible. It couldn't be."

"Who in the world would that girl kill?" Charlene guided Bailey to sit at the table. "You're shivering. Poor thing." She went to the living room and grabbed the crocheted doily off the sofa. She came back and placed it around Bailey's bare shoulders. She filled a glass with water and set it in front of her. "All right. Start from the beginning."

"Elsa was arrested. The sheriff busted in there like she was a sworn criminal and carried her off, saying she was under arrest for killing a man found in the river."

"What man? Who?" Charlene asked.

Bailey began to cry. Charlene was back on her feet, this time searching the drawer for a clean towel. She pressed it into Bailey's hands. "It's all right. It's okay. All right. Listen, she has a family with a lot of money. They're not going to let anything happen to her."

"I was there. I saw what he did to her," Bailey said through a choppy sob.

"Drink some water. Drink," Charlene told her. "You saw what . . . Bailey? What did you see?"

"I saw him attack her."

Charlene sat back against the chair, confused. She placed a hand on her chest. The last thing she wanted to hear was that Bailey was involved in any way. "You saw someone attack Elsa?"

"In my vision. It was . . . yes, an attack. At first I thought they were having their moment. Normal. Like I see . . . their bodies wrapped around each other. But this time . . . the room turned dark gray, deep, like a storm. Then I saw them fighting, wrestling. Connor raped Elsa."

"He raped her? Oh, sweetie, you saw this happen? That must've been awful."

"But I still don't believe she would kill him, or anybody." Bailey kept her eyes down while she kneaded the towel and rolled it back and forth. "I should tell someone what I saw."

"Ah, I beg your pardon? No, ma'am. No."

"I have to tell what I saw. It might help her."

Charlene leaned as close to Bailey's face as she could without pressing nose to nose. "You will *not* tell a soul. Not a word to anyone. We've gone over this. Visions. Seeing prophecies. Announcing any of that now with something this serious going on—no. They'll figure it out."

"But—"

"Bailey, it's late. Let's talk about this in the morning. All right? You need to get out of this dress and into bed." Charlene stood and pulled her niece to her feet. It was odd to have a child raised by her hand who was a full head taller now. But she was still her Bailey Bear. She wrapped an arm around her waist and escorted her down the hall.

After managing to get Bailey into bed, Charlene went to the living room. She stood over the telephone, staring, wishing she had a way to call Matty. No matter what she'd just said to Bailey about leaving the Grimes family alone to fend for themselves, she was worried. But nothing could be done tonight, so she went to bed herself and did her best to sleep.

THE ALARM CLOCK RANG. Charlene awakened before the sun rose completely. She had an early appointment to do a wash-and-set. Saturdays were her busiest day. She had four clients on the schedule.

She got up and stretched with a solid yawn. Last night had taken most of her energy, worrying about Bailey and whatnot.

She peeked in on Bailey, still sleeping. *Thank goodness.* She'd normally have been up and off to the Regal Gown an hour early, but Charlene wanted her to sleep in, get more rest. Not to mention, she wanted more time to have a good-sense word with her.

While she prepped the kitchen for her first client, she couldn't help thinking about the entire dilemma. It wasn't like she could call up the block and get the news. Folks on the other side of town kept their gossip to themselves as best they could. It didn't travel fast, but eventually the information would make it to the Eastside after a housekeeper overheard a few gems and passed them along. Charlene would just have to wait it out.

It wasn't likely that Matty would call her and want to see her under these dire circumstances, not while his daughter was being charged with murder. Charlene had surmised the girl was trouble but had no idea she was capable of doing that kind of wrong. *For goodness sake! Murder.*

The scratching sound at the back door sent Charlene scooting over in her slippers. It was still early; her first client was not due for another half hour or so. When she opened the door, she saw a man in gray overalls with his hat in his hand.

"Yes?"

"Hey there, I'm . . . um . . . the handyman, Walter," he clarified, pulling his lips back and forcing a smile.

"Walter. I'm Charlene, her aunt. It's a bit early, don't you think?"

"I'm supposed to get started on the floorboards."

"Well, my niece is still asleep and I want to keep it that way, so can you come back later?"

He squinted as if confused. "She's asleep? She usually likes to get to the gown shop early. I figured I'd get here before she left so I could be working while she was out."

"Yeah. Not today. She's getting some much-needed rest," Charlene said, slightly disturbed by all the conversation. "So come back later. A couple of hours should be fine." She went to close the door.

"Ah, ma'am, I think Bailey would want me to start the work." His fingers rested on the doorframe, gambling that Charlene wouldn't slam the door shut on his hand.

"Man, are you deaf? Get on out of here." Charlene wasn't used to back talk. Certainly not from the likes of a handyman. *Handyman?* She paused, and gave him a once-over. "Oh, you're that handyman! Bailey's beau," she announced. "Walter." She spoke his name with a smile.

"Auntie." Bailey's voice came from behind her.

"Now look what you did! You woke her up."

Bailey nudged Charlene out of the way. "This is Walter," she said, still in her housecoat. "Come in. I'm sorry. I must've overslept. Come," she repeated.

"I'll be right back. I need to get my tools."

Charlene let out an exasperated sigh. She closed the door to make sure they'd have privacy. "He's a bit pushy."

"He's really not. He's very polite."

"Ah, if that's what you call not listening to a damn thing I said."

"I have to get to the shop."

"Can't you take one day off?"

"No, I can't," Bailey said, stomping off toward her bedroom.

Charlene was on her heels. "Listen. You can't talk about what we were talking about last night. Not one word, you understand?"

Bailey nodded. "Yes. Got it," she said; then she must have felt Charlene still staring daggers at her and turned around.

"Good. Now, I'll babysit your man, make sure he gets the work done, but if he gives me more attitude, he will be meeting these hands." Charlene held up her fists. Her antics got a smile out of Bailey, and that was all she'd wanted.

39

INGRID PACED IN SHERIFF GALE'S OFFICE, her pointy heels pivoting on the waxed linoleum tile. She pulled out a cigarette and her silver lighter. The first drag lightened her stress. Today was supposed to be the wedding day. Every close friend and relative was supposed to be gathered at her home at this very hour to see how triumphantly Ingrid's life had turned out. Instead she would forever be remembered as the mother of Elsa the murderess.

Ingrid's cashmere coat collar felt scratchy for the first time ever. She took it off and flipped it over her arm. What was taking so long? She leaned to peek past the partition. No sign of Matthias or their lawyer. Only the clacking of typewriter keys and whispers she couldn't make out.

Ironically, up until now her only goal in life had been to be rid of Elsa, but now all she wanted to do was take her home. She couldn't begin to fathom what kind of evidence they'd found to lead to Elsa's arrest. And so quickly. Every few steps, she blew out smoke.

On one of her turns, Ingrid noticed a manila folder on the sheriff's desk. She sidled over to the side of the dull oak table to get a better view. Her daughter's name was written across the top of the folder. She flipped it open and saw a single piece of paper.

Inscribed pearl necklace
Threats heard
Three witnesses to her proximity to victim on day he disappeared.

Ingrid heard the soles of hard shoes squeaking against the linoleum and closed the folder. She moved to the center of the office and stood still. The list played in an endless loop in her head. *Pearl necklace. Threats. Witnesses.*

"Here she is," Matthias said, proud of his accomplishment. Elsa looked lost as usual, that bewildered look, wondering how she'd ended up there. She still wore the pink chiffon dress from the party, but now it had a broken zipper and gapped open at the side.

Ingrid tapped out her cigarette and left it in the plastic ashtray on the desk. "Come here, darling. Oh my goodness! Look at you. Poor thing."

Elsa slumped against Ingrid.

"She can go home, for now," Glen, their lawyer, announced.

"For now?" Ingrid shrieked. "She's not coming back here. Ever."

"All right, calm down," Matthias said, looping his arm through his wife's. "We'll talk when we get home."

Elsa was the one who needed guiding. She could hardly stand. Ingrid pulled away from her husband and went to her aid. Slowly, they walked together out of the station.

Once they were outside, Elsa began to cry. Ingrid could barely keep it together herself. Matthias opened the back door of the car, and Ingrid slid in next to her. She wouldn't leave her girl's side, not until Elsa was in her warm bed and fast asleep. Ingrid vowed to make up for all the times she wished she was somewhere else, anywhere else but with her child.

"I'm so sorry, darling," she whispered against her temple. "Did you tell them anything?" she asked, also against her ear.

"No. I don't know anything," Elsa said, pulling herself away. She wiped at her eyes, but wouldn't look at Ingrid directly. "I'll be fine. Thanks for asking."

Matthias kept a watchful eye on them in the rearview mirror, making the drive even longer. If he focused on the road they could get to their house quicker, Ingrid thought. She had a plan rolling in her head. She'd have Oda Mae run a bubble bath for Elsa. She'd make sure she took a long soak with a shot of brandy in her tea.

"Can you drive any faster?" Ingrid asked.

Matthias didn't bother answering. He pushed ahead only slightly, doing his best to annoy her, she presumed. She pressed a finely manicured fingernail to her temple and decided to relax. There was no need to hurry. Elsa was safe now.

IT TOOK FOREVER for Elsa to finally fall asleep. Ingrid had sat in the chair across from her bed and stared at her list of the apologies and courtesy calls she'd have to make.

"Is she asleep?" Matthias asked when Ingrid entered their bedroom.

"Yes. I had to give her a sleeping pill. I put it in her tea. Nothing else was working."

"She needs to sleep." He walked to the window and stared out. "We've got to get the best attorney. I'll make some calls. There's no way this should go any further."

"I was thinking about that. I don't think we should throw the artillery at this. If we get the most expensive criminal lawyer we can find, it's going to look like she's guilty. Like we need the most high-powered defense because she actually did it."

Matthias turned around. It was odd seeing him without a drink in his hand. But even though he hadn't slept more than a few hours, he still looked more alert and present than he had in months, years. He was listening.

"I believe we should ask Glen to handle everything," Ingrid said. "I saw the file in the sheriff's office. They have no evidence."

"What'd you see?"

"I saw a folder. It had Elsa's name on it. It listed a pearl necklace and witnesses to threats," Ingrid said with a chuckle. "I mean, that's what they have against her. Hearsay and a pearl necklace. I'm thinking this whole thing is really being pushed by the Salleys. You know how they are. And Sheriff John Gale is Gweneth Salley's brother-in-law. Not to mention, the sheriff's wife died of lung cancer last year. He blamed the fire, you know. He didn't have the balls to join the lawsuit because he was up for reelection. But oh, he was flaming mad. And now here he is, finally getting his revenge."

"Right," Matthias said, remembering the connections. Yet he still appeared preoccupied.

She wanted him to focus. "Matthias, this is more of their anger coming out toward us. That's all. They're vindictive and jealous. Heaven forbid the Salleys find out Elsa's pregnant with their grandchild.

Though that won't be the case after Monday, I assure you." Ingrid paused, realizing Matthias knew nothing about the planned trip to the Pawnee clinic. He didn't respond, thank goodness, and she was already on to a new idea. She might as well have been talking to herself anyway. "Wait. Wait a minute. Maybe we should tell them. Maybe that's exactly what they need to back off . . . What if Elsa keeps the baby? We tell them they're having a grandchild. Surely they'll want to preserve any chance of having a piece of their son."

"That's not—no," Matthias said firmly, suddenly listening. "We're not going to barter with them. There's enough bad blood between us as it is. They lost their son, but they aren't getting our grandchild as compensation."

He rubbed at his graying temples. "I think we need to keep our distance. I'll talk to Ed and Bill in legal, have Glen sit in, and let them suggest what kind of lawyer we need."

Ingrid shook her head. "I'm telling you what kind of lawyer we need. Why can't you listen to me for once?"

"That's all I do is listen to you," he said. "I'm done." He grabbed his coat and walked to the door.

"Where are you going? We need to talk about this. We have to figure out what to do about Elsa."

"We're going to let the lawyers handle it." He left, slamming the door hard enough to shake the wall.

Ingrid ran behind him. She yanked the door open and followed him down the hall. "Don't you dare leave this house!" Her fingers gripped the banister as she realized there was no one to hear her. Matthias had gone. Oda Mae had gone after getting Elsa to eat a bite of breakfast.

Now Ingrid felt completely alone in the monstrosity of a house. For the first time, she was afraid to be there. Too much space, too many corners and walls. She pushed her back against the wall and sat vigilantly on the stairs.

40

THE REGAL GOWN, like the rest of Main Street, was empty on the weekend. Garments had already gone out earlier in the week. Miss Jackson rarely came to the boutique on a Saturday, and they were closed on Sunday. Bailey was expected to handle any inquiries, which were rare.

She appreciated the quiet more than usual, simply wanting to sit alone. She felt helpless, wondering about Elsa. When her auntie made her promise to not speak a word of what she saw in her vision, she knew it was the right thing to do. Stay silent. The exposure would only land Bailey in trouble. Who was she to speak up for one of the richest white ladies in Mendol? And what exactly had she planned to say: that the man Elsa killed deserved exactly what he got?

She'd read enough crime stories in *True Detective* to know that her statement would be nothing more than hearsay. She had nothing but her dreams and what Elsa had told her. She really hadn't witnessed anything. Not really.

In the afternoon, Bailey had her lunch but didn't have much of an appetite. Outside in the alley, she ended up giving her entire sandwich to the birds. What they left behind, she scooped up and dumped in the trash can. "Y'all being wasteful," she told them.

"Bailey."

She turned around. She still held the trash can top. She could use it as a weapon if she had to. "What're you doing here, John?"

"I didn't mean to scare you," he said, standing with his hands in his jacket pockets. He took a step closer.

"Well, you did. You do—you scare me, popping up anytime you like. I've told you I don't know anything."

"I was wondering if you could touch my hand. I was thinking about it, that you might be able to see something about Alice. You know, you might have a vision about her."

Bailey slammed the can lid down. The clang sent the pigeons fluttering, jumping to their perch on the edge of the Regal Gown doorframe. "Fine. Then will you leave me alone?"

"I . . . I just want to find her."

"But what if she doesn't want to be found? What if she's in her house, trying to be a wife and doing wifely things? Do you even know where she lives? Have you seen or met anyone who knows about her life? She might be perfectly happy." Bailey knew what she was saying, that Alice might be fine and good without having John wasn't what he wanted to hear, but she continued, "What if she's more than capable of getting in touch with you, but chooses not to?"

He shook his head. "I have been there. I know where she lives. Her husband comes and goes, but she never does. There's never been a sighting of her. I've asked the people at church—casually, you know, not to spark any attention—if they've seen her, and everyone says no. Not in a while."

"How long is a while, exactly?"

"Six months. I'd already been watching her house long before I came to see you to ask if you knew anything. You think I want to be here? I just don't know what else to do."

She moved to stand in front of him. "Give me your hands."

He laid his calloused palms against her hands. She closed her eyes before gripping his hands. She tried something she'd never done before. She asked aloud, "Where is Alice?" partly for theatrics, and partly to show John she was trying her best to give him what he wanted.

She wasn't expecting anything but light, a swirl of colors, like always. Images came at night if they were going to come at all.

But not this time. She saw Alice. Though her face was blanketed by moving shadows, she saw Alice clearly. Her face was different— tired, drained, and truly sad, but it was Alice. A slice of light opened wider, continuously blooming into a full view of a room, a kitchen. A table setting with flowers. Sunflowers and daisies.

"What is it? What do you see?"

Bailey's eyes flashed open. She lost her concentration and let go of his hands. "I saw her. She was in a kitchen. I saw wallpaper with sunflowers and daisies. That's all."

"That's the wallpaper in her house. I've seen it."

Bailey swallowed. "You've been that close, looking in?"

He shook his head, no. "Well, *yes*. I mean, it was only once. But I remember the yellow-and-white wallpaper. It was definitely daisies and sunflowers. What does this mean?"

Bailey shrugged and her voice quivered. "I don't know. If I knew anything more than what I just saw, I'd tell you. To be honest, I'm surprised I saw what I did. Visions usually come to me in my dreams, at night. I promise you, if I see anything else, if something comes to me, I will tell you."

She didn't wait for him to walk away. She went inside and bolted the door. She leaned against it, listening. Not that she would have heard much through the heavy door. She just wanted him to be gone.

If she hadn't been the only one in the store, she would have closed the shop and gone home. Four more hours were required of her.

Four more endless hours of relying on her own thoughts for company. That meant she had to depend on herself to say nice things. *You're not a bad person. You told John what you saw. You did what you could.*

However, it wasn't the entire truth. She didn't mention that Alice looked beaten down. She was a far cry from the confident young woman who'd known every detail of how she wanted her wedding. That woman was not the same person she just saw.

Then it dawned on her that she had expected to see nothing. Bailey closed her eyes and settled into the amazing thing that had just happened. She asked, "Where's Alice?" and she saw her . . . just like that.

Nothing like that had ever happened to Bailey before. Something magical had just occurred—for the first time. She wrapped her arms around herself, almost as congratulations. As if complimenting herself on a job well done, when in actuality she didn't know whether it was a good thing or bad. She just knew that it happened and it was real.

It wasn't hearsay.

Or speculation.

It was real. And she saw it in real time. This was new. And different.

Bailey didn't wait for closing hour. She couldn't wait. What she'd learned, what she was capable of, made it impossible to sit around another minute. She had to share the news with Aunt Charlene. She locked the golden doors and headed up the block to the Olds. The car started, and before she knew it she'd turned onto Baker Street.

She saw the Wag truck parked in front of her house. She'd tell Walter too. It wasn't something she had ever wanted to talk about. Men had an innate fear of their secrets being exposed. Having a lady in his life who might know more about him than he was willing to offer freely . . . She paused. That wasn't something a man wanted to hear from a woman. Bailey didn't want to scare him away. Maybe this tidbit should wait, she decided.

"Auntie," she called out automatically, since there was no sight of her in the kitchen. She heard rummaging and the remnants of conversation coming from under the house and took the stairs down to a flood of light. Walter was on a stepladder, and Aunt Charlene stood off to the side, a human lantern, holding the spotlight for him.

"Hey! What're you doing here so early?" Aunt Charlene asked. "Or is it past five? I've lost all track of time down here. I see why you like it so much. It's like having a tiny world all your own."

"She's going to like it even better when this ceiling's not set on falling on her head." Walter climbed the few steps down. "Thank you, Charlene. I can take that from you." He took the bright electric lantern and hung it on a hook. "I wanted to get finished before you got home. I had a surprise planned."

"I closed the store early. There was no point in me being there another couple of hours. No one ever comes downtown on Saturdays. This looks great, Walter," she said, doing her best not to appear anxious. But she wanted to talk to Aunt Charlene.

"Thank you. Thanks to my assistant." He smiled and winked.

Aunt Charlene smiled back, almost coyly. "You're welcome. I'm pretty handy. One time I built a bookshelf. Well, it was mostly just stacked boards and bricks, but it worked."

"Auntie, can I talk to you?" she asked, pointing up.

"Oh, sure. Let me know if you need any more help, Walter."

"Sure thing," he said. "But I think I've got it handled from here."

Bailey led the way up the narrow staircase and into the living room. She wanted to put as much listening distance between Walter and the two of them as possible.

Before Bailey could say a word, the phone began to ring. *Must be for Aunt Charlene,* she thought. Bailey couldn't remember the last time someone rang her on the line. Sometimes Gabby called ahead before stopping over. They did most of their talking while sitting together on the back porch.

Mostly, calls were ladies scheduling hair appointments. Bookies calling in losses—she'd never won, as far as Bailey knew. There'd been only a few callers that Bailey couldn't identify by her auntie's tone when she answered the phone.

"Hold on, this might be a client," Aunt Charlene said.

"Can it wait? I really need to say something."

"Won't take but a minute."

Bailey was left sitting on the couch, eager to present her case. Ready to tell her story about what had happened with John and seeing Alice. She was ready to declare that she was much more than a reader of heartstrings. She could *see,* actually *see* people and situations, and where they were. It was all real, she told herself again, not wanting to lose her courage. It meant what she saw happen to Elsa was truly something she witnessed, whether it came as a vision or not. "I'm a witness," she whispered.

"Yeah. All right. I'll be there. I'm leaving right now," Aunt Charlene said into the phone, her voice low but resolute. She hung up and came a few steps shy of where she'd left Bailey on the couch.

"I have to go, Bailey. It's kind of a . . . a hair emergency. Miss Hillary won't leave the house . . . so, I'm about to head over there." Aunt Charlene kept her eyes forward, avoiding direct contact with Bailey.

She was lying, of course. But Bailey nodded okay and told her she'd be there when she got back. What else was she to say? *You're not being honest . . . again.* What else was new?

When the phone rang a second time, after Aunt Charlene had already gone, Bailey picked up the receiver with irritation. "Hello?"

The voice on the other end of the line was unexpected.

"BAILEY, IT'S ME." Elsa sat on the edge of her bed, cradling the phone, keeping her voice low.

"Oh my goodness. I've been worried about you."

"Yeah. Some party, huh?"

"Elsa." Bailey breathed her name through the phone line. "I can't believe you're calling me. I've been so worried. You're home now?"

"I'm home. Did you get my note?" she asked.

"Your note?"

"I sent someone over with a note. Her name is Rochelle."

"Elsa, you're calling about a note right now? My God, you were arrested for killing someone!"

"Did you see the note or not?" Elsa tried to keep her irritation at bay.

"There was kind of a lot going on at the time. I got a note."

"The note asked that you touch Rochelle's hand. I doubt if you'll get another chance. I mean, I guess you could go to her house. She lives at 41 Route 12. It's on the Eastside too, not far from you."

"Elsa," Bailey snapped. "I am not going to a stranger's house and knock on their door to ask if I can touch Ro—"

"Yes, Rochelle," Elsa finished for her. "She's the one. But I guess I'll never know. And what does it matter anyway? I'll probably be spending some time away from here."

"Don't say that. Don't even think it." After a pause, Bailey softened. "Rochelle, huh? Tell me her address again."

"Thank you, Bailey."

That was the only thing keeping Elsa from sinking into sorrow: the possibility that she and Rochelle could have a life together. The three of them, she thought, while her palm circled the growing bump in her middle. One small thread of hope could be a lifeline.

After she hung up with Bailey, she crawled back under the covers. When she closed her eyes, she waded back to the long night in the sheriff's office. The endless questions and accusations weren't completely farfetched.

"You killed Connor out of vengeful anger. After he'd used you for his pleasure, he wanted nothing more to do with you and made sure everybody in your circle knew what a whore you were. Isn't that what happened, Elsa?"

And hadn't she told Connor Salley that she'd kill him if he touched her again? Yes. Enough people had heard her say it. The witness at the Tire Gas and Pop said Connor did indeed touch her, right there at the gasoline pump: *"The other fellas tried to pull her off of him."*

"That's not what happened," Elsa said to the sheriff. "Niles hit Connor. Did anyone talk to Niles? *They were in a fight . . . over me.*" She hadn't meant to say this out loud. She wasn't trying to blame Niles. She only wanted the sheriff to speak to him, ask Niles what really happened. Anyone else would be unreliable in this town. He was the only one who'd stand up for her, just as he did at the gas station. But then again, she remembered his condescending tone. *Nah, have fun,* he'd sneered. Maybe he too had finally turned on Elsa, decided she was too different from the rest of them and wasn't worth fighting for, just as Connor had said.

The questions kept coming. The notes the sheriff made had nothing to do with her answers. What about the necklace with the inscription on the silver clasp, *To Elsa with Love, Mommy and Daddy*? The necklace was found at the water's edge. When had she lost it? Had he yanked it off her neck the night of the party when he'd attacked her? Was it now a message to tell the world who'd killed him?

What about the gun found under the driver's seat, right next to her pocketbook? She'd borrowed her mother's car, hadn't she?

"And what about *all that money* the clerk said you withdrew?" Sheriff Gale asked.

Elsa never carried a pocketbook. It was only because she had to pay Bailey and didn't want to carry a wad of money out of the bank in her hands.

"You borrowed your mama's car the same day Connor was last seen alive. Was all that money for your plan to pay him for his silence? Stop the rumors of your relations? After all, you were supposed to be marrying Niles Porter. You couldn't have a sullied reputation on your wedding day." *Too late for that,* Elsa had thought. She'd stayed strong throughout the questioning, mostly because she was numb.

But now, Elsa wiped her nose and tried not to cry out loud, "Why? Why is this happening to me?"

41

CHARLENE ENTERED THE MOTEL ROOM and wondered how long Matty had been there. He wasted no time embracing her. She couldn't distinguish whether the room or Matty was the source of the odors of stale alcohol and cigarettes.

She leaned back. "I heard about Elsa. Are you all right? Do you want to talk? I'm here. I'm listening." She stroked his wide back. "I'm so sorry you have to go through this." She meant every word. Seeing your child hurt had to be the greatest pain.

While she did her best to soothe him, he was busy pulling her toward him. "Matty," she said, touching his face. "I know you're hurting."

He ignored her words. His eyes remained closed as he selfishly pulled at her blouse. He leaned away just enough to unbuckle his belt. He pulled and tugged her skirt up, then turned her around, pushing her onto the bed. She hadn't expected this, but moaned, anticipating his firmness. Her arms locked and braced to keep from falling too hard under his weight.

By the time he'd entered her, she'd already felt the stirring of a climax. She wanted to slow down, slow him down, but they were at it like tomorrow wasn't promised. She bit her lip to keep from saying his name. But she wanted to. She wanted to say his name out loud with the words *I love you* right behind it. The surge of dizzying warmth rose over her body, closing around her. Only a brute, guttural gasp erupted from her throat.

He panted, catching up to where Charlene had already raced ahead. He pulled away and collapsed next to her on the bed. She curled against his body, missing his heat, the friction between them. He wrapped an arm around her. His chest rose and settled in long, deep breaths. Then the rhythm changed. It became staggered and jolting.

She rose up to see if what she thought was happening was really happening. Matty covered his face, but it didn't stop the tears from sliding past his cupped hands.

"Oh . . . sweetie," she said, pulling him into her arms. "Oh, baby. It's going to be all right."

He responded with a hoarse sob. "I should've been taking care of her."

Charlene had never seen him cry, never heard him lose all hope. But this was what it looked like.

She cradled his head and smoothed his hair away. "You're going to get through this. You know that. Your daughter is going to get through this. Elsa is strong and she's smart," Charlene said, not knowing if what she was saying was true. What she did know was that nothing lasted forever. Pain, sorrow, or joy—they were all temporary. No guarantees from one day to the next. She'd sometimes experienced the entire array in an hour or less. Mostly, sorrow had been her friend. She understood his sadness.

"I only wanted the best for her," he said. "I wasn't there. I didn't stop it."

"You've been a good father. Look at the life you've provided for her and—" She stopped, unable to say his wife's name. Though she knew it, she couldn't bring herself to even refer to his wife. Charlene's hypocrisy could only go so far. Here she was, consoling the man she loved, who was married to someone else. A claw of jealousy reached down and twisted in her chest.

"Matty, we have a daughter too," she blurted. "She's twenty-eight now. She's married, got a son and another baby on the way. That makes us grandparents," she said softly, as if the news would land better that way.

Matthias rose on his elbows. The stream of tears stopped. His face became unreadable. He sat up, gathered himself, but remained silent.

"I know you're probably never going to forgive me," Charlene continued, her words tumbling out before she could stop herself. "When you didn't come back . . . or when I thought you didn't come back, I didn't know what else to do. I couldn't raise her by myself. I left her in good hands, Matty." She wiped her eyes. "Say something. Please."

"What's her name?" he asked, looking away from her and staring at the ceiling.

"She goes by Sage. Sage Murray is her married name. She's a schoolteacher. She and her husband live in New Orleans."

Matty's dark eyes narrowed. "She's been there the whole time?"

Charlene nodded and attempted to take his hand. He pulled away, as she knew he would. "I'm so sorry. Last I saw her, she was thirteen, and even then, we'd agreed, the Broussards and I, we shouldn't mention who I was. They wanted to tell her in their own way, but that time never came." She paused. Every word she'd uttered seemed to have drained more life out of him.

"You never gave me a chance." His voice filled the room with something far more than anger—desolation.

"I wished I'd been able to keep her, Matty. I really did. I wanted us to be a family. I was young and so stupid." She squeezed the last budding moisture from her eyes. "I call every year and ask about her. They tell me updates. That's how I know she's doing really well. Really, really well," she said, believing it was possible to make up for the heartache. *Look how well she turned out.*

Charlene had no idea what she had meant to accomplish, dropping this heavy package at his feet at a time when he was already broken.

Matthias shook his head, as if in a daze, then rose from the bed and found his shoes. He tossed his coat over his arm, grabbed his keys, and left the room.

There was nothing Charlene could do but let him go. She watched him walk out of her life for the second time. The whiskey bottle on the tiny round stand sat half full. She unscrewed the top and tilted it to her lips, feeling the immediate burn in her throat. Her eyes watered, and she could blame the alcohol. The second gulp brought about a full stream of tears. The third satisfied her need for numbness. She sat and waited for the lightness to come from being still. Silent. No such luck. The past never went away. No matter how much distance and time she'd put between herself and that terrible thing, it never left her side.

Her numbness traveled back to sadness and then rounded comfortably to rage. How dare Matthias play the victim? Charlene was the one who'd run away from her family to be with him. When her daddy died, she'd been too ashamed to show her face for his burial. Then her mama passed, and soon after, Sammie, like she'd caused some terrible curse. She'd lost them all without ever telling them "I love you" or "I'm sorry."

42

SUNDAY MORNINGS WERE A GIFT to Bailey, a reward for making it through the workweek. She couldn't explain the way it felt, that it was a job just being alive. But once a week she put on her Sunday best to give her thanks and drove to the edge of Mendol where the oil drillers had yet to erect their towers, where farmland remained untouched, filled with tall, golden grass. A grove of pecan and walnut trees had survived the violent wreck of tornadoes the previous year, when the rest of the area had been flattened.

Zion Tabernacle sat on a small portion of the land purchased by the church for one dollar in 1902. The fifty-year-old church had been torn down twice and was newly rebuilt. The current version had twenty-foot ceilings and arched windows, a modern resurrection. Bailey parked the Olds and walked along the straight concrete path to the entrance.

She could readily remember sitting in a church service next to her mama, starting from the age of pigtails and bows. She remembered her mama more vividly here in the Zion pews than she did anywhere else. And that was saying a lot, since she thought of her often. But this Sunday, she was thinking of Aunt Charlene, who hadn't been heard from since she'd left to tend to "the emergency hair incident" phone call that sent her scurrying out the door. Bailey woke up with her mind spinning with possible scenarios.

What with worrying about Aunt Charlene and Elsa, she'd been a wreck, so outside of herself she'd sent Walter home without a kiss and a thank-you. "But don't you want to see what I've done? Your space is ready." He'd beamed proudly.

"Not right now. All I want to do is take a soak and climb into bed," she'd told him.

Now, she figured she'd find solace in the pews.

She perked to attention when the offering basket landed under her nose. She threw in the coins she had at the ready. "We are nothing without our walls and a roof over our heads. God provides you a way every day so you can give and keep receiving," the reverend reminded his flock.

Bailey sheepishly returned to the shifting images of her mama, safe there in the memory of Sammie's arms, the spatter of moles up the side of her neck, and the scent of jasmine on her wrists.

By the second sermon, Bailey gave in to the pull of sleep. Her head nodded forward in jerking motions. This was where she felt most comfortable, where she could rest and feel safe. In church, where she knew her mama's spirit rested, she could be at peace. And all she wanted was a little rest. She was going to need it in the coming days.

"You keeping late nights, ma'am?" the familiar voice asked as the choir belted out a lively intro to "Blessed at the River." Bailey jumped unsteadily to her feet and began clapping and singing along with the congregation. A tap on her shoulder came with a nudge, letting her know the voice asking about her late nights hadn't been God.

It was Gabby, sliding into her pew. Bailey hugged her and released a breath she didn't know she'd been holding. She'd been concerned about Gabby too, not having seen her in the choir. It was best to keep a straight line of who to worry about first. Aunt Charlene was still missing and first on the list. Elsa was at least home, safe. But Gabby should have been in church, wearing her gold-and-white robe. These were things Bailey depended on, and lately all that she'd taken for granted was slipping from her hands.

"I had a late start," Gabby whispered back. "I got something to tell you. It's about Charlene. I know who she's been keeping company with."

Under normal circumstances, leaving church before the last offering felt like a deplorable offense. However, Gabby's carrot of information was an impossible temptation to resist. Hesitation be damned. Bailey picked up her handbag and scooched out of the row, stepping over Sister Tamara, who was never without a baby in her arms. Six in all. Little feet were scattered along the aisle.

Once they were out the double doors and into the sunlight, Gabby started talking. "I found out who your auntie's been keeping time with."

The echo of the reverend's voice followed them through the glass panes.

"Aunt Charlene was gone this morning. I mean, she left Saturday and didn't call. I haven't heard from her. What do you know? Tell me."

"Hold on. No need to panic. She's fine. Your auntie is just fine." Gabby kept walking.

"Tell me whatever it is you're trying to say," Bailey demanded, keeping up with her friend's pace. Some parking lot gravel landed in her shoe. She had to stop to shake out the stones. "Just tell me what you know."

Gabby opened her car door. "We're here. Get in."

"I have my car here."

"Get in. We not going nowhere. You don't want anyone to hear what I'm 'bout to tell you. You know the wind carry out here, and I don't want you cursing in front of the house of the Lord. Get in."

Bailey slid inside the Chevy Gabby drove only on Sundays, her deceased daddy's car. "Now what?" She'd lost all patience. The night had dragged on as she lay worrying about Elsa and Aunt Charlene. She had very little energy left.

"All right. Here it is. Your auntie been seeing the Senate Oil dude. Elsa's father. The one—"

"Yeah, I know who he is. Why would you say that? How's that possible? They don't even know each other!" Bailey felt hot around the butterfly collar of her white blouse. She took off her gloves and used them to fan herself.

Gabby dropped her eyes and took a deep breath. "My cousin Bonnie work at the 98th Street Motel. This the third time she said she seen them together. That's where they meet. How come you didn't know what was going on . . . you know, with your mind reading and everything? Please don't tell her I told you. I don't want to be banned from visiting or getting my hair done. Charlene's the only one know how to bump my ends."

Bailey rested against the dash. "No, no" was all she could say. She couldn't accept what she was hearing. "I don't believe it."

"Well, ma'am, it's the truth. So now you know."

Truth, Bailey thought. What exactly made something true? What you saw with your own eyes, or what you felt and knew in your bones?

"I have to go," Bailey said and got out, slammed the door, and stomped over to her Olds.

Gabby rolled down her window and called out, "Don't blame the messenger."

Bailey drove home from church, listening to the gospel in between the crackling static. The same was played on every station, with equally bad bandwidth, so she didn't bother turning the dial. She pulled up to see gray smoke swirling from the backyard.

The distinct acrid burn of trash hit her nostrils as she got out of the car. She leaned a shaky palm on the back gate and pushed through. "Hey, there," she said.

Aunt Charlene was in the midst of emptying a canful of trash into a metal barrel. Flecks of fire leaped up. They didn't have trash service in the Eastside. If the residents wanted refuse properly disposed of, they had to carry it five miles to the town dump themselves. Or they could burn as much as would fit in the can.

"Hey there, yourself," Aunt Charlene said, barely looking up. "How was service? Anything new? Will our sins be washed away with redemption?" she asked smugly.

When Bailey didn't answer, Aunt Charlene looked up. "I made some fried chicken for you. It's still warm."

Bailey stood firm, holding her handbag and Bible.

"Well?" Aunt Charlene said. "You want me to go in and put it on a plate for you or what? I'm not your servant, child. Food's getting cold while you're standing there." She slapped the side of the barrel with a stick to make sure no debris escaped being burned.

Bailey watched a flash of embers sail upward and disintegrate before they could attach to the dry roofing of their house.

Aunt Charlene looked up. "I got some coleslaw in the fridge too. Are you gon' tell me what's on your mind or not?" When Bailey didn't answer again, Aunt Charlene left her smoke-filled barrel and went inside, letting the back screen door slam shut.

Bailey followed, not to be outdone. She stood there too, arms folded over her chest and Bible. The foil over the chicken was smooth, but the scent of the goodness inside had escaped and made her head swim. She was starving. She wondered if she could continue her protest after she ate. Over the years, their squabbles were neat and tidy, since Aunt Charlene didn't do a lot of disciplining. What little parenting she'd done was dutiful, so as not to be accused of neglect. *Go to bed by eight on a school night. Don't wash your whites with colors.* They fought over silly things only when their moods soured, and that most likely had nothing to do with the other person.

Bailey held fast and left the food untouched. She went to her room. She couldn't bring herself to ask about what Gabby had told her at church. She just couldn't do it.

"All right. You want to talk, let's talk," Aunt Charlene blurted minutes later from the other side of the closed bedroom door. She knocked, then kept talking. "You know what, doors are a luxury. Me and your mama didn't have a door. This here was your grandma and papa's room. Your great-gran and pop were in what's now my room. Me and Sammie, we shared one bed in the middle of the living room floor. We used to whisper secrets to each other so as not to wake up everybody. Those are good memories. I miss your mama. I truly do." There was a pause. "I'm coming in," Aunt Charlene announced.

Before she came inside, Bailey hopped into bed fully dressed and lay still with her eyes closed and the quilted orange bedspread tucked under her chin.

"Girl, open your eyes. Nobody believe you sleep that fast," Aunt Charlene said. She cleared her throat. "*Ahem* . . . Come on, now. If I remember correctly, somebody's ticklish." Her fingers crept under the blanket to the soles of Bailey's stocking-covered feet.

"No. Stop," Bailey ordered. The wire bed frame squeaked with the weight of Aunt Charlene climbing on top of her.

"You want some more?" she threatened with loose and fast fingers. "Talk to me or you're going to get tickled to tears."

Bailey dodged and wiggled free, though she loved every minute of it. She could simply cry just from Aunt Charlene's touch. She sat up and threw her long legs over the side of the bed, then hugged her auntie fiercely tight.

"Oh, sweetie. Talk to me."

Bailey knew she was far too old to say what she felt out loud. *I'm scared, Auntie.* She was as vulnerable as if every step she took might swallow her up. She was still that twelve-year-old girl who'd found her mama no longer breathing, heart no longer beating. "When did you plan on telling me?" was what she said instead. "Did you ever plan to tell me about Mr. Grimes and you?"

Aunt Charlene looked back with questioning eyes.

"You didn't have to sneak around," Bailey said.

"I didn't?" Aunt Charlene replied, frowning, her eyes quickly turning glossy. But she tightened up, refusing to let her sassy status be quelled for too long. "Grown folks' business is grown folks' business."

"So it's true?"

"There's so much I should've told you, Bailey. But it was a long time ago. We knew each other when we were young and . . . well, he and I are over now."

"Nothing. Not a word. You never even hinted that you knew Elsa's father."

"Did you see something? Feel something? How did you know?" She picked up Bailey's hands and held them in hers.

Bailey squeezed her auntie's hands, but not in a good way. Her nails dug in. "Gabby told me," she blurted. "She said people been seeing you two at a motel. He's married. And you don't care about none of that, do you?"

Aunt Charlene took her hands back. "Well, Miss Holier-Than-Thou, I've known Matthias Grimes far longer than anyone, including his . . . current family. There's more to it than meeting and sneaking around at a motel, trust me."

"Why? Why would you start seeing him now? You made me feel like I had no business being friends with Elsa and then you do this." Bailey watched as her auntie's face drew a blank, as if she wanted to speak but forced herself not to.

"It really doesn't matter now."

Bailey had to resist the urge to beg. She wanted to know how and what brought them together after *so long ago* happened. She thought of the other secret her aunt was hiding, the vision of a baby she'd never told Bailey about, and figured there was so much more she'd never know or understand. *To each his own*, she thought. If this was the way Aunt Charlene wanted it, so be it.

"You have your life and I have mine," Bailey said. "So, I want you to know, I'm going to put what I know about Elsa and the man who attacked her on record. I don't know how he died, but I know what kind of man he was. I know what he did to her, because I saw it in my dreams, and it's just as real as anything. And it's eating me up inside to stay silent."

Aunt Charlene reeled backward. "No. No. Absolutely not. I care about Matty . . . Matthias, and Elsa too, but you are my first priority. There's no way I'm going to let you throw yourself on a heap of fire. There's got to be another way."

Bailey pushed herself back against the pillow. "How? What am I supposed to do? Nothing?"

"The Grimeses can handle their problems their way. Trust me, it's all going to work out. You have to know that. Okay? Do you understand? It's all going to work out," Aunt Charlene said before getting up to leave.

Bailey knew no such thing.

43

INGRID REACHED OVER and picked up the receiver, and offered her cheeriest voice for a Monday morning. "Hello, Grimes residence." She'd insisted on answering the phone herself, just this week, knowing that crank callers were likely to be on the other end of the line. She wanted them to know she was strong and unbothered. Her family had survived worse. What was new about being called murderers or heathens?

"Ingrid, it's Glen."

"Oh, hello, Glen. Is there news?"

"As a matter of fact, yes. The prosecutor has dismissed the case against Elsa," he calmly stated. "Insufficient evidence."

"Well, of course. Oh, oh, this is wonderful!" What other outcome was she expecting? They'd paid Judge Lerner handsomely, a thick wad of cash in an envelope slipped into the man's morning paper. Glen hadn't balked at the idea, calling it "the best alternative," as though it were standard practice. Matthias would soon enough see the money missing from their bank account and cry foul, but he'd thank Ingrid later. They were up against a town of angry crybabies. A jury of Elsa's peers would convict her if they got the chance. Downright ungrateful, the whole damned lot of them. One little fire and they'd forgotten about all the jobs and prosperity Senate Oil had brought to Mendol.

"Indeed. You can share the good news with Matthias. I tried reaching him first, but to no avail. Go on, you tell him and Elsa. You all have plenty to celebrate."

Ingrid covered her face and forced herself to stop feeling guilty. "Thank you, Glen. Thank you so much."

She kicked her legs free from the silk duvet. Now that the situation had been rectified, there was no need for guilt. She didn't want to be one of those women skulking around all day, drinking and blaming herself.

A fresh new start was ahead. She had to let go of the hope of marrying Elsa off, let go of her goal of perfection.

She'd fallen so far from the heights that her feet had almost touched the dry, desolate path where poor little Ingrid Fredrick had begun. Onward and upward. She pulled out her planner and began to jot down notes.

Now that there was zero possibility of Elsa being married off, she'd have to plan the trip to the Pawnee clinic. Getting Elsa there without anyone knowing plagued her thoughts. Even if the clinic listed the service as an emergency D&C, everyone would know the true reason was an unplanned pregnancy being resolved.

When her bedroom door swung open, Oda Mae appeared, surprised to see Ingrid awake and in good spirits.

"Good morning, Miss Ingrid. You're looking well rested today!" Oda Mae made her way across the room, ripping open the curtains and tying them back on the hooks.

"I'm wonderful."

"Coffee and toast for you?"

"Just coffee, Oda Mae. Thank you. How's Elsa? Did she already wake up?"

Oda Mae didn't answer, at least not quickly enough for Ingrid. She knew what the hesitation meant and didn't bother with her robe or slippers. She made her way down the hall and saw Elsa's door cracked open. Before looking inside she knew what she'd find. Elsa was gone.

Oda Mae met her in the hallway. "She took my car. Didn't say where she was going."

"For heaven's sake. If it isn't one thing it's another," Ingrid fumed. She went to her room and dialed Matthias. She at least could share the good news with him.

"Good morning, office of Mr. Grimes."

"Let me speak to Matthias, and don't you dare tell me he's in a meeting. Get him on the phone."

"Mrs. Grimes, he's unavailable," Mrs. Kenner answered coolly.

"Unavailable? As in, he's there, but not taking my calls?"

"No, ma'am. *Unavailable* as in 'not here.' He hasn't come in yet this morning."

Ingrid pressed the receiver button and began dialing again. "May I speak to Mr. Porter?" she said, knowing the two men were thick as thieves. He'd know the whereabouts of Matthias. Besides, she'd wanted to talk to Layton. She hadn't apologized for the catastrophe personally. Vera and Layton really were first on her list to call with regrets about—well, about everything. The Porters and the Grimeses would not be united as a family.

"Who may I say is calling?" Layton's secretary asked.

"Mrs. Grimes," she said. "I will not be put on hold. Get up from your desk and tell him I am on the phone."

"Yes, ma'am," the secretary said. Now, she was a well-trained secretary, Ingrid thought. Mrs. Kenner had to go. When things settled down, she'd make Matthias fire her. "Ma'am, Mr. Porter is in a meeting. Can I take a message?"

Ingrid gritted her teeth. "Is he there with Mr. Grimes? Are they in a meeting together?"

Her questions were met with silence. "Ma'am, can I leave a message for you?"

"What are you, a machine?" She slammed the phone, yanked the wire out of the wall, and threw the entire thing across the room.

How was she supposed to fix everything, repair their lives, and put them back in social graces if her chances were being blocked at every turn?

44

BAILEY HADN'T SEEN THE WORK Walter had finished in her house, too preoccupied to focus on what he'd described as "a work of art."

But now, as she stepped into the basement, the peaceful quiet greeted her along with the smell of cut wood. She did a small dance, seeing what he'd done. Shoring up the basement ceiling, and thereby the entire house, was only the beginning.

She couldn't believe all that he'd done, far beyond the new beams. There was a wide new desk, sanded smooth, and a tall sitting stool underneath it. She'd already dressed for work and had a cup of coffee in her hand. She sat on the stool, opened her sketchbook, and grabbed a heavy pencil. Sitting there with the excitement of a Christmas morning, she began to draw.

Sometimes she didn't know what was going to come to the page. Her hand wielded the pencil in loops and soft shifts until a billowing chiffon skirt with a scalloped edge appeared. She did the same treatment for the sleeves and made a fitted, ruched bodice. She didn't usually give her models faces, but this time she completed her, head to toe.

When she was done, she signed her name in the lower right corner, *Bailey Dowery*. She folded the sketchbook closed and left it on her new desk. She organized an area for her tools. She didn't want to leave. She could absolutely live down there in her new room and draw for hours.

But duty called. The Regal Gown was her first priority, and she'd promised Miss Jackson there'd be no more unusual circumstances, so she especially didn't want to arrive late.

"I'll be back," she whispered to her crisp new room before flicking off the light.

At the Regal Gown, she peeled off her coat and scarf and began her morning routine.

In the workroom, she flicked on the light. The new brightness made her think of Walter, and she smiled. What Alice had said about John came to mind: *Everything lights up when I'm around him.* Pleasant tingling ran over her. She folded her arms around herself.

But with all that was going on, she didn't have time for daydreams. By the time Miss Jackson arrived, Bailey wanted to have completed all the work she'd left undone the day before.

"Good morning," Miss Jackson said. "Well, I told you—" she began.

Bailey looked up from her sewing machine. "Ma'am?"

"—what a train wreck that Elsa Grimes would be. Didn't I say, 'It'll be a miracle if she gets married at all'? To think she's going to get away with what she did to that young man! I bet her family paid someone off. To have the entire charge dismissed, and pouf! She's free as a bird." She set the copy of the *Chronicle* down where Bailey could see it for herself. "What about that poor boy's family? I'm not one to assume, but it really does come down to what you can afford in this town."

That poor boy raped Elsa, Bailey thought.

Bailey followed Miss Jackson to where she began setting up her cookies and sparkling wine. "What do you mean, the charges were dropped?"

"It means she's free to wreak havoc on others, that's what it means."

"Do they have other suspects?" Bailey asked.

"Suspects?" Miss Jackson scoffed. "Who else would have done such a thing? Now that this Elsa Grimes business is behind us, can we please get on with doing what we do best around here?"

"Yes, ma'am. Absolutely," Bailey said. "We can." She fought the urge to rush over and hug Miss Jackson.

"All righty, then. Off you go. Apron. Gloves. Our schedule is tight today. We still haven't caught up since the upgrades. You never even said how much you liked the new dressing area. Mr. Graves built the additional dressing room."

"Yes. He does fine work."

Bailey got on with her preparations for the day.

As she tugged and pinned, conversations swirled over Bailey's head about Elsa and Connor Salley. Miss Jackson had a different perspective to offer with each new customer. It was all anyone wanted to talk about.

"*I guess there could be other suspects. But Niles is far too timid to do such a thing. His brother, Leo—now that one should be questioned.*"

"*They say the Salley boy had abrasions around his wrists from being tied up. Maybe there were two people involved.*"

"*I guess. Yes. Mr. Grimes could've done it. Matthias Grimes certainly has a reputation for making his own rules.*"

By the end of the day Miss Jackson had her own list of suspects, and it wasn't quite as unbelievable as it had sounded at first.

"*I mean, for all intents and purposes, anyone in that family could've done it.*" There were endless theories of why and who would have done such a thing. The Grimeses and the Porters were capable of anything.

Bailey craved the simpler days when all she had to care about was someone wanting their heartstrings read. But then business as usual happened far quicker than Bailey would have liked.

"I hear you can tell someone what their true heart desires, Bailey," Kathryn Cline said, impulsive and indiscreet. "I've heard people say that you're the reason Connor Salley was killed."

Bailey had been caught off guard. She peeked around the curtain, realizing Miss Jackson was nowhere to be found to save her. This woman never would have mentioned such a thing if Miss Jackson were around. Bailey pulled the waistline tight against the woman's rib cage and placed a clip.

"That's a bit too much. I need to breathe occasionally," Kathryn chided.

That was exactly what Bailey had intended: to squeeze the air from the woman's lungs so she'd think twice about speaking.

Once she released the clip, Kathryn continued. "I think it's impressive that you can see someone's true love. Obviously, it was Niles Porter. He did it out of jealousy. He didn't like what you told the Grimes girl, that Connor was her one true love. Better to be rid of the competition altogether. I promise whatever you say to me, I will take to my grave. I won't share a word." She faced Bailey. "I drove an hour from Bartlesville. Alone. Slipping away from my family and fiancé for an entire afternoon. No easy feat, as you can imagine. Price is no object."

Of that, Bailey had no doubt. The oil families were spread far and wide in and outside of Mendol. Miss Jackson had been excited when the call came for Kathryn Cline's appointment. "She's a Cline. One of the richest oil families in Washington County, coming here. I always knew word would spread about my beautiful shop. Thank goodness I'd already planned for the expansion."

"Give me your hands," Bailey said, after a few seconds of contemplation.

"Just like that? Right now? We're doing this?" Kathryn asked.

"Yes." Bailey shoved her gloves into her apron pockets. Her palms faced up, waiting for the woman's hands to lie upon hers. Her eyes darted in Miss Jackson's direction, offering the notion that what she was doing was forbidden. Miss Jackson was on the telephone, scheduling more appointments and cheering her good fortune, no doubt. "You might want to hurry."

"Oh. Yes. Oh my. This is exciting."

Bailey took a deep breath, eyes closed, and braced for the lights flooding beneath her lids. She'd expected the swell of sharp colors in ribbons. But the pictures, the images and voices, were new. Like when she'd touched John to see Alice, and she understood right away. This was her way now. She didn't have to wait until she was lying in the darkness on her pillow. She was there, right there.

"I saw you," Bailey said, dropping her hands to her pockets. She quickly pulled her gloves back on.

"And?"

"It's forty dollars," Bailey said effortlessly. She turned Kathryn to face the mirror and resumed the fitting.

"Well, yes. That's fine. But I'm dying to know. I'm just dying to know. Can you describe him? Tell me. His hair, was it lush, dark curls? Did he have a mole, here?" She pointed just above her brow line.

Bailey stayed silent. She waited as the woman carefully stepped away in the gown to reach her dressing room. In the reflection, she saw her reach into her handbag and come out with bills, which she folded to fit in her hand.

"With something extra." She beamed, pressing the cash into Bailey's apron pocket.

"Yes," Bailey said, simply. "Yes. That was him. He's your true love." She'd seen exactly who Kathryn Cline had described, the two of them holding hands, sharing their breath in short, heated kisses. But what difference did it make?

"I knew it. I knew it," Kathryn announced, pushing the tears across her cheeks. "We're getting married. I knew we were always meant to be together. How often does one find their soul mate?"

"It's very rare," Bailey answered. She couldn't explain that finding one's soul mate wasn't so unusual. It was actually being free to love him or her that was the rarity. She reached for the folded squares of tissue she usually kept in her left pocket, but they weren't there. Having turned skeptical and entirely bitter over the tears spilled at her feet in vain, she hadn't bothered to put them there. Instead she felt the folded bills Kathryn Cline had shoved into her pocket.

"Thank you. You have no idea what this means to me." A tear rolled down Kathryn's cheek, and she dashed it away furiously, lest it drop onto the silk of her dress.

"Me too," Bailey said, suddenly choked up. "Let me get you— *us*—some tissues."

45

ELSA TURNED ON BAKER STREET and couldn't be sure, but she knew what her father's car looked like—a shiny beige Studebaker, the same as the one she was driving. What could he possibly be doing at Charlene and Bailey's place? She parked and got out. She'd come to find Bailey, and the one car she expected to see—Bailey's—wasn't there. It was late enough for her to have returned from work.

Elsa looked over her shoulder to see an elderly gray-haired man across the street wave. She waved back. She knocked lightly on the front door, then tried the knob, happy when it turned easily. Oda Mae had told her once, "We don't lock our doors on the Eastside. We all neighbors and watch out for each other. No need to keep each other out. If someone coming, they know they welcome."

"Hello," she called out. "Bailey, it's Elsa." She smelled the aroma of tea. Someone was home. "Miss Charlene?"

Bailey's aunt appeared at the kitchen door. "Elsa? What're you doing here?"

"Hi. Sorry if I scared you. I was looking for—" Elsa stopped talking when her father came and stood directly behind Charlene. "Daddy?" He was dressed in his usual dark suit, white shirt, and tie, like he was going to the office. He wasn't wearing his glasses and could have been ten years younger, standing casually in a house where he didn't belong. Father and daughter looked at each other like two perfect strangers who had recently met.

Here, her father was relaxed and calm. He didn't have a drink in his hand or make glib, forced comments. Charlene stood unbothered by the closeness of her father, her shoulder pressed squarely against his chest.

Matthias stepped forward quickly, as if he could tell Elsa had noticed. "What're you doing here?" he asked.

Her question seemed more important than his. "How do you know Miss Charlene and Bailey?"

"We're old friends. I've known Charlene for years," he said, running a hand over his face. "Does your mother know you're here?"

"No. I left. I couldn't do what she wanted, and . . . I just couldn't do it." Elsa felt her mouth go dry. There was so much she'd come to tell. How she'd disappeared and refused to go to the clinic with her mama. How she'd finally gotten the nerve to ask Rochelle straight-forwardly, "*Do you want us to be together?*" But she kept all that to herself.

"You're *friends?*" she managed to rasp out instead. She hadn't thrown up in a few days. The mornings of waking up with nausea and dizziness had ended, or maybe she'd been too busy to notice. But now, she felt the stirring in the pit of her stomach.

Charlene gestured to the couch. "Why don't you sit down, Elsa? We have tea, and I already know how you like it," she said kindly. Elsa noticed how she suddenly seemed less standoffish than on her last visit.

Elsa plopped down, still unsettled by the realization: These two have known each other, as what . . . What kind of friends?

Her father hiked his pants and sat beside her. He put an arm around her shoulder and kissed her forehead. "I want you to understand something. I love you more than life itself. I don't want to see you go through a minute of heartache. I've stood by and watched you be hurt. I'm not going to do it anymore. I'm not going to turn a blind eye anymore."

Elsa balled up her fists. She didn't know what else he was about to say, but she didn't want his pity. He was trying to turn things around and make them about her. And right now, she certainly didn't want to be exposed in front of Charlene. She wasn't sure what she knew, or how much Bailey might have already shared about Rochelle, the baby, and the infamous murder charges. For now, Elsa wanted to maintain some semblance of dignity, of privacy. "I'm not a child. Can you just talk to me like an adult and tell me what you're doing here?" She unhooked her father's arm from around her.

Charlene set the tea in front of her on the coffee table and then sat in a chair, kitty-corner but next to her father.

Elsa's eyes flicked between them, back and forth, waiting for the explanation. The unlikely scenario that surfaced in her mind made little or no sense. How would her father know Charlene Dowery? In what world would they have ever connected or been friends?

Her father reached out and took Charlene's hand. An olive branch came to mind, the way her father's soft, alabaster hand connected to the brown skin of Charlene's hand. He folded his fingers with hers.

"Matty," Charlene whispered and stood, nervous for what was about to be disclosed, as if it hadn't become obvious.

"It's all right. Years ago, before I met your mother, this lady was in my life," he said, sounding genuinely enamored. "We were discussing things . . . a future together. We . . . we have a daughter." He paused, waiting for Elsa's reaction. When she said nothing, he continued, more relaxed. "Unfortunately, I never had a chance to meet her. But I hope to, one day," he said, looking up at Charlene. "I hope we all get to meet her."

Elsa picked up her cup of tea and took a sip to hide her shock. She took a moment to collect herself before speaking. "So, you're saying I have a sister?"

Relief left her daddy's lungs. He reached over and hugged Elsa again. This time she didn't shrug him off.

"Yes. You do," he said. "You have a sister. She lives in Louisiana."

"That's not far at all," Elsa said. She took a deep breath. "Does that make me and Bailey cousins?" she asked with a hard grin.

"Close enough," Charlene said. "But for now, can you keep this secret between us? I haven't told Bailey. Not that she doesn't know . . . something, with her skill and all to see what's at the heart of the matter, but I want her to hear everything from me."

"Hi." The soft voice came from the edge of the small living room. Bailey stood there shocked, even more perplexed than Elsa had been when she had first walked in.

They all waved and moaned, "Hi," right back, as if it were a normal evening.

But it was Elsa who got up and went toward her. "Welcome home, cousin." She hugged Bailey.

"What in the world are y'all doing here?"

Charlene shook her head.

"Oh yeah, I wasn't supposed to say anything. Your aunt has something to tell you," Elsa said, nearly bursting at the seams. Even with the turmoil of her life, she couldn't have been happier.

IT ALL MADE SENSE once Aunt Charlene finished telling Bailey about her history with Matthias Grimes. The blank spots between the pictures Bailey had seen of a baby being born were now filled in with a life of expectation and loss. It also explained why Aunt Charlene would tense up anytime Bailey went for a hug. She knew that a touch of her skin could reveal all the pain and love in her life.

"Once I knew you had the gift, it made me afraid. I didn't want you to see the worst of me," she said that night, after Matthias and Elsa had gone home.

"It's not the worst of you, Auntie. It's the best. You had a child, a beautiful baby, and you did the best thing for her. There's no shame in that."

That night they hugged the longest hug they'd ever shared. Neither wanted to be the first to let go. But when they did, and faced one another, it was in a new state of understanding. Bailey couldn't help but be happy for Aunt Charlene. The burden of keeping her secret had been released.

46

IT HAD BEEN A RESPECTABLE SIX WEEKS since the sheriff had crashed Ingrid's party—Elsa's party, technically. It was time to make amends in her own circle and start rebuilding relationships.

The Rose Society breakfast was on Ingrid's calendar the first Saturday of every month. The ladies looked surprised when Ingrid entered the doors of the clubroom. She had donned her canary yellow tweed suit and a pair of gold leather pumps. Lucy had given her a root touch-up and lightened the rest of her hair, correcting the brassy color from the do-it-yourself washes over the past month, all because Ingrid had been afraid to be seen out in public. With Matthias coming home later and later in the evenings and Elsa holed up in her room, it was time to find her voice, to speak, smile, laugh. She had every right to be there.

She approached the white linen–covered table that sat five, where her regular seat was empty and waiting.

Vera Porter stood and leaned in for an air kiss. "Ingrid, so good to see you. You're looking well. I'm so sorry to have missed your calls. I've been inundated with returning gifts and writing thank-you notes. You understand."

Ingrid ignored the three other ladies at the table since they hadn't had the decency to stand and greet her as was customary at the Rose Society.

"Same here, of course." Ingrid nodded that she understood. But she didn't. Weeks' worth of calls left as messages. Vera was the closest thing to a friend she had. A return phone call wasn't too much to ask.

"How is Niles doing?" Ingrid asked and genuinely wanted to know. Niles deserved none of the drama thrust upon him.

"Honestly, he's doing remarkably well. I don't know that I've ever seen him this happy to wake up in the mornings. I'm hoping this is a new era for him." Vera knocked gently on the table for symbolic luck. "Well, how are you and Elsa doing?"

Ingrid couldn't offer the same cheery update. If she even uttered her daughter's name out loud, she might burst into tears. Her daughter was at home, soon to be an unwed mother, determined to bring shame and embarrassment on their family name. Ingrid had no one to talk to about it, no one to call and tell her side of things. Matthias wasn't listening to her wishes.

"Can't we force her to get on the plane?" she'd pleaded with him. All she needed was a little backup. The boarding house in Tennessee was known for good midwifery and discreet adoptions. Ingrid had done her research, which was a gut-wrenching process. Asking strangers how to deal with a pregnant daughter with no prospects of a future had been humiliating.

"She's an adult, plain and simple. We can't force her to do anything," Matthias had replied. His stance was ridiculous. As long as Elsa was dependent on Ingrid and Matthias, that made her a child, and a child needed guidance.

"Good morning. Welcome, ladies." The voice burst into the sunroom over the two small speakers on the upper landing.

To Ingrid's relief the meeting was underway. "We'll finish catching up later," she whispered to Vera. She sat down and sipped the coffee that seemingly had been poured yesterday. She surveyed the room, taking in the jutted chins and upturned noses. She'd fought so hard to belong with these women, who, by the way, were no better than she was. Ingrid might have been from a penniless family, but she had style and gumption. She had the foresight to marry Matthias when he was only beginning to shine, because she knew potential when she saw it. Not one of them in the room would have anything if it weren't for Matthias and Senate Oil. She deserved their respect and loyalty.

The icy temperature in the room wasn't just because of the botched wedding, the scandalous arrest and further accusations around Connor Salley's death, or about the refinery that had gone up in flames and scorched their very lives. No. It was old-fashioned greed.

Every family's bank account was dwindling right along with the company's stock and revenue. Matthias and Layton held the majority shares of Senate Oil, but a portion had been divvied up in private stock, which had made them all rich.

"Let's put our hands together for Deanna Diplo, who has put forth the most donations for our upcoming Winter Carnival."

The applause pounded against Ingrid's beginning headache. She clapped along with the rest and displayed an appropriate smile. She wished to be back home in her day coat, drink in hand, dancing around the room with Perry Como's "Papa Loves Mambo" turned to the highest volume on the record player. The vinyl had scratches at the end but she didn't mind. The longer it played, the better, even if it skipped and repeated.

"I am honored. Thank you," Deanna said at the podium. She wore a silver lamé waist jacket over a black dress that accentuated her hips. Ingrid guessed that wasn't her goal.

Across the table, Bunny and Laura put their heads together to whisper. Normally, the word would have traveled among them, each person hearing a shorter version than the previous one. The last person responding loudly with, "*Oh, behave!*"

"I have always given my all when a task is at hand," Deanna said. "You ladies continue to inspire me to give from the heart."

More applause followed. The servers began to fan out with decanters of hot coffee and trays of glossy pastries. Vera had turned to face Louise, on the other side of her, while Bunny and Laura made an effort to remain huddled shoulder to shoulder. Ingrid stared awkwardly straight ahead.

When a hand came to rest on her shoulder, Ingrid went directly into gratitude mode, turning with a smile. It was Deanna Diplo. "My goodness, it *is* you!" Deanna exclaimed. "I could only make out the back of your head from over there."

Ingrid was slow to her feet, but managed a two-hand hold with an air kiss.

"Nonsense. Give me a hug, Ingrid. You've been through so much." Deanna's arms wrapped tightly for a firm grip. "Let me look at you. Yep, gorgeous as usual."

"Thank you, Deanna. Same to you. Good to see you." Ingrid slipped back into her seat, but knew the short exchange was too good to be true.

"I'm so sorry for not reaching out sooner," Deanna said, leaning in to her ear, "with all that's going on with you and Matthias and Elsa. Well, my goodness, can you believe how life goes full circle? Matthias and his long-lost maid. Then there's Elsa and that woman's niece tied at the hip. My goodness. I've been getting the scoop from my house lady, Annie. She gets her hair ironed there in that woman's kitchen. Let me see . . . what's her name . . . Charlene? Well, if you ask me, Ingrid, you're taking it all with exceptional grace. You look younger than the last time I saw you, for heaven's sake! What is your secret?"

Ingrid's smile stayed on her face, frozen almost into a grimace, as she turned away. Long after the breakfast was over and everyone had gone, she'd continued to sit there, wondering if she could stand, even if she wanted to.

47

THINGS WORKED OUT, just as Charlene had said they would. Was it possible Charlene was the one with the second sight? It was a family trait, after all.

This was the first time they'd all been together to celebrate the dismissal of the criminal case. However adamant Bailey had been about doing her part, ultimately there really had been nothing she could have done to save her friend. It had been safer not to get involved.

Bailey took a swig of her warmed tea and gave the dumplings one last stir.

"Dinner's ready," Charlene called.

Settings for five were spread on the unsteady oak dining table. Matthias was late. He'd urged Charlene to carry on without him. He didn't want to be responsible for the food being served cold. Bailey, Elsa, and Walter pulled their chairs out and sat.

"Wait. Let's say grace," Elsa said. She opened her hand for Bailey on one side, and Charlene came to the other.

"Really, now?" Charlene chided.

"Yes. Families say grace together, and that's what we're doing."

Elsa loved the idea of their one big happy family and became a regular visitor at the little house on Baker Street. She made her way over in the afternoons and hung out in the spare bedroom with its twin-size bed, which Bailey had slept in as a child. Now the sunken mattress was Elsa's happy place, where she spent her days writing down baby names and staring out the window at the sky. In between Charlene's hair appointments, she'd come out, rubbing her round belly and asking if she could cook something. She never got to cook at the Grimes home. Her specialty was grilled cheese with onions. Charlene had to admit the sandwiches tasted pretty good.

"Thank you for letting me hang out here."

Charlene would shake her head, miffed. "It's all right, Elsa. You stay as long as you like."

They'd become a family in their own way. Charlene still had the nagging feeling the other shoe was bound to drop. She couldn't think of a time when she'd ever gotten a single thing she'd asked for in this life, and she wasn't about to drop her guard now. The bigger the hope, the bigger the disappointment.

"Well now, seems I came just in time." Matty stepped into the kitchen from the back door, walked over to Charlene, and kissed her on the forehead.

Charlene offered him a lopsided smile. "Matty, have you ever been on time for anything?"

She nudged out of his wrapped arms. She'd asked him to keep his displays of affection private.

"They're not children," he had replied. "I think they get the point of what's going on."

"I don't care. I'm trying to keep some dignity around here," she'd told him.

Dignity was a luxury, she'd learned a long time ago, but it didn't stop her from trying to hold on to what little she had. Loving Matty had always come with a price. In fact, not much had changed. There was still nowhere in Mendol, or the entire state of Oklahoma, where they could hold hands, let alone move into a home and live together. Regardless of how many times he'd promised they'd be together, that he was working on it, she remained a pragmatist. She let Matty do what he did best. Dream big. She was in charge of her own life, regardless.

He reached over the prayer circle and shook Walter's hand. "Matthias Grimes. Good to meet you."

"You too."

"Now, where were we before my daddy came in late and interrupted my supper prayer?" Elsa picked up where she left off. "Thank you for our blessings and giving us this food to nourish our bodies and giving us peaceful dreams. Amen."

"Short and sweet. Let's eat," Matty said, loosening his tie and then pulling it over his head.

"You're in a fine mood, sir."

"I am. Yes. I got some good news today. I got some movement with our wonderful US government representative, who wants to hear what I have to say about the oil price-fixing." He scooped a heap of chicken onto his plate. "They've been at this for a long time. The infamous Seven Sisters. That's what they're called. The top seven monoliths that are controlling the flow of oil so the supply squeezes out any competition, domestic or foreign." He glanced in Charlene's direction. "But I think we're here for a celebration. All that oil talk can wait."

"Yes. But I like hearing your good news. Everybody, raise your glasses. We're going to have a toast," Charlene said, holding up what beer was still in the bottle. She waited until Bailey and Walter poured sweet tea into their cups. When she saw Matty had nothing in his glass, she poured an ounce or so of beer for him. "So, we are celebrating. Like Elsa said, family. Being together like this is a reason to be thankful. I'm so glad the dark times are behind us, and may we move forward to a brighter chapter."

"Cheers," a lilting voice called from the back screen door.

Charlene hadn't expected a gate-crasher for the evening. It could've been anyone. Neighbor. Client. Friend. But seeing Bailey rise from her chair and then stand frozen, not sure if she should run or scream a warning, grabbed her full attention.

"Hello, Mrs. Grimes." Bailey's voice went high and off pitch. "Hello, Alston. Good to see you."

"You too." The wiry young man came from behind the slender white woman. He handed a large wrapped box to Bailey; then he rushed back out the door. He moved like a man who wanted to get out of the way.

"I'm here in peace. I promise. I followed the voices. Matthias, hello," Ingrid said before turning to rest her eyes on Charlene. "Do you want to introduce me to your friend?"

"Ingrid, you shouldn't be here," Matthias croaked, still sitting. "How—"

"You shouldn't be here either. Should you? But Elsa, well, that's a different story. This is probably where you belong." She rested a hand on her hip. Her nails matched her lips. She looked like she'd spent the entire day in the salon just for this appearance. Charlene couldn't help but feel flattered that Ingrid had gone through so much trouble primping just to make her acquaintance.

"Matty, I think you should go and take her with you before things get out of hand," Charlene said carefully.

"Things have already gotten out of hand, haven't they?" Ingrid's facade of calm cracked.

"Ingrid." Matthias was finally on his feet. "That's enough. This isn't what I wanted. For you to . . . to walk in here and—"

"Catch you? You didn't want to be caught. This is a married man," she announced to the room. "This is my husband. This is my family." Her eyes glistened with sharpness. "How dare you? All of you. All the sacrifices I've made for this family. All I've done is take care of both of you. This is so much like you, Elsa, but you, Matthias Grimes! God! I trusted you to care enough about me, about what we've built, to not embarrass me this way. Everybody knows. How do you think I knew to come here? Everybody in Mendol knows about you and this . . . this . . ."

"My name is Charlene. And you're in my house, so I'd be careful about the words you choose."

"Charlene, honey, I hope you don't think you've won any prize here, because you haven't," Ingrid spat, moving a little too close for Charlene's liking.

Charlene pushed up from her seat and leaned forward on her balled fists. "Get out of my house."

"To think, I brought a house warming gift, only to be treated this way."

"Mrs. Grimes." Bailey tried again to be the voice of reason. "We don't want any trouble."

Walter reached over and gripped Bailey's hand. "How about we go out on the porch and let these kind folks sort things out?"

Bailey ignored Walter. "Mr. Grimes, please, if you don't mind, will you take Mrs. Grimes home with you?"

Matty moved swiftly to take Ingrid by the arm. "Let's go," he said.

Ingrid pointed her finger at Elsa. "All I've done is try to protect you. You know that. How could you let your father treat me this way?"

Elsa began to back away. There wasn't much room before she hit the wall of cabinets behind her.

"And you . . ." she said before wrestling away from Matty. Her body twisted completely out of his grasp. She lunged forward and grabbed a butcher knife off the counter.

Charlene saw the knife held high but stood frozen. As much as she told herself to act, to move, her limbs refused to obey. Everything around her felt thick and in slow motion. Then there was Elsa's piercing scream.

"Oh, my God! Oh, my God!"

Bailey sprung forward, clutching Ingrid's arm with both hands. The knife finally came down, but landed on the floor with a clang.

Bailey's body jolted, bent, doubled over, and then she heaved with a groan as if she'd just learned to breathe again. She took in her surroundings and looked first at Elsa and then at Ingrid.

"Bailey!" Charlene rushed to the other side of the table. She touched Bailey's face. "Sweetie," she said, sliding her hands over her shoulders and arms, searching for any wounds. "Are you all right? Babygirl, look at me."

"Let go of me!" Ingrid writhed against the hold Matthias had around her waist.

"I saw you. *You and Connor,*" Bailey almost shouted at Ingrid, shaking her head in disbelief. "You loved him," she said more softly, swallowing back the shock. "He was your lover. You were in love with Connor. I saw what you did." Bailey covered her mouth, already regretting that she'd said any of this out loud. Her eyes shifted to Elsa.

Ingrid stopped struggling. Her straight shoulders folded. The fight drained right out of her. She didn't push back or have any last words as Matthias tightened his grip around her waist and carried her out the door. No one breathed until the screen door slammed shut.

"What did you see?" Charlene asked. "What?"

"I can't." Bailey looked over to Elsa, who'd slid to the farthest corner of the room and was crouching there. Safe. Within herself. "She's gone, Elsa. She left." It took both Bailey and Walter to get her to her feet.

Elsa stood shakily, trembling. "We did it. Me and my mama killed Connor," she whispered against Bailey's shoulder. "I'm sorry. I'm so sorry."

Charlene gripped the back of her chair. It was her turn to feel unsteady. In her wildest dreams she hadn't seen such a thing. A mother and daughter?

Bailey walked Elsa out and down the hall to the small room and its bed. Walter began picking up the knocked-over chairs and gathered the broken plates that had fallen from the table. Their house had no room for such devastation.

Charlene went to the screen door and pushed the hook in place. It was the first time she'd ever used the back lock, but from now on, she thought, there'd be no more surprises.

"You want me to go check on Mr. Grimes?" Walter asked.

"No. I'm sure he'll be fine," she said before she made her way to the living room. She sat heavily on the sofa and took a minute.

The only thing she'd ever been sure of was that nothing came easy. And she had been right.

48

*LOOK WHAT HE DID TO YOU. **You hate him,*** Ingrid said.

Elsa gasped. She could hardly breathe, suffocating from her own fear. The memory came pouring over her: her mama waking her up in the middle of the night and whispering, "I got him. Get up. Come on." Elsa, still wearing her pajamas, had climbed in the car. They drove to the Cross Creek dock, where their boat sat in the still water. They only took it out once a year, in the summer. That's where her mama had Connor tied to a pole, head bent forward as if he were already dead. She told Elsa that she put two of her sleeping pills in his beer, then waited until he was knocked out and tied him up and left him there, tied with nylons around his mouth. More nylons around his wrists, which held him against a dock post.

Elsa had been so shocked to see him there, looking helpless. He wasn't so tough now. She hated thinking that. It only lasted for a moment. Then she went back to shock.

Her mama had put a gun in her hand. Elsa had never held a gun in her life and didn't know anything about them, except that it was heavy.

"Look what he did to you," Ingrid said. Elsa held the gun in her shaking hand while her mama waited, but she couldn't do it. She dropped the gun and ran. The sound rang out seconds later. It echoed like an explosion. She smelled the metallic heat in the moist air.

Her mama came to the car, where Elsa was curled in the back seat. The car started and moved along the road slowly and casually. When it stopped, they were back home, parked in the circular driveway. They walked through the front door of their home arm in arm. Elsa remembered the kiss on her cheek and feeling immensely grateful. Her mama loved her. That's what she told herself before she lay down in bed. Before sleep took her away.

The next day her mama said, "Good morning, darling," and acted like nothing ever happened, so perfectly calm and proud that

Elsa wasn't sure herself. She might well have dreamt all of it. *Wishing someone dead doesn't make it so,* she'd told herself.

But then, seeing her mama with that knife in Charlene's house, with that look in her eyes, with her so close, Elsa saw it all. She smelled the harsh gunpowder smoke in her nostrils. It might as well have been yesterday, instead of months ago. She thought for sure she was next.

"I . . . I never wanted anything like that to happen to Connor," she sobbed against her father's chest. That morning, he'd returned to Charlene's with a suitcase filled with Elsa's things.

"This wasn't your fault," he said, holding her. "None of this was your fault."

Elsa ached all over. Her head throbbed. Her bloodshot eyes stung. "If she comes back, what am I going to do?" She'd barely slept. Every little noise pushed her eyes open. She relived each word they had spoken. In the middle of the night, she'd gone to Bailey's room and sat there, wanting to know what she had seen. She wanted every detail.

When Bailey first stirred, Elsa pounced on the edge of her bed. Bailey nearly jumped out of her skin. But she wasn't mad. "Tell me what you saw," Elsa had whispered.

"Your mother and Connor were lovers. She loved him, Elsa. That's all I know."

Elsa began to put the lines straight in her head. She went back to the way Connor had stared at her that day at the party. She ran through it over and over again.

"*You just don't know what's good for you,*" she heard in Connor's voice and then in her mama's, until they became all one. He was doing her a favor.

"He thought he was doing Mama a favor. She wanted him to stay quiet about it," Elsa blurted. She wiped at her wet eyes. She had dozed off again and had gone down a spiral of nightmares.

"What?" her father asked. "Who was doing who a favor?" He sat at the foot of the narrow bed. She was still at Bailey's house and couldn't fathom leaving.

"Connor thought he could change my mind about wanting to be with women instead of men." It was the first time Elsa had spoken the words so plainly. "He wanted to teach me, change me." Her lips shook as the words poured out. "I think Mama told him about me loving Rochelle. As if I could be changed," she sputtered. "I've been trying to change all my life. Did he truly believe he could make me a different person by . . ." She trailed into hiccuped sobs. "I hated him. I hate Mama too. I do."

"Oh, sweetie," her father said, rocking her in his arms. "It's okay. You don't have to worry about anybody trying to change who you are, you understand? I'm not going to let anybody hurt you. Your mama's not going to be doing any pushing. She's not going to be showing up. You don't have to be scared."

"How do you know?"

"She can't have people finding out what she did. She'd rather disappear than stick around for a fight."

Ingrid had packed up her things and left without a note or word of regret, knowing this didn't make Elsa feel any better. She knew what her mama was capable of.

Elsa swiped her nose, which was red and stung. Her lips had gone dry. "There is no place to go, no place far enough away to forget what we've done."

"Stop saying *we*. You had nothing to do with it, do you understand?"

Elsa nodded. But she would never forget. She knew that now. Her arms wrapped around the child who would soon come into the world. She had no idea what she'd tell him or her about their father.

ISABEL GRIMES WAS BORN on April 8, 1955. Elsa left Connor's name off the birth certificate. What was the point? He was gone, and she didn't want to be reminded of what he'd done to her each time she wrote her child's name. She called her "Issy" from the start. One day, she'd have to tell Issy the truth of where she came from, how she'd come to be, but for now all that mattered was that she was here, healthy and loved.

Matthias bought a small house for Elsa and Issy in the central part of Mendol, a short distance away from Baker Street. That afternoon, Elsa and Matthias had spent the day in the office of his team of lawyers, tying up loose ends, as he put it. He had set up a trust for Issy and Elsa. Iron-clad, he'd said. "Whatever happens, you two will be taken care of."

It sounded dire, but she knew her father didn't plan on leaving her anytime soon, not when he was this happy. She'd never seen him the way he was around Charlene, always joking and smiling. He said they were taking it slow at Charlene's request, but Elsa could see— anyone with eyes could see—how they felt about each other.

When they pulled up to Oda Mae's house to pick up Issy, Elsa didn't wait for the car to stop moving completely; she swung the door open and hopped out running. Oda Mae stood outside, holding the little ray of sunshine. That's what Issy looked like with frilly yellow sleeves and a pink bonnet over bunches of brownish blond curls.

"She's so big. She's so big!" Elsa shrieked.

"Girl likes to eat," Oda Mae said. She was working a few days a week for another family, since no one was staying at the Grimes place. Matthias hadn't decided what to do with the house just yet, since Charlene was afraid to live in it. "Too many windows," she'd said. Elsa understood all too well.

"You literally were gone for only a few hours," Rochelle said, stepping out and onto the porch. She wrapped her arms around both Elsa and Issy. "She do like to eat, though. Like her mama."

"We're going to get ice cream. Y'all want to come?" Elsa asked, the enticing question mostly directed at Rochelle. They'd had a chance to talk at the behest of Bailey. Elsa understood what Rochelle was facing.

"You know I care about you," Rochelle explained. "But I can't live that way. I can barely live in my own skin. Ain't nobody going to accept me that way too." Besides, she'd been accepted at a nursing residency program in Oklahoma City. Only a couple of hours away, so they'd still see each other.

Rochelle refused the ice cream offer. "No. You go on. I'm helping

Mama get the house ready. Moses is coming in for a visit. We're making all his favorite plates." She squeezed Elsa's hand. "What? What is it?"

"I really . . . I wish . . ." Elsa shook her head.

"We got a long road ahead. I'm not saying it's impossible. I'm scared, is all. People gotta do things in their own time."

Elsa smiled. "Yeah, I'll say. At this pace, we'll be grannies."

"It's going to be okay. You going to have your hands full taking care of Issy. You're a good mommy."

That was all Elsa truly wanted. She wanted to be a good mother. "I wish my mama and I could've liked each other."

"She loved you, Elsa. I believe that, and you should too. What do you think is going to happen to her?"

"I don't know. She once told me I'd never survive in a constant state of need. I think she was talking about herself. She would die in a prison cell, if anyone ever found out the truth." Elsa let out a jagged breath. She stroked Issy's cheek. "I'm going to do better."

"We got to get a move on." Matthias trotted to open the car door. "Thanks for everything, Oda Mae."

Rochelle took a step toward Elsa, but then stopped.

"See you around," Elsa said before she slid in the front seat with Issy. She began the talk she'd longed to have with her daughter. "Hi, my sweet girl. You are my angel and I can't wait to give you the world. That means you own it. Whatever you want to do with your life is your choice."

49

INGRID HADN'T DARED give the sheriff the chance to come sniffing around with accusations. She'd left that night, hurriedly packing only the essentials. She'd driven through Texas and figured it would be safer to leave from the Dallas airport. She told herself she'd go wherever an available flight would take her. The next morning, she boarded a plane and then landed in Guadalajara.

She was weary, having traveled by car and plane for the last ten hours. Ingrid heard the men chatting behind her in Spanish. She knew very little of the language, but she was sure she heard one of them say "Marilyn Monroe" with a roll of the tongue.

Wait. Yes. She'd heard it for the second time. The real Marilyn was far younger than Ingrid, but she didn't want to disappoint them. She pushed the wide-brim hat lower over her face and adjusted her sunglasses in case the men were bold enough to approach her. The locals were usually kind and respectful to Americans. As long as she didn't hear her actual name called, she was safe, for now.

She held her passport in her hand as she waited for the customs officer. A cute family, a man, wife, and a little girl, were in line in front of her. It was hard to see a perfect little family without thinking of Elsa and Matthias. The early days had been good. Those first years of marriage—when she'd felt like there was nowhere to go but up—had been a dream come true.

She'd give anything to start over, to go back to the way things were.

But there was nothing left of her life back in Mendol. She'd had no choice but to leave. As she had always tried to teach Elsa, being without choices was the lowest of the low, and that's where she had landed.

The shame alone was enough to send her running. Matthias carrying on with that woman with everyone knowing about it would have led a weaker woman to do something even more desperate. Ingrid wasn't about to hurt herself over a man's infidelity. What she did feel bad about was leaving Elsa in the clutches of people who would always judge her. She was sorry she could no longer protect her daughter.

Not that she'd done a great job of it.

She'd done the unspeakable and still had failed. All she'd wanted Connor to do was show the tiniest bit of remorse. All she'd asked was that he confess and stop lying to her face. *"Now look who doesn't know what's good for him,"* she'd told him. She should have let him go. Cut him loose and walked away. But she wanted Elsa to see what he'd been reduced to: a whimpering coward. She'd pulled Elsa out of the house and had driven her back to where Connor was tied to the boat post.

"Look at him. He's nothing. He's not worth ruining your life for," Ingrid told her. "You want to carry a loser's baby?" She wanted Elsa to see reason. Being saddled with Connor Salley's baby and giving up any chance of a decent future would bring a lifetime of misery.

"I was just doing your mama a favor," Connor said, his words slurred. He was still under the influence of the beer cocktail she'd made him. She'd gotten seductively dressed for the ploy. A low-cut top and sleek pants. She was standing barefoot over him after giving up the ruse.

"Shut your mouth," she ordered.

"I did what she asked me to. Right, Ingrid baby? My love for you made me crazy. I'm sorry. Please, I'm sorry."

Ingrid hadn't expected his soliloquy. She panicked. "He's a liar and a coward."

"She said if you had someone like me, you could learn a thing or two."

And there was that grin. Ingrid had pulled out the gun she'd had no intention of using. If he tried anything or got away, she wanted protection. But it was obvious he could never leave that place. Elsa might believe him. Worse, Matthias would learn of their affair and how his ridiculous attack on Elsa had been Ingrid's fault.

"You said you hated him for what he did to you." Ingrid pushed the gun into Elsa's hand, but she dropped it and ran. "Come back here,

Elsa," she cried. She saw Connor lurch forward, pulling his wrists loose from the knotted stockings she'd used to hold him. They struggled. Ingrid didn't know her own strength. That's when he must've pulled the necklace off her neck. She got to the gun before he could reach it and pulled back on the trigger.

Her eyes were squeezed closed.

"Señora, madam," the attendant said, "you are next." He waved her over to the customs window.

Her heart was racing. She picked up her suitcase and moved forward. This was her punishment: exile. She could never return home. She didn't have a home to return to, even if she'd wanted to.

"Ingrid Grimes," the officer said with exact pronunciation.

"Yes," she said nervously, anticipating the moment he told her to wait as he requested someone arrest her. She kept a hand on the charm around her neck. She was wearing yet another one of Elsa's necklaces. Of all the things she'd taken out of the safe—cash, passport, and jewelry—Elsa's jewelry meant the most to her. Each piece signified a time when Ingrid had shopped and put her heart into the gift, always adding a personal touch, a personal inscription. If she hadn't been wearing the pearls with the words *To Elsa with Love, Mommy and Daddy* inscribed on the clasp the night at the boat dock, the sheriff never would have come for Elsa in the first place.

"Welcome to Guadalajara, Señora Grimes."

"Thank you," she said in barely a whisper.

She had enough money for a few months' stay at a modest resort, but she hadn't planned to remain there that long. She wasn't sure if anyone was looking for her. Having used her real name to travel to Mexico, she'd be easy to find. But until then, she'd watch the ocean waves crash and roll away. At the lonely six-week mark on the shores of a foreign beach, exiled, she'd finally had a nibble on her line.

"The señor over there has asked you be given this complimentary bottle," the server said, placing a bottle of something that looked expensive and a wineglass at her side. She wore a white bathing suit and a matching chiffon layer. She looked over her shoulder to see.

"Who?" She peered around and saw no one.

"There," he said, pointing nearly behind her.

A dark-haired man waved. He was older. She gathered from his open floral shirt that he was too embarrassed to take it off at the beach. But she wasn't in the picky business. She waved back, then held up the glass.

"Tell him to join me," she told the server. She hadn't planned on spending the rest of her life alone. She'd suffered enough.

The man eventually came, kicking up sand as he arrived. "Hello, I am Arturo," he said.

"Ingrid," she said. "Pleasure to make your acquaintance."

"May I join you?" he said with accented but perfect English.

"You may." She kept her sunglasses on.

"You are as beautiful as I imagined from afar," he said.

50

BAILEY, GABBY, AND CHARLENE SHARED a booth at Queenie's. Enough food to feed five or six people covered the shiny red table-top: platters with fried catfish, mashed potatoes and gravy, smoked greens, and piles of toasted bacon-covered mac and cheese.

"Keep it coming," Gabby told the server with a wink. "I'm starving. Feel like I haven't eaten for a week, worrying about you people. I couldn't believe it. Her own mama was going to let Elsa go to jail."

"I hope they find her."

"They not going to do nothing to that lady. Besides, I might've done the same thing somebody mess with my child like that," Gabby said, with a spoonful of creamy potatoes ready to launch. "Now we can get back to our lives?"

"Yes. Please. No more talk about that woman. Bailey is going to take the money from the bank of Matty Grimes and start her own dress business. You, Gabby, are going to ride out of here to Chicago and become a famous singer," Charlene said.

"I can't take that money, Auntie," Bailey said.

"Matthias said it was for you from the very beginning. I was just too ashamed to give it to you, ashamed to tell you where it came from. That money is yours. Well, less the fifty I put on Gray Beard."

"Don't tell me—the horse was this close to winning," Bailey teased.

"*Uh-unh*. I won. I just gave it back, is all."

"Ladies," a familiar voice said.

Bailey stood up. "Walter," she said, surprised, leaping into his arms and kissing him longer than she should have, knowing Gabby and Charlene were watching. "You want to join us?"

Gabby rolled her eyes and muttered, "Walter, sit with us."

"You ladies enjoy your girl time." He and Bailey kissed again, quick and light. "I'll see you later."

Bailey sat back down, gushing with pride and a tiny bit of embarrassment.

"Oh, lawd," Gabby said. "You truly are smitten, aren't you?"

"Why has he won everybody over except you? Aunt Charlene likes him. And you know she's quite the judge of character."

"I don't know all about that, but I do like Walter. He's sweet," Aunt Charlene said with an approving nod.

"Well, I just happen to know bull crap when I smell it," Gabby said.

"Give it till you're thirty or so," Aunt Charlene said confidently. "A bit more time and you won't know the difference between bull crap and roses."

They ate until their stomachs were at the bursting point. Bailey thought about the past year and knew she couldn't have made it without the two of them by her side. She put out her hands and grabbed Gabby's left and Aunt Charlene's right. She closed her eyes and didn't bother bracing herself for the light. "Are we going to be together forever?"

Aunt Charlene pulled her hand away. "That's not the right question."

"Yeah. If we're doing this I got my own question: 'Am I going to Chicago to have a singing career?'" Gabby asked.

Bailey put a napkin to her head for drama's sake, closed her eyes, and let out a deep cleansing gasp. "I see it! I see your future. The answer is yes. You will be a big success."

Gabby bumped her shoulder. "I actually believe you."

"Good. Because it's true." Bailey picked up her iced tea and pushed her glass against theirs, one at a time. "May all our dreams come true."

IT HAD BEEN a few weeks since Charlene had seen Matty. He'd been traveling on business and working around the clock. She'd even seen him on the television while he was speaking in front of the United States Congress. He looked smart and handsome, even while being asked tough questions about an oil price-fixing conspiracy that his company had suffered from, which had lost them millions of dollars.

He'd been back in Mendol for a few days. Since he had his hands full, she wanted to give him space. But today, she had news she wanted to share.

Charlene sat on the back porch and sipped her beer; then she took a drag on her cigarette. She heard the car doors slam, then the voices and the footsteps.

She took one more quick puff, then put out her cigarette. She rose to her feet. "Bailey, they're here," she called into the house. She marched through the hallway to get to the front door, opening it before they could knock.

"Well, look a here," Charlene said, taking the baby out of Elsa's arms. "How's our pretty girl?"

"I'm doing just fine, thank you," Elsa quipped.

"I'm not talking about you, girl," Charlene said with a smirk, then a hug. "But you are pretty. That new haircut suits you," she said. Elsa had given herself a not-so-blunt pageboy and Charlene had cleaned it up with an even trim. It was her first time cutting straight hair like Elsa's, and it gave her the confidence to put *Haircuts* on her flyers.

Matty came inside holding a bouquet of flowers. "These are for you."

"Stop. I'm just turning twenty-one again. I don't need flowers."

"Happy birthday," Elsa said.

"Thank you, sweetie."

Bailey rushed up the stairs from the basement. She came toward Charlene, arms outstretched.

"No, ma'am. I just got her," she said, swinging Issy away. "Wait your turn."

In the kitchen, plates were already set out. The roast was resting and the muffins were cooling. They sat around the table like a family, and Charlene could hardly contain the joy filling her chest.

"So, I was thinking," Charlene said after they'd finished their dinner. "I'm planning to go to Louisiana. I'm going to see Sage. I don't know if it's the right time or not, but I can't wait any longer."

"Yes. We'd love to go," Elsa announced quickly.

"Well, no. That's not quite what I was thinking."

"I'm in," Bailey said.

"We'll drive. Road trip. Three dames, a guy, and a baby," Matty added, with his thick eyebrows doing a dance.

Charlene looked at Matty and then exchanged a look with Bailey. "What would that look like, us traipsing on the highway, the four of us? Through the South. We'd be a target for sure. It's not safe."

"It'll be fine. No one will ever know you're the love of my life. I'm just the driver escorting these fine ladies to their destination."

Love of my life. Charlene tried to stop the hiccuped sob from spilling out. She tried and failed. She rose up and dropped herself in Matty's lap. "I don't know if she'll even want to see me. I . . . I reached out to her mother . . . I mean Phoebe. She said she'd talk to Sage, and I haven't heard back. It's just my decision. I want to go. You sure you want to come?"

"I'm sure. I wouldn't miss it. Even if we have to go up and back ten times, she's eventually going to have to accept she has two other parents who want to be in her life."

"And a sister," Elsa said.

"And a cousin," Bailey said, eyes gleaming. "I can't wait. When do we leave?"

BAILEY WAITED AT THE CURB while Walter put her brown suitcase in the car alongside all the other luggage and food packed for the trip. "I wish you were coming with us," she said.

"I'll be right here when you get back. Not right here. I don't want to look too needy, waiting on your porch."

"Have no fear, I will find you." She put a finger to her head. "I have second sight."

"You'll know I'm thinking about you then." He pulled her close. When she had finally told Walter about her ability, he simply said, "I already knew about you, Bailey Dowery. I heard about what you do. That day I met you sitting with them birds, I thought, 'Here she is, the famous Bailey. Seer of all things beautiful.'"

"Why didn't you say anything? You acted like you'd never met me before," she asked.

"Because I hadn't met you before. You can't believe everything you hear. People say a lot of things. Don't mean any of it's true. But now

I know, and all I can say is, a natural gift shouldn't be squandered. If you know how to read hearts and minds, do it. Don't hide it. But don't give it away. No one values what they don't have to pay for."

It was precisely what she needed to hear. Walter's wisdom sometimes amazed her.

Instead of fighting her visions, Bailey had let them come in whatever form they wanted. Once she was no longer afraid to see whatever she was meant to see, it all became pure and natural. There were so many untold stories hiding in folks, scared to come out for fear of judgment or pain. She couldn't control when or how it was going to happen. If she could do a small part to bring them into some peace and knowing, she'd do it.

She loved the feeling almost as much as—or maybe more than—creating a beautiful dress. She had plans to do both. Bailey and Walter had talked about moving to Oklahoma City together. There, she planned to set up her own dressmaking business. And if heartstrings wanted to be read, she'd do the honors—for a small fee, of course.

"Can y'all kiss already? We got to get on the road," Aunt Charlene called from the open window. Elsa, Isabel, and Matthias were already in the car.

Bailey did as ordered and planted a smooch on Walter. He rocked back on his heels, animated. "I'm missing you already, girl."

"I will be back before you know it," Bailey said, getting into the back seat with Elsa. She blew him a kiss as they drove away.

"I'm so glad you two are coming with us," Aunt Charlene said from the front seat. "I'm going to need all the support I can get. I'm so nervous."

"I wouldn't be anywhere else," Bailey said. She rolled down the window and let the wind make her ends flutter. When she opened her eyes, she saw two people sitting on a park bench. *Alice and John?* She blinked and focused. They were definitely there, side by side, heads together, sitting under the shade of a sprawling oak tree.

Bailey fell back against the seat and let what she'd just seen sit with her for a moment. *Sometimes true love prevails.*

51

THEY DROVE STRAIGHT for four long hours and stopped to get gas. When nightfall came, Charlene drove another bit of distance before the sign appeared: Texas. The Lone Star State. A tickle of excitement ran through Bailey. She had never been outside of Oklahoma. She had barely left Mendol.

They rode straight through Texas without stopping, to Bailey's disappointment.

Matthias drove for another few hours before they pulled in to a diner. They were starving and hadn't eaten since they'd run out of peanut butter and jelly sandwiches a hundred miles back.

The four of them walked into the diner that flashed a BREAKFAST sign right along with OPEN. It was nearly midnight, but they'd all agreed they'd sleep better with full stomachs. Aunt Charlene looked apprehensive, unsure, when they sat in the booth.

"What's wrong, Auntie?"

"Just waiting for the tap on the shoulder to tell us we can't sit here. Me and you, anyway."

Matthias reached across the table and took her hand. "We're here now. All right? It might've taken nearly thirty years, but we're here."

Bailey knew exactly what he was referring to, having heard their story, even though it was told in bits and pieces. She knew that, as an interracial couple, they had faced even bigger risks being together than they did now. But what Matthias said seemed to put Aunt Charlene at ease. A waitress with a long gray ponytail came over with menus and welcomed them. "If you've got big appetites, I suggest the Number One. You get the pancakes, hash browns, eggs, and bacon."

"We'll take four of those," Matthias said. "With four coffees."

"I'd like two glasses of milk," Elsa said.

"She's been so good," Bailey chimed in after the waitress left with their orders.

"I know. She practically slept the whole way. But you're hungry now, ain't cha, sweet girl." Elsa looked up. "You mind holding her while I go to the restroom?"

"Oh, my pleasure." Bailey took Issy in her arms and then took hold of her little hand. She wasn't prepared for the wave of light that rushed through her. A tremble passed between them. Bailey closed her eyes to wait.

"Bailey, you all right?" Matthias asked. His voice came as an echo.

"It's all right. She's fine," Aunt Charlene said, from what sounded like a hollow chamber. Her voice seemed an infinite distance away. "She's seeing something."

Bailey settled into the bright lavender field of flowers as if she were there, right there with Issy. Seeing her laugh and run. She saw Elsa waiting with arms open wide.

It felt like an eternity, serene and quiet. When Bailey opened her eyes she realized that only seconds had passed. She was overflowing with the same emotion she'd witnessed: joy.

Aunt Charlene and Matthias stared at her as if waiting for a full report. "Well?" they said at the exact same time.

"Happiness. I know what it feels like. That's all." She was so grateful to know that Issy and Elsa were happy. Bailey had felt like she had let Elsa down in the love department. Inwardly, she'd wanted Rochelle and Elsa to find each other, meet somewhere on the same foundation, but it wasn't there. Maybe in another time, another place, but for now Elsa had Issy, and the kind of unconditional love that could sustain her for a lifetime.

"That's it?" Aunt Charlene questioned, waiting for the fireworks, the do-tell.

"Yeah," Bailey said, taking a firm hold of Issy's hand. "That's it," she said, grateful even for a small glimpse of what bliss looked like.

THE NEXT DAY it took only an hour's drive before they were parked in front of what looked like the perfect home. The Broussard family, who had raised Aunt Charlene's daughter, Sage, lived on a pristine street with weeping willows shading the path to the front door.

"This is it," Aunt Charlene announced shakily. "This is where we're supposed to meet." She checked Matthias's watch. "She should be here. I mean, we're early, but she's probably already inside. Or should we wait, or come back?" she asked, obviously anxious.

"We're going in. It's going to be fine," Matthias said. He reached over to the glove box and pulled out an envelope.

"What is that? You're not bringing her money, are you? Matty, you can't buy everybody." Aunt Charlene shuddered.

"This is a letter, as a matter of fact. I wrote it a few weeks ago when we decided to come. I wrote it to her, explaining . . ." He paused. "I wanted her to know I would've been there if I had known. In case she doesn't want to talk to me." His voice cracked slightly.

Aunt Charlene's tears began to well up. "Well, we're one fine mess, aren't we?"

Bailey leaned forward. Someone needed to take control of the situation. "You two go in first. Me and Elsa will wait here. Just go and take as much time as you need. It's going to be all right. I know it. Just go," she said.

They nodded, both opening their car doors at the same time. They walked up the path, Matthias leading the way, holding Aunt Charlene's hand. It didn't take long after the doorbell was rung for the door to swung open. Bailey and Elsa climbed over each other to get a good view.

"Is that her?" Elsa whispered.

The lady who answered had a short, curly hairstyle pushed up and pinned at the sides. She wore a frilly white blouse and high-waisted slacks.

"I think that's her, because she kind of looks like my mama," Bailey said with amazement.

Aunt Charlene leaned in to the lady for a hug, and Matthias piled on.

"Yep. That's her. Looks like she's happy to see them."

"All right. Let's go," Elsa said, already gripping the door latch.

Bailey had to stop her. "Let's give them some time. Just a little. Meanwhile, you and I can relax and talk."

Elsa put her head down to focus on Issy, even though she was sleeping soundly.

"Look at us. We're here."

"As we should be," Elsa said proudly.

"It's strange, because I always felt you and I had a connection," Bailey said. "We were tethered, and I couldn't figure out why. Now it seems like it was the only way all of this was going to happen, Aunt Charlene and your daddy reconnecting. I don't think it would've happened had we not fallen into that foxhole together."

Elsa nodded. "I'm sorry I wasn't honest with you up front about Rochelle. I wished I could've just told you how I felt. But like you said, if we'd taken any shortcuts, we wouldn't have ended up being a family. Us. We're a family, Bailey. Right here and now. That's all that matters."

The knock at the half-open car window startled them both. They grabbed their hearts and then started laughing.

"Come on in and meet your sister and your cousin," Aunt Charlene said. "She's dying to meet y'all."

Bailey saw Sage up close and immediately felt their kinship. She was tall like Bailey and looked so much like Charlene it made her heart skip. They hugged a nice long time, and then Elsa did the same. They sat around and talked breezily about the easy things, what kind of work they did and what their plans were. None of them mentioned how the last year had consumed their lives, or how all the tragedy had brought them together. Seeing Aunt Charlene's wide, unabashed smile with Sage in the center made up for the tumultuous road traveled. And, like Elsa said, all that mattered was that they were here.

Acknowledgments

I'M GRATEFUL TO SO MANY PEOPLE for helping this story become a book.

For reading my many drafts, no matter how many times I change one word for another, I thank you, Cameron Thomas, for your service. None of my books would see the world without you. For reading and always having the perfect words of encouragement, Gail Ragen, I thank you with all my heart. Kimberla Lawson Roby, I appreciate your check-ins. You make me stop and smell the roses.

I'm grateful to my editor Rachel Kahan and the rest of the team at William Morrow, whose support and faith in me as an author and in this story have made all the difference from a good book to an amazing book. Thank you, Ariana Sinclair, Bonni Leon-Berman, Dale Rohrbaugh, Allison Hargraves, associate publisher for fiction Jennifer Hart, and publicity director Eliza Rosenberry. I am grateful to Kayla Dunigan for her insight and advice.

I'm super happy to thank my agents and team at Folio Literary Management. Thank you, Jeff Kleinman and Claudia Cross, for your cheerleading and ability to make everything look easy when I know it's not. You two complete me! Thank you, Sophie Brett-Chin, for being there and working tirelessly on my behalf.

To my family, who have way too many copies of my books in their garages, I appreciate your many trips to the bookstore. Mom and Dad, thank you for giving me this life to make of what I pleased. I could not have been blessed with better parents. I love you dearly.

About the Author

TRISHA R. THOMAS is the author of the popular Nappily series. Her debut novel, *Nappily Ever After,* was a finalist for the NAACP Image Award for Outstanding Literary Work; was chosen for *O, The Oprah Magazine* as a Book That Made a Difference; and became a Netflix Original film starring Sanaa Lathan.

She is a Literary Lion honoree by the King County Library System Foundation. She has written fourteen novels and has been featured in *O, The Oprah Magazine; Glamour;* the *Seattle Times; Essence;* and the Mary Sue. Trisha fearlessly explores the complexities of human relationships, delving into topics such as love, family, identity, and societal issues.